THE BIG BOOK OF Summer Sizzlers

THE BIG BOOK OF Summer Sizzlers

REDFOX

THE BIG BOOK OF SUMMER SIZZLERS
A RED FOX BOOK 0099 456370

First published in Great Britain by Red Fox,
an imprint of Random House Children's Books

Love on the Rocks and *Love Money* first published by Red Fox 1998
Caught in the Act first published by Red Fox 1997

This edition published 2003

3 5 7 9 10 8 6 4 2

Red Fox Books are published by Random House Children's Books,
61-63 Uxbridge Road, London W5 5SA,
a division of The Random House Group Ltd,
in Australia by Random House Australia (Pty) Ltd,
20 Alfred Street, Milsons Point, Sydney, NSW 2061, Australia,
in New Zealand by Random House New Zealand Ltd,
18 Poland Road, Glenfield, Auckland 10, New Zealand,
and in South Africa by Random House (Pty) Ltd,
Endulini, 5A Jubilee Road, Parktown 2193, South Africa

THE RANDOM HOUSE GROUP Limited Reg. No. 954009
www.**kids**at**random**house.co.uk

A CIP catalogue record for this book is available from the British Library.

Printed and bound in Denmark by
Nørhaven Paperback A/S, Viborg

Contents

Love on the Rocks   7
Anne Harris

Caught in the Act   159
Kate Cann

Love Money   315
Sarra Manning

Love on the Rocks

Anne Harris

Talent Spotting

'Have you two read this?' Jez waved the outdoor centre activity holiday brochure at Bronwen and Lara as the minibus swerved around a tight corner. 'It says that most of the meals served at the centre are . . . vegetarian. Does that mean no burgers at all?' he asked, pale with horror.

Lara patted his hand consolingly. 'It's only for five days, Jez.'

'Look on it as a personal challenge.' Bronwen grabbed the brochure out of his hands, and flicked to the accommodation section to check that the whole place was centrally heated. For the end of April it was still kind of chilly. Even chillier since they'd crossed the border into Wales with its snow-capped mountains. She could live for five days without a trip to McDonald's, but some things – like warm dorms – were essential. They looked all nice and toasty in the photos. Thick carpets and big feathery duvets.

'I hope they have hair dryers too.' Lara rested her chin on Bronwen's shoulder, studying the brochure. 'I forgot to pack mine.'

'You should get your hair cut short, then you wouldn't need one.' Jez rubbed a hand over his cropped brown hair. 'See, softer than a baby's bottom.'

'We'll take your word for it,' Bronwen grinned, turning to the activities section. She'd been looking forward to this holiday for ages. Rock climbing, camping out under the stars, canoeing, orienteering and late night gossiping sessions in the dorm. Potholing sounded a bit cold and scary, but she was willing to give it a go. A whole week of fun with her mates. Bronwen couldn't wait.

'Are we nearly there yet?' Jane crouched down beside Lara.

'With Mr Rodol driving . . .' Bronwen rolled her eyes.

'Next time I'm going by donkey,' Jez said, dangling his arms over the seat. 'It would have been quicker.'

Jane couldn't help smiling. They should have been at the centre hours ago. But thanks to Miss Havistock, who was completely useless at navigating, they'd taken three wrong turnings and almost ended up in Bristol. Which was ironic, considering she was the Geography tutor at college.

Mr Rodol – Head of English, boring old fart – wasn't much better at driving: creeping up the motorway at 40mph, and stopping every thirty minutes for a crafty cigarette and a wee.

'I'll go and see if Miss Havistock knows where we are,' Jane sighed. Like she'd have a clue. Jane walked unsteadily past Jez, Luke, Tim, Dean and Shona and sat behind the driver's seat at the front of the bus.

'Good news, Jane,' Miss Havistock shouted over her shoulder, above the sound of crunching gears. 'We should be there in the next half-hour.'

Jane groaned loudly. Miss Havistock had been saying that for the last three hours. It was getting beyond a joke. How were they supposed to pass the time? They'd already played cards, listened to hundreds of tapes and had a minibus picnic. It was a good thing she'd kept an emergency supply of sweets in her bag. And this was definitely an emergency.

'Does anybody want to share a bag of Mini Dime Bars?' she said, squeezing past Jez again. Technically speaking, half of them were Dave's too. But Dave had been asleep for ages. And by the time he discovered they'd gone, she grinned to herself, it would be too late.

'Don't just sit there,' Jez prodded her playfully with his trainer. 'Go and get them.'

Jane wobbled unsteadily back to her seat, almost falling on top of Dave as the minibus lurched around another tight corner. He was sprawled out along the back seat, fast asleep. Short, blond hair stuck to his face in clumps.

'Urrh?' He woke up suddenly as they hit a bump in the road. 'What's going on?' he blinked, looking confused.

Jane hid the Mini Dime Bars quickly behind her back. 'Nothing. Just go back to sleep.'

'Can you move your rucksack?' he yawned, rubbing his eyes. 'I'm getting squashed here.'

He was already taking up the whole seat. Where was she supposed to sit, on the roof-rack?

'Please, Janey.' Dave stretched out his long legs, yanking off his trainers and dropping them on the floor. Jane picked them up and threw them right back at him.

'What did you do that for?' he asked.

'Because your feet stink.'

'They're not that bad.'

'Dave,' she gasped, holding her nose, 'they're cheesier than a packet of Mini Cheddars.'

'So what's the problem, you love cheese,' he teased, wafting his foot under her nose. 'Go on, take a sniff, you know you want to.'

Jane hid quickly under her jacket. The smell from Dave's feet could knock a girl unconscious in five seconds flat. 'Just put your trainers back ON!'

'Yeah.' Bronwen peered through the gap in the seats, wafting the smell back towards Dave with her magazine. 'And while you're at it, could you get your feet vacuum-packed, for the sake of humanity?' It was bad enough being squashed on to a minibus with eleven other people, without being forced to inhale toxic boy fumes.

'I'll put them back on if Jane shifts her rucksack.' Dave peeked under her jacket, his face close to hers. 'Please?' he kissed the tip of her nose.

'OK, OK,' Jane laughed, giving in. He could be quite sweet, when he tried. She just wished he'd try more often.

'And don't eat all the Dime Bars,' he grinned, settling down for another snooze.

Damn. He'd caught her out.

'I heard you rustling the bag,' he added, tugging at the hand she was hiding them in. He knew her too well. They'd been going out with each other for eight months now. It had been great. Spending cosy nights in at her house, just smooching on the sofa, sharing a pizza and a big tub of ice cream. Going out to the trendy gig venues in town.

But lately . . . Jane sighed. She used to get that tingly, loved-up feeling just thinking about Dave. Ringing him five times a night to hear his sexy voice. Daydreaming about his cute smile when she should have been doing her homework. But now, all they ever seemed to do was bicker. They never held hands at lunchtime any more, or met in the college library before classes, for a private chat and an early morning cuddle. And the only time she ever got butterflies now was when she thought about exams.

'Where's Lara?' She sat next to Bronwen, giving Jez a Mini Dime Bar.

'She's gone to sit with Fil. Do you think we should go and check on her too?' Bronwen asked anxiously.

Jane hesitated. Poor Fil. It wasn't her fault she got travel sick. They'd been on the minibus for so long now, she was vomming up stuff she'd eaten in a previous lifetime.

They both peered cautiously over the seat in front. Fil still had her head in a big paper bag. They sat down again swiftly.

'It's probably best just to leave Lara to it.'

'Right,' Jane agreed thankfully. 'Three's a crowd.' And Lara was good at stuff like that. She was sweet, caring and sensitive. Jane wouldn't be much help. Watching other people puke made her feel queasy too. She'd only end up needing her own paper bag – extra large.

Jane stared out of the window. 'So what shall we do now?'

'I know,' Bronwen smiled. 'How about a quick dip into . . .' She produced a small book from her bag: 'Ta-dah!' And waved it in front of Jane. 'The Destiny Guide. Everything a girl needs to know about her future and more.'

Jane glanced over her shoulder at Dave. 'Does it tell you how to rediscover life on planet boyfriend?'

'Page thirty-two,' Bronwen chucked the Guide in Jane's lap. 'Fifty top tips to turn him into a little sparkler.'

Jane sighed. If only it was that easy. She and Dave were on the verge of a permanent break-up. They both knew it. It had been on the cards for ages now. But so far, neither of them had had the guts to end it.

She couldn't exactly dump him before they came on holiday, when they'd be forced to spend a whole week together. It wouldn't have been fair on Dave. She didn't want to hurt him any more than she had to. And, if she were really honest with herself, it would be too painful for her too.

That's why she'd decided to put her boyfriend dilemma on hold, until they got back to college.

Holidays were supposed to be fun. And Jane was determined to enjoy this one.

Bronwen collapsed on her bed in the girls' dorm and wrapped the warm duvet around her shoulders. Heaven! After seven and a half hours on the puke-mobile they'd finally arrived at the centre, just in time for dinner.

It was even better than in the brochure: soft lights, nice smells, and a kettle and some mugs by the door so they could make hot drinks. It was like having their own private hotel. Except it wasn't exactly private.

They'd found out five minutes ago that they had to share it with some girls from another college. One of them had already pinched the best bed – in its own little alcove overlooking the boys' dorm. Still, it could be a laugh.

'Wake me up when it's time to eat,' Jane yawned, diving head-first into her pillow.

'I wonder what the lads from the other college are like?' Lara squashed up beside her, staring at the ceiling. 'I mean, do you think we'll get to see them much?'

'I know exactly what you're thinking,' Bronwen teased.

'I was just curious.' Lara chucked a pillow at her, grinning. 'They might be a real laugh.'

'They might be cute, too.' Bronwen hugged her pillow and pretended to snog it.

'Very funny,' Lara smiled. 'If you've finished being stupid I'm off to have a shower.'

'Not if I get there first.' Jane scrambled off her bed and grabbed her shower gel. After a close encounter with Dave's whiffy feet she was desperate for a wash. She dashed down the dorm after Lara. Bronwen beat them both to it and flung the door open wide.

'Oh yuck!' she groaned, turning on the light.

The place was a total bomb-site. There were shampoo and conditioner bottles everywhere, make-up smeared across the basins, and wet towels flung across the floor.

Bronwen ran a hand quickly under the tap. No hot water either. Jane and Fil would go ballistic. They'd been dreaming about hot bubble baths for the last hundred miles.

'Even *I* don't make this much mess in a bathroom,' Jane gasped in the doorway behind her.

Bronwen almost choked. 'Yeah, right!' she sneered.

'I think I'll skip the shower,' Lara said, picking up a wet towel and throwing it over the side of the bath. 'What about the mess?'

'Leave it.' Bronwen flicked off the light and closed the door. 'It isn't ours. Let's just go and find the lads.'

'Maybe we could use their shower?' Jane suggested.

'Forget it.' Bronwen dropped her shampoo back on her bed. 'You can risk it if you want to, but count me out.'

They wandered along the corridor to the main building and found everyone sitting in the TV lounge. Bronwen sat on a spare chair next to Jez.

'What's going on?' she asked. 'Are we watching a video or something?'

'Introductory talk before dinner,' Jez said.

Bronwen looked puzzled. 'Nobody told us about it.'

'Probably didn't want to lower the tone,' Jez grinned, ducking swiftly before she thumped him.

'Who's that at the front?' Bronwen squinted, trying to focus on a short bloke with a straggly beard who was setting up chairs.

'Your dream boyfriend?' Jez jiggled his eyebrows wickedly.

'As if,' Bronwen snorted. 'I fancy him about as much as you'd like a date with Miss Havistock.'

'She could be quite attractive if she shaved off her moustache,' he whispered. 'Do you think she combs it before she goes to bed at night?'

Bronwen stifled a smile. 'It's not that bad.'

'Are you kidding? It's like the eighth wonder of the world. She could charge people money to see it.'

'I'd pay you to keep your mouth shut for five minutes if I thought it would work,' she whispered, digging him in the ribs. The bloke at the front of the room was trying to catch their attention.

'Hi, everybody,' he said, scratching his beard. 'I'm Chris, the chief instructor.'

Bronwen was disappointed. Outdoor sporty types were supposed to be tall and gorgeous. Chris was more like a garden gnome.

'I know you're all hungry so I'll keep this short.'

'Good,' she whispered.

'We only have two rules here at the centre. Rule number one, if you have any questions at all, don't be afraid to ask.'

'I've got a question,' Jez mumbled in Bron's ear. 'Why don't they have burgers on the menu?'

'Shhh!' Bronwen nudged him.

'The second and most important rule, no channel hopping while I'm watching my favourite soap.'

'Uh-oh,' Jez mumbled. 'Prat alert.'

'Take a schedule of the week's events from the pile over there,' Chris pointed to the back of the room, 'and I'll see you all later.'

'Is that it?' Bronwen whispered.

'Come on.' Jez dragged her to her feet. 'Let's get out of here before he changes his mind and gives us a lecture on walking boots. I'm starving.'

'Is that all you ever think about?' Bronwen asked. 'Food?'

'No, I think about other stuff too.'

'Like what?' Bronwen grinned. 'Cars, girls?'

'And footie.'

Typical lad. If he couldn't eat it, drive it, or kick it around a field, he didn't want to know. Bronwen pushed him down the corridor towards the dining room, before he started telling her everything she'd never wanted to know about Man United.

They headed for a table at the far side. Lara and Filiz were saving them seats. Jez made room nervously for his double portion of garlic bread and lasagne, the non-vegetarian variety. He'd discovered with relief that there'd been a misprint in the brochure. It was supposed to read 'many' meat-free meals, not 'most'.

'Is it safe to sit this close to Fil?' he asked Bronwen. 'She only stopped barfing an hour ago.'

Fil tutted loudly. 'Thanks for bringing that up again.'

Jez grinned. 'I thought you were the one doing that.'

Fil cringed. 'Can we talk about something else please?' Throwing up in front of her mates was bad enough. But discussing it over pasta sauce and fruit salad! 'What are we doing tomorrow?' she asked Bronwen, trying to change the subject.

Bronwen unfolded the schedule and weighed it down on the table with her cup. 'Tomorrow we're . . . canoeing on a lake.'

'All day?'

Bron nodded. 'All day.'

'On a watery type of lake?'

'Is there any other kind?' Bronwen stared at her. 'Fil, are you OK?'

Fil suddenly looked pale and anxious, fiddling with her long brown hair. Ever since she'd sunk to the bottom of a swimming pool when she was little, she'd been terrified of water.

'I can't help it,' she explained. 'It brings me out in goosebumps just thinking about it.'

Fil wasn't too keen on heights and closed-in spaces either. She wasn't really the adventurous type. In fact, she was a real wuss when it came to stuff like this. She'd really only come on the holiday because her best mates were going and she didn't want to miss out. But, suddenly, it didn't seem like such a great idea.

'Maybe I can just watch?'

'No spectators allowed,' Jez spluttered through a mouthful of lasagne.

'Didn't you realise we'd be going canoeing?' Bronwen asked.

'Well yeah, obviously. I just . . . I just . . . Oh, I don't know, I suppose I just tried not to think about it . . .' But, it was too late to back out now.

'The only way you'll ever get over your fear of water is by getting in a canoe tomorrow,' Jez said, waving a fork at her.

It was alright for him, he wasn't scared. Fil took a deep breath, trying to pretend she wasn't either. She nudged Lara's foot gently under the table. 'Have you spotted any talent yet?'

Lara brushed a strand of baby blonde hair out of her eyes.

'Maybe.'

'Oh my God, that means yes.' Bronwen shuffled her chair round to Lara's side of the table. 'Who is it? No wait, let me and Fil guess.' She huddled up close to Fil and they scanned the room together.

'Cut it out, he'll see you,' Lara hissed, embarrassed.

'Just one guess each. Go on,' Bronwen begged.

'What about him?' Filiz pointed to a cute-looking

guy on the far side of the room with long, surfy ringlets.

'Not even close,' Lara giggled.

'OK then, the one with the big brown jumper and the eyebrows.'

Bronwen stared at Fil in disbelief. 'Are you crazy?'

'What's wrong with him?'

'He's a total geek!'

'Will you two keep it down?' Lara hid inside her jumper. She'd have to tell them who it was, before they started making a big deal of it. 'If you must know, it's the guy in the blue T-shirt.'

'Wow!' Bronwen gasped. 'Spunky!'

'I know,' Lara smiled. She was in the middle of the longest boyfriend drought in history. She hadn't been on a single date since Chet Mallory at the beach, last summer. It wasn't her fault. She'd tried everything. Getting herself invited to loads of parties and being super sociable. It was all a total waste of time. Every guy she'd fancied in the last six months was either attached, or completely oblivious to her existence. She just wasn't meant to have a boyfriend. In the college New Year Honours List, she'd even been awarded the 'Single Chick of the Year' prize.

Well maybe her luck was about to change. She'd spotted blue T-shirt guy in the TV lounge earlier.

She'd squeezed past him to the empty seats at the end of his row, and tripped over his feet. He was perfect. Huge brown eyes, floppy hair, cuter than a shop full of cuddly koala bears. He'd been watching her all through dinner and smiling.

And now . . . Lara looked up and caught her breath. Now, he was collecting his tray and leaving the dining room.

Bronwen had already noticed. 'Quick! Don't let him get away.' She piled up their empty plates and cups. Fil grabbed Lara by the wrist and dragged her towards the door.

'Fil!' Lara pulled away. They were charging after him like a herd of elephants. Not exactly subtle.

'You haven't got time to be subtle,' Bronwen warned, as they followed him into the TV lounge. They stood by the coffee table where they could get a good look at him. 'You've got five days, Lara. Go and talk to him, or regret it for the rest of your life.'

Lara regretted mentioning him in the first place. Still, Bronwen had a point. Five short days and the cutest guy who'd ever walked into her world would be gone forever. Unless she got her butt into gear and talked to him.

'Do it now.' Bronwen pushed her gently. 'We promise not to watch.' Yeah right. They'd be pulling up chairs and getting out the popcorn as soon as she took a step towards him.

'OK then, I'll come with you . . . no, wait a second,' Bronwen squeezed her fingers excitedly, 'he's coming over!'

Lara's stomach flipped. He was heading straight towards them, his long fringe hiding his eyes, and his big cuddly jumper with room enough in it for two.

'What do I say to him?' she panicked. She hadn't had much practice since Chet at the beach.

'You'll think of something,' Bronwen giggled. 'We'll just disappear and leave you to it.'

'Wait!' Lara dragged her back. 'Don't make it look so obvious.'

'OK, OK, calm down,' Bronwen said. 'You get talking to him and we'll just slip away. You won't even know we've gone, I promise.'

He stopped at the far end of the coffee table and flicked on the kettle. Lara's knees wobbled dangerously. He was even more gorgeous close up. He had a sprinkling of stubble across his chin, and extra curvy eyebrows that gave him a mischievous look, like he was about to do something he shouldn't.

'Lara,' Bronwen put a hand on her shoulder. 'We're just going to, um . . . watch something very, very important on TV. We'll catch you later,' she winked, dragging Fil and Jez with her before Lara could stop them.

Bronwen was *so* embarrassing. What was all that stuff about not making it obvious? Lara hovered awkwardly by the table, fiddling with her pendant. If she made a run for it now she'd look like an idiot. She'd have to stay and talk to him.

She glanced over her shoulder. Bron, Jez and Fil weren't even pretending to watch the TV. She glared at Bron, mouthing, 'Go away!' then turned back to blue T-shirt guy, hoping he hadn't noticed.

He smiled shyly at her. 'Hi.' He looked embarrassed. 'Do you want a coffee or something?' he scratched his head nervously. The light caught his hair making it shine, all silky and soft.

'Thanks,' Lara nodded. She hated coffee, but so what? He handed her a mug. She stirred in four heaped teaspoons of sugar to hide the horrible taste and took a sip. Yuck! It was totally disgusting. She swallowed it quickly and burnt the roof of her mouth.

'Is it alright?' he asked, looking at her concerned.

'Fine.' Lara could feel her face going red. 'It's just a bit hot,' she gasped.

'Have mine instead, it's cooler. Here.' He handed her his mug carefully. 'I'm Jake, by the way.'

Jake. Yes! It was perfect. Sweet and kind of sensitive.

It sounded amazing next to Lara too. Like there had always been an invisible gap beside her name and he'd just filled it. Lara and Jake. Jake and Lara. It was fate.

She turned the mug around and took a sip from the side his mouth had already touched, wondering what on earth to say next. Jake wasn't exactly being over chatty. But he was just the kind of boy who gave her butterflies.

'Are you canoeing tomorrow?' she said, after an awkward pause.

'Yeah,' he nodded. 'I think we're in the same group.' Wow! He'd obviously checked. Lara gripped her mug tightly to stop her fingers from trembling.

'I've done it before, it's good fun,' he said, looking up at her properly for the first time. His big, brown eyes locked on to hers for a split second, smiling.

Lara put down her mug and held on to the table for support. If he looked at her like that again she'd pass out into the sugar bowl.

Jane walked into the TV lounge and sat on the sofa next to Bronwen.

'Shhh!' Bronwen said, before she even had a chance to speak.

'What?' Jane asked.

'Lara's met someone.' Bronwen nodded towards the coffee table. 'His name's Jake,' she whispered. 'I couldn't hear anything else. They're too far away.'

'You've been listening in on their private conversation?'

'Of course not.' Bronwen shook her head.

'Yeah right,' Jane smirked. 'That's why you're holding the Destiny Guide upside down.' She turned it the right way round and handed it back to Bronwen.

'OK, so I may have listened for a second or two,' she admitted sheepishly. 'But don't you think they look sweet together?' Jane nodded. And if anyone deserved a nice guy it was Lara.

'So what have you done with Dave?' Bronwen finally turned her attention to Jane.

'He went back to the dorm to find his sweatshirt.'

'The boys' dorm,' Bronwen raised an eyebrow. 'Maybe we should go and help him look.'

'You didn't want to go anywhere near it earlier,' Jane reminded her.

'For a shower, no,' Bronwen smiled. 'But for a quick look around . . .'

Dave walked into the TV lounge as she said it. He wasn't alone. He was talking to a tall girl with long, dark hair. She was laughing at one of his terrible jokes.

'Who's she?' Bronwen hissed.

'I thought she was with that Elliot guy,' Jane mumbled. 'She was all over him earlier in the dining room.'

Elliot was sitting on the other side of the TV lounge now, watching them closely. Then they walked towards Bronwen and Jane.

'Hey you two.' Dave sat down on the end of the sofa. 'This is Kim.'

'Hi,' she smiled, perching on the arm next to him.

'Kim's in our canoeing group tomorrow,' Dave explained.

Jane frowned. 'Really?' Kim was also edging her way up along the arm of the sofa. If she got any closer to Dave they'd both be wearing her jeans.

'Dave is really funny,' Kim giggled. 'Tomorrow should be a right laugh.' She swung her legs inwards, brushing up against him. 'Just tell me if I'm squashing you, Dave.'

He shifted uneasily. But not before Jane caught a quick smile crossing his lips. 'It's OK.' He struggled up off the sofa. 'I was going to talk to Jez anyway, see you later.'

Kim watched him go, looking disappointed. She shrugged it off quickly, then turned towards Bron and Jane. 'You two must be in *my* dorm.'

Bronwen bit her lip. Cheeky cow! She made it sound like they were trespassing on private property. 'Bet you a tenner she's the bathroom trasher,' she mumbled quietly to Jane. Anyone who could sit that close to Dave when his girlfriend was watching wouldn't think twice about taking over the bathroom.

'Dave's kind of cute.' Kim glanced over at him.

'He is, isn't he?' Jane agreed. 'That's why I'm going out with him.'

Kim looked surprised. 'I didn't know he had a girlfriend.' Not that it mattered, she thought to herself, it had never stopped her before. She stood up, flicking her long hair over her shoulder. 'I'd better go and find some old clothes for canoeing tomorrow. Or maybe I could just borrow something from you?' she said, looking over at Jane, critically.

She walked out of the TV lounge before Jane had a chance to answer, and wandered back to the dorm to paint her nails. Give her five minutes alone with Dave, and he'd soon forget Jane had ever existed.

The Kiss of Life

'Quick!' Fil waved at Jane, yelling urgently, 'Get out of the way!'

Jane paddled like mad in the opposite direction. Fil was racing towards her on a canoe collision course. 'Back up!' she shouted.

'I don't know how!' Fil managed to swerve at the last second, just scraping the back end of Jane's canoe with hers. 'Sorry,' she grinned sheepishly over her shoulder. She hadn't quite got the hang of manoeuvring a canoe yet. She could paddle forwards, but going backwards, emergency stops, and three point turns – forget it. She'd already caused a major pile-up when she'd ploughed into Dave, Jake and Lara. But how was she supposed to know which way they were going to turn? She wasn't a mind reader.

'Get ready, I'm coming alongside,' Jane warned, slowing her canoe to a stop and grabbing on to Fil's with both hands. It wobbled dangerously.

Fil gripped her paddle, trying to hold it steady. 'Can you get seasick in a canoe?' she gasped.

It had taken Chris fifteen minutes to persuade her to get into the stupid thing on dry land. Another twenty to actually launch her out on the lake and get her to open her eyes. But once she'd messed about in the shallows for a while and got used to the way it bobbed about, it wasn't as bad as she'd imagined. She hadn't even capsized.

'Could you give me a bit more warning if you're going to scare me like that again?' Jane grinned. With Fil on the loose it was more like a bumper car ride than a canoeing lesson.

'It wasn't that bad,' Fil smirked. 'I think I'm getting the hang of it now.'

Jane looked doubtful. 'I'll race you back to the shore, if you think you can handle it.'

'OK, you're on.' Dry land! She couldn't wait. Her leggings were wet through and she needed to stretch her legs. And as long as she could paddle in a straight line and nobody got in her way, she might even win.

'No pushing, no cheating and no ramming,' Jane grinned at her. 'Are you ready?'

Fil tensed her muscles and sat forward ready to get a good start. 'Ready when you are.'

'Go!' Jane yelled. Then she dropped her paddle as Fil crashed into her.

'Sorry,' Fil grinned innocently. 'It was an accident.'

Jane made a dive for her paddle and tried to catch her up. 'Move over!' she shouted from behind, clipping Fil's paddle and throwing her off stroke.

Fil wobbled, splashing Jane with water as she tried to keep her balance. 'I thought you said no cheating?'

'Change of rules,' Jane giggled, speeding past her mate with a big grin. Her arms were killing. She was laughing so much she could hardly paddle and there was more water sloshing about in the bottom of her canoe than in the lake.

They were getting in close to the shore now. She'd have to glide the rest of the way in. She skidded up on to the pebbly shore and stopped with a jolt.

Fil bumped up behind her, laughing. 'Call it a draw?'

'Call it what you want.' Jane struggled out of her canoe, breathless. 'But I won.'

'You got in my way.'

'I did not.' Jane shook her wet hair over Fil.

'I want a rematch,' Fil demanded, shoving Jane playfully close to the water's edge.

'Let's ask Lara who won. She can decide.' Jane

scrambled across the pebbles to the grassy bank where Lara was sitting and collapsed beside her.

'Did you see the race?' she panted.

'What race?' Lara looked at her blankly.

'Me and Jane,' Fil said, shaking loose stones out of her trainers.

'Sorry,' Lara shrugged. 'Must have missed it.'

Fil was speechless. They'd been paddling across the lake yelling like mad. 'How could you possibly miss it?'

'Take a wild guess.' Jane nudged her and pointed out to the lake where Jake was messing about with Elliot, his wet hair falling all over his face. From where she was sitting, Lara had a bird's eye view.

'You are *so* smitten with him,' Fil teased.

'I am not.' Lara hugged her knees to her chest, grinning. 'Well, maybe just a little bit.'

Ever since he'd handed her a coffee in the TV lounge, accidentally touching her fingers, she'd been in a complete love trance. Tingle factor ten. She couldn't get Jake out of her mind. She'd been replaying the melty moment over and over again in her head, like a scene from a slushy movie, with the hand-touching moment in slow motion.

'I even had a dream about him last night,' she grinned. She'd been bursting to tell Fil and Jane all morning, but this was the first time they'd been alone. 'He was playing football on the beach with the England squad, scoring loads of goals. Then at half-time,' she paused suddenly, looking embarrassed.

'Well go on,' Fil urged. She couldn't stop now, when it was just beginning to get interesting.

'At half-time, he came over to the beach hut where I was sitting, and that's when I realised,' she lowered her voice, 'he was wearing shorts.'

'Is that it?' Jane sat back on her heels, disappointed.

'No, I haven't told you the best bit yet.' Lara made sure nobody else was listening, then beckoned Fil and Jane closer, whispering, 'They were made of digestive biscuits!'

'Oh my God!' Jane screamed.

'Every time he moved, a little piece of biscuit just crumbled away and fell off.'

'I wish I had dreams like that,' Fil gasped. All hers were about boring, everyday stuff, like college.

'So what happened next?' Jane grabbed Lara excitedly. 'Did he take you into the beach hut for a romantic little smooch?'

'No,' she sighed. 'I woke up.'

Fil leaned forward, chewing on a piece of grass. 'Have you spoken to him since last night?'

'He's been with his mates all morning.' She wanted to

get him alone, this time without an audience. 'Anyway, if I see him now he might guess about the dream.'

'You're right,' Jane teased, inspecting Lara's face closely. 'You've got CRUMBLY SHORTS stamped right across your forehead. Quick,' she took off her sweatshirt and wrapped it round Lara's head, 'cover it up before he sees.'

Lara pulled it off again and threw it back at Jane. 'Stop messing about.'

'Hey! Girls!' Dave called, bounding along the shore towards them.

'Whatever you do, don't tell Dave,' Lara whispered as he crashed out next to Jane. Dave would tell the whole centre. Including Jake. He could be really sweet and funny sometimes, but discreet? It just wasn't Dave's style.

'What's going on?'

Lara shifted to one side. Dave was blocking her view of Jake.

'Why's it suddenly gone all quiet?' Dave propped himself up on one elbow, grinning mischievously. 'I bet you lot were talking about me, weren't you?'

Jane rolled her eyes. 'Why on earth would we do that?'

'Because I'm cute and irresistible and you just can't help it?'

'If you must know, we were talking about canoeing,' Fil lied.

'Yeah, pull the other one.' Dave ruffled his scruffy blond hair. 'It must have had something to do with lads.'

'Dave . . .' Jane warned. He was always barging in on their conversations uninvited.

'It's OK, just pretend I'm not here. I'll cover my ears up if it starts getting too juicy, I promise.' He made himself comfortable. He loved sitting in on their girlie chats, it was much more fun than discussing goal averages. He'd learnt loads of useful stuff too. Like why girls got so angry with lads if they didn't phone when they'd promised. And how to make a facial scrub using oatmeal and sugar.

'We were having a personal chat actually,' Jane said, hoping he'd take the hint and leave them to it.

'My lips are sealed,' Dave promised.

'Isn't there somebody else you'd rather go and talk to?' Jane signalled over to his mates, winking.

'No.' Dave looked confused. 'Have you got something in your eye?'

Jane sighed. Sometimes he was so slow. She'd have to put it another way. Spell it out clearly so even Dave would get the message. 'Will you please just go away?'

'Why, what have I done?' Dave sat up, looking hurt.

'We were having a private conversation,' Jane gasped. 'That means you weren't invited.'

'OK,' Dave tutted. 'I don't get all moody when you sit with my mates.'

'All your mates talk about is music and footie, it isn't exactly deeply personal, is it?'

'So I was right,' Dave grinned. 'You were talking about lads. Which one?' He scanned the lake. 'Elliot? No, Tim?'

'Dave, just go!' Jane ordered, pulling him to his feet.

'OK, keep your hair on. I know when I'm not wanted.' He jumped down on to the pebbles and marched off along the shore, to join the rest of the group.

'Dave . . .' Jane called after him. Perhaps she had been a bit hard on him. She hadn't meant to hurt his feelings. But what else was she supposed to have done? Let him sit there and listen in?

'I wouldn't lose any sleep over it,' Fil said. Dave had sprinted over to Kim, and was helping her undo her life jacket.

'She doesn't need a life jacket,' Fil added, watching. 'She's got enough buoyancy in her bra to keep a whole canoe school afloat.'

'OK, everyone,' Chris called, interrupting their chat. 'Get yourselves over here please.' They walked along the grass and slipped into the group between Tim and Dave.

'I'm glad you three found time to join us,' Chris said, doing a head count to check that nobody else was missing. 'We were just talking about safety. What's the first thing you have to do before paddling off across the lake, Fil?'

Fil stared at him blankly. Was he expecting an answer? The first thing you had to do . . . 'Check for leaks?'

'Good answer,' Chris nodded. 'Unfortunately not the right one, but nice try.'

'If he already knew the answer, why did he ask me?' Fil mumbled.

'The first thing you have to do is learn how to capsize, then we can tackle eskimo rolls. We'll be working in pairs, so if you could all partner up,' he grinned at Fil. 'Sorry to disappoint you, but I'm already taken. Better luck next time.'

'Is he trying to be funny?' Fil whispered.

Jane shrugged. Chris' dire sense of humour was the least of her worries. She had more important things to think about, like how to make things up with Dave. She was determined not to let one stupid argument spoil the whole holiday. They were here to have fun. Not start a bickering marathon. She nudged him with her elbow. 'Are we still friends?'

Dave shrugged, refusing to look at her.

'Do you want to partner up?' she asked.

'Sorry,' he said moodily. 'I can't.'

'Why not?'

He glanced over his shoulder. 'I've already asked Kim.'

'Kim?'

Kim appeared beside him right on cue, grinning at Jane and Fil.

'Hi.'

'Is she talking to us?' Jane mumbled. It was funny how she only spoke to them when one of the lads was around. She'd been a crabby cow in the dorm the night before. And she'd used up all the hot water again that morning. She hadn't been so friendly when Bronwen had asked her to leave them some dry towels. But now, she was acting all sweet and girlie in front of Dave, like Miss Butter Wouldn't Melt.

'You don't mind me stealing Dave for the safety training, do you Jane?' Kim smiled at her, molars glinting in the sunshine. 'I promise I'll bring him straight back. Haven't you got a partner?' she asked, pretending to look all concerned.

'Don't worry, I'll find someone,' Jane smiled through clenched teeth. She was such a cow.

'We'd better go,' Dave said. 'Before we get in the way of another private chat.' He walked away, laughing at something with Kim, and glancing over his shoulder to make sure that Jane was watching.

'Dave's just blowing off steam.' Fil put a friendly arm around Jane's shoulders. 'Do you want to partner up with me instead?' Lara had vanished into thin air in the middle of the whole Dave drama, and Jane was good at holding her breath underwater. 'You can give me some tips on how to avoid drowning.'

Lara sat on the grassy bank overlooking the lake, fiddling nervously with her pendant. Jake was sitting just two inches away from her, his hand resting beside hers. He'd pulled her away while Dave, Kim and Jane were talking, and asked her if she wanted to be his partner. Stupid question. She'd been dying to see him all day. So far they hadn't done much talking. Jake was humming a tune quietly to himself.

'Sorry,' he stopped suddenly, looking self-conscious. 'I heard this song on the radio the other day and I can't get it out of my head.'

'No, I like it,' Lara smiled. His voice was so gentle

and dreamy it could melt icebergs. She could listen to him humming for hours. 'So what kind of music do you like anyway?' she asked. Apart from the fact that he was absolutely gorgeous, Lara knew nothing about Jake. And she wanted to know everything, from his favourite colour to his compatible star signs.

Jake turned to face her, arms hooked lazily around one knee. 'I like all kinds of stuff really, dance, indie, soul. I used to be in a band,' he grinned. 'I was the drummer.'

'Really?' Lara gasped. Jake in a band? She couldn't imagine it.

'We weren't very good, we never even played a gig,' he said.

'What were you called?' Lara was getting all curious.

'Promise you won't laugh?'

'Cross my heart,' she giggled.

Jake hid his face, embarrassed. 'We were called the Red Leicesters, after the cheese.'

'No wonder you never played any gigs,' Lara laughed out loud. Maybe he wasn't quite so shy after all.

'So what about you?' he asked, gently tapping her leg.

'I have *never* been in a band,' Lara grinned. A cat howling on the tiles at night could carry a tune better than she could. She brushed a stray hair out of her eyes. Jake was so cute. Last night by the coffee table they'd both been flustered and nervous. This was the first proper chat they'd had without an audience. It was nice.

'Everybody's walking down to the lake,' Jake said, nudging her with his shoulder. Lara held her breath. They were sitting so close now she could feel him breathing in and out. The hairs on his arm were tickling her skin.

'I suppose we should go and see what's happening.' Lara stood up reluctantly, wishing they could sit like that a bit longer. She hadn't even asked him about star signs yet.

They walked side by side down to the water's edge, where Chris was getting ready to demonstrate capsizing.

'Let's get started,' he said. 'I showed you what to do if you capsize in a canoe, now I need a volunteer to demonstrate.' Luke and Dave put up their hands. Chris ignored them and pointed over at Fil. He waved her into the water. Fil's heart was racing. Paddling about on a flat calm lake was one thing, but turning upside down in the water? She wobbled into the canoe as Chris held it steady. Her palms were all sweaty and she suddenly wished she hadn't eaten such a big breakfast.

He pulled her out into the lake until he was standing chest deep. 'Just remember what I taught you.'

Fil couldn't remember a thing. She was too scared to think.

'One final tip,' Chris said. 'Keep your mouth closed.' Fil clamped her jaw tight and gripped the sides of the canoe with shaky white fingers. This was it. The moment of truth . . . She took a deep breath as Chris flipped her over.

'Excellent!'

She resurfaced five seconds later, her hair plastered against her face, and water running down her nose.

'Perfect example of how to exit your capsized canoe, well done!' Chris said, patting her on the back.

Fil waded back to the shore, gasping for breath. She'd done it! She'd actually capsized her canoe. The rush of cold water up her nose had been a bit of a shock to the system, but apart from that . . .

She shook her hair and galloped up to Jane and Lara. 'I did it!' She hugged them both tightly. 'Did you see me?'

'Congratulations,' Jane laughed, pushing Fil away before she completely soaked her to the skin.

'Are you ready to have another go?' Chris asked.

'Keep still,' Jane said, holding Lara's hand out flat. 'How can I read your palm if you keep scrunching it up?'

'I can't help it, I've got finger cramp.' Lara shook her hand, then held it out so Jane could study it properly.

'That's your love line.' Jane traced it with her finger as she spoke.

'It tickles,' Lara giggled.

'It ends just below your index finger,' Jane said.

Lara looked at her anxiously. 'What does that mean?'

Jane checked the Destiny Guide. 'It means that you're going to get married eleven times.'

'Eleven?' Fil gasped.

'Sorry, no, seven.'

'Give me that.' Fil snatched the Destiny Guide out of Jane's hands and inspected Lara's love line herself. 'This is so simple even a four-year-old could work it out, look,' she pointed to the diagram on the page. 'Lara's is like that one there, see?'

'So I'm not getting married seven times?' Lara asked, trying to read it upside down.

''Course not.' Fil twisted her palm to the light.

'According to this you'll be happy with one guy when you've met him.'

'When am I going to meet him?'

'Maybe you already have,' grinned Fil.

'How about mine?' Jane stuck her hand under Fil's nose. Fil took a good look at it, then consulted the Destiny Guide.

'Are you sure you want me to do this?'

'Why, what's wrong?' Jane suddenly looked pale.

'It says that any girl who has a love line like yours is a hopeless case.'

'Where does it say that?' Jane grabbed the Destiny Guide and flicked through the pages in a panic.

'Nowhere,' Fil grinned. 'I just made it up.' Jane swatted her on the head with the book. 'I'm sorry! I'm sorry!' Fil giggled, trying to fight her off.

'So you should be.' Jane chucked the Destiny Guide on the grass with a sigh of relief. She rolled on to her stomach, then suddenly wished she hadn't. Kim was sitting directly in her sights, talking to her mate Roshi.

'How come her hair looks perfect?' she said. Everyone else's had gone flat or frizzy after several million dunkings in the lake, but Kim's still looked immaculate.

'It's a wig,' Fil giggled.

'That doesn't explain why her make-up is still perfect too.'

'I wish I had a wig,' Lara tried to detangle her frizzy mop. She took a strand and sniffed it. 'It smells like eggs!'

Fil leaned over and took a sniff. 'Eeww!' she giggled. 'Don't worry, unless Jake runs his nose through your hair, he won't even notice.'

'Very funny,' Lara smiled, giving up on it and stuffing it down the back of her jumper.

Fil's smelt even worse. She didn't care. Because today, for the first time ever, she'd spent a whole morning up to her neck in water, without having a panic attack.

The biggest surprise of the day – after she'd got the hang of manoeuvring the canoe – was that she was good at it. Even Chris had said so. Fil rolled over on to her back, wondering what was for lunch. Swallowing half the lake had made her ravenously hungry.

A dark, bearded shape loomed over her, blocking out the sun. 'I haven't finished with you lot yet,' Chris said cheerfully.

'What about lunch?' Fil asked.

'You can have some food after first aid training.' He called the others over. 'Get into pairs again so you can all have a practice.'

'First aid training?' Fil whispered to Lara. 'Does he mean mouth to mouth resuscitation?'

'Right, basic resuscitation techniques,' Chris said, gathering them around in a tight circle. 'Useful to know for the rest of the week anyway. Lara and Jake, you can demonstrate while I talk you through it.'

'Oh my God,' Lara grabbed Fil and Jane. Why couldn't he pick on somebody else?

'Have either of you ever done the kiss of life before?' Chris asked. The kiss of life! In front of everyone. Lara glanced quickly at Jake.

'Don't look so worried,' Chris teased. 'It's only a practice, not the real thing. Lara, can you pretend you need resuscitating?' She wouldn't have to pretend. This was going to be so embarrassing.

Lara lay down on the grass and closed her eyes. The first time she'd actually got within kissing distance of Jake and they had an audience. Why didn't Chris just sell tickets?

'Now, Jake, tilt her chin backwards.'

Jake did it gently.

'Open her mouth to check for obstructions,' Chris continued, 'and if the airway's clear, that's when you'd start resuscitation.'

Jake bent over Lara. She still had her eyes closed tight, lashes flickering nervously. Her hair was frizzy and out of control, like she'd spent the day in an open top car with the wind blowing through it. It didn't matter. She looked gorgeous anyway. He couldn't believe she didn't have a boyfriend back home.

He smoothed the curls gently away from her face and concentrated on her mouth, just inches away from his. Chris was still talking in the background, explaining how the kiss of life worked. But Jake wasn't really listening.

He closed his eyes and smelt her warm skin. The kiss of life. The kiss. Kiss . . . He brushed Lara's lips softly, melting into the slow, sweet snog that he'd been dreaming about since she'd fallen over his feet in the TV lounge. She tasted like apples. Smooth, smiling, kissing him back.

He finally pulled away from her, grinning. Jane, Fil, and the others were watching, speechless.

'You'd better put her in the recovery position, Jake,' Chris said, looking surprised.

'I think she might need it,' Jane smiled.

Just Joking

'Fil, will you get your big fat bum out of my *face*!' Bronwen gave her a helpful shove with her foot.

'If you hadn't taken up half the tent with your sleeping bag, I wouldn't need to do this.'

'Watch it!' Jane said, rescuing her rucksack before Fil squashed the packet of crisps she'd been saving for later. 'Fil, you're treading all over my bag.'

'It's not my fault. This tent isn't big enough for the four of us,' Fil crawled back over Bronwen and collapsed in a corner of the tent next to Jane.

'Would you rather go and share with Kim?' Jane asked.

Fil considered it for a second. Maybe sharing with Jane, Bron and Lara wasn't that bad after all. Except that Jane – and there was no easy way of saying this – snored like a wart-hog. And guess who was sleeping right next to the wart-hog? It was bad enough in the dorm, but out here, in the middle of nowhere, without walls . . . The noise would be deafening.

'It's just Jane's snoring . . .' Fil began.

'I do not snore!' Jane snorted. 'Bron, tell her!'

Bron giggled. 'Just sleep with your head outside the tent, Fil, it won't sound so bad from there.'

Jane whacked her with her rucksack. 'Maybe I'll go and share with Kim if that's the way you feel.'

'Don't let us stop you,' Bronwen teased. 'More room for the three of us.'

Fil stretched out, yawning. 'Just as long as nobody keeps me awake. I'm knackered.'

They'd been canoeing all afternoon. Fil had loved every second of it. Racing the guys across the lake, practising her capsize. After spending hours upside down in the water she'd discovered it wasn't really that scary after all. Just great fun.

Chris had taken them back to the centre so they could get a change of clothes and a quick shower, then he'd driven out to the middle of nowhere, to camp overnight. Their tent was tiny. Barely big enough for the four of them, let alone the army of spiders and creepy-crawlies they were sharing it with. It was like sleeping in a wildlife park.

'I thought we were playing Truth or Dare,' Jane said. They'd been in the middle of a game when Fil had decided to rearrange the tent. Lara was on the brink of telling them about 'The Kiss'.

'So what kind of a kisser is he?' Bronwen shone the torch on Lara's face so they could interrogate her properly.

Lara squinted into the beam. She couldn't stop grinning. The muscles in her cheeks ached from the constant smile on her face. 'It was nice.'

'What kind of a word is *nice*?' Bronwen nudged Lara with her knee. 'Give us some details.'

Lara shrugged. 'Like what?'

'Did you know he was going to do it?'

'No,' Lara twisted her hair round her finger absently, 'it just kind of happened.' One minute she'd been lying on the grass with her eyes closed, wishing she was somewhere else, and the next thing she knew . . . She still couldn't believe he'd done it. He obviously had hidden depths.

Lara leant back on one elbow and ran a finger over her lips. They hadn't stopped tingling since it had happened. She could still feel Jake's gentle kiss, so sweet and perfect it was almost as if she'd dreamt it. Lara sighed happily. She already knew what she wanted for her birthday. A plaster cast of his lips.

'Earth calling Lara.' Bronwen was shining the torch

in her face again. 'You were about to give us some details, remember?'

Lara rested her chin on her knees with a secret smile. 'Let's just say he was really sweet and gentle, and he can give me mouth to mouth any day.'

'Marks out of ten?' Jane demanded.

'A definite ten.'

'So are you two an item now?' Fil opened a bag of Mini Mars Bars and passed them round.

Lara hadn't even thought about it. She was still in shock. She'd spent the rest of the day with Jake, messing about on the water, having a laugh, eating lunch. They'd sat on the grassy bank, sharing a packet of Jaffa cakes, talking about loads of stuff. But neither of them had actually said anything about being an item. You could tell a lot about a boy from a first kiss though. And this one had definitely been the I-want-to-get-to-know-you-better kind. Not just a quick time-filler.

'We'll see,' she smiled, stuffing three mini chocs in her mouth at once to hide another enormous grin.

'I still can't believe I missed it.' Bronwen thumped her sleeping bag. 'You couldn't get him to do an action replay could you?'

'No way,' Lara giggled. From now on, any kissing between her and Jake was going to be done in private.

'OK, it's Bronwen's turn. Truth or dare?' Jane rolled over to face her mate.

'Truth. Go ahead, ask me anything.'

'Don't rush me.' Jane flapped her arms about. 'I have to think of a good question.'

Jane loved playing Truth or Dare. They hadn't had a really good game of it since High School. And after the day she'd just had with Dave, she needed a laugh with her friends to take her mind off everything.

'OK, I've got one,' she grabbed the torch out of Bronwen's hands. 'If you had to go on a date with one lad from the centre, which one would you choose?'

'Only one?' Bronwen grinned, reaching for the chocolate. She needed brain food to answer a tricky question like this.

'What about Jez?' Fil suggested.

'Why would any sane person want to date Jez?' Bronwen spluttered. 'He'd just talk non-stop and drive you mad.'

'So who would you pick then?'

Bronwen shuffled forward on to her stomach and considered it carefully. Dave could be a bit immature sometimes and, anyway, he was still going out with her best mate. Luke was too short. Lara had already snapped up Jake – unfortunately. Elliot was quiet and moody. And none of the other lads from his college had really caught her eye. Which just left two possibles.

'It would have to be Tim or Dean,' she said finally.

'Yeah, but which one would you most like to date?' Jane asked, trying to pin her down.

Difficult choice. Bronwen unwrapped another chocolate. Both of them were cute, and available. 'Tim,' she said eventually. 'He's got a nice smile.'

'I would have gone for Dean. He's got a nice older brother,' Fil informed them.

Jane shone the torch in her eyes. 'Trust you to know something like that.'

'You never know when it might come in handy,' she giggled.

'Nobody took a dare.' Jane threw another Mini Mars Bar at Bronwen. 'Why don't we all do one together?'

'Count me in,' Fil grinned. She was still on a high from her canoeing triumph.

'Me too,' Bronwen leaned in closer.

Lara peered over her shoulder. 'What's the plan?'

'How about a water-bomb attack on Kim?' said Jane.

Bronwen laughed out loud. 'You're joking, right?'

'I never joke about water bombs.'

'Excellent,' Bronwen giggled.

It was a brilliant idea. It wouldn't stop Kim flirting

with Dave or using up all the hot water at the centre, but it was worth doing just to wipe the smug smile off her face. They were all getting fed up with the way Kim behaved. She might be able to fool the lads with her silly, girlie act, but they'd seen the real Kim. She was self-centred, shallow and greedy, and that was just for starters.

Bronwen tipped the emergency supply of chocolate out of a large paper bag she'd been hiding in her rucksack. 'Who's got the water?' she beamed.

Jane grabbed a half-full bottle from her sleeping bag. 'There's another empty one outside.'

'I'll go fill it from the stream.' Fil crawled out of the tent with the torch, then stuck her head back through the flap. 'Promise you won't go anywhere without me.'

'Scout's honour,' Jane grinned.

'I can't believe we're doing this.' Lara put on her trainers. 'Who's going to chuck it at her?'

'We could draw straws,' Bronwen suggested.

'No way, it was my idea. I should get to throw it,' Jane said as she scrambled out of the tent. Fil was waiting with the other bottle of water.

'I'll hold the tent flap back so you can just throw it,' Bronwen whispered. 'She's in that one straight ahead with Roshi.'

'What about me and Lara?' Fil hissed.

'Just sit back and enjoy the show.'

Jane filled the paper bag and ran carefully across the field with it, giggling like a maniac. Kim was about to get the shock of her life.

'We should get a medal for doing this,' Bronwen hissed, tripping over a tent-peg in the dark. She hopped around in a circle clutching her foot in pain. 'Ow-ow-ow, ow-ow-ow.'

'Shhhhh!' Jane put her finger to her lips. Then she mouthed silently, 'There's somebody in there, I can hear them moving around.'

Bronwen gave her the thumbs up and grabbed hold of the tent flap. 'Are you ready?'

Jane nodded. Oh yeah, she was more than ready. As Bronwen yanked back the flap she saw a head turn towards them in the shadows. 'NOW!' she shouted.

Jane launched the bomb. It flew gracefully through the air and exploded, bull's-eye, right on target, all over . . .

'HEY! What the . . .' a deep voice suddenly spluttered. Jane swiftly let the flap fall back again. That didn't sound like Kim. She had a stupid, squeaky, girlie voice.

'Oh my God!' she gasped. 'We got the wrong tent!'

'What? We can't have done,' Bronwen hissed.

'Well, take a look inside if you don't believe me.' Jane stood behind her friend for protection as a damp figure emerged from the tent, a wet jumper clinging to his ribs, and his nose dripping like a leaky tap.

'Dave, mate,' Jez said, appearing behind them. 'You should have told me you were going swimming. I would have come with you.'

'Dave?' Bronwen gasped.

'What did you do to him?' Jez asked, with a huge grin on his face.

Dave held up the burst paper bag, scowling. 'They water-bombed me.'

'Just look on the bright side,' Bronwen grinned. 'At least you won't need a shower in the morning.'

Jane tried to stifle a smile. 'Would it help if we said sorry?'

'No,' he glared at her, reaching back inside the tent. 'But this might.' He picked up a can of Coke and started shaking it up.

Jane backed away, grabbing Bronwen's sleeve and yelling, 'RUN!' She made a dash for it across the field, tripping over her laces, trying to keep up with Bron in the dark. They made it back in record time and hid behind the tent-pegs.

'Is he following us?' she gasped. Bronwen held her breath and listened. Silence. Dave had given up and gone back to his tent. Luckily for them.

'Phew! That was a close one,' Jez sighed.

Bronwen spun round surprised. 'Jez! What on earth are you doing here?'

'Jane said run,' he panted. 'So I did.'

'She didn't mean you, dumbo!'

'I didn't want to take any chances,' he said, still trying to catch his breath. 'Dave looked pretty angry.'

'I think it's safe to go back now,' Bronwen teased, patting him on the shoulder.

Jez didn't look convinced. 'You go over first and see if he's calmed down.'

'No way!' Bronwen gave him a shove. 'He's your mate, you go.'

She crawled back into their tent when he'd wandered off again, and collapsed on her sleeping bag with a big sigh. 'Phew! That was a close one. I can't believe we got the wrong tent.'

'Dave wasn't happy.' Jane sat beside her, her heart still thumping fast. Why couldn't it have been Jez, or Luke in the tent instead of Dave? He was already in a mood with her. This little incident wasn't exactly going to help.

'Maybe we should take him a peace offering,' Lara

said, peering out into the dark to see if Jez had got back safely to his own tent.

'How about a dry jumper?' Fil suggested.

Jane shook her head. 'It wouldn't do any good.'

'Why not?' Lara asked.

'Because, let's face it, me and Dave, it's as good as over,' Jane said sadly. 'I've decided to finish it.'

Fil dropped the torch. 'Are you serious?' Jane nodded.

'But you two have been together forever,' Lara said.

'I know.' Jane shook her head. 'It just isn't working any more.' Dave used to make up stupid songs about college to make her laugh. They'd done loads of mad stuff together, like snowboarding down his driveway on tea trays in winter, having food fights and jelly-baby eating competitions.

Not any more. They'd drifted into the boredom basement without even noticing. All they ever did now was get on each other's nerves and argue. The whole canoeing saga had been the final straw. They'd had yet another stupid row, and Dave had stormed off and partnered up with Kim, just to get her back. They hadn't really spoken since.

She'd been hiding from the truth for long enough. It was time to face facts. She and Dave were finished, finito.

'I can't believe it,' Lara said, shaking her head. 'You two were perfect for each other.'

Jane hugged her knees. 'Not any more.'

'Are you sure this is what you really want?' Bronwen asked.

Jane nodded. She had no choice. It was over, and now that she knew it for sure, she couldn't just stick her head in the sand and ignore it. 'How am I going to tell him?' she sighed, looking round at her mates for some advice.

'Are you going to do it now?' Lara asked.

Jane shook her head. 'I'll wait till we get back from Wales.'

She couldn't just march over to his tent, break the bad news, then pretend he didn't exist for the rest of the week. She didn't want to hurt his feelings any more than she had to.

'You could send him a letter,' Fil suggested. 'We could write it now.' She rummaged around her bag for a pen and some paper.

'She can't just leave a note in his locker at college,' Bronwen said.

Lara shone the torch on Jane. 'You'll have to tell him face to face.'

Jane knew she was right. She was dreading it already. What if she said something stupid and messed it all up?

'Are you OK?' Fil asked, giving her hand a friendly squeeze.

'Here,' Bronwen chucked her a sweet. 'Comfort food.'

'I think I'm going to need more than that,' Jane smiled sadly.

Bronwen dumped the whole packet in front of her. 'Have as many as you want. Only don't eat all the red ones,' she grinned. 'They're my favourites.'

Bronwen was being really sweet. And Jane was going to need all her mates over the next few days. Being around Dave, knowing that it was over, wasn't going to be easy. She'd just have to patch things up for now and make the most of the holiday. Jane unzipped her sleeping bag and got in it to keep warm.

'Good idea,' Lara shivered, doing the same. 'OK, own up,' she unzipped it all the way to the bottom, 'who's been eating biscuits in my bed? It's full of crumbs.' Fil sat guiltily on an empty chocolate crunch packet.

'Fil.' Bronwen pulled it out from under her. 'Didn't you save us any?'

'I was hungry,' she said sheepishly.

'Give me the bag, I'll shake it outside.' Bronwen was closest to the tent flap, and she needed to have a private think about Jane and Dave. She dragged it out into the dark after her and shook out the debris. Poor Jane. Breaking up with Dave, after all this time. They'd been so good together. Like Romeo and Juliet, always sneaking off at parties for a private cuddle.

Bronwen should have seen it coming. Just lately Jane always seemed to be in the middle of a row. They'd been driving everyone else mad too. But breaking up? It was like the end of an era.

'Caught you!' Jez said, suddenly appearing beside her out of the dark.

'Jez!' Bronwen thumped him hard. 'Don't *ever* do that again.'

'Sorry,' he grinned, rubbing his arm. He loved scaring Bronwen. She was so shockable, it was almost too easy to make her jump. But he just couldn't resist it. 'You can do my sleeping bag too if you like, Dave's been clipping his toe nails in it.'

Bronwen cringed. That was gross. 'Why doesn't he do it in his own bag?'

'He can't, it's still drying out.'

Bronwen smiled. 'We thought Kim and Roshi were in that tent.'

'Kim asked us to swop. We didn't have much choice. Kim's kind of persuasive.'

'I've noticed.' Bronwen gave Lara's bag a final

shake and folded it up. 'She's been hanging around with Dave a lot today.'

Jez nodded. 'No accounting for taste. I offered myself as a stand-in but she turned me down,' he jiggled his eyebrows wickedly.

'Can't say I blame her,' Bronwen teased.

'Thanks a lot.' He looked hurt. 'For your information there are loads of girls who'd kill to kiss a good-looking guy like me.'

'Pah!' Bronwen snorted. 'Name two.'

'Jinny Ringwald.'

'Jinny Ringwald doesn't count, she'd snog any-body.'

'OK then,' Jez screwed up his eyes, thinking furi-ously, 'Filiz.'

'Fil!' Bronwen screeched.

'Last Christmas she said I had a cute nose.'

'Yeah maybe, but that does not mean "please kiss me Jez".' How on earth did they get into these mad conversations? Nobody else in the world could start off talking about toe nail clippings in a sleeping bag, and end up by wondering if Filiz fancied him.

Jez was one of her best mates. He made her go trick or treating at Hallowe'en. He gave her Chinese burns when he was bored. He practically lived in the kitchen at her house, eating everything that wasn't nailed to the fridge. She could cope with him copying her homework and making fun of her when she sang out of tune. But this whole conversation was getting way too complicated. It was late. She wanted to snuggle up in the tent with her sane friends, and talk about normal stuff.

'Just go to bed, Jez,' she said, turning him round and pointing him back towards his own tent.

'Don't I even get a goodnight kiss?' He closed his eyes and puckered up, messing about.

Bronwen pushed him away. 'You'll get a kick in the pants if you don't get lost.'

'Do you think Fil might be game for a quick snog . . .?'

Bron chased him across the field with Lara's sleeping bag, laughing. Jez was such an idiot. It was kind of reassuring in a way. Because whatever happened at college, whoever broke up or drifted apart, she knew for certain that Jez would always be the same.

Tunnel of Love

'So, let me get this straight.' Fil peered nervously into the dark narrow hole before her. 'You want me to climb down that pothole on a wire ladder?'

Chris nodded. 'Yep.'

'Into the wet and the dark?'

'Uh-huh.'

'Without a safety net?'

Chris put a hand on her trembling shoulder. 'Fil, trust me, I won't let you fall. I'll have you on a lifeline, and I've already sent Dave down so you'll have something soft to land on.'

Fil wasn't convinced. Tight spaces made her nervous. She got claustrophobic in the multi-storey car park lift. She'd even panicked in a sauna once. And she'd never actually been underground before. Except in London on the tube, but that was different. Tube trains had lights and comfy seats, with big red emergency stop buttons. They pulled into huge stations with escalators and handy exists. There wasn't much chance of them stumbling across a group of buskers or a chocolate machine down a pothole.

For the first ten minutes it had been quite exciting. They'd walked into the cave-like entrance, where sunlight warmed the sides of the rock, and they had checked their miner's helmets, head lamps and safety equipment. But the further they'd walked into the cave, the darker and colder it had got. And now, Chris wanted her to climb down a bottomless hole.

'You can see the bottom, look, there's Dave's lamp.' Fil couldn't look. She kept her eyes firmly shut as Chris attached her to a lifeline.

'OK, are you ready?'

She'd never be ready. She might have conquered her fear of water but this was totally different. It was in the dark for a start.

'Ready when you are, Fil,' Chris said.

It was too late to back out now, she had to do it. She climbed slowly down the wire rungs, gripping them tightly, the cold, wet walls getting narrower and narrower as she went.

'What if I get stuck?' she yelled back up in a sudden panic.

'No problem,' Chris shouted. 'We'll just come back for you in a week, when you've got thinner.'

He was supposed to be an instructor, not a comedian. Why couldn't he just give her a straight answer for once? She felt Dave's hand wrap around her waist as she got to the bottom.

'It's a bit of a tight squeeze,' he grinned, sending the line back up, 'but you'll be OK as long as you don't breath out.'

She'd have more room for breathing if she wasn't wearing half her wardrobe at once: T-shirt, shirt, woolly jumper, trousers, thick knitted socks, wellington boots, and an attractive orange boiler suit for insulation over the top of everything. Fil felt like a giant, inflated vegetable.

'I don't like this.' Lara squeezed up beside her. 'What if we get lost?'

'Did you have to say that out loud?' Fil whispered. She hadn't even considered the nightmare possibility of getting lost.

'Stop panicking you two.' Dave banged the top of Lara's miner's helmet. 'Chris knows this system like the back of his hand.'

Fil spluttered. 'Have you seen the back of Chris' hand? It's covered in hair.' She shifted further along the tight, narrow tunnel to make room for Jez, Bron,

Jane and Jake. It was getting more and more like a tin of sardines.

'Right, is everyone OK?' Chris was at the bottom with Luke and Shona.

'Depends what he means by OK,' Fil mumbled. If OK meant shaking like a leaf, feeling sick and being generally terrified then she felt on top of the world.

'Before we set off, I want you all to close your eyes tight,' Chris said. If this was his idea of a joke and they'd all disappeared when Fil opened them again, they'd be in deep trouble.

'Now, turn off your lamps and open your eyes again.' Fil opened her eyes. At least she thought she had. She suddenly wasn't sure. It was blacker than when she'd had them shut.

'Dark isn't it?' Chris' voice sounded twice as loud in the tunnel. 'Now you can see why we need these.' He flicked his lamp back on again, Fil followed with a sigh of relief.

'That wasn't funny,' Lara whispered.

Jane grabbed them both. 'Can anyone else hear running water?'

'That's one of the reasons you're wearing welling-ton boots. Underground streams. But don't worry, Jane,' Chris grinned at her, 'if it gets too deep you can borrow my Donald Duck armbands.'

Jane rolled her eyes. 'Does he actually think he's funny?'

''Fraid so,' Bronwen smiled. 'He laughs at all his own jokes.' He might be a bit of a prat, but she had to admit he was a good instructor.

'It will take us about twenty minutes to get to the end of this narrow tunnel,' Chris informed them. 'Watch out for the low ceiling near the end.'

Jane let the others walk past and waited for Dave at the back. He was still in a mood about the water-bomb incident. He'd completely ignored her at breakfast. And he'd grabbed the last vegi sausage before she could fork it. It was time to patch things up.

OK, so she'd decided to break up with him when they got back from Wales. But, technically speaking, he was still her boyfriend. And for the next three days, she was going to make an extra effort. Declare herself a non-bickering, Dave-friendly zone. Splitting up with him was going to be hard enough without ignoring each other for the next three days.

She tagged on to his boiler suit as he squeezed past. 'Cut it out, Jane,' he scowled.

He clearly wasn't going to make this easy for her. 'Dave,' she said quietly. 'Will you just let me apologise?'

He stopped and turned round, his arms folded sulkily. 'Go on then.'

Jane took a deep breath. 'We got the wrong tent last night, we didn't do it on purpose. And I'm sorry for snapping at you yesterday, OK?'

'Is that it?' Dave asked.

Jane nodded. 'What else do you want me to say?'

'You could at least say it like you mean it,' he tutted.

Now he was just being awkward. One apology was all he was going to get. He could take it or leave it. 'Look, are we friends again or not?' she asked, hands resting on her hips. She was starting to get annoyed.

Dave scratched his chin thoughtfully. 'I'm not sure. I'll have to think about it.'

'Dave . . .'

'OK,' he grinned mischievously. 'I suppose so. I just wanted to watch you squirm.' He kissed the top of her miner's helmet and gave her a quick hug. 'I'm sorry about yesterday too, you know, with Kim,' he said, avoiding her eyes. 'I only did it to make you jealous.' It was the closest Dave ever got to an apology. She pinched him round the waist playfully. At least they'd sorted things out – for now.

Dave suddenly pulled her closer, whispering, 'Have

we got time to make up properly?' He went to kiss her, but Jane ducked swiftly and moved out of his reach.

'I don't want to kiss you down a pothole,' she shivered. 'It's all cold and horrible.'

'OK, it can wait,' he shrugged.

Jane sighed with relief. Kissing Dave now wouldn't feel right. Not when she'd already made up her mind that they were finished. It would be like lying.

'We'd better catch up with the others,' she said, manoeuvring him along the tunnel. Thank God Kim wasn't in their potholing group. Things with Dave were complicated enough without Kim, the incredible flirt, stirring it up again. They stopped suddenly behind Lara and Jake. 'What's the hold-up?' Jane asked over Dave's shoulder.

'Low ceiling,' Lara explained. 'We're just waiting for Luke and Shona to go through.'

Lara crouched down behind Jake, walking carefully as the rock above their heads started sloping downwards. Even in a boiler suit Jake managed to look yummy. Broad shoulders and long legs.

He turned round to check she was still behind him and reached for her hand. 'I hate being alone in the dark,' he whispered, locking their fingers together tightly.

Lara smiled secretly to herself. It was the first time

they'd held hands properly. His fingers were cold and wet from the damp rocks, but she didn't care. It still felt good. And as for being alone in the dark . . . It was a different kind of dark, sort of cold and thick like you could cut through it with a knife.

Not that Lara minded. It was a good excuse to cuddle up close to Jake. Like last night. When the others had finally stopped yakking and fallen asleep, she'd sneaked out of the tent to say goodnight to him. They'd sat by the campfire, his sleeping bag wrapped around them like a blanket, cosy and snug in the warm glow of the embers. They'd talked for ages. Jake was really easy to talk to, once he got going. Not shy at all – but she'd already discovered that at safety training the day before!

Jake was sweeter than she'd ever imagined, making sure she was warm enough, lending her his jumper when she got cold. She'd never met any boy like him before. He was sensitive, gentle and so huggable. She got goosebumps just being close to him. They'd sat looking up at the night sky for ages.

'See that line of stars over there?' he'd said, pointing out the different constellations. 'That's the Orion belt. And the tiny red star above it and the blue star below?'

'I see it,' Lara had lied. She didn't have a clue what

she was supposed to be gazing at. They all looked the same to her. Just tiny dots of light millions of miles away that went all blurry when she concentrated too hard. Not that she could concentrate on anything, sitting so close to Jake, except the heavenly way his hair tickled her face.

'Those two are called Betelgeuse and Rigel,' he'd whispered, brushing her cheek with his silky soft lips.

She'd looked at him in disbelief. 'Did you just make those names up?'

'No, that's what they're called,' he'd said. 'Honest.'

'What's that one over there then?' she'd asked, pointing to the brightest star in the night sky, just so she could get close to him again.

'That's called the Celestial Diamond,' he'd said.

'Really?' Lara had breathed, taking a long look at his gorgeous profile.

'No, I made that one up. I only know the Orion belt,' he'd grinned. 'Sounded good though, didn't it?'

Smooching under the stars with Jake had been the perfect way to end an amazing day. Romantic, cosy, just the two of them. She'd even finally asked him about his star sign.

'Do you believe in all that stuff?' he'd asked, sounding interested.

'Some of it,' she'd nodded. 'So what sign are you?'

'Gemini.'

'Me too!' she'd said. They were just meant to be together!

He turned around as the ceiling got higher again, his miner's lamp shining in her face. 'When I woke up this morning I could still smell your perfume on my sleeping bag,' he told her quietly.

'It's a good job you like it then,' she smiled, squeezing his hand. Oh my God! She'd been the first person he'd thought about that day. She hadn't stopped thinking about him all night either. Cuddling the jumper he'd loaned her and wondering what he was dreaming about.

'We're coming to the end of the tunnel,' he said.

Lara was disappointed. She liked having Jake all to herself. By campfires, down potholes, in canoes, she wasn't fussy where. He let go of her hand to squeeze through an extra narrow bit. She followed him through and out, suddenly, into a huge cave-like chamber.

'This is incredible!' Lara gasped. She'd forgotten all about being scared. She hadn't expected to see anything so amazing as this. 'It's like standing in a cathedral.' She turned round in a circle, looking up. The cave walls were wet and shiny, with strange rock gargoyles jutting out at all angles. Stalactites hung from the ceiling, like long strands of frozen rain.

Jane stumbled up behind them. 'WOW! It's like being in Santa's grotto. Magical,' she whispered in awe.

'She still goes every Christmas, just to sit on Santa's knee,' Dave teased. 'What present did you ask him for this year, Janey?'

'A tall, good-looking boy,' she giggled, looking him over. 'But I guess he couldn't find one.'

Dave grinned. 'I love you too.'

'This place gives me the creeps.' Bronwen appeared from the other side of the chamber. 'Have you seen the witch's fingers?' She showed them five delicate stalagmites pointing up from the rock-bed like a long, bony hand. Bronwen shuffled up closer to Jane. The whole place was spooky. It gave her the shivers.

'WA-HA-HA-HAAA!' Jez jumped out in front of her, making scary monster shadows on the rock.

'Jez!' She clutched her boiler suit to her chest. 'You almost gave me a heart attack, you idiot!'

He grinned mischievously. 'You should have seen your face. Anyway, I was just getting you back for earlier.'

'Does this mean we're even now?' she asked.

'OK,' Jez put his hand on his heart in a solemn promise, 'I swear I won't do it again.'

He was such a liar. If he lasted ten minutes without

trying to spook her it would be a miracle. Not that Bronwen really minded. It was a laugh creeping up on each other, and waiting for it to happen. That was half the fun.

'Have you seen the bit we've got to crawl through next?' Jane said, dragging them over to the far side of the chamber.

'Did you say crawl?' Lara asked. 'As in crawl on our hands and knees?'

'As in crawl on your stomachs.' Chris crouched down next to the gap in the rock and gathered them round for a closer look. 'Welcome to the Cheese Press,' he grinned, shining a torch into it. 'Twenty centimetres high, one and a half metres long, you go in round and come out flat.' He gazed around them all. 'Who's going to follow me through first?'

'Jez will,' Bronwen volunteered him before he could nominate her. 'This should be good,' she whispered, nudging Jane. 'If he gets his fat head through that it'll be a miracle.'

'I heard that.' Jez adjusted his helmet and squeezed into the tiny gap, wriggling along on his stomach, head sideways, feet disappearing into the dark.

'Maybe there's another way through,' Jane said hopefully.

'You mean like a revolving door,' Dave grinned.

'What's the matter, are you two afraid to tackle the Cheese Press?'

'Yes!' Jane laughed.

'You're next, Bronwen,' Chris shouted from the other side of the tunnel.

Bron knelt down and peered into the dark. She didn't like the look of it. 'Do you think anyone has ever got trapped in there?'

'Only after eating Mars Bars,' Dave teased.

'Very funny,' said Bronwen. He knew she'd eaten one earlier. 'Wish me luck.' She squashed her head flat against the wet rock and crawled forwards slowly, her elbows scraping on the low ceiling above. She slithered over a small smooth rock in the middle. It was hard work. If this was what cheese had to go through before it appeared in her sandwiches, Bronwen decided she was switching to peanut butter.

'Stretch your arms out and we'll pull you through,' Chris said, suddenly close. Bronwen could see his light. She breathed a sigh of relief and thrust her arms towards him. Chris and Jez tugged on her sleeves – she didn't even move a millimetre.

'Stop gripping the sides with your feet,' Chris said.

'I'm not gripping with anything,' she shouted back.

They tried again, nearly pulling her arms out of her sockets this time. She didn't budge.

Chris beamed in at her. 'Just a temporary blockage. Don't panic. We'll get you out.'

Bronwen closed her eyes and groaned. Total humiliation. She was stuck. Wedged tighter than a cork in a bottle.

'If the others push from that end and we pull from this side . . .' Chris was enjoying this, she could tell. And Jez would never let her live it down.

'One, two, three and . . . PULL!' Chris shouted.

'STOP!' Bronwen yelled. Dave, Jane and the others were pulling too. 'You're supposed to push,' she explained. At this rate she'd end up eight centimetres longer.

'OK, this time,' Chris yelled. 'And go!'

Bronwen was suddenly free, her head and shoulders clear of the Cheese Press. She scrambled out quickly and sat on a rock, checking she was still in one piece.

'It'll be much easier going back the other way,' Chris said, patting her on the back.

Bronwen stared at him in disbelief. 'You mean I've got to go through that *again*?'

'Don't worry, we'll grease up your helmet, you should go through it like a bat out of hell.'

Jez sat beside her, stifling a grin.

'Don't say anything,' she warned, wiping mud off her face.

'I wasn't going to.' He held up his hands in defence. 'I'm just glad I remembered my waterproof camera.' He swung it before her face. 'Got some great pictures. Maybe I'll pin them up in the common room when we get back to college.'

Bronwen made a lunge for the camera and missed. 'Put those up and I'm never speaking to you again.'

'Promises, promises,' he laughed.

'I mean it, Jez. If one person sees those photos . . .' She snatched the camera out of his hands and opened it up. 'There's no film in here.'

'I know, I used it up ages ago.' He patted his boiler suit pocket. 'I just wanted to get you worried.' He pulled her to her feet before she could thump him. 'Your hands are freezing.' He blew on her fingers then clamped her hand under his armpit.

'Jez,' she struggled to unclamp it, 'what are you doing now?'

'It's a well-known survival technique.'

'Just give me my hand back and stop messing about,' she hissed.

'Huh-hum,' Chris coughed.

Bronwen spun round. Chris, Jane, Dave, Lara, Jake and Fil had all made it through the Cheese Press in one piece and were watching the whole spectacle, highly amused.

'Don't let us interrupt,' Dave sniggered, shining his miner's lamp on them like a spotlight. 'What is it, some kind of ancient armpit ritual?'

'Looks like fun. Can anyone join in?' Jane raised an eyebrow at Bronwen.

'Very funny,' Bronwen stepped away from Jez, wondering why she suddenly felt so flustered.

They walked behind Chris down a wider tunnel this time, following the path of an underground stream.

'It's cold,' Bronwen gasped, as they waded through it, the water rushing round her feet, trying to trip her up.

Jez took her hand again and squeezed it. 'If I go under, you're coming with me.'

'Ha!' she said. 'If you go under you're on your own.'

Jez's hand was warm. He'd never held her hand before. It felt kind of nice, just being connected. They'd been close all day. Scaring each other in the dark, having a great laugh. Potholing wouldn't have been half as much fun with anybody else. And speaking of scaring each other in the dark . . .

'Before we sort out the equipment, I think we should all give our star potholer a big round of applause.'

Chris pulled Filiz to the front where everyone could see her. 'Take a bow, Fil.'

Fil took a bow, beaming round at everyone. Potholing was fantastic – once she'd got used to the feeling of being squashed underground. And the chamber with the stalactites – wow! It was the most amazing thing she'd ever seen in her life. She'd taken masses of photos.

She'd also discovered a hidden talent for wriggling through tiny holes and impossible spaces, clambering over boulders, and wading knee-deep in water. She'd even kept up with Chris, most of the way round. Claustrophobia eat your heart out! She wanted to go potholing again, now.

'OK, that's enough applause,' Chris shoved Fil back into the group playfully. 'We don't want her getting too big-headed. Dave, can you take the safety ropes and put them back in the store cupboard. The rest of you, give your boots and helmets a good wash down under the taps over there.'

Jane tried to pull off her wellies. They were stuck to her wet socks. They wouldn't budge. She'd have to sleep in them. She flopped back in the grass as Bron sat down next to her, yawning.

'You pull my boots off, and I'll do yours,' said Bronwen.

'Do mine first,' Jane propped herself up on her elbows, 'and it's a deal.' Bronwen grabbed her left boot and yanked it off.

'Ah! That feels so good,' Jane sighed, wriggling her toes and plonking her right foot in Bron's hand.

'I can't wait to sleep in a proper bed tonight.' Lara collapsed on the grass beside them. 'Camping out in sleeping bags is not my idea of fun.'

'No, but snuggling up to Jake round the campfire is,' Bronwen laughed. 'We saw the whole thing.'

Lara was stunned 'But you lot were asleep, I checked.'

'All that smooching woke us up.' Jane patted her leg. 'What was he doing, pointing out interesting cow pats?'

'Stars actually,' Lara thumped her arm.

'Next time, turn down the sound effects so we can all get some sleep,' Bronwen teased.

Fil pushed in next to Lara. 'Well, I think it's sweet.'

'Thanks. Now can we stop discussing my love life please?' Lara smiled. At least she finally had one to discuss. But she didn't want to tell Jane, Bron and Fil absolutely everything. She wanted to keep the best bits to herself and daydream about them all over again. Some moments were private, between her and Jake alone. That's what made them so special.

'So have you and Dave called a truce?' Fil asked Jane.

Jane nodded. 'He even apologised for going off with Kim, sort of.' They'd had a good day. Teasing each other and having a laugh. It made a nice change from bickering. He could be great company, when he tried. 'If only it could be like that all the time,' she sighed. She wasn't in the mood to talk about it now, not with Jez and Luke hovering close by. She didn't want Dave to hear it from somebody else. It wouldn't be right.

'Has anyone seen Dave?' Jez asked, sitting on the grass next to Bronwen.

'He took the ropes back to the cupboard,' Bronwen yawned.

'That was ages ago.'

'I'll go and look for him,' Jane volunteered. 'Don't use up all the clean towels,' she warned, picking up her boots and hobbling off across the grass.

'Hey, what about my boots?' Bronwen waved her leg at Jane. 'We had a deal, remember?'

'Get Fil to do it,' Jane said, walking away from them backwards.

'Do it yourself,' Fil snorted. 'I've got boot problems of my own.'

Jane left them to it and wandered round the back of the centre to the main store cupboard, her wet woolly socks squelching on the tarmac. She was desperate for a bath. Camping out overnight and crawling about down potholes played havoc with a girl's hair. Not to mention her feet.

She stopped outside the store cupboard door. It was shut. Dave had probably gone straight back to the boys' dorm to get a shower before the others. But Jane decided to check; she might as well since she was already there.

She opened the door. It was dark inside. She fumbled for the light switch on the wall and flicked it on, then did a double take.

Dave was standing right in front of her. But he wasn't alone. Kim was with him, firmly attached to his lips. They hadn't even noticed she was standing there.

'Jane!' Dave gasped, leaping away from Kim, his face completely white. 'This isn't how it looks. I mean we were just . . .' He took a deep breath, staring down at his feet. 'I think we need to talk.'

Jane stood frozen to the spot. The time for having cosy chats was over.

It's All Over

'Jane, just let me explain,' Dave said shakily, wiping his mouth hastily on his jumper sleeve. 'It was just one tiny kiss.'

Jane finally found her voice. 'It didn't look like that from where I was standing,' she said, trying to keep it under control. She faced them both with her arms folded. Dave stood shamefaced in front of her while Kim stood behind him looking like the cat who'd got the cream.

'It was just a kiss,' Dave repeated, blinking sheepishly in the light. 'It didn't mean anything.'

'So why did you do it?' she asked angrily.

Dave shrugged. 'It just happened.'

Unbelievable. He'd be telling her next that it wasn't even a kiss. That he'd tripped and fallen smack on to Kim's lips in an accidental snogging position. One kiss or a hundred, it made no difference. A kiss was a kiss. End of story. God, how could she have been so stupid? She'd made a point of trying to be extra nice to him all day, when all along he'd been planning a secret rendezvous with Kim.

'It wasn't planned,' Dave said. 'Kim was just going back to the dorm and . . .'

Jane cut him short. 'And you weren't exactly fighting her off.'

'Janey,' he sighed, reaching out a hand to touch her arm. She pushed it away and whacked him hard with one of her boots.

'Jane.' He ducked. 'Can't we just talk?' he pleaded.

'No!' She whacked him again, on the shin.

'Ow! That really hurt.'

'Good,' she hissed, getting ready to clobber him a third time. 'Now you know how it feels.' How could he do this to her, with Kim?

'Will you just give me a chance to explain?' he pleaded.

She glared at him. 'Why should I?'

Dave hobbled towards her, clutching his bruised shin. 'I promise it'll never happen again.'

'Don't make promises you can't keep,' Kim butted in, wrapping her arms around him.

Jane had almost forgotten about Kim. She'd been keeping a low profile, skulking behind Dave with a Cheshire cat smile on her smug face. 'Why don't you get on your broomstick and bog off?' Jane hissed.

'No.' Kim tightened her grip on Dave. 'He wants me to stay.' She stared up at him. 'Don't you, Dave?' She was loving every second of the whole drama. Clinging on to Dave like she'd won the star prize in a raffle.

'Can't we go somewhere quiet and sort this out?' Dave glanced anxiously over his shoulder at Kim, wriggling out of her grip. 'Just the two of us.'

'No. Forget it, Dave, it's over.'

He gripped her arm tightly. 'You're dumping me?'

'What did you expect, a gold medal?' Jane pushed him away. Dave wasn't stupid, he knew it was over. 'I was going to finish it days ago,' she said, marching out of the store cupboard. To think, she thought to herself, I was afraid *I'd* hurt *his* feelings. Ha! What a joke. Dave's feelings were written all over his lipstick-smothered face.

'Jane, wait!' Dave made a dash for the door, but she'd already gone.

Kim reeled him back in slowly. 'Forget about Jane, she's not worth it. Stay here and keep me company instead.' She stroked his face with the tips of her fingers.

Jane might have been Dave's number one once upon a time, but now Kim had him all to herself, and she intended to make the most of it. She kicked the cupboard door shut with her foot and flicked off the light. 'Now, where were we before we got interrupted?'

'Poor Jane,' Fil said, ripping open a packet of crisps. 'She's really upset.'

Bronwen sighed. 'Is it any wonder? I mean, how could Dave be so insensitive? Jane's been really nice to him all day and then he goes and does something stupid like this.'

'And with Kim of all people,' Lara chipped in.

'She probably planned the whole thing,' Bronwen tutted. 'She's been flirting with him from day one.'

Fil nodded. 'But you can't just blame it all on Kim. Nobody forced Dave to kiss her.'

Bronwen sighed again. Fil had a point. And now everyone would assume that Dave had dumped Jane for Kim. It was so unfair. No wonder Jane was upset. If she told everyone the truth, who would believe her now? It would just look like a bad case of sour grapes.

That's why they'd sneaked out to the local pub, to try to cheer Jane up and give her some support.

'Don't you think she looks happier than when we came out?' Fil said.

Lara shook her head. 'She's just putting a brave face on it.'

On the way to the pub Jane had gone all quiet. And since they'd arrived at the Flag and Lamb she'd eaten four packets of peanuts and two bags of smoky bacon crisps. It wasn't a good sign; Jane hated smoky bacon crisps.

'We'll just have to try and make her laugh,' Fil suggested. 'Take her mind off it.'

Bronwen thought about it for a second. 'What else are we supposed to talk about, the weather?' Dave and Kim. Nobody could believe it. It was the shock/horror event of the holiday.

'We'll have to think of something fast.' Lara lowered her voice. 'Shhhh, quiet, she's coming back.'

Jane sat down on the stool next to Bron. 'What?' She looked around the table at their anxious expressions. 'Have I got something on my face?' She rubbed her nose, checking for stray snot.

'Your face is fine,' Bronwen reassured her. 'We just don't know what to say about . . .' She stopped short of saying, 'Dave and Kim'. They sounded too much like an item already.

Jane leaned on the table with a sigh. 'If you want to talk about butt face and Dave, go right ahead. I don't care.' She tapped her fingers restlessly on the table. 'I'm going to get another packet of crisps.'

'This is awful,' Fil whispered, as soon as she'd

gone to the bar. 'We've got to do something to make her smile.'

Jane sat back down again and opened her crisps. No one spoke for a minute. Bronwen nudged Fil, mouthing, 'Talk to her.'

'About what?' Fil said silently back. She couldn't think of anything to say.

It was Jane who broke the silence. 'I mean, I can't believe he kissed her,' she suddenly blurted out, making them all jump. 'God, after *eight* months. It wasn't supposed to end like this.' Jane ate another crisp moodily. Ever since last night she'd been thinking about how to finish with Dave and she'd finally got the whole thing figured out.

She'd decided to take him out for a pizza when they got back to college, break it to him gently over a cheese and ham crispy crust, and in that way she hoped they could still be friends.

But now Dave – the moron – had ruined every-thing. How could he just go off on a snogging spree while they were still an item? She'd been trying so hard not to hurt his feelings. Didn't he care about hers? And how could he prefer a cow like Kim to her?

'Typical lad,' Bronwen said, pinching a crisp. 'He just couldn't say no to a kiss.'

'That's not fair,' Jez appeared beside Bron. 'That's like saying every girl on the planet wants to be a super model.'

'Are you saying it isn't true then, about boys?' Fil asked.

Jez shifted uneasily. 'I didn't say it wasn't true. I'm just saying it isn't fair.'

'Jez, you're not helping,' Bronwen muttered under her breath.

'Do you want me to disappear?'

Bronwen nodded. 'Got it in one.'

'Bad timing?' he asked, escaping behind her stool.

'Couldn't have been worse.'

Jez made a quick exit back over to Jake. He didn't want to get involved in a big girlie discussion about lads. 'You would not believe what they're talking about,' he grinned. 'Stay well clear, mate, unless you want your head bitten off.'

'Look at it this way,' Bronwen said, trying to cheer Jane up when he'd gone. 'At least you don't have to worry about how you're going to dump him now.'

'And it means you can flirt with any boy you want,' Fil chipped in.

'Great,' Jane sighed. 'Except I don't feel like flirting with anyone else, ever again.'

'You're just out of practice,' Bronwen nudged her gently, trying to coax a smile out of her mate.

'How about the guy behind the bar?' Fil suggested. Jane turned round reluctantly to look at him.

'Nice bum, good teeth, fairly bad taste in T-shirts but we can overlook that,' Fil said.

'He's quite cute,' Lara chipped in. Bron stared at her. 'You've already got a guy, greedy.'

'Until the end of the week,' she fiddled with her beer mat gloomily. 'Jake lives two hundred miles away, I'm never going to see him.' It wasn't fair. Jake was the most amazing boyfriend she'd ever had. He made her feel so special. At dinner earlier, he'd come to sit at their table with Fil, Bronwen, Jane and her, making a real effort to get on with her mates. He'd sat next to her, nudging her leg under the table, his elbow resting against hers. She could have sat there all night just listening to the dreamy way he asked Fil about potholing.

After her mates had gone off to get changed, she and Jake had sneaked into the empty TV lounge and watched a chat show in Welsh, trying to understand what it was about.

'I think they're talking about tractors,' he'd said, concentrating on the screen.

She'd got up to find the remote control so they could switch channels.

'I was watching that,' Jake had teased. 'It was just getting interesting.' He'd wrestled her for the remote control, tickling her feet until she'd collapsed in a heap on the floor.

'Are you OK?' he'd grinned down at her from the sofa. 'We can watch something else if you want.'

In the end they'd turned it off and just sat cuddling up together, talking quietly, until Dave and Jez barged in on them.

She could really talk to Jake like a mate. He didn't go on and on about himself all the time either, like some lads did. They connected. They understood each other. It was like fate or something. She'd finally broken her boyfriend drought, and on Friday, she'd have to wave goodbye to him.

'Haven't you heard of the telephone?' Fil grinned.

'And,' Bronwen added, 'you can write long sloppy letters to each other, with secret little messages. It'll be dead romantic. Long distance love.'

Lara hadn't thought about anything else. Of course she'd write to him everyday and ring up. But it wasn't the same as being together, in the same room. She couldn't reach over to brush his hair out of his eyes or hold his hand in a letter.

'Two hundred miles isn't that far away,' Fil said.

'Lara, he isn't going to forget about you,' Bronwen

added. 'He's floating around on a fluffy little love cloud, look.'

Jake was hanging around by the pool table with Jez. The instant Lara turned and glanced over, he looked up and grinned.

'I rest my case,' Bronwen took a bow.

The big farewell was only three days away. It was going to be horrible. 'Maybe we should head back to the centre,' Lara sighed.

Right now, they were supposed to be in the TV lounge, watching a video of Chris' kayaking trip to Alaska. The Flag and Lamb wasn't exactly an exciting pub anyway. Tiny and smoky, in the middle of nowhere, with horrible brown wallpaper and no light bulb in the toilets.

'The jukebox selection hasn't been changed since 1950 either,' Fil said as they rounded up the lads and piled out of the door. 'Woah!' She stopped suddenly in her tracks. 'Who turned out the lights?'

When they'd gone into the pub it had just been getting dark. But now it was total pitch blackness. The Flag and Lamb was in the middle of nowhere. It didn't even have a street lamp.

'I can't even see what I'm walking in,' Fil said.

'It's called dung.'

'Jez.' Bronwen thumped him.

'We've got to walk back through the woods yet,' he cackled in a deep scary voice. 'It's probably full of werewolves just waiting to pounce.'

'It's a pity Dave didn't come to the pub with us.' Jane linked arms with Fil. 'One look at his ugly face and they'd all be running for cover.'

'Maybe we should call a taxi,' Fil suggested nervously as they turned on to the dirt track that led through the woods.

'It's only a ten-minute walk,' Bron said. 'And there's no such thing as werewolves.'

'How do you know?'

Bronwen thumped Jez again. 'Will you stop scaring Fil?'

'Sorry,' he grinned sheepishly, holding Bron back until the others were out of earshot. 'What's going on with Jane and Dave?' he asked.

'Dave didn't tell you?'

'Tell me what? He's just been really quiet since we got back from potholing.'

Bronwen sighed. Didn't boys ever communicate with each other? 'Jane caught him giving Kim a tongue sarni in the store cupboard,' she explained.

Jez looked shocked. 'How did that happen? Kim's way out of his league.'

'Jez,' Bronwen tutted, 'that's not the point.'

'It isn't?'

'The point is,' Bronwen said it slowly so even Jez could grasp it, 'Jane's really upset and she's dumped Dave.'

For some reason Bronwen was sad about the whole drama too. Jane and Dave used to be brilliant together, really close and cute. Cuddling up all the time at college. Buying each other little presents. She couldn't get it into her head that they weren't an item any more. How could people be so horrible to one another?

Jez held back a branch so she could duck underneath it. 'Not everybody ends up like Jane and Dave.'

'Name one couple who doesn't?' Bronwen demanded; she needed real examples.

'Lara and Jake.'

'They've only just met. They don't count.'

'Alright then,' Jez shrugged, 'what about us?'

Bronwen spun round on her heels crashing straight into his chest. 'Us?' she gasped surprised, rubbing her nose.

'Yeah, us, as in you and me – friends. We spend loads of time together and we don't argue like Dave and Jane. Why, what did you think I meant?' Jez teased.

'Nothing.' Bronwen looked away, flustered. For

one crazy split second she'd thought that he'd meant
. . . She walked ahead, quickly catching up with Jane,
Fil, Lara and Jake before she had any more insane
ideas.

'What's up with you, Bron?' Fil asked.

Jez bounded up behind them. 'Bron thought I was
going to propose to her.' He got down on one knee
and grabbed her hand, gazing up into her face. 'Oh
Bron, Bron, say you'll be mine. I can't live another
second without knowing we'll always be together,
until the end of time.'

Bronwen pushed him over.

'I'll take that as a no then,' he grinned, brushing
dirt off his jeans.

'You can take that as a never. Not even if I had to
choose between you and a train-spotter.'

'Just as long as I know where I stand,' he joked.

'Shhhh, everybody, what was that noise?' Fil
whispered as the moon came out from behind a
cloud, shrouding the woods in an eerie silvery glow.
They all stood still, listening. 'There it is again,' Fil
gasped, digging her nails into Jane's arm.

'Must have been a werewolf,' Jez whispered.

'Werewolves don't go terwit terwoo, dumbo,' Jane
slapped his cheek playfully. 'Now can we please hurry
up, I'm dying for a wee.'

They sneaked in through the ground floor window of the boys' dorm so they didn't bump into Chris by accident.

'What a tip,' Fil said, looking round the room. Dirty washing and muddy trainers were thrown all over the place. Not to mention the smell of stale socks. Luke and Dean were playing cards. Dave was nowhere in sight.

'Thank God,' Jane sighed. 'I don't think I could face seeing him again right now.'

'We could have a game of cards,' Luke suggested, making room on his bed for them all.

Bronwen shook her head, muttering to Jane, 'I'd rather go and check out the bathroom.'

'Are you crazy?'

'Come on, it'll be fun.' She dragged Jane down the end of the dorm and flung the door open. 'Oh my God . . .' She looked round the room amazed.

'I know,' Jane sniggered. 'They've got more junk than we have.' She picked up a bottle of aftershave. 'Pooh! What's that supposed to be, Eau de Rat's Breath?'

Bronwen was inspecting the impressive facial wash collection by the sink. 'This one smells gorgeous. Ahhhh!' She sniffed it again. 'Like grapefruit.'

'I didn't know they bought all this stuff. Look at

this.' Jane picked up a flash-looking bottle. 'They could open their own branch of Boots.'

Bronwen checked her hair in the mirror. 'I'll know where to come if I run out of moisturising shower gel. Do you reckon we could use this shaving foam on our legs?' She turned round. Jane had suddenly gone very quiet. 'What's up?' Bronwen asked.

'I've just found this in Dave's stuff.' She handed Bronwen a strip of photo-booth snaps. She and Dave had squashed into the tiny booth together ages ago, pulling stupid faces, almost getting chucked out of the shop for making such a racket. They'd laughed about it for ages afterwards. 'I didn't know he'd kept them.' Jane sighed, then stuffed the photos back in Dave's wash bag and zipped it up again. It was no good; they'd never be friends now. Dave had dented her pride badly. And she wasn't sure she could ever forgive him.

Young, Free and Ladless

'Have you got the Destiny Guide?' Bronwen prodded Jane. 'I want to look something up.'

Jane yawned lazily. 'Do you need it right now? I'm using it.'

Bronwen rolled on to her side to face her mate. Jane was lying flat on her back, eyes closed, soaking up the sunshine before they started rock climbing.

'What have you done with it?' Bronwen asked, checking in Jane's rucksack. She still hadn't read the sections on lucky numbers, special colours and feng shui yet. If Jane had lost it, she was in big trouble.

'Don't panic, it's right here.' Jane took the book from behind her head and handed it back to Bronwen. 'I was just using it as a headrest,' she grinned. It hadn't been much use as a Destiny Guide, or it would have warned her about Dave and Kim. Dave had been keeping a low profile all morning, avoiding her like the plague.

He didn't want to talk to her. Well, the feeling was mutual.

But Kim ... Late last night in the dorm, she'd been whispering about boyfriends. She hadn't actually mentioned any names, but it didn't take the Brain of Britain to work out who she was talking about. Jane had put on her Walkman in the end, to drown out the sound of Kim's stupid voice.

'Come on,' Bronwen said, tugging at her sleeve. 'Chris is waving us over.'

'Welcome to Heartbreak Ridge, everybody.' Chris slapped the rockface they were about to tackle with the palm of his hand.

'More like Break a Leg Ridge,' Bronwen mumbled, squinting anxiously up to the top.

'Take a good long look at the surface before we get started,' Chris said.

'Does he seriously expect us to climb that?' Bronwen gasped.

'Sure, why not?' Chris beamed over her shoulder. 'Heartbreak Ridge is an easy beginner's climb.'

'Easy?' Bronwen spluttered. That was like calling the Sahara Desert a sand pit. Even Spiderman couldn't make it to the top without extra suction pads and a winch. 'Why on earth did they call it Heartbreak Ridge?' she wondered.

'Ah, I'm very glad you asked me that. Gather round, children,' Chris joked, perching on a boulder. 'And I'll tell you how it got its name.'

'Who's he calling children?' Jane whispered. Chris was the biggest kid of them all. When was he going to grow up and start acting like an adult for a change?

'Local legend has it that a long, long time ago, a man called Bryn Davis climbed up to the top here, and wept for seven heartbroken days and nights, after losing his beloved Gwyn.'

Jane glanced over at Dave. He didn't even look remotely red around the eyes after losing her. He'd probably been too busy with Kim to even think about anything else.

'So what happened to him after seven days and nights?' Bronwen asked.

'He climbed down and went home to his wife.'

'But . . .' Jane was confused. 'I thought Gwyn was his wife.'

'No,' Chris grinned, 'his sheepdog.'

Everyone groaned loudly and Jane folded her arms with a weary sigh. What a pile of crap. Only a guy could make up such a stupid legend. It probably wasn't even called Heartbreak Ridge.

'Are we doing any climbing today or is he just going

to sit around telling us fairytales?' she whispered to Bronwen.

'What's wrong with fairytales?' Bronwen asked. At least they were less scary than climbing cliffs.

She looked up at the ridge again. Chris had already talked to them about climbing techniques and shown them how it was done. He made it look easy. But Bronwen had a feeling it was going to be a lot harder than canoeing.

'Uh-oh!' She suddenly grabbed Jane's sleeve. 'Don't look round now. Dave's coming over.' He was walking towards them, hands in his pockets, head down, looking up sheepishly under his fringe. 'Do you want me to disappear so you two can talk?' Bronwen asked.

'No.' Jane held her firmly to the spot. 'If he's coming over to apologise, he can forget it.' She slipped behind her mate. 'I'm going to see Luke and Dean. Just tell him I don't want to talk about it.'

'OK,' Bronwen promised. 'Jane doesn't want to see you,' she said, as Dave stopped beside her. 'Congratulations, you've made a real mess of things.'

'Thanks for reminding me.' Dave stared over at Jane. 'She won't even hear my side of the story.'

'Do you blame her?'

'Not really,' he admitted, scuffing the soil with

his shoe. He hadn't planned to snog Kim. She'd just followed him into the store cupboard, fooling around, sticking to his side like glue. One minute he was putting the ropes back and the next thing he knew . . . It had just happened. He hadn't done it to hurt Jane. But Kim was kind of sweet and really friendly, making it obvious that she fancied him. What was a boy supposed to do?

And now Bronwen was giving him a hard time. Maybe if he tried to explain it to her . . .

'Jane's been a bit moody lately,' he sighed.

'So what are you saying,' Bronwen interrupted before he could finish, 'that this is all Jane's fault?'

'No.' Bronwen folded her arms, looking totally unconvinced.

'It was just a kiss. It didn't mean anything,' Dave tried to explain.

'So do you fancy Kim or what?' Dave opened his mouth but nothing came out.

'Are you planning to kiss her again?' Bronwen asked.

'Stop asking me questions.' Dave was confused enough without Bronwen giving him the third degree. 'Just tell me what I should say to Jane.'

Bronwen thought about it for a second. 'Tell her the truth. That you're a two-timing git. That you'd totally understand it if she never wanted to speak to you again.'

'I have to say all of that?' Dave ran a hand through his short blond tufts. 'Even the bit about being a git?'

'Nothing but the whole truth.' Bronwen prodded him in the ribs.

'Do you think she'll give me another chance if I tell her I'm sorry?'

Bronwen shrugged. 'Do you want another chance?'

Dave wasn't sure. Things with Jane had been rocky for weeks. One long string of rows and arguments. Jane sat with her mates in college instead of him. They'd stopped phoning each other up for long talks. They both knew it couldn't last much longer. Dave had been hoping that Jane would finish it, so he didn't have to. That way they could still be friends. But now, he'd really messed things up.

He scratched his head, confused. Why was life suddenly so complicated? How could he tell Jane he was sorry if she wouldn't even speak to him? They'd been together for eight months. They couldn't just end it like this. He'd miss Jane too much. She might have been getting on his nerves a bit just lately but he didn't want to lose her completely.

She was standing with Luke and Dean now. She'd

been hanging out with them all morning. What was the big attraction all of a sudden?

'Thanks for the advice,' he said quickly, before Bronwen could have another go at him. 'I'll catch up with Jane later.' He wandered off to get roped up, ready to tackle the rockface. It was easier than tackling Jane.

Jane linked arms with Luke and glanced over her shoulder to make sure that Dave was watching.

'Are you OK?' Dean asked. Jane nodded. She'd been letting Dean and Luke pile on the sympathy. Well, why not? The whole centre knew about Dave and Kim, mainly because Kim – the smug cow – had run around quicker than an Olympic Flame Bearer, telling everyone. Why didn't she just get it announced on the radio, so the whole of Wales knew that Dave preferred Kim to her.

'I've just had a cosy chat with Dave,' Bronwen reported back to Jane the instant he'd gone. 'He's claiming it didn't mean anything.'

'He would say that, wouldn't he?' Jane sighed. He was hardly going to admit anything else to Bron.

'And he says he's sorry,' she added.

'Sorry' was wearing thin, thought Jane. Any idiot could say it. It wouldn't make up for his store-cupboard antics with Kim.

Bronwen glanced over at Dave. 'He was asking me for grovelling tips too.'

'He's wasting his time,' Jane said. 'I don't want to hear it.' She was still too angry to speak to him; they'd only end up having another row and what good would that do?

'Let him do a bit of grovelling. It might make you feel better,' Bronwen said, shielding her eyes from the sun. Jane smiled. Bronwen had been trying to make her laugh, to take her mind off Dave and Kim, all morning. But it was a bit difficult to think about anything else when Kim was walking around with a huge grin on her face. She'd been hanging around all morning, gloating. And now she was edging closer still.

'She's trying to wind you up,' Bronwen said. 'Ignore her.' Impossible. Kim was determined to be a pain. How could Jane just ignore her?

'Hi, Jane,' Kim said, looking her over critically. 'I thought you'd chicken out of this today. I mean, it must be hard enough climbing stairs with those chubby little knees of yours, never mind a rockface.' She rolled up her leggings, showing off her skinny legs. 'Dave says I've got very sexy knees.'

'Dave's a compulsive liar.' Jane gave her a sarcastic smile.

'OK, you lot.' Chris appeared with helmets, handing them out to everyone before Kim could say anything else. 'Kim, you're climbing next. Jane, you can go with her on the other rope.' Jane groaned. That was all she needed. 'And just remember, this is not a competition,' Chris said. Yeah, but beating Kim and her spindly legs to the top would be the highlight of the holiday.

'See you at the top.' Kim flicked her hair in Jane's face. 'If you make it that far.'

'Eat my dust,' Jane muttered under her breath, as Chris attached her to the safety rope.

'You're ready to climb,' Chris said, tapping her on the shoulder.

Jane glanced quickly over at Kim, she was still fiddling with her helmet. Time to get a head start. Jane found her first foot-hold and pushed herself up. So far so good.

'Now look for your next hand grip before you move,' Chris said below her. 'Climb with your eyes first and take your time.'

She didn't have much choice. How on earth was she supposed to move from this awkward position without falling?

'Grip the surface with the side of your foot. There's a hand-hold just above your left shoulder,' Chris said calmly.

Jane slid across and up. Yes! Now she was getting the hang of it. She remembered what Chris had told them earlier. Short decisive moves. Well, that nifty little manoeuvre couldn't have been shorter or snappier. She looked over at Kim. Damn. She was pulling ahead.

'Concentrate on what you're doing,' Chris yelled. 'Forget about Kim.' Was he crazy? How could she forget about Velcro lips? Jane was determined to get to the top before Kim did.

She found a perfect foot-hold to the right and hauled herself up. Her arms were aching already. The top of the ridge was still miles away. How was she supposed to make it up there without them dropping off with exhaustion?

'Given up already?' Kim called across. She was still ahead – but only just. 'Or are your chubby knees slowing you down?'

'At least I could find a helmet to fit my head,' Jane whispered, climbing away from her to the right.

'Good move,' Chris shouted somewhere below her. Jane looked down to wave to Bron and Jez. Bad move! Her legs turned to instant jelly. She shut her eyes tight and clung to the rockface. How come she was so high up already? She had to move quickly before she lost her bottle and chickened out completely. She couldn't give Kim the satisfaction.

She grabbed a hand-hold just above her right shoulder, sliding her foot into a handy crevice. Her next two moves were obvious, staring her in the face. She paused to check where Kim was now. Yes! Jane was pulling ahead by a mile. Kim was having all kinds of problems keeping her balance. Good. It served her right for making fun of Jane's knees.

Jane made it to the top first, no sweat, and scrambled over the edge, collapsing on the grass. Her legs and arms were killing, shaking with the effort. But she'd done it! Beaten Kim and completed her first climb ever.

She took off her helmet and let the cool breeze blow her hair. The view was amazing. Green valleys and rolling hills as far as she could see. Who needed Dave when she had all this? She was young, free and ladless. It felt brilliant. From now on, she could do what she liked. She didn't have to worry about Dave being in a mood any more. Or go and watch football round at his house, when she really wanted a night out on the town. She could see more of her mates at college. Flirt with the guys in the coffee bar. Stay in to watch weepy, romantic films without Dave fidgeting about, and getting bored. It would be like starting again, a whole new boyfriend-free life.

'Great climb, I was watching you.' Dave knelt down beside her, spoiling the moment.

'What do you want, Dave?' she mumbled, still catching her breath.

'I wanted to say sorry for, you know, what happened with Kim.' He made it sound like an accident. Like he'd run her over on his mountain bike, not snogged her on purpose in a cupboard.

'You said sorry before, remember?' she sighed.

'I know,' he nodded. 'But this time I really mean it.' He thrust a bunch of dead-looking wild flowers at her. 'I picked these for you.'

She stood up, brushing him aside. 'Just get lost, Dave, I'm not in the mood.'

'Don't you want the flowers?' He followed her, looked hurt. A handful of wilting cowslips wouldn't make up for what he'd done. She walked away from him without looking back. Lads! Who needed the hassle?

'You've only just *had* a rest,' Jez called up at Bronwen.

'So?' she yelled back. 'I need another one, OK?' She was halfway up Heartbreak Ridge, her feet wedged into a gap. Even the muscles she didn't know she had until today were aching.

Rock climbing was harder than she'd ever imagined. Jane had got to the top in record time. But Bronwen just couldn't grasp the basics.

'Come on, Bron.' Jez was level with her now. 'Get a move on, it'll be dark in eight hours.'

'My hands hurt,' Bronwen sighed.

'Don't grip so hard then,' he said. 'We can finish the climb together if you like.'

Bronwen shook her head. 'It's OK. I can do it by myself.' She'd got this far without having to be rescued; she had to try and make it to the top on her own. She reached up to the small shelf-like ledge above her head then stopped.

'Urgh!' Bronwen yelled. 'A bird just pooped on my head.'

'Hazard of rock climbing. Birds use you as target practice,' Chris laughed from the ground below. It was a bit late to tell her that now.

'Just be glad you weren't looking up.' Jez was having hysterics, practically falling off the rockface.

Bronwen couldn't help smiling. When Jez laughed it was kind of infectious. 'Just get on with your own climb and shut up,' she giggled, wiping her hand on her leggings. Yuck! Why did it have to pooh on her? Kim was a much better target. She couldn't wait to have a bath back at the centre. Climbing was a sweaty, dirty sport.

'Think about your next move, Bronwen,' Chris shouted up at her. 'And remember your feet.'

She'd had trouble balancing, putting her weight on the wrong foot when she moved. Jez was a natural, scaling the rockface like he did it every morning before breakfast. She felt across the smooth surface to her next hand-grip and dragged herself up.

'Use your legs,' Chris said. 'They're not just there for decoration.'

'I know, OK? Stop yelling at me!' Bronwen answered back. It wasn't her fault. How was she supposed to remember everything at once? It was kind of difficult when she was dangling from a rockface in a nappy-shaped harness.

'There's a good grip to your left.' Jez was suddenly above her head, looking down over the top of the ridge. Great. Now he was going to lie there watching every mistake she made and comment on it.

'Don't put me off,' she warned.

'I won't, I promise,' Jez grinned.

'Stop pulling stupid faces then!'

'This is my normal face,' he laughed.

Bronwen concentrated on the last stretch of her climb, taking it slowly. It wasn't easy with Jez checking his watch every couple of seconds to see how much longer it was going to take her.

'About time too,' he teased as she reached the top. He grabbed her hand and helped her on to solid ground, slipping his other arm around her waist to hold her steady. She leaned against him, thankful to be on terra firma again.

She'd never been this close to Jez. His eyes were incredibly green and his smile . . . why hadn't she ever noticed it before? His hand felt warm and cosy in hers, almost like it belonged there.

Bronwen's heart did a tiny somersault. She held her breath. Something strange was happening. Jez was just a mate. She wasn't supposed to get butterflies just because his palm was resting in the small of her back. And maybe she was just imagining it, but wasn't he holding her gaze longer than he had to?

He finally let go of her hand, embarrassed. Even stranger. Jez never got embarrassed, about anything. She took off her helmet, playing for time until her pulse rate came back down to normal. What was going on?

'Let's go and see what's for lunch,' Jez said, punching her arm, back to his normal jokey self.

'It's too early for lunch,' said Bronwen, checking her watch. 'We only had breakfast a couple of hours ago.'

Jez shrugged cheerfully. 'It's never too early for lunch.'

'I'll catch you up later,' Bronwen said, taking a

big lungful of fresh air. She turned round to look at the view from the top of the ridge. It was pretty spectacular, almost worth the climb just to see it.

'OK, but don't blame me if there's nothing left,' Jez called, running away from her backwards, almost crashing into Fil, Jane and Lara coming the other way.

'Where's he going?' Jane asked, looking at the view again with Bronwen.

'Looking for food, as usual.'

'Did anybody else catch their knee on that lump of rock that sticks out halfway up the climb?' Lara said, showing them her impressive graze.

Bronwen inspected it. 'You were supposed to climb round that, not over it.'

'Seriously?' she said. 'Nobody told me.'

'Chris told everyone, you just weren't listening,' Fil smiled. 'Too busy thinking about Jake.'

It was true. Lara couldn't think about anything else at the moment, except that there were only two days left of this holiday, and once it was over, she didn't know when she'd see Jake again.

Last night they'd talked for hours, promising to write and phone. Jake had mentioned something about meeting up in the summer, but that was months away, and he'd been kind of vague about it.

They both had to study for exams. Lara didn't have a job and it would take forever to save up the train fare to visit him. Jake worked on Saturdays anyway. It wasn't going to be easy to keep their relationship going.

Lara had been awake for hours panicking about it. What if Jake was having second thoughts? What if he'd decided it was too much hassle to keep in touch after all? What if it all just fizzled out, or he met someone else and she never saw him again?

She gazed out at the amazing view from the top of Heartbreak Ridge with a heavy sigh. Most holiday romances didn't last. But this was more than just a five-day fling, wasn't it?

♥

Routes to Trouble

'Sorry, guys, but we'll have to bump the minibus out of the mud,' Chris said, jumping out of the driver's seat to see just how deep they'd sunk. They'd been driving across swamp-like fields to get to the start of their orienteering course, when the wheels had suddenly started spinning and they'd ground to a halt.

'The sooner we get bumping, the sooner we can start the orienteering,' Chris grinned at them all.

'What's all this *we* business?' Bronwen queried, doing up her waterproof jacket. Chris was the one who'd got them stuck. So Chris should be the one to 'bump' the bus free. 'How come we have to do all the dirty work?'

'Because I say so. And,' he said, jangling his keys in front of them, 'I'm the only one who can drive the minibus.' He climbed back into the driver's seat then stuck his head out of the window. 'Well, come on, you lot, don't just stand there staring at it, start bumping.'

'What are we supposed to do?' Fil asked, lining up along the bumper with Jez.

'Typical girl,' Jez joked. 'Doesn't know a thing about cars.'

Jane squeezed in between them. 'We bounce it up and down so the wheels can get a better grip and then Chris can drive it clear.'

'How did you know that?' said Jez.

Jane patted him on the shoulder. 'Girls don't just play with Barbie dolls and tea sets.'

'Jez is really proud of his Ken and Barbie collection,' Bronwen joked behind them.

'Very funny,' Jez grinned, making room for her. 'That's the last time I let you play with Malibu Barbie's beach hut.'

Bronwen laughed and grabbed hold of the bumper. She was still aching all over from rock climbing the day before. Jane and Fil had practically carried her down to breakfast that morning, her limbs were so stiff.

And it had taken her ages to scrub the bird poo off her helmet too; it had gone all dry and hard in the sun. They wouldn't have that problem today. It had been raining all night and now the sky was just grey and drizzly.

'We'd better swap places,' Jez said, positioning Bronwen next to the wheel.

'I'm not falling for that one.' Bronwen held him firmly by the shoulders and manoeuvred him back round again. 'If the wheels start spinning I'll get covered in mud.'

Jez wiggled his eyebrows. 'Well, you wouldn't want me to get all dirty, would you?' He squeezed in beside Jane, pushing Bronwen up to the wheel again.

'Jane, help me,' she giggled, trying to budge him.

'I can't,' Jane laughed. 'He's digging his heels in the mud.'

'Will you lot stop talking and start bumping?' Chris yelled from the driver's seat.

'Alright, keep your beard on, hippy,' Jane sighed.

'If I get so much as one speck of mud on my clothes, you're in deep trouble,' Bronwen warned Jez.

He grinned at her. 'Don't worry, I'll hose you down when we get back to the centre.'

'If we don't start bumping soon we'll never get out of here,' Fil said, getting bored.

Bronwen grabbed hold of the bumper again and helped the others. There hadn't been anything in the outdoor centre brochure about spending half the day in a mud bath.

'I could feel it shifting. One more time, boys and girls.' Chris gave them the thumbs up.

Bronwen stopped to give her arms a quick rest.

She'd be too knackered to do any orienteering by the time they'd bumped the minibus free. They tried it again.

'Yes!' Jez shouted as the tyres suddenly gripped, and Chris drove on to solid ground. 'Told you there was nothing to worry about.' He turned to Bronwen.

Bronwen folded her arms. 'Only because I jumped out of the way at the last second.'

'Looks like Fil didn't move quick enough,' Jane said, pointing over to their mate.

'Oh my God!' Bronwen gasped. Fil was a mess. She was covered from head to toe like a swamp monster.

'It's soaked right through to my T-shirt. Ew!' Fil shook her head, spraying them all with dark flecks of mud.

'Here.' Jake came to the rescue with a spare jumper. 'You can wear this.'

'Thanks,' Fil spluttered, cleaning mud off her teeth with her finger. 'But how am I supposed to take this one off?'

'Easy,' Bronwen said, taking a corner between her finger and thumb. Jane grabbed hold of the other and they pulled it carefully over Fil's head.

'Isn't deep sea mud supposed to be good for your skin?' Bronwen grinned and wiped her face clean with a tissue.

'Yeah, but what about Welsh field mud?' Fil cringed. What was that going to do to her complexion? Probably block up her pores and give her spots. Fil sighed. She didn't want to think about it.

'Jake's jumper is gorgeous,' Fil said, cuddling up inside it. 'Lara is so lucky.'

'I know,' Jane sighed. Lara was sitting just inside the open minibus, talking to Jake. They were holding hands, whispering to each other and smiling. When Jez had walked past them humming the theme to *Love Story*, they hadn't even noticed. It was so sweet. The perfect match.

'Are you thinking about Dave?' Fil linked arms with her. 'Or are we not allowed to mention the "D" word now?'

Jane smiled. She was trying hard not to think about Dave. She didn't want to spoil what was left of the holiday. He hadn't said one word to her since the dead flowers incident on top of Heartbreak Ridge yesterday. And if that was the best he could do . . .

'What are you going to do when we get back to college?' Fil asked. 'You and Dave are in all the same classes.'

'Don't remind me,' Jane sighed. But right now she

didn't feel like calling a truce. Every time she looked at Dave she remembered what he'd done and got angry all over again. It wasn't that easy just to forgive and forget. Dave hadn't exactly considered her feelings before he'd gone off and kissed Kim. How did he expect her to feel? Her mates had been brilliant. Cheering her up, keeping her company. At least they understood.

'Are you OK in that jumper?' Jake walked towards them, laughing at Fil. 'It's a bit big on you.'

'It's fine, really.' Fil hugged it closely. Jake's jumper and Jez's spare pair of jeans. It was better than borrowing the musty old rugby shirt and saggy jogging bottoms Chris had offered to lend her.

'Does anybody know which groups we're in yet?' Lara asked, holding Jake's hand.

'Haven't got a clue,' Jane said, looking round for Chris.

'Does anybody know how to use a compass?' Jez asked, appearing out of the trees to their right.

'Chris showed us five minutes ago,' Jane said.

'I must have missed it,' he grinned. 'Call of nature.'

'Are you lot ready?' Chris called, waving them over to the starting line. 'The team who makes it round the course in the quickest time using a map and a compass, wins. Team A have already gone. Team B,' he pointed at Dave, Kim, Lara and Fil, 'Get ready to go in precisely one minute's time.'

'Dave and Kim in the same team,' Jane said. 'What a coincidence.'

'Don't worry, we'll keep an eye on them for you,' Fil whispered.

'Team C,' Chris said, nodding at Jane, Bronwen, Jez and Luke. 'You'll be starting five minutes behind team B, so you won't all be tripping over each other. Team B get ready to go.' Chris counted them down at the starting line with a stop watch. 'Three, two, one, go-go-go!'

Jane watched them run off down the sloping field into the forest below. Fil was already lagging behind, tripping over Jez's long jeans.

'I bet we beat them round the course,' Bronwen said, trying to suss out which way to read the map.

'Let me look at that.' Jane grabbed it off her and studied the route. 'Why don't we take a short cut, straight through the middle of the forest. Nobody will ever know.'

'Good idea,' Chris whispered, creeping up behind them and nearly giving Jane a heart attack. 'Except you have to mark a card at each checkpoint with a special pen, so we know you haven't been cheating.'

'Do we look like the kind of girls who'd cheat, just to win a race?' Bronwen tried to act all offended.

'Yes.' Chris handed the compass to Jane. 'I'm making you responsible for the map reading.'

'Piece of cake,' Jane said. She'd just get Luke to help her if she got stuck. He did Geography so he was bound to be good at stuff like that.

'And I'll be testing out your knowledge at the finishing line to check you really did it.' Damn, Jane sighed.

'If Jane's doing the navigation, I want to change teams,' Jez grinned, standing next to her along the start line.

'I can read a map,' she snorted.

'It helps if you hold it the right way up first,' Chris turned it around and held it out to her. Jane took it back and put the compass round her neck. He was such a smart arse.

'Team C, are you ready?'

Ready for a hot cup of coffee, a piece of Mississippi mud pie and a chat with her mates, yes. Ready to hike around all afternoon looking for a bunch of special pens – definitely not.

'It'll be a laugh.' Bronwen forced the corners of Jane's mouth up, trying to make her smile. 'Just give it a go. We can't let Dave and Kim win.' Jane hadn't thought about that. She checked the compass one more time and got into a starting position.

'Five, four, three, two – wait for it,' Chris held them back. 'Go!'

Bronwen followed Jez across the field. Running was hard work in the mud; her feet were sliding all over the place.

'Where do we go when we get to the bottom?' she yelled over her shoulder to Jane.

'There should be a path to the left, no, the right. Or it could be left.' She'd dropped the map when they'd set off. Now she wasn't sure which way to hold it.

'Make up your mind.' Jez clambered over the stile and into the trees. There were two paths. 'Which one do we take?'

'Left.'

Luke looked over her shoulder. 'Yep, she's right.'

'Of course I am.' Jane clipped him over the ear with it. Maybe this map-reading stuff wasn't so difficult after all.

'Admit it, that was just a lucky guess,' Bronwen teased, waiting for her to catch up. 'Told you it would be fun.'

Fun? It definitely got the adrenaline pumping round her body. And at least she hadn't got them lost yet. 'Wait!' Jane held up her hand and called them back. 'I think we're supposed to go left again, up that track.'

'Are you sure?' Jez panted. 'It doesn't look very wide.'

She sighed. 'I'm just reading the map, I don't make the paths.'

'Come on, we're wasting time.' Luke set off down the narrow path. Jane followed close behind with Jez and Bron bringing up the rear.

Jane clutched the map tightly so she wouldn't drop it again. Jez, Bron and Luke desperately wanted to win this. She didn't want to let them down.

'Dead end,' Luke yelled suddenly, stopping up against a tall wire fence marked 'Private Property'.

'It can't be.' Jane checked the map in a panic.

'There must be another left turn further along the path we were on,' Bron said, following the route with her finger.

Jez turned around and retraced his steps. 'We can still make up the time if we run.'

More running. They should have had mountain bikes or a Jeep with a chauffeur. Jane hadn't done this much running . . . ever!

'Come on, keep up!' Luke yelled. Jane couldn't go any faster. She only had little legs. They were on the main path again, running hard, leaping over fallen branches and tree stumps.

'Left here!' Jane shouted. This time she was positive. There were fresh footprints in the mud from teams A and B. She'd even checked it with the compass.

'I can see the first checkpoint!' Jez yelled from the front. Jane stopped suddenly, gasping for breath. Bronwen crashed into the back of her.

'Sorry,' Jane panted, clutching her side. 'Got a stitch.'

'You haven't got time to have a stitch,' Jez said, running back to see why they'd stopped. 'Give me the marker card. We'll meet you at the checkpoint.'

Jane handed it over with the map. 'You can work out where we have to go next while you're at it.'

'But Chris said you were supposed to do it,' Jez teased.

'Chris doesn't have to know,' she said, still breathless. 'Just take the stupid map.' She pushed it into his hand. She couldn't see straight anyway; running always made her eyes go funny. If they took one more wrong turn they could kiss goodbye to the fastest time. And she didn't want Kim to get it. Bronwen sat down on the ground beside her as the lads ran off down the track.

'Just give me a minute,' Jane gasped, trying to breathe normally.

Bronwen let her sit quietly. It was good to stop for a minute anyway. This was the first chance she'd had to think all day. Since yesterday she'd felt kind of uneasy around Jez. Things were fine when he was being all jokey and stupid, but when he went quiet . . . She never knew what he was thinking anyway. It had never bothered her before. But now, all of a sudden, it did. And she couldn't figure out why.

'Are you ready to go again?' she asked Jane, helping her to her feet.

Jane took a deep breath, testing out her lungs. 'Do we have to run?'

'How about a slow jog?' Bronwen suggested.

Jane gave her the thumbs up. 'You're on.' She had to save her legs for the rest of the course or she'd be crawling across the finish line.

'You two took your time,' Jez said as they finally made it to the first checkpoint. 'We can't afford to lose any more time if we want to win.'

'Well, what are we hanging about here for?' Jane said, grabbing the map out of his hands and studying it carefully. 'The next bit's across open country. We have to get out of the forest. It's a straight line that way.' She pointed north. She set off down the muddy path with Luke, checking her compass.

Jez followed behind with Bron. 'I'm glad I've got you alone. Any news on the Jane and Dave situation?' he asked.

'Nothing's changed,' Bronwen puffed. 'Jane's still really angry. Has he said anything to you about Kim?'

Jez shook his head.

'Haven't you asked him?'

'No.' Jez looked surprised. 'Why, was I meant to?'

Bronwen stopped running. 'Haven't you talked to him about it at all?'

'Well, yeah, sort of.' Dave hadn't gone into details. Jez didn't really want to get involved. That's why he was asking Bron.

'Remind me not to get a girlfriend,' he sighed, starting to run again. 'They're way too much hassle.' What did he mean by that? Bronwen wondered, following more slowly behind. Was he trying to tell her something?

Jane, Luke and Jez had stopped in the middle of the path, and were looking at the map.

'What's wrong?' Bronwen asked, catching them up.

'The path just disappears,' Jane explained.

'So why don't we use the compass?' Bronwen suggested.

'Because there's another clear track we could take, down that slope. It comes out in the same place.'

'But it'll take twice as long to get there,' Jez said, measuring it out with his fingers, looking all hot and bothered.

'Not if we keep running,' Bronwen argued.

Jez wasn't convinced. 'Why can't we just carry straight on and use the compass?'

'Because we'll still get lost,' Jane said. They'd already managed it once and without a proper path to follow . . .

'Let's just take a vote on it,' Bronwen suggested. 'All those in favour of taking the new route . . . three to one. Jez, you're outvoted.'

'Let's go!' Luke was already halfway down the slope, slipping and sliding all over the place in the thick mud. Bronwen clung on to Jane for support. One false move and they'd both end up covered in the stuff.

'Watch out for the tree roots,' Jane said as they reached the bottom. They were sticking up all over the place.

Bronwen glanced back over her shoulder. 'What did you say?' She tripped over a tree root and went crashing to the ground, clutching her ankle.

'Are you alright?' Jane knelt down beside her.

Bronwen shook her head; she couldn't speak. It was taking everything she had just to stop herself from crying. She'd twisted her ankle badly when she fell. If she even moved it a millimetre it sent shooting pains right up her leg.

Jane groaned. 'This is all my fault. I made you come this way. We should have gone straight through the forest.'

Bronwen managed to gasp, 'I was the one who wasn't watching my feet.'

'Bron?' Jez and Luke ran back, crowding round her, looking concerned. 'How bad is it? Can you still walk?'

'I can try,' she winced as the lads put her arms around their shoulders and lifted her up. She steadied herself then put her foot down, testing it gently.

'Ow!' she squealed, hopping quickly back on to the other foot. It hurt too much to put any weight on it. They sat her down again on a tree stump. There was no way they were going to win the orienteering now. 'Sorry, everyone,' she sighed.

'We would have lost anyway with Jane's map reading,' Jez joked.

'I'll pretend I didn't hear that!' Jane thumped him. 'We'll have to go and get help.' Jane looked at the map. 'If we follow this route out the other side of the forest and down to the river, it takes us straight to the finish line.'

'Don't leave me here alone,' Bronwen panicked. What if they couldn't find her again and she had to sit out all night?

'I'll stay with you,' Jez volunteered.

'Thanks.' Bronwen shifted uneasily.

'Jane and Luke can go fetch Chris,' Jez added.

'We'll be as quick as we can,' Jane promised, leaving them two bags of crisps and a half-eaten Snickers bar. 'There's a bit of fluff stuck to the end but it's still edible.'

'Great.' Jez picked at the fluff and took a large bite out of it.

'Don't let him eat it all,' Jane frowned. 'And don't go wandering off.'

'There isn't much chance of that,' Bronwen said.

'Sorry.' Jane bit her lip. 'Here, you might need this.' She gave Bronwen her Walkman. 'Ear defenders, in case Jez starts telling his awful jokes.'

'They're not that bad,' he argued, kneeling down to inspect her ankle as soon as Jane and Luke had gone. 'This might hurt a bit,' he said, unlacing her boot, gently easing it over her foot. Bron held her breath. It was agony. Like the time she trapped her fingers in a car door, only worse.

'Are you OK?' Jez asked. She nodded, tears escaping down her face.

'Please don't cry,' he panicked. 'Here, dry your eyes on this.' He handed her a piece of furry tissue that looked like it had been in his pocket since 1989.

She blew her nose loudly on it and gave it back. 'Thanks.'

'Keep it,' he grinned. 'Call it an early Christmas present.'

He peered up at her from under his eyelashes, studying her face. Bron was always so controlled, in charge of her emotions. Now and again she yelled at him, but most of the time they just had a laugh. But this . . . her nose had gone all red and swollen, her eyes had disappeared under puffy lids, and she'd smeared a string of snot across her cheek with the back of her hand. He took the soggy tissue and wiped it clean.

'Don't worry,' she sniffed, wiping her eyes on her sleeve, 'I'm not going to cry again.'

Jez sighed with relief. It was horrible seeing her so upset. He didn't know what to do. He touched her ankle gently, testing where she'd injured it.

'Does that hurt?' he asked.

She shook her head.

'What about there?' he said, placing his hands gently round the sides.

'OW!' Bronwen gasped.

Jez let go of her ankle. He took off his jacket and rested her foot on it.

He was being incredibly gentle. The same un-familiar Jez who'd slipped an arm around her waist on the top of Heartbreak Ridge. She'd never seen this sweet, sensitive side to him before. He hadn't even cracked a joke about her ankle. She'd expected him to attempt at least one Long John Silver impression by now.

'So what shall we do?' he asked, squashing up beside her on the tree stump. 'We could play Name that Tune.'

Bronwen shook her head. 'I'm not really in the mood.'

There was an awkward silence. Bronwen fiddled with the toggle on her hood, trying to think of something to say. Usually she didn't have to think at all. She felt so at ease with Jez she could say anything she wanted. But this was different. Jez was carefully avoiding all eye contact. And, she suddenly realised, they were squashed together so closely, his leg was pressing up against hers. It sent a warm tingle through her body.

'Crisp?' he said, opening a bag of prawn cocktail flavour crisps and offering her one.

Bronwen shook her head. 'I'm not hungry.'

'Me neither,' he agreed, and stuffed the packet in the top of his rucksack. His hand was shaking nervously.

Bronwen stared up at him, trying to control the

sudden butterflies in her stomach. She locked on to his deep green eyes, holding his gaze. This time he didn't look away.

He bent his head towards her. Bronwen held her breath, this couldn't be happening! She closed her eyes as he kissed her softly, barely brushing her lips with his. Bronwen kissed him back, pushing the wet hair out of his eyes, her pulse racing faster than the Monaco Grand Prix winner.

'Is that your heart thumping or mine?' He pulled away from her smiling, hand on his chest.

Bronwen was still in shock. Jez had just kissed her! A proper, melty kiss that had almost blown her into orbit. WOW!

'How long do you reckon we've got before the cavalry arrives?' she smiled wickedly.

'Long enough for another kiss?' Jez grinned.

'Looks like team B have already finished,' Luke nodded over at Fil and Lara, who were already sitting in the minibus. Fil was fast asleep, her mouth wide open, catching flies. Chris was marching over to ask what was wrong.

'I'll go and tell him about Bron,' Luke took the map and sprinted across the grass to meet him halfway.

Jane let him go. She had something else to sort out. Fil and Lara were only one half of team B. What had happened to the other two, Dave and Kim? Surely they couldn't still be in the forest. All teams had been told to finish together. Unless it was Jane's lucky day and aliens had zoomed down from outer space and kidnapped Kim – Ha! no such luck.

Jane clambered over some rocks to get a better view of the area.

That's when she saw them. Locked in a crafty kiss behind a tree on the river bank. They were really getting into it. Eyes closed, lips merged, Kim's fingers playing with his tufty blond hair. Snogging for all they were worth.

Jane stared in disbelief. This time they'd gone too far. She'd had enough. She marched towards them, rolling up her sleeves ready for action. Kim saw her coming and broke away from Dave.

'Well, if it isn't Dave's ex,' she said, with a triumphant look. 'Sorry, Jane, but he's not up for grabs. He's with me now.'

There was only one way to wipe the spiteful grin off her face. Jane took a step towards them and before they realised what she was planning to do, pushed them both straight into the river. They made a spectacular splash, disappearing bums-first into the freezing cold water.

'You cow!' Kim erupted, staggering to her feet, waist deep in the river. 'Look what you've done to my clothes.'

Dave was floundering about beside her, still breathless with the cold water shock.

'Do something, Dave!' Kim screamed, waving her arms and splashing him in the face. 'Don't just let her get away with it.'

Jane was laughing so hard that her sides ached. Tears streamed down her face. This was the best thing she'd done all week. At last Kim was a mess. Make-up was running down her face, and her hair was drenched and stuck to her head. Little Miss Perfect had finally lost her cool. She was throwing a tantrum in front of Dave and it wasn't a pretty sight.

'Tell her, Dave!' Kim yelled, her face screwed up in anger. Dave pushed dripping wet hair out of his eyes, blowing water down his nose.

'Tell her what?' he shrugged, looking up at Jane. 'I guess I deserved it.'

Kim was furious. 'You big wuss!' She shoved him in the water again, then waded towards the river bank. 'Just stay away from me,' she scowled, scrambling on to the grassy bank, her feet sliding all over the place in her wet boots. 'And don't bother talking to me again.' She turned her glare on Jane, flicked her drenched hair over her shoulder in a mega strop, and squelched off towards the minibus for some dry clothes, rearranging her wet clingy knicker line as she went.

Dave stood dripping on the grass beside Jane, shaking his hair like a wet dog. 'Are you going to push me in again, or have you finished trying to drown me for the day?' He was half smiling. Not exactly devastated at the loss of Kim. He hadn't even attempted to stick up for her. He was more embarrassed at the sniggers coming from Fil, Lara, Luke and Chris.

He sat down on the grass and took off his boots, wringing out the excess water. 'I'm sorry about Kim,' he said shaking his head. 'It's all my fault; I really messed things up, didn't I?'

Jane sat down beside him. 'Yep.'

'I didn't want it to end like this.'

'Me neither,' Jane sighed.

'I just got caught up in things.'

Jane hugged her knees. Dave was actually trying to apologise. 'Did you mean what you said, about wanting to finish it days ago?' He looked straight at her.

Jane hesitated. It was time to come clean. Their

relationship was well and truly over. They both knew it. Kim or no Kim. And now that she'd pushed them both in the river and evened up the score, she didn't want to fight with Dave. What was the point?

'We can still be friends, right?' She grabbed his hand and squeezed it.

Dave looked relieved. 'Course we can, Janey.'

'Good.' She kissed his wet cheek. 'There's just one condition.'

'Name it,' he grinned.

'Stop calling me Janey, or the whole deal's off and you're going straight back in the river.' She pulled him to his feet. 'You'd better put on some dry clothes before you freeze.' They walked back towards the minibus, side by side.

'Is it OK if I call you Janey Waney?' he teased flicking water at her.

'No,' she shoved him playfully.

'Well, how about Jane the Pain?' He swerved out of her reach before she could hurt him again.

'Dave.'

'What?' He put a friendly arm around her shoulder.

'Just shut up before I smash your face in.'

New Beginnings

'I can't believe we're going home, it feels like we only just got here,' Fil shouted above the noise of Bronwen's hair dryer.

'Speak for yourself,' Jane said. She'd had a roller-coaster week full of emotional ups and downs. But she'd still managed to have a good time and, now that everything was sorted out with Dave, she wished they were staying for another five days so she could do it all again. Especially the rock climbing.

'I wish we were staying too,' sighed Lara. Five fantastic days with Jake just weren't enough. She yanked at the zip on her bag. 'This stupid thing won't do up.'

'That's because you've got my jumper in there.' Fil rescued it before it disappeared forever and found a new home in Lara's wardrobe. 'Now try it.'

'Wait!' Bronwen turned off her hair dryer, and fished her shower gel and facial wash out of Lara's bag too.

'Sorry,' Lara smiled. 'I guess I must have been thinking about something else when I was packing.'

'Or some*one* else,' Jane said, sitting next to her on the bed and putting an arm around her shoulders. Poor Lara. She'd finally found a special lad and he lived two hundred miles away. It was so unfair. He'd been stuck to her side like superglue the whole week.

Jane flopped back on the bed. Her mind drifted back over the week's events. Lara had definitely won first prize for grabbing the tastiest boyfriend – no question. Bronwen loved canoeing, Jane had done well at rock climbing. But Fil had been the star all-rounder of the week.

'Fil, you were brilliant at everything this week,' she said.

'What can I say,' Fil grinned. 'Some of us just have natural ability.'

'What's your next challenge then?' Jane teased. 'Mountain trekking, white-water rafting?'

'My mid-term geography assignment,' Fil sighed. After everything she'd done this week it would feel kind of weird doing something so normal and ordinary. She couldn't wait to go potholing and canoeing again. As soon as she got back home, she was going to join the local clubs and save up for their next weekend away. Fil was proud of herself and amazed that she hadn't even panicked once. She'd had a brilliant holiday.

'Shall we go and get some breakfast?' she suggested.

'I've got something to tell you first,' Bronwen grinned, sitting down next to Jane and hugging a pillow.

'Can you make it quick?' Fil said, her stomach rumbling loudly round the room. 'If we leave it too late the lads will eat all the toast.'

'This won't take long,' Bronwen promised. This was the first chance she'd had to tell them about Jez. Yesterday, after Chris had taken everyone back to the centre, he'd driven her straight to the hospital to get her ankle checked out. Luckily it was only badly twisted. But it had taken hours to sort out.

By the time they'd returned to the centre and had something to eat, everyone, including Jez, had been in the TV lounge. She could hardly tell her mates about the kiss while he was there.

And when they'd gone back to the dorm later, Fil and Lara had been firing questions at Jane about her pushing Dave and Kim in the river. It was 3am by the time they'd finally gone to sleep. This was the only private moment they were likely to get all day. She had to tell them now.

'Come on then,' Jane said, checking her watch. 'What's so important that we have to miss breakfast for it?'

'Jez kissed me,' Bronwen whispered.

'He did what?' Fil almost choked.

'Yesterday in the forest, after I twisted my ankle,' she smiled, remembering every single second of it.

'Is this a wind-up?' Jane gasped.

Bronwen shook her head. 'Jez kissed me and I wanted him to.'

'But how . . . when . . . I mean, why didn't you tell us something was going on?' Jane shrieked.

'Never mind that, what was it like?' Fil grabbed her arm and squeezed it.

'Are you sure it was Jez?' Lara's face was still in shock.

Bronwen grinned. 'I think I might have noticed if it had been somebody else.'

'So tell us how it happened?' Jane said, her eyes wombat-wide with anticipation. 'Did he just pounce on you without warning? What did he say? Do you fancy him or what?'

'Don't leave anything out,' Fil added eagerly.

Bronwen blew a stray hair out of her eyes and smiled. 'We were just sitting there chatting. Then he offered me a crisp . . .'

'How romantic,' Jane teased.

'Shhh!' Fil nudged her. 'I want to hear this.'

'And all of a sudden,' Bronwen continued, 'we were kissing.'

'And you had no idea it was going to happen?' Lara asked.

'None,' Bronwen shrugged.

At the beginning of the week he'd still just been Jez, her mate. The guy who sat burping famous TV theme tunes on her sofa, who borrowed her tapes and never brought them back. Somehow, since they'd arrived in Wales all that had changed. She'd seen a gentler, sweeter side to him. A different Jez to the one she thought she knew. They'd got closer than they ever had before, then yesterday . . . kissing him had just felt right. Kind of natural.

'So what was it like?' Fil asked again, edging closer.

'I bet he stopped in the middle to tell you a joke,' Jane said.

Bronwen closed her eyes so she could picture the whole little love scene again. 'I can't really describe it,' she grinned, hugging her knees. 'It was just special.'

'I just can't imagine it,' Fil said, laughing. 'You and Jez, together.'

'Well I think it's brilliant.' Jane gave her mate a big hug.

'You two were made for each other.'

'Do you really think so?' Bronwen asked. The whole idea was still pretty new to her. She needed some back-up from her mates.

'Definitely,' Jane said. 'You get on great, and let's face it, who else would put up with Jez?'

'Good point,' Bronwen smiled. She stood up, pulling Jane and Lara with her. 'Breakfast?' She felt much better now she'd told her mates about it. She'd fill them in on the details later, when they'd got over the shock.

She linked arms with Jane as she hobbled carefully down the corridor. Her ankle still hurt a bit, but it wasn't too bad. Thinking about Jez helped to ease the pain considerably!

'Why didn't you tell us all this last night?' Jane asked her.

'I couldn't get a word in edgeways,' Bronwen teased. 'You were talking about Dave, remember?'

'You should have told me to shut up.' Jane raised her eyebrows.

They stopped as they entered the dining room. 'There he is!' Jane whispered. Jez was sitting by himself. 'Are you going over to sit with him?'

'With everyone watching?'

'We're the only ones who know,' Jane reminded her. It wouldn't stay that way for long. By the end of breakfast the whole centre would know about it.

'It isn't a secret, is it?' Fil asked.

'Not exactly,' Bronwen said. She just hadn't got used to the idea of fancying Jez herself yet.

'Well, what are you waiting for?' Jane gave her a gentle push.

'You won't be able to have any private chats on the minibus.'

'Not with Big Ears here listening in,' Fil teased, pulling Jane's hair back to expose her lobes.

'Well, when you put it like that,' Bronwen grinned. 'I'll see you three later.'

She limped across the dining room, her pulse rate rocketing as she got closer and closer to Jez. They'd had breakfast together loads of times before, round at her house on a weekend watching TV, at college, in town. But this was the first time ever that she'd been more excited about seeing Jez than ordering hot cinnamon muffins before they sold out.

'Hi,' he said, pulling out a chair so she could sit down without hurting her ankle. 'How is it this morning?'

'Getting better,' she said, looking up at him nervously. He was smiling at her, his gorgeous green eyes twinkling.

Bronwen smiled back, hoping he couldn't see her heart thumping through her shirt. She sat fiddling with the cutlery. They'd never been this quiet with each other before – except when Jez had had his wisdom teeth out, but that didn't count.

Usually they sat around throwing jokey insults at each other, messing about. But this wasn't just an ordinary, everyday breakfast. They were both thinking about the kiss. It was kind of difficult not to. Bronwen was still reeling from the shock. One thing she knew for sure, the days of her and Jez being just good friends were over.

'Didn't you want any breakfast?' Jez asked.

Bronwen shook her head. She'd walked straight past the serving counter without even noticing the queue of hungry people beside it.

'You can share mine if you like.' Jez pushed his plate between them and handed her a fork. He'd never offered to share any meal with her before. It usually went straight down to his stomach without touching the sides of his mouth.

'Are you OK?' she asked.

'I'm just not hungry,' he explained, looking up at her with a cheeky grin. 'It's all your fault. If you hadn't thrown yourself at me yesterday . . .'

'Ha!' she grinned, relieved that he'd mentioned it

first. 'I did not. It was the other way round.' She grabbed the plate and pulled it over to her side of the table.

'Give me back my scrambled eggs,' he teased, holding her wrists so she couldn't move the fork up to her mouth. He brushed her skin with his fingers, then pulled her slowly towards him across the table, kissing her gently.

He'd been lying awake all night dreaming about kissing her again. He still couldn't believe it was happening. The biggest shock of all was that Bronwen felt the same way too. She was funny, gorgeous, a great mate – how come he'd never noticed how sexy she was before? He must have been blind.

'I think you'd better go and get some more toast,' Bronwen smiled, feeling flustered. She'd just discovered that kissing made her hungry.

*

'Did you see that?' Fil nudged Jane and Lara as Jez kissed Bronwen across the table.

'It's so sweet,' Jane said, amazed that Jez could be so cute.

'This calls for re-fills.' Fil gathered up their coffee mugs and dived over to the serving area. She couldn't take in shock news like this before 10am without extra caffeine and another round of toast. 'Have I missed anything?' she asked, when she returned and handed round the mugs.

'They're just talking,' Jane informed her. 'Not that we've been watching or anything.'

Lara rolled her eyes. 'Jane's been holding up a spoon and watching them in the reflection.'

'I was just polishing it,' Jane laughed. How could she not look? Her best mate was having a romantic *petit dejeuner* with Jez. Bronwen couldn't drop a bombshell like that, then expect them to sit and talk about the weather.

'Have you seen Jez and Bron?' Dave squeezed up next to Jane with his breakfast tray. 'How long has that been going on?'

'Since yesterday,' Fil said, shuffling her chair to the left so she could see.

'If we all moved over there,' Dave nodded to an empty table right next to Jez and Bron, 'we could hear everything they say to each other.'

'Don't be so nosey,' Jane said.

'That's rich coming from you.' Fil picked up a spoon and waved it in front of her face.

Jane pinched a slice of Dave's toast, grinning, 'That's different, I was being subtle.'

'There's a first time for everything, I guess,' Dave

joked. 'OW!' He jumped up out of his seat as Jane poked him gently in the bottom with a fork.

'Serves you right for being so sarcastic,' she smiled. It would take some time to get used to being single again and seeing Dave just as a friend. She'd been afraid that it would be awkward after all that had happened with Kim. But so far, things were going fine. Breaking up had been the right thing to do. Now they could wipe the slate clean and try to forget about Kim.

'Kim hasn't spoken to me since yesterday,' Dave told her, concentrating on his cereal. 'I think she's still a bit annoyed. I'm glad you pushed us in the river though,' he added, grinning. 'I was wondering how to get rid of her.'

'She dumped you,' Jane reminded him.

He shrugged. 'Same difference. Toast?' He offered her a half-eaten slice. She took a bite and chewed it as Kim walked past their table, nose in the air, ignoring everybody. She sat down next to Elliot, cuddling up close to him like they'd never been apart.

'Good luck to him,' Dave mumbled under his breath. 'He's going to need it.'

Lara waited for Jake in the empty TV lounge, flicking

♥   151   ♥

restlessly through the channels on the television. They'd arranged a last private rendezvous to exchange addresses and say goodbye properly. She wasn't looking forward to it. She didn't want to leave Jake. She was having too much fun.

And she still didn't know for sure how much he really liked her. They'd spent tons of time together just talking and cuddling and having a great laugh. But now it was all over . . . they were going to have to go their separate ways. It didn't make sense.

'I haven't got long,' Jake said, eventually appearing in the doorway. 'We're leaving in a few minutes.'

Lara nodded and handed him a slip of paper with her address and phone number on it, written in big block capitals so there was no chance of him getting it wrong.

'Thanks.' He put it in his pocket. 'Is it OK if I give you a ring tonight?'

'Ring any time after eight. Mum goes out on a Friday,' she said. She didn't want everyone listening in on their conversation.

He took an envelope addressed to her out of his back pocket. 'My address and everything,' he sighed. Lara held the envelope close to her chest. It was thick, more than one page long. More than just an address. The first love letter he'd written her.

Jake looked embarrassed. 'Don't open it now,' he grinned. 'Save it for later, when you're alone. Some of it's a bit . . . personal.'

'Really?' Lara wanted to rip it open and get straight to the personal bits. But she slipped it into her pocket instead.

'I've got something else for you. Close your eyes and no peeping,' he smiled.

Lara closed them tight, wondering what on earth he was doing. It sounded like he was getting undressed. She opened one eye carefully to see. He was taking off his sweatshirt and throwing it on to the sofa. He pulled his T-shirt over his head.

Lara took a sly peek at his bare chest. It was just as gorgeous as the rest of him.

'This is for you.' He handed Lara his favourite T-shirt. 'I thought you could, you know, sleep in it or something.' He put his sweatshirt back on and looked at her, unsure. 'It probably needs a wash.'

Wash it, when it still smelt of him? Was he mad? It was never going near a packet of Ariel. 'I love it, Jake.' Her voice was breaking up. She gave him a huge hug. She didn't want to let go. He was so gorgeous. It might be months before she got this close to him again. That's if she ever got this close to him again.

'I'd better go before they leave me behind,' he said, taking her hand and leading her to the door.

'I wish they would,' she sighed, resting her head on his chest. Then he'd have to go home with her and their feelings wouldn't have a chance to fizzle out.

Lara pulled away from him. She had to know if he was planning to see her again or not. 'So, are you coming to visit me in the summer?' she asked anxiously, watching his face.

Jake took a deep breath and sighed. 'No.'

'No?' Lara felt sick. That was it then. It was over. He must have decided that with them living two hundred miles apart, it simply wasn't worth it.

'But I was thinking,' Jake said, fiddling with his hair, 'maybe when I've passed my driving test, I could borrow my brother's car and come over to see you then.'

Lara stared at him in shock. She didn't even know he was having lessons. 'Why didn't you tell me?' she whispered.

'I had to ring my brother and do a lot of crawling,' he explained. 'I didn't want to tell you until I was sure he'd say yes.'

'When do you take your test?' Lara brightened.

Jake grinned. 'In two weeks' time.' Two weeks! If he passed his test they could be driving out to the beach, sharing an ice cream and messing about in the waves in less than twenty days. Yes! Everything was going to be great. Jake wanted to see her as much as she wanted to see him. She was so relieved.

'Here.' She undid her pendant and tied it around his neck. 'Good luck charm for the test. Don't lose it,' she smiled. 'I need it for my exams.'

'Thanks.' He tucked it safely inside his sweatshirt. 'I really have to go.' He smoothed her cheek gently with the back of his hand.

Lara tilted her chin upwards. She reached up to him on tiptoes and brushed his warm lips softly. 'That's so you don't forget me,' she smiled.

'There's not much chance of that,' Jake grinned. 'I'll ring you tonight.' He gave her hand a quick squeeze then dived out of the door.

Lara hugged herself tightly with both arms, spinning round in a little celebration circle. Life was so weird. She'd been in the middle of a record breaking boyfriend drought when they'd arrived at the centre. And now – she did another quick twirl – she'd just said *au revoir* to her luscious, new, long-distance boyfriend.

He burst suddenly back through the door, practically knocking Lara off her feet for one last cuddle.

'Jake!' she grinned, hugging him tightly, melting

into his warm body. 'Just make sure you pass your driving test first time round!'

'I don't want to worry anybody but I'm feeling a bit queasy,' Fil said, rubbing her tummy.

Bronwen looked at her pale face warily. 'But we've only been on the bus for ten minutes.'

'Open a window,' Jane suggested. 'Fresh air might help.'

Lara pulled a packet of travel sickness tablets out of her bag and chucked them at Fil. 'I bought these specially for you.'

'Thanks.' Fil sighed with relief.

'Poor Fil,' Jane whispered. 'Do you think she'll be alright?'

'Just keep your fingers crossed,' said Lara.

'And a plastic bag handy,' Dave grinned, poking his head over the back of his seat as they hit a bump in the road. 'Will you lot keep it down, I'm trying to get some sleep.'

'Dave needs all the beauty sleep he can get,' Jane teased, pinching his cheek.

Dave was just annoyed because she'd managed to grab the back seat of the minibus for the journey home. Fil, Lara and Bronwen were sharing it with her.

Jez was at the front, trying to show Miss Havistock a quicker route home.

'Good news,' Jez said, collapsing in the seat beside Dave. 'I think I've finally taught Miss Havistock how to read a road map.'

'Maybe you could start on Jane now,' Bronwen giggled.

'It should only take us about four hours to get home,' Jez moved Lara's bag and sat next to Bron, quietly taking her hand in his.

Bronwen smiled. It had been quite a week.

Caught in the Act

Kate Cann

Curtain Up

Aisha threw her bag into a corner of Philly's living room, chucked her coat after it, and fell on the sofa. 'I'm knackered,' she groaned. 'Three hours non-stop rehearsal. Trying to look like I'm in love with that jerk Joel the whole time. D'you realise the effort that takes?'

'Yep. Superhuman,' said Philly, collapsing beside her.

'Well, don't ask me for sympathy,' put in Tasha, squeezing on the end of the sofa. 'I've been sewing stupid glittery wigs all day.'

'I saw them,' said Philly. 'They looked fantastic. Are they for my scene? Beauty School Drop Out?'

'Yeah,' grumbled Tasha. 'And it can drop *right* out as far as I'm concerned. My hands look like they've been grated.'

'Oh, stop moaning,' said Aisha. 'You wanted to be in charge of costumes.'

'Well, *you* wanted to be leading lady.'

'Yeah, but not opposite Joel. If he was any more up himself he'd turn inside out. He's such a pain.'

'Can't you just ignore him?'

'*Ignore* him? Tasha, I have to spend half my life mauling him. I can't take any more.'

'Well, *I* can't take any more cutting and stitching and . . .'

'God, you *miseries*!' exploded Philly. 'It's all worth it. It's going to be brilliant. It's going to be the best production of *Grease* the world has ever seen.'

'Maybe,' grunted Tasha. 'Right now I'm too tired to care. And I'm starving. And dehydrated. Who's going to get the drinks?'

'That's all the way to the fridge,' moaned Aisha. 'You go.'

'No. You.'

'Philly – it's your house. Come on. We're guests.'

'Uninvited!'

'Go on. Philly. Please.'

There was a silence as all three girls settled deeper into the sofa. Finally Philly staggered to her feet and stomped off to the kitchen. She came back with three cans of lemonade and three bags of crisps, saying, 'Here you are, you lazy cows.'

'Lifesaver Award to Phillippa Howard,' said Aisha gratefully, reaching for her share. 'Thanks, Philly.'

'Yeah, thanks,' said Tasha, crunching furiously. 'Oh, that's better. Nourishment. Liquid. And I guess my wigs do look OK, even if my hands will never be the same again.'

'They looked fantastic,' said Philly. 'And that's the last time I'm telling you.'

'So, what d'you think of the new girl?' asked Aisha suddenly.

'Ness? Far too pretty. Hate her,' said Tasha.

'She's all right,' said Philly firmly. 'I think she's fitted in brilliantly. I mean – it's no joke, coming into a production half-way through. It's no joke coming to a college half-way through.'

'Philly, you're always so *fair*. And positive. It's dead irritating. What I mean is – is she as good as Jan?'

Philly rolled her eyes skyward. 'She's better,' she said, 'and you know it.'

'Yeah well – this glandular fever thing, it must have been dragging Jan down these last weeks – her voice had gone, and . . .'

'Aisha, Ness is a better actress than Jan will ever be. With or without glandular fever. Everything's taken off since she took over as Rizzo.'

'She's perfect for Rizzo,' agreed Tasha.

'Some compliment,' Aisha muttered. 'Rizzo's a queen-bitch slapper with a smoking problem. And yeah – Ness *is* good as her.'

Tasha burst out laughing. 'Oh dear. We're not likely to get any objective criticism from you, are we, *darling*? What's the matter? Feeling a little upstaged?'

'No,' retorted Aisha, glaring.

'OK, then – you're jealous because Ness has to snog loverboy on stage, and she really puts herself into it. You're scared Sean'll get blown away and realize what he's been missing for the last six months, give you the heave-ho and . . .' Tasha broke off with a squeal as a cushion landed in her face. Laughing, she lobbed it back at Aisha.

'You're not really jealous of Ness are you, Aisha?' asked Philly, all concern. 'You can't be. Sean's mad on you. He wouldn't even look at anyone else. Everyone knows that.'

'Da-da-dada,' intoned Tasha, singing the Wedding March. 'Da-da- da*da* . . .'

'Tasha, I'm *warning* you – No, Philly. I'm not jealous. I feel so secure with Sean I . . .'

'What?'

'Oh, nothing. I feel very secure, that's all. And Ness is fine. It's just – I mean, she throws herself around so much.'

'She's got energy.'

'Yeah, but there's no need to spew it over everyone so much, is there? That last dance scene with Sean – she nearly went into orbit.'

'Oh, Aisha,' said Philly, giving her a friendly shove, 'leave it *out*.'

The girls stayed motionless on the sofa for a while, chatting about the rehearsal, watching the early evening soaps on the TV and gratefully accepting Philly's mum's offer of a sandwich. Then at about seven, Aisha and Tasha heaved themselves to their feet, slipped reluctantly out into the dark, wintry streets and plodded home.

Aisha let herself into her house, staggered upstairs

and flopped back onto her bed. Slowly, she pulled the band off her long, blonde hair, letting it fall loose and heavy over the pillow. Then she put her arms behind her head and gazed up at the ceiling where she'd taped a large photo of Sean. He looked down at her, grinning, one corner peeling off. He had sandy hair and a great smile, with grey-blue eyes and a mouth that was made to be on the move.

It was their six-month anniversary in a week's time. Six months since that amazing party when they'd finally got together after weeks of eyeing each other in the college canteen and walking slowly past each other in the corridors.

You're a looker, all right, she thought, staring up at him. You're a real looker. And you belong to me. She closed her eyes and thought about the way he said her name whenever they met up, always pleased and somehow surprised, as though he couldn't get over the fact that they were an item. She thought about the way he got her by the elbows and pulled her in close and kissed her. She told herself how nice it was, never having to wonder what you were doing at the weekends, always having someone to go to clubs and parties with, always having someone there at the end of the phone.

'I am so lucky,' she whispered up at the photo. 'I've got you, and I've got the lead in *Grease*, and everything's going right for me.'

Then she rolled over onto her side and sighed, as though something inside her wasn't convinced.

♥

Sporty Boys

Rehearsals started at ten sharp the next morning for the boys in the cast. They were running through one of the fast numbers and working on the choreography. The girls had been told to turn up at twelve to do the café scene, but Aisha and Philly drifted in around eleven. They wanted to see how the lads were doing.

The two girls found themselves a seat at the side of the drama studio and settled down to watch. Music was pounding out so loudly it made the air vibrate. Up on stage, Sean, Ian, Charley and Joel were lined up, learning the steps.

'Sean – easc it off a bit!' yelled the director, Bill. 'I know I said I wanted it raunchy, but those hip movements are obscene!'

Aisha laughed as Sean mimed an even more

obscene movement at Bill's back and then waved to her, a big smile splitting his face. 'He'll be worse now you're here,' grinned Philly.

'OK,' shouted Bill. 'One more time. From the top. And remember – it takes *discipline* to move like a bunch of kids who don't know what the word discipline means – and not end up in a heap on the floor, OK? GO!'

'God,' said Aisha. 'Why does Bill have to be such an idiot. He's so over the top.'

'I know,' said Philly. 'All that "hey – I'm one of you guys" stuff. It's embarrassing. Blimey – look at them go!'

The dance routine the boys had worked out needed all their skill and energy. They jumped in the stage car, they jumped out, they threw each other about – and all the time they were singing, loudly. It looked like chaos, but each movement had to fit the main pattern, so timing was crucial.

'Look at them all,' breathed Aisha. 'Just watch Ian move.'

'Who d'you think I'm watching?' hissed Philly. 'Yes! He did it. He's been practising that back flip all week.'

'Must have been fun for you.'

'It was OK. Jesus – Charley nearly crashed off the stage then.'

'Joel's out of place. Again. Look – he's thrown them.'

'I love this number,' said Philly happily, nodding her head to the beat. 'It's corny, but I love it.'

'Hey – *HI*!' came a shrill voice from behind them.

'Oh God, what does she want?' grumbled Aisha.

'Have the new chorus guys turned up yet?' the shrill voice continued.

'There's your answer,' smirked Philly. 'That's what she wants. *Hi*, Karina. Come to watch?'

Karina was blonde, voluptuous and voracious for new talent. Male talent. She plumped herself down beside Aisha and Philly. 'Oh, it's just that lot still,' she said dismissively, eyeing the stage with distaste. 'Bill said he was bringing in some more guys just to fill out the scene, you know, at the back.'

'Yeah, he is,' said Aisha. 'Real rough types. He wants authenticity.'

Karina brightened. 'He does?'

'Yeah. One of them's six-six, apparently. Muscles like Schwarzenegger.'

'*Yeah?*'

'Scars all up his arms, one ear missing . . .'

'Oh, shut up, Aisha,' Karina complained. 'You're always taking the piss. It really gets on my nerves.' She glared at Aisha with hostility.

Karina played Marty in the show, and still hadn't got over Aisha being given the lead instead of her.

'I think he's got three guys lined up,' said Philly. 'God knows how he got hold of them.'

'Ah, it'd be no problem, luring them in,' said Aisha. 'The drama department is famous for its female talent.'

Philly laughed. 'Too right. Anyway – they're here. We're going to have some serious moving going on for the big dance sequences now.'

'Mmmm,' breathed Karina. 'Sounds *good*.'

'Tasha's got her hands on them at the moment, in the green room. Trying to turn their number threes into fifties quiffs.'

Karina scrambled to her feet, scooping up her bag from the floor.

'Off to the green room, Karina?' laughed Aisha.

'I need Tasha to take my skirt in,' she shrieked back over her shoulder. 'I've just been losing *so* much *weight*.'

'Pass, the sick bag,' groaned Aisha as, up on stage, Bill called a break. Sean and Ian jumped down and headed for their girlfriends. Aisha smiled as the two boys loped towards them. They moved well, like dancers – supple and powerful. They were both great looking guys, Ian a bit shorter than Sean, and much darker – perfect for Philly with her cropped, white-blonde hair. When the four of them went out together, people turned to stare at them.

'Hey, Aisha,' said Sean, coming to a halt in front of her. He was still panting from the dance routine.

Aisha stood up and moved forward to give him a hug. His back felt hot and damp from all the exercise and she could see sweat running down his neck. 'You need a shower, mate,' she said, wrinkling her nose, and he laughed and grabbed her. She slotted under his arm so naturally now, so smoothly, as though they'd been made to fit together.

'That was all right, that routine,' she said. 'You looked good up there. It's coming together, isn't it?'

'Think so,' said Sean. 'God knows what'll happen when we get the beef up there with us though. We're bumping into each other all the time as it is.'

'Have you met them yet?'

'Yeah. They seemed OK. Seemed to think it was all a big laugh.'

Ian raised his head from a lengthy hello kiss with Philly. 'Joel can't understand it. Can't see why they're needed. Mind you – he'd like the whole thing as a solo.'

Sean laughed. 'Yeah. He was saying to me how he never knew what to do in all the gaps. I told him I thought it was pretty tight production – turns out he meant the gaps when he wasn't speaking!'

'Oh, Sean,' said Aisha impatiently. 'He's not that bad.'

'He is,' said Philly. 'Anyway. Are you guys free after this next session?'

'Yep,' said Ian. 'I've had it up to here.' He put

his arm round Philly, pulling her in close. 'Go back to your place? I'm only two weeks late on that economics assignment. One more night won't make any difference.'

Philly put her arms round his chest and squeezed him hard, looking mockingly up into his face. She loved the way he always gave in to temptation – especially when it involved her. 'It's so tough being a stage star *and* still be expected to work, isn't it?' she said.

'Really tough.'

'OK. What about the pub tonight?'

'Yeah. Then we could get a Chinese,' said Ian. 'It's a real laugh, watching you try to eat with chopsticks.' Philly smiled, and hugged him a lot tighter. 'Ouch. What about you two?' he added, turning to Aisha and Sean.

Sean smiled down at Aisha. 'Sound good to you?' he said.

Aisha smiled back, nodding, feigning enthusiasm. And the words came into her head: How cosy. A foursome. *Again.*

'All right, you slackers, back on stage!' yelled Bill. 'I want you four – and Charley and Joel.

Where's Ness? Isn't she here yet? We'll have to go without her.'

Ness was standing in the girls' toilets, gripping the edge of the basin, staring at her face in the mirror, trying to turn herself in to Rizzo. First she had to slow her breathing right down and clear her head of all the shrieking fear and jangling worries and self-doubt. She needed a calm, clear space in there, to let Rizzo in. Only then could she walk out and face everyone.

In the green room, Tasha was trying to keep her cool under pressure. She was penned in by large, well-muscled males. One was seated in front of her, duplicated by the mirror, and two more were standing on either side of her. They had their arms folded and they were leaning towards her, watching her every move.

The mirror reflection frowned as she tugged hopelessly at its hair, trying to make it quiff upwards. 'Maybe it'll be OK,' she said doubtfully.

'I mean – you'd never be able to grow it in time, would you? And some blokes in the fifties had crew cuts. Only I think the ones that did were all in the army.' Oh, *God*, Tasha, stop whittering, she thought.

'But we're not meant to be soldiers, right?' said the guy to her left.

Great grasp of the script, she thought, wondering how to answer that – then she was saved by Karina bounding through the door.

'This skirt is *huge* on me,' shrieked Karina, 'it practically *falls off* – oh *hi* guys!'

'Hi,' said the three sporty boys, in deep unison.

'I'm Karina,' she gushed. 'I play Marty. And you're . . . ?'

'Dave.'

'Chris.'

'Andy.'

'We fill up the background in the dance scenes,' Chris said.

'I bet you do! Fan*tastic*. Have you rehearsed yet?'

'We haven't even learnt the basic steps yet,' said Dave. 'We're sp'osed to be in the gym . . .'

he checked his watch. 'Christ! Fifteen minutes ago.'

'You'd better go,' said Tasha hastily. 'I've done my bit.'

'I was thinking,' said Chris. 'What about side-burns? I can grow them really quickly.'

'Ooooh, can you?' said Karina.

'Good idea,' said Tasha. 'You need to look kind of . . . sleazy.'

'No problem for Chris, that,' laughed Andy. 'Sleaze is his middle name.'

'Oh really? said Karina, coy as hell. 'Why's that, then?'

There was a silence, during which everyone but Karina looked embarrassed. 'What gear d'we have to wear?' Andy asked.

'Oh, jeans and white T-shirts,' said Tasha. 'And you'll just need basic stage makeup.'

This caused loud laughter and the usual run of *ooh-sweety* comments from the three lads as Tasha opened the door and ushered them out.

Karina collapsed petulantly into the chair that Chris had just vacated. 'What d'you have to sling them out so soon for?' she grumbled.

'I didn't. You heard them – they had to get to the gym.'

'Well, you didn't have to remind them.'

'Yes I did. I had to get them out before you got completely embarrassing. You're like something out of a *Carry On* film sometimes, Karina, I swear. And this skirt is fine on you. If anything, it's tight.'

'Oh, lighten up. I just wanted a reason to come and see you.'

'See *me*? Sure it was me!'

Karina shrugged happily. 'Who cares. That Chris guy was lush. You're *sooo* lucky, getting to tart up all these guys, stripping off their shirts, measuring their inside legs . . .'

Tasha grinned. 'Yeah, well. I need some compensations in this job.'

'So – which one did you go for?'

'I didn't. Not my type.'

'None of them?' Karina was incredulous. 'You're joking. They were all so *fit*. You know what your problem is, Tasha? You're far too choosy. Mind you . . .' and she sneered sideways at Tasha, 'I suppose you do have very distinctive taste.'

This was a comment on Tasha's style. She had richly coloured, wavy hair that she wore differently every day. She liked experimental makeup. She wore three earrings in one ear and one in the other. And she *never* bought her clothes from high-street stores.

'I'm an art student,' said Tasha drily. 'I have to look like this. It's in the contract.'

'Oh, ha ha. Hey – can anyone go to the gym? Only I was thinking – I wouldn't mind starting a weights programme. Just to tone up, you know.'

'Karina,' Tasha groaned, 'why don't you just go and look up the word 'subtle' in the dictionary – and then try to *be* it a bit more?'

Karina smirked and tossed her blonde hair back from her face. 'No one ever got anywhere good by being subtle,' she retorted – and left.

♥

Minefield

'Sorry I'm late,' Ness called out from the back of the hall. She was speaking in the voice she used for Rizzo – gravelly, confident, a bit aggressive.

'OK,' said Bill. 'Try to make it on time next time, OK? We're just getting to you now.'

Ness walked up to the steps, aware that everyone was staring at her. Not with hostility – but just the staring was daunting enough. 'People are bound to stare,' she said to herself. 'You waltz right into a starring role in your second week here – and you attract attention. Just use it, work it, use it for yourself.'

She strutted onto the stage, forcing herself to be brave. A few of the cast smiled and 'Hi-d', and Bill clapped his hands for everyone's attention. 'OK. We've been through this café scene a few times before, and it was good but it's got to be better. It's all on you in this scene, Rizzo. You're the centre. You're scared you might be pregnant – and the way I see it – you're even *more* scared Kenickie might dump you if you are. So what do you do?'

'I dump him first,' said Ness quietly. 'I hurt him before he can hurt me.'

'Good. And Sean – what do you feel? What's going through your mind?'

Sean grimaced. He hated it when Bill started his cheesy method-acting stuff.

'Come on Sean – what do you *feel*?' Bill repeated.

'Well – when she says it's not mine, that's it, right?' muttered Sean. 'I'm so hurt I can't even see straight, right?'

'Right. You're not a subtle guy.'

There was general laughter. Sean and Ness were staring at each other, thinking their way into their characters.

'OK,' said Bill. 'So we need hate and love and fear all mixed up together, Ness. It's a tall order. Let's go from the beginning.'

Aisha's eyes were glued on Ness as she crackled her way through her lines, throwing off anger and need like electric sparks, being somehow hateful and loveable both at the same time. 'OK,' she said to herself, 'I admit it – you can act. You can *really* act.' She could see Sean was charged by Ness's performance, lifted by it. She watched as he grabbed hold of Ness, pulling her against him, making her look at him, face so close to hers they could have kissed. They held that position for a long time, much longer than they'd done before. The passion between them made the air shake, made everyone else on stage fade into the background.

When the scene was finished there was a silence, then Bill shook his head, as though he couldn't quite believe it, and started clapping. 'That was brilliant, kids,' he said, 'you've cracked it. We can't better that. Hold on to it. *Hold on* to whatever you were feeling when you did that scene – it was magic.' He took a deep emotional breath, then beamed round at them all. 'OK – let's break for today.'

'Whooo!' said Philly, as they all clambered down

from the stage, 'that was something else. That got top marks. I've never seen Bill so disgustingly happy about anything.'

Joel glared at Philly. 'You weren't here last Thursday. My reunion scene with Sandy. He said I was superb.'

'Bill doesn't use words like superb, Jo,' said Sean. 'Ever.'

'It's Jo-EL,' Joel snapped. 'Jo-EL. Is that so difficult for you to remember? It's only two syllables, for Chrissake.'

'Sorry, Jo, er . . . Jo-EL. I just don't know why I have a problem with it. Do you, Ian?'

'No idea. It's a great name.'

'Shut *up*,' laughed Philly, whacking Ian on the back.

Joel. He drove everyone up the wall, particularly the girls. They couldn't get over why such a superb physical specimen should be such a total *jerk*. It was such a waste. He had a face carved by an artist, a body fit for a model – and a mind that short-circuited whenever it was asked to consider more than just his own sweet self, self, self.

'Let's go to the canteen,' said Charley. 'Let's celebrate the star performance.'

'Count me out,' sniffed Joel. 'I have lines to learn. *Some* of us have more lines to learn than others,' and he stalked off.

'What a prima donna,' breathed Ian, as they all watched him go. 'Can't bear the spotlight on anyone else.'

'He's a good-looking bloke,' Ness ventured.

'Don't,' said Philly. 'Don't even think about it, Ness. Aisha'll tell you. She went out with him last year.'

Aisha groaned. 'Oh, thanks, Philly. Shout my crap taste from the rooftops, why don't you. It was before I knew what he was like, Ness. I mean, you're right – he is good looking.'

As she was speaking, Aisha slid her eyes over to look at Ness, taking in her incredible green-brown eyes and mass of auburn hair. Joel isn't the only good looker around here, she thought, ruefully.

'So what happened?' said Ness. 'How long did it last?'

'Two dates,' Aisha said. 'That's all I could stand.

Joel's dad's quite a big actor – he must've told you. He tells everyone.'

'Yeah, he did,' admitted Ness. 'All that stuff about acting being in his blood . . .'

'Right. Well on the second date he took me home and sat me down in front of a video of one of his dad's tired old costume dramas. And while I was watching it, trying to keep awake, his *dad* came in and sat down right next to me on the sofa and started asking me what I thought of it!'

'So that was why the second date was the last date?' asked Ness, laughing.

'That and the fact that he snogs like a sink plunger.'

'I reckon he still fancies you,' said Ian, stirring. 'Those stage kisses aren't just for show.

'What?' said Sean. 'I'll kill him.'

'Oh, leave it out,' said Aisha. 'I've warned him – any tongue, and I'll knee him. I feel like getting the mouthwash out each time as it is. But he's a bit slow to get the message – I don't think he can believe I'd go for Sean over him.'

'None of us can, Aisha,' said Ian. 'Serious taste lapse there, girl.'

'Yeah, right,' said Sean. 'Very funny. Now come on – let's go and get a drink.' And he put an arm round Aisha's shoulders and steered her towards the canteen, with all the others following, still chatting about the rehearsal and laughing about Joel.

They bought drinks and headed for a table at the side. Ness and Charley sat opposite each other, up against the wall; Sean slid in after Ness and Aisha followed Charley, then Sean reached over and held Aisha's hand across the table.

'Stop luvvy-doveying Aisha and budge up,' said Ian, shoulder barging Sean as he tried to sit next to him. 'Come on. My arse is halfway off the seat.' Sean moved nearer to Ness, but he still left a gap between them, a space.

A space like a minefield, Aisha suddenly thought, a space too dangerous to cross. Why was Sean so scared of sitting near Ness? It was as though all the passion from the scene they'd acted together was still there between them.

Ian attacked his milkshake with a long, drain-like gurgle and said, 'What time are we meeting tonight, Philly?'

'If you keep making disgusting noises like that we're *not* meeting. Ever again.'

'OK. What time?'

'Eight?' said Philly. 'Eight, Sean?'

'Eight OK, Aish?'

Aisha nodded, smiling at him, trying to look enthusiastic. Then she finished her drink. Over the rim of the glass she watched Sean and Ness as they didn't look at each other and didn't touch.

Sean's Gorgeous

Sean and Aisha and Philly and Ian all turned up together at the pub at the same time. They found a free table in the corner and collapsed round it with their drinks and packets of crisps.

'God, it went so well today,' said Sean. 'It was almost worth feeling this knackered for.'

'Almost,' agreed Philly. 'And I'm glad Ness came along with us, after the rehearsal. It was like – I dunno, we hadn't been that friendly before . . .'

'Yeah?' said Ian. 'Well, don't blame Sean and me. I can just imagine the reaction from you girls if we'd been *too* friendly. She's a babe. Joel's on her tracks already. Good job you warned her off, Aish.'

Aisha shrugged. 'It's not up to me to tell her who to go out with. Maybe she fancies him.'

'I don't think so,' Sean said. 'I found her hiding from him the other day, in the props room.'

Aisha looked at Sean, suspicion in her eyes. 'Yeah? Did she say that was what she was doing?'

'Sort of. Well, she said she just went in there for some space, but I saw Joel prowling around outside.'

'Maybe she did just want space. I think she's a bit of a loner.'

Sean shrugged. There was a pause, then Philly stood up. 'Coming to the bog, Aish?' she said.

'Do they synchronise their bladders or something?' grumbled Ian, as the girls headed off.

'Nah,' said Sean. 'They just like to go places in pairs.'

'Weird. Want me to come with you to get the next round in?'

'Yeah, funny. No, I don't.'

'What's up, Aish?' asked Philly, as they leaned across the sinks and examined their faces in the dingy mirror.

'What d'you mean – what's up?' said Aisha.

'I dunno – you just seem a bit down tonight.'

'Oh – I'm tired. That's all. Why – have I been really boring or something?'

'Well – not exactly a barrel of laughs. Never mind.' Philly spiked her fingers through her hair and turned to grin at her friend. 'Well, how are you going to celebrate it then? And can I come?'

'Celebrate what?'

'You *know* what. Next week – you and Sean have been together six months!'

'Oh, *Philly*,' groaned Aisha. 'How come you remember that?'

'Because I was there when it all started. When you two finally got it together. Oh, it was dead romantic . . .'

'Philly – don't make me *cringe* . . .'

'. . . *and* a huge relief. All you'd *done* up 'til then was whitter on about how fit Sean was but you were too scared to speak to him . . .'

'Christ, was I that bad?'

'Worse. And then that party came along, and the two of you disappeared for ages, and then walked back into the room, hand in hand . . . *Gaaaad*! The start of a perfect relationship.'

'Oh, leave it out,' Aisha snapped.

'Come on, how you going to celebrate? Big party? Hoards of people – loads of nosh?' joked Philly.

'I kind of think it'll be just the two of us, OK?'

'OK. Your loss.'

The girls left the loo and went back to their table. Sean was still at the crowded bar. Philly wrapped her arms round Ian's waist and nuzzled her face into his neck, and then they started chatting about the great party they were going to have once the show was over, a last-night party to end last-night parties. Aisha smiled to herself as she listened to them laughing and flirting together. Philly and Ian had been together for over a year, the original match made in heaven. They're so good together, Aisha thought, they still get such a buzz out of each other. When you listen to them chat, you know the spark's still there.

And suddenly she felt like a cold hand had got hold of her, somewhere deep inside. She looked miserably over at the bar. Sean was standing there, one foot propped on the rail, trying to get the barman's attention. Face it, she thought, it's not like that for me and Sean, not any more. Not like it is for Ian and Philly. I've stopped feeling any sort of spark.

She sighed and looked down at the table. You haven't just had a down patch, she said to herself, or been fed up, or tired, all the things you said to yourself to explain why you never really wanted to kiss him any more . . . why you always pulled away before it went any further . . . why he's been getting on your *nerves* so much lately. You just don't feel hooked on him any more.

She looked sadly over at Philly and Ian, who were talking together, nose to nose. What am I going to do? she thought. I can't just – end it. It'd be horrible. Even thinking it is horrible. How do you tell someone you've just – gone off them? I can't hurt him, I can't. He's such a good bloke. And not so long ago being with Sean was everything, it was all I wanted. Oh, God. *Why* can't that feeling come back?

Ness was stretched full length on her bed, with

the bedroom door barricaded against her two little brothers and her Walkman plugged in against the din of the television downstairs. She subsided into the music, feet moving to the beat, hands behind her head, and realised she felt happy.

The feeling of happiness hadn't been around much since her family had had to up stakes and move right to the other side of the country. At first, she'd missed her old friends so badly she'd felt she was going crazy. Then, when she'd landed the role of Rizzo in the Christmas production, she'd been scared but delighted. Acting meant almost everything to Ness. She was determined to prove herself and today – with that scene with Sean – she was just beginning to think she was pulling it off.

Ness rolled over onto her side, then slid off the bed. She felt restless, energised. Today, she thought, when we went to the canteen – I almost felt part of it. I felt accepted. They're a good crowd. Aisha's brilliant – a bit cool, maybe, but I really like her, and Philly and Ian are dead friendly when they're not stuck to each others' faces.

She sashayed a few steps round the room, nodding her head to the music. Then she threw herself down in front of her dressing table, leaned her face in her hands and stared at her reflection.

'He shouldn't be allowed out,' she mouthed. 'He should be branded with a health warning. Oh, *God*, he's gorgeous. I love the way he moves – when he dances on stage, and I love when he hardly moves at all, the way he just lounges in a chair, as if he's so relaxed with himself. I love his voice, I love the way he laughs, the way his eyes crease up when he laughs, that lopsided smile he's got . . . And, *oh God*, when he gets hold of me, when he kisses me, when we dance, I'm going to pass out with it one day, it's too much, he's gorgeous, Sean's *gorgeous*.'

♥

Frosty!

The next day, Tasha arrived at the green room early with an original Coca-Cola shirt someone's grannie had found up in the attic. Five minutes later Charley turned up to meet her, as arranged.

'Here,' she said, holding the shirt out to him. 'This is why I wanted to see you. It's such a find, Charley. It's authentic fifties.'

Charley looked at it and grimaced. 'Yeah, but it's also seriously tacky. Look at the *collar*. Why do I have to be the one to wear it?'

''Cos Bill's decided Putzy is a bit of a geek, OK? Come on, try it on.'

Grumbling to himself, Charley peeled off his T-shirt and slipped the shirt over his back. 'It's way too tight,' he said, pleased. 'Look – the buttons don't even meet.'

'Charl -ey,' remonstrated Tasha. 'Make an effort, can't you? Look – you haven't even got it *on* properly.' She reached up to his shoulders, tugging the shirt material round his chest. 'C'mon – I spent a whole half hour last night mending a tear in it.' She started to do up the buttons.

Charley leaned towards her, letting her hair brush his face. '*Mmmm,*' he said. 'You smell expensive.'

'Yeah? Well, it isn't expensive. Where would I get the money for good perfume from?'

'I dunno. Maybe someone bought it for you.'

Tasha shook her head and carried on fastening up the buttons. 'I can always move these over a couple of centimetres,' she said, 'give you a bit more space.' Just as she got to his navel, Charley grabbed her hands, pressing them up against him.

'Don't,' he said, 'I'm ticklish down there.'

'OK, you do it then. C'mon, Charley, let go of my hands.'

'Come out with me, Tasha,' he said, pulling her closer. 'Go on. Just one date.'

'Charley, we've been through this.'

'But how can one date hurt?'

'No. I told you. I just want to be friends. Now come on. Let go.' But she didn't pull her hands away. It felt good, pressing her hands to his stomach, feeling the muscles there, the tension in them. It's so long, she thought, since I've been held by a boy. Since I've been kissed. Then this desire to just reach up and kiss Charley came over her and she pulled away from him, abruptly.

'Whooo,' Charley said. 'Frosty.'

'Oh shut up,' Tasha snapped. 'Why do blokes always say stuff like that when girls don't fall at their feet?'

'Hey, calm down. I was only joking. I just think we'd have a good time together, Tasha, that's all. I think you'd enjoy yourself. I mean – what are you saving yourself up for?'

Then he unbuttoned the Coca-Cola shirt in silence, took it off and threw it on a chair, put on his T-shirt and left the green room, look-ing sulky.

He's right, thought Tasha, what *am* I saving myself up for? Charley's a nice guy. He's funny, sweet . . . She sighed and picked up the shirt

Charley had discarded, smoothed out the creases and hung it on a hanger. Maybe old happy-slappy Karina's right, she thought. Maybe I *am* far too choosy.

In the drama studio, rehearsals were in full swing. Everyone knew that things had shifted up a gear. The countdown had started; there were less than three weeks to go now until opening night. Bill went into panic overdrive, working everyone really hard all morning. He wasn't a bit satisfied with Joel and Aisha's love scene at the drive-in.

'Come on Aisha,' he said, 'put a bit more into it. You're completely *bonkers* about this guy. The attraction's so strong it's broken through all your prejudices about boys like him.'

Joel smirked in her direction and flicked back his perfectly cut hair. It'd take more than attraction to break through my prejudices about him Aisha thought sourly. She stomped back to the wings to make her entrance again, muttering about it taking more than just talent to act like you were mad on Joel.

Five minutes into the scene, Bill sent her back to the wings again. 'Come *on*, Aisha,' he said. 'You look like you're kissing your grandma. Give me some passion, can't you?'

Aisha scowled and headed once more for the side of the stage. While she waited for her cue, she noticed Sean and Ness chatting at the side of the hall. Plenty of passion going on there, she thought uneasily. *Great* body signals. She watched Ness throw back her head and laugh. Ness couldn't seem to keep still on her feet; she was drawing spirals in the air with her hand as she explained something, all happy animation. Sean was laughing too. He had his arms folded, as though he needed to protect himself from something.

This time, Bill let the scene run its full course. He announced he still wasn't satisfied, but it was getting better. Then he told everyone to break for lunch. Aisha jumped down from the stage and joined Sean and Ness. 'Hi,' she said, taking Sean's arm a bit possessively. 'Having fun?'

'It's happened,' Sean said, laughing. 'Joel asked Ness out.'

'Oh, *no*! What did you *say*?'

♥   199   ♥

'*No*, of course! But he couldn't seem to understand it. It was like I was talking in Martian or something. He kept trying to, like, *interpret* what I was saying as a *yes*.'

'He'll think you're really weird now. Or blind,' said Sean.

Ness laughed. 'Or totally lacking in taste – or *gay* – or . . .'

'C'mon, Sean,' interrupted Aisha. 'Let's get lunch. I'm starving.'

'Want to join us?' Sean asked Ness.

'No,' said Ness. 'Er – thanks. I'll see you later, OK.'

Don't worry, Aisha, Ness thought, as the couple swung out of the room, arms round each other. I don't go in for trying to steal other girls' blokes. Anyway, I wouldn't stand a chance. How could I match up to you? I can see how relaxed you are with him, how confident. I can be that as Rizzo – scrape my fingers across his back, get hold of his chin, pull his face round to mine and kiss him. But in real life? That's different. That's totally different.

Serious Second Thoughts

Dave, Chris and Andy, the three sporty lads who'd volunteered to swell out the background in some of the dance scenes, had their first rehearsal with the rest of the cast. It was chaotic and noisy – and a success.

When they'd finished, all the lads jumped down from the stage, laughing and chatting. Immediately, Karina whisked into the middle of them, yelping congratulations. Tasha had wandered by with an armful of clothes and stayed to watch; Andy made a beeline for her and started asking for her opinion on how he'd done. Ness was laughing with Charley; Joel was chatting up two of the chorus girls.

Sean got hold of Aisha's hand and together they stood in silence, watching all the ducking and weaving. It's like we're kids who can't join in the fun, thought Aisha, miserably. We have each other, so we're out of the game. And it suddenly hit her how much she really missed all that, the silly, meaningless fun of it, the excitement – flirting and fooling around and just having a laugh.

'Hey, Aisha,' said Philly, wandering over, 'you know that essay you said you'd help me with . . .'

'Did I?' Aisha replied unenthusiastically. 'Oh, yeah. How far have you got?'

'The opening line?'

'Oh, *Philly*.'

'It's a good line! Honestly, it's a *great* line. But I've got no idea how to continue. I've done the research, honestly Aish, but I've got writer's thingy – you know, block. Serious writer's block. And I thought if you wouldn't mind . . .'

Aisha's mind drifted off as Philly tried to talk her into helping her out. Sean had slipped her hand and had gone to join Ness and Charley. She watched him walk up to them: from the minute he joined them, it was as if Charley was sidelined. Out of the picture. Sean stood right in front of Ness, close, and she turned all her attention to him, and Aisha, watching, had this sense of an energy field between them, communicating all sorts of unspoken things.

Sean and Ness started laughing together, really cracking up over something Sean had said. Sean put his hand on Ness's arm, as if he might fall over if he didn't have someone to support him, and Ness's eyes were wide and wild and fixed on his face.

And Aisha felt the cold hand again, pressing down on her. Face it, Aisha, she thought, we never have fun like that any more. Never. If I had the guts, I'd finish it, only I'm scared that'll make me feel worse. Then she turned away, depressed.

'OK, kids, listen up,' said Bill loudly, coming to the front of the stage and clapping his hands. 'We have a lighting boy at last. I'd better introduce you to him.' He spun round and shouted towards the back of the stage, 'Aidan! Aidan? You back there? C'mere a minute will you?'

There was a long pause, then a bad-tempered thud, as though someone had dropped something heavy on the ground from a great height. Then Aidan appeared through the curtains.

He was black, about six foot two, long, long

legs, broad shoulders. Expressionless face, carved, symmetrical, perfect. Strong nose, strong chin, deep, deep, dark eyes.

For at least five seconds, Tasha forgot to breathe. He's the one, she thought, half in delight and half in sheer panic. He's the one I've been waiting for . . .

Karina had been smitten by a similar affliction. She goggled at Aidan, open-mouthed, and then she giggled.

'This is Aidan,' said Bill, in a matter of fact tone. 'He's doing art and he's a genius with lighting – he's already come up with some good ideas for the show. So help him out when you can, guys, OK? He's going to be around a lot in the next couple of weeks. Right, Aidan?'

'Right,' said Aidan. 'I s'pose.'

He had a deep, dark voice, all soft and resonant. When she heard it, Tasha sighed with yearning. Karina clutched the arm of the girl standing next to her and mock-swooned. Aidan gave one long, expressionless look at the group in front of the stage, then he turned silently on his heel and stalked off, back behind the stage curtain.

'Blimey,' said Sean. 'What's his problem?'

'Dunno,' said Ian. 'Having to work with Bill?'

'Maybe. He's got a real chip on his shoulder about something.'

'Chip on his shoulder?' put in Joel. 'He could supply *McDonald's*.' He went off into a peal of self-satisfied laughter.

Sean turned to look at Joel. 'That joke doesn't really work,' he said. 'They're called fries in McDonald's, not chips.'

'And it makes it even *less* funny when *you* laugh at it,' added Charley. 'It kind of makes the fact that no one else is laughing a lot more obvious.'

'Not planning on a career as a stand-up comedian, are you mate?' said Ian. 'Stick to straight.'

Joel spun on his heel, swung his bag angrily over his shoulder and stomped out of the hall 'No offence, Jojo!' Sean shouted after him.

'Aw,' said Philly. 'I could almost feel sorry for him.'

'Don't bother,' said Ian. 'He's been really pissing us off. You try dancing next to him. It's a nightmare.'

'The only good bit today,' added Sean, 'was when Chris put him out of action for half an hour by landing on his foot.'

'By accident?' Philly gasped.

Ian shrugged. 'Who cares?'

Who indeed? thought Tasha, as she floated back to the green room. Right now she didn't care about anything, anything at all, but getting another glimpse of Aidan. If he's doing art, how come I haven't seen him before? she wondered. Someone that completely, breathtakingly fabulous doesn't just blend into the crowd. Just where has he been hiding?

'Come on girls,' shouted Bill from the stage. 'Let's have one more run through of the dreaded sleepover scene. Full bitch mode, OK?'

Sean and Ian watched as the Pink Ladies and Sandy clambered back on the boards. 'This scene gives me the shivers,' muttered Sean. 'D'you think they're really like that – on their own I mean?'

Ian laughed. 'We'll never know.'

'We could bug one of their bedrooms.'

'I think I prefer not knowing.'

'Yeah. Maybe you're right.'

There was a silence. 'So,' said Ian, 'what are you getting Aisha for your six-months' thing then?'

'What?'

'You could get jewellery. Girls really like that. A necklace or something.'

'Hmm. Earrings, maybe. She's had her ears pierced again.'

'Yeah – earrings'd be good.'

There was a pause. 'And?' said Ian.

'And – what?'

'What are you going to do to celebrate?'

'Oh, for God's sake. I dunno. Nothing.'

'That'll be fun. Aisha'll really know where she stands then.'

Sean looked up, annoyed. 'What're you saying?'

'Oh, work it out Sean,' Ian snapped. 'You'd have to be stupid not to see what's going on.'

Sean lowered his head and glared at the floor. There was a burst of music from the stage. Ness was belting out her 'Sandra Dee' song, all mockery and exaggeration.

'It's her, isn't it,' said Ian.

Sean shook his head, as if to shake something away. 'Oh, God,' he burst out. 'She's – she's so – she's – I don't know. Look at her. She's gorgeous. She blows me away. Oh, God, I don't know. I don't know what to *do*.'

Lights, Action

When the scene was over, Ness smiled patiently as Bill gushed out congratulations on her song, then she hurried from the stage, calling out an excuse about having to get home quickly to babysit her little brothers.

'You're going to blow it, Ness,' she muttered to herself as she raced away, 'you're really going to blow it if you don't watch it. Why d'you have to go and get the hots for him, you idiot? You were just beginning to feel part of the group – and now this happens. Aisha's hardly going to want to chum up with someone who's after her bloke. She probably thinks there's something going on already, the way we . . . the way we . . . what *is* going on anyway? Does he have any *idea* what I'm feeling?'

* * *

News of Aidan's arrival had spread like wildfire through the girls in the cast; it seemed he was all anyone could talk about. Groups of girls hung out backstage just on the off-chance he'd slope by; they'd stare fixedly as he climbed up and down his ladder; and they'd sit in huddles in the canteen, discussing him. His long legs, his broad shoulders, his gorgeous face, the way he moved, his total air of mystery. No one had seen him smile and no one had yet got him to open his mouth, but this just strengthened his appeal.

Tasha didn't like being part of a fan club, especially one with Karina as a leading member, but she had to admit she was as hooked as the rest of them. She had only to catch sight of him and her heart speeded up. She'd met Aisha for lunch and talked of nothing else but Aidan for the whole hour, leaving Aisha really amazed, because Tasha had a real reputation for being impossible to please as far as guys went.

'You mean there's *nothing* wrong with him?' Aisha had asked, incredulous. 'Nothing you'd change at all?'

'Nothing,' Tasha had said mournfully. 'It's an obsession, Aish. It's eating me up.'

And as if being eaten up wasn't enough, she was having big problems with the costumes, too. She wanted to go really over the top with the 'Beauty School Drop Out' scene, but the boy playing the Teen Angel said he couldn't move in the Elvis-style shirt she'd designed for him. They'd met to work out a compromise but it had practically ended in a fist fight. Tasha had wound up yelling abuse and telling him to make his own damn costume. Then she stormed back to the green room, dumped the costume and locked up for the night.

'I've had it with this place, and this stupid play,' she grumbled to herself, as she stomped along behind the stage to the exit. 'You get no thanks, no gratitude, no acknowledgement that you're giving up *all* your free time . . .'

Suddenly a pair of very long, jeans-clad legs swung down in front of her face and Aidan dropped like a vampire from the rafters, landing on his hunkers right next to her.

It was a completely thrilling appearance. It so shocked Tasha she couldn't breath for a second or two.

'Sorry,' he grinned, standing up straight. 'I dropped

my screwdriver.' He bent to pick it up off the floor. 'You were looking like I feel, girl. What's up?'

'What's –? Oh. I – er – I just had a row with someone.'

'Boyfriend?'

'Oh . . . no . . . someone I've made a costume for. He hates it. Says he can't move in it.'

Aidan shook his head. 'Typical. Actors. It's all ego with actors. I hate 'em.'

Tasha laughed, delighted. 'Yeah, me too. Well, right now, anyway.'

'They don't see broader than their own selves. All those big egos, up on the stage together, banging into each other. It stinks.'

'Yeah. I mean – I wouldn't have minded so much if I hadn't spent so *long* on it. But he just chucked it aside like a – like a *rag*.'

Aidan shook his head. 'It's like all that counts is their performance. They don't rate what anyone else does.'

'Yeah. Anyway.' She cast her mind frantically around for some more conversation. Anything to keep this fantastic creature in her line of vision a bit longer. 'How're you getting on with the lighting?'

'OK. But they won't let me do anything interesting with it. I had this great idea, this grim lighting, for one of the sad scenes – and that dark-haired guy, that Joel?'

Tasha groaned. 'I know him. Biggest ego of the lot.'

'He said it made his face look sallow. Jesus. He was checking in this mirror on the side of the stage – I couldn't believe it. I told him to put more blusher on. He didn't like that either.'

'No, he wouldn't.'

There was a pause. Tasha could feel her blood racing. 'Well' said Aidan. 'I'd better get back up there. Screw in some more 40-watts.'

She laughed and watched him as he turned his back on her and started clambering up the side ladder, hauling himself up with incredible ease. She stared after him, oblivious to anything else, hoping he wouldn't turn round and catch her staring.

He *talked* to me, she thought. He actually opened his mouth and *spoke*. Then she floated out of the drama studio and into the street, high as a helium balloon.

*　　*　　*

'It's happened, we've talked, I'm in *love*!' Tasha screeched down the phone to Philly. Then she went over the whole scene she'd had with Aidan, second by second, nuance by nuance, in a non-stop, pleasure-filled monologue. She analysed everything. When he'd said 'You were looking like I feel' it *had* to mean he'd been watching her before he jumped down, it *had* to. Which meant that seeing her had to be *why* he jumped down, it absolutely *had* to. She described in detail the dazzling moment when he'd just dropped out of the rafters and landed beside her. Whoooo, she breathed, remembering the impact it had had on her. Whoooo-*ooooo*.

On the other end of the phone, Philly was enjoying a slow foot massage, courtesy of Ian, and she managed to 'mmmmm' and 'aaaah' with real feeling in almost all the right places. 'So when are you going to ask him out?' she said, when Tasha finally let her get a word in.

'Ask him . . . ?! You've got to be *joking*. I couldn't just *ask him out*.'

'Why not? He's just a guy.'

'Philly,' said Tasha firmly, 'Aidan is not "just a guy". He's – I don't know what he is.'

'A god? A sex hologram? An alien from planet *Lurrvvv?*' suggested Philly, while Ian laughed.

'Get lost, Phillippa Howard. If you're just going to take the piss . . .'

'Aw, Tasha. I'm not. Honest. It's brilliant. *He's* brilliant. I think he definitely fancies you and you should ask him *out*!'

'No. Never. I couldn't. I'd – I'd sooner – I *couldn't*. I mean – if I tried to – I'd – no, I *couldn't*.'

'So what you going to do, then?'

'I don't know. I just don't know. But I have to get him. *Somehow*.'

After ten minutes more of this Philly managed to put the phone down. 'Tasha's found someone she really fancies at last,' she told Ian. 'I've never heard her this blown away about *anyone*. She's really got it bad.'

'Me too,' murmured Ian, moving slowly up Philly's leg.

Girl Talk

The next morning's rehearsals went along at a great pace. Bill announced that they'd really got the whole thing together now and that all that was needed was some ironing out here and there. Then he told them to clear off for an early lunch.

Joel cornered Aisha just as she was disappearing out of the door to fetch her coat. 'Aisha!' he said gushingly, laying a hand on her arm. 'Aisha, we really have to talk.'

'We do?' said Aisha reluctantly.

'Yeah. Our scenes. They're just not as – they're not as *hot* as they should be. I think we need to practise.'

Oh, spare me, thought Aisha. She suddenly felt incredibly weary. 'Well, you know, Joel,' she said, 'I don't know about hot, I'm kind of playing Sandy as *very* virginal, you know? Very reluctant. I mean – I think that's what attracts Danny. Don't you?'

'Well – yes,' said Joel. 'But at the end – when Sandy gets all tarted up – that's when she really comes alive, surely. Physically.'

'Yeah – but she's inexperienced, remember. She's shy. I think it should all be *implied*.'

'But there are more *direct* ways of implying it,' said Joel.

'I'm not sure that makes sense, Joel, does it? Bit of a logic-gap there. You can't say . . .'

'My dad said he'd run through it with us if we wanted,' interrupted Joel. 'Maybe give us a few tips.'

Over my dead body, thought Aisha. 'That's . . . nice of him, but . . .'

'He knows a lot about this kind of acting. How to . . . Well, you saw him in that telly-drama, remember?'

It's etched on my memory with acid, thought Aisha. 'Joel, I really don't think . . .' she began.

'Oh, Aisha. You didn't always find it hard to get passionate with me. Did you?' And he moved closer to her, smiling.

'Look Joel, just cut it out,' said Aisha warningly. 'That was ages ago.'

'Only seven months.'

'Joel, there's nothing between us. You *know* that,' she said, backing away.

'I've changed a lot in those seven months, Aisha,' he replied, following her. 'I've really – *matured*.'

He'd somehow managed to manoeuvre her into the wide space between two sets of lockers in the corridor, blocking her escape route. Oh, blimey, she thought, I'm going to have to smack him one in a minute.

Joel put his arm snakily around her shoulder. 'Come on,' he murmured, 'I'm only talking about an extra rehearsal.'

Aisha pulled away and saw Ness standing there watching them, one hand frozen on her locker door, mouth hanging open.

'Hey – *Ness*,' squawked Aisha. 'Come to find me? I'd forgotten I'd said we'd have lunch. Joel – I'll catch you later. OK? C'mon, Ness.' And she pushed past Joel, grabbed Ness by the arm and towed her along the corridor towards the exit.

'Sorry,' she breathed, as soon as they got outside.

'I had to do that. I had to. He'd started to get all nostalgic about me and – *whoo*. I mean – I could've just kneed him, but that would have made acting opposite him a *bit* difficult – even more gruesome than it is now.'

'It's fine,' said Ness. 'I understand. It's just I thought I was hallucinating when I saw you two together.'

'Yeah, well – I wish you *had* been hallucinating. God, what a slimeball. What a *creep*. Saying he wanted to rehearse the love scene with me. *Urrgh*!'

Ness laughed. 'Well, you handled it brilliantly. Queen of diplomacy.'

'You think? Yeah – maybe you're right.'

'I *am* right. You put the show first. That's just so unbelievably *noble*, Aisha!'

'Totally self-sacrificing, right?' laughed Aisha. 'Anyway – thanks for playing along with it. I am *so* glad you appeared when you did!'

'S'OK. Glad to help out. OK then . . . I'll . . . I'll see you . . .'

'Ness, look – why don't we have lunch anyway? Let's get out of this place, just for an hour or so.'

'Well – yeah . . . OK.'

'Café des Amis, in town. Have you been there? It's great. *And* cheap.'

'OK, I'd love to,' Ness grinned. 'Come on, let's go.'

The two of them hurried out of the college grounds and into the centre of town. Aisha started yakking away about how Joel was so oblivious to the difference between acting and reality he was convinced her smitten onstage act was for real and that was why he'd tried it on again. Ness made her laugh telling her how Joel was still unable to grasp the fact that she, Ness, didn't want to go out with him and how he kept suggesting different places to go and telling her not to be so shy.

'Shy!' said Ness indignantly. 'He really thinks the only reason I've said no is because I'm *shy*!'

'It's really sad, when you think about it,' said Aisha. 'I mean – he's so one-dimensional. Half-dimensional. Can you be half-dimensional?'

'Joel can.'

'He just wants a girlfriend, but it's going to be hard finding someone who thinks as much of him as he does himself. Come to think of it, it's scientifically *impossible*.'

This is weird, Ness thought, as they turned into the café and found an empty table. We're getting on really well together. *Can* you get on really well with the girlfriend of the guy you've fallen for? Aren't there laws about things like that?

The girls ordered open sandwiches and juice and settled down to eat. 'Ness – I'm going to come clean,' Aisha suddenly announced. 'I don't think I was as friendly to you when you first joined the cast as I should've been. And that was totally unfair of me. I mean, you can't help your looks, can you?'

For a moment, Ness looked stricken. 'My . . . ?'

'*Or* the way you act.' Aisha burst out laughing. 'You should see your *face*! Your *good* looks, dummy! And you act brilliantly. You know you do.'

'*Oh*! Er – thanks. So do you. I mean . . .'

'And we have something in common now, right?'

Ness's stomach felt as though it had gone into seizure. 'We *do*?' she whispered.

'Yeah. The honour of having Joel hitting on us.'

'Oh. Right. *Right*!'

'Cheers,' said Aisha, clinking her glass into Ness's.

'Cheers,' Ness replied, relieved. Aisha's great, she

thought. I'd really like her as a friend. No wonder Sean's so into her. Oh, *God*.

'So,' went on Aisha, 'what do you make of the cast then? And are you drooling over the new lighting boy, like everyone else is?'

Ness shrugged. 'Not really. I mean – I can see he's gorgeous, but . . .'

'Gorgeous? He's *sensational*. He must work out five hours a day to get a body like that. Or maybe it's all the clambering about he does, fixing the lights. Everyone's getting in a real state about him, it's amazing. Even Tasha's lost it, and her standards are well high . . . and Karina's just about doing herself in over him.'

'Karina? I thought she was after Chris . . .'

'Karina always has lots of possibilities lined up. She gets through about eight men a week. Well – maybe not eight, but you know.' Aisha shrugged. 'I dunno. I envy her in a way.'

Ness's mouth dropped open. '*You* envy *her*? But you've got – you've got . . .'

'Sean. Yes I know. And he's great. It's just – sometimes I miss really partying, really going wild, you know? I don't mean completely crazy, like

Karina. Just messing around, having some fun.'
She leaned over the table to Ness, smiling. 'Hey
– you know Dave – the big guy at the back in
"Greased Lightning"?'

Ness nodded, wide-eyed.

'I really like the look of him. He's cute. Oh, not
for anything serious, just to have a laugh with. Just
to get off with at a party and . . . snog each other
senseless!' She laughed; then she threw herself back
in her chair and sighed. 'I shouldn't be *feeling* this,
right? Not when I'm going out with Sean.'

'No, but – you can't help what you feel,'
stammered Ness.

'I just – I just feel so *tied down* sometimes,' Aisha
almost exploded. 'I feel like I'm standing on the
edge, watching it all go by without me. Oh, it was
brilliant to start off with, absolutely brilliant, with
Sean and me. He was absolutely all I wanted – I
even taped his photo to my ceiling, so I could go
off to sleep gazing up at him – I mean, besotted or
what? But the last couple of months it's just been
– oh, I don't know. I'm beginning to feel – I feel I
want to move . . . I'm – I'm *bored.*'

Under cover of the table, Ness was digging the

nails of one hand into the palm of the other. It was as though she was being given some very precious information – information she didn't quite know what to do with yet.

'He gets on my nerves sometimes like – like – *anything*,' Aisha rattled on. 'I feel such a bitch, but I can't help it, he irritates me, and I snap at him, and – oh, I don't know, we just don't seem to have a laugh any more. It's all got really samey. I used to wait for him to phone as though my life depended on it, and now half the time I'm all, oh God, what does he want again . . . and yet he's so sweet, and we still have good times, it's just . . . *Jesus*, Ness, d'you mind me going on like this?' Aisha said, suddenly, leaning over the table towards her. 'It's just – it's easier sometimes, talking to someone you don't know. Know that well, I mean,' she corrected herself, catching Ness's downward glance.

'No – it's – really, it's fine,' croaked Ness.

'Tasha can't get her brain round anything that isn't Aidan at the moment. And Philly – she just thinks we're perfect for each other. I tried to talk to her the other night and she went on as though feeling like this was something that would just go away – like it was a silly phase I was going through. I mean – to her, splitting up with Sean is completely unthinkable. She said you can't *expect* it to be as exciting six months on as it was at first. Well – I want it to be. I want to feel those goosebumps again!' Then Aisha stopped and looked at Ness, almost in surprise at everything that had just poured out of her.

'It must be awful,' said Ness, with real sympathy.

'It is. I'm really messed up about it.'

Ness made herself meet Aisha's eyes and said, 'And you don't know how he feels?'

'No. But then – I don't suppose he knows how *I* feel. I mean, I don't think I've been acting all that different when I'm around him. I just don't want to *hurt* him. I'm so fond of him. And it's not his fault.'

Ness took a deep breath. 'You should talk to him,' she said. 'You should tell him. It's just not fair not to. Not fair on you or – or him. I'd hate to be with someone who was with me just 'cos they felt sorry for me. I'd *hate* it.'

Aisha looked down at her plate. 'Yeah, I know

you're right. It's just – suppose it really hurts him? I mean – just how *do* you tell someone you've gone off them? It's horrible. It makes me feel sick just to think about telling him. I wouldn't even know where to *start*.'

'Maybe if you start talking,' began Ness, 'maybe you'll find he feels a bit the same. I mean – if the spark's gone, maybe it's gone for both of you.'

Aisha looked up. Her face looked suddenly drained and wan. 'I've got to do it, haven't I?' she said. 'I can't let it go on like this. It's eating me up inside. It's like living a big lie.'

There was a long pause. 'We'd better get back,' said Ness abruptly, checking her watch. 'Look at the time. I've got a class at two.'

The girls left the café and made their way back to college. At the doors, Aisha said goodbye and thanks to Ness, then she stood and watched her as she hurried down the corridor. Well, Aisha, she thought, full of self-amazement, you really let it all hang out then, didn't you? You really let the floodgates open. To the one girl who probably has most interest in Sean being single again. Freudian or *what*?

*   *   *

Ness didn't go straight to the classroom. She ducked into the girls' toilets and stooped over a basin to splash cold water on her face. Then she dried her skin and looked at her reflection in the mirror. It stared back at her, eyes wide. The conversation she'd had with Aisha had torn her in two. She felt almost hysterical, as though she wanted to cartwheel round the room; she felt guilty and happy and sorry for Aisha and mad with excitement, all at the same time. 'Now what?' she whispered to herself. '*Now* what?'

The Big Break-up

'I mean – he's incredible,' Karina was burbling, sprawled on the old sofa in the green room. 'Like a panther. He's so strong – you should see the way he lifts things, all those heavy lights and things. And he has the best arse in the world.'

Tasha groaned and pulled a box of stage makeup towards her. She was supposed to be sorting it out and making a list of stuff she needed to replace.

'He gave me *the* most seductive look the other day,' Karina droned on. 'I mean – I really think he's noticed me.'

'Yeah?' snapped Tasha, throwing kohl sticks into a tin. 'And what about Chris?'

'Chris? Oh, he's yesterday's. He has nothing like the shape that Aidan has. That guy is gorgeous. He has pecs like I've never *seen*. He has legs that just go *all the way* and . . .'

Something in Tasha cracked. 'You know what, Karina?' she said. 'I'm just about sick of listening to you. You're like some old lech, pulling dirty mags down off the top shelf. You should hear yourself. Cute butt, great pecs, good legs. It makes me want to throw up, it really does.'

'Well, *sorreee*!' said Karina sarcastically. 'I certainly didn't mean to sicken you.'

'You *dissect* them. I mean – you're like some kind of butcher. You think that's all there is to a bloke.'

'I do not!' Karina's eyes were wide with indignation. 'I just appreciate good looking lads. What's the matter, Tasha?' she added nastily. 'Don't you?'

'Yes. But I don't bleat on and on about it, and I don't embarrass them by . . .'

'By what?'

'I saw you! Hanging round right underneath Aidan's ladder, ogling up at him, making all those comments . . .'

'Look – I was just showing my appreciation . . .'

'Yeah? Well, *you're* pretty quick to get snotty if any bloke talks about you that way.'

'Not if it's the right bloke, I'm not.'

'Oh, for heaven's sake. Hasn't it ever occurred to you that people are more than just their *bodies*?'

Karina gawped at her. 'You doing philosophy or something?' she said. 'I thought you were textile art.'

Ness walked into the canteen, saw Sean, Ian and Charley sitting in the corner together and panicked. She cast one look of sheer longing at Sean then she went to the counter and took a long, long time choosing a salad.

'Look who's come in,' said Ian meaningfully.

'I can see her,' said Sean.

'What?' said Charley.

Ness put her salad on a tray, got a drink and paid. She stood looking anywhere but at Sean, then she waved frantically to a girl in a green dress who was sitting on the other side of the canteen. The girl was a bit surprised, because she and Ness had barely spoken to each other before, but they were in the same history group, so she smiled and beckoned Ness to join her.

The three lads watched Ness cross the floor and sit down with her back to them. 'Avoidance tactics,' said Ian, even more meaningfully.

'Look – shut up, you smug git,' said Sean.

'What?' repeated Charley.

'Well, why didn't she sit with us, eh?' went on Ian.

'Maybe your ugly face put her off, mate. Maybe she's heard about Charley's burping problem.'

'Or maybe . . .'

'Look – just *shut it*. You don't know what you're on about.'

'Oh yes I do,' said Ian.

'What's going *on*?' said Charley.

Once Aisha had decided she had to talk to Sean about their relationship going nowhere, she knew she had to get on with it fast, before her courage failed her. She phoned him and arranged to meet him in the pub that night. As she got ready to go she kept rehearsing over and over in her mind what she had to say to him, until the words got jumbled up and senseless and meant nothing.

I wish I could have a script for this one, she thought. I wish I could just say my lines, and he could say his, and it would all be predictable and the curtain would come down and we could go off home and forget it.

She was so nervous by the time she got to the pub she was actually shaking. Sean was already at the bar, with two drinks in front of him. When she came up beside him he smiled and kissed her and gave her one of the drinks. Then he put his arm round her and steered her towards an empty table by an open window. A thin, cold breeze was blowing in from outside. Aisha inhaled it thankfully, hoping it would clear her head.

'So,' said Sean, 'how's things?'

'Fine. I – fine. Bill is *finally* satisfied I'm putting enough passion into my last scene with Joel.'

'Not too much, I hope,' said Sean, in automatic-boyfriend-mode.

'No chance of that. How's your dad? Has he got over his flu yet?'

'Yeah – well, nearly.'

'Still in bed, still driving your mum mad?'

'Yes. Well – he got up to watch the footie last night.'

'Good. That's good. Who was playing?'

'Er – Arsenal. And Tottenham.'

'Right. Good match?'

There was a pause. Suddenly, Sean pushed his chair away from the table and sat back. 'OK, Aisha, what is this?' he said. 'Since when have *we* made small talk?'

'What d'you mean?'

'What did you want to see me about? You sounded dead weird on the phone and you're acting it now.'

Aisha was silent. She looked down wretchedly at the table, twisting her glass round and round in her hands.

'What is it, Aish? What's happened? Come on – you're scaring me.'

At last Aisha found the courage to look up at him. 'Oh. Christ,' she said. 'I don't know what I've come here to say. It's just – it's just – we've been together nearly six months now and – and . . .' Suddenly, Aisha seemed to collapse. Tears started spooling down her face, one after the other, a steady stream of them.

'Aisha, what's *wrong*?' said Sean desperately. He reached over and got hold of her arm, squeezing it. 'What *is* it, Aisha?'

'Oh, Sean, I feel such a cow,' she wailed, dabbing frantically at her eyes. 'You're so sweet, and you're so nice, and – and . . .'

'And what? You're dumping me?' He said this almost teasingly, as though it couldn't be true.

There was a long pause. She glanced up at him miserably.

'Oh,' he said. He looked pale, as though all the blood had suddenly drained from his face.

'It's just not the same any more, Sean,' she whispered. 'Is it?'

'Isn't it?'

'It's not that I don't like you any more. I think you're great. Really great. I'm really fond of you, Sean, honestly. But that's it. It's like you're a friend – a really, really good friend, not a . . . not a . . .'

'Not someone you fancy?'

Aisha took a big breath. 'No. Not any more. I'm *sorry*. It's just got – stale. You must feel that, Sean. You *must* feel it too. We don't even kiss like we used to. Do we?'

Sean was staring down at the table, hard. When he looked up his eyes were wet, too.

'It's like – we spend time together just 'cos we're *together*,' Aisha rushed on, as though she could somehow talk away the pain, 'just 'cos we're a *couple* and the thing is, I don't always want to be that, not deep down.'

'I liked it,' said Sean. 'I liked being a couple with you. I really liked it, Aish.'

Aisha started crying again and got hold of his hand. 'Oh, Sean, so did I. But – but – don't you think it's time to move on? Don't *you* ever feel you want to break out a bit, flirt a bit, do something with someone else?'

Sean looked away from Aisha, and Ness's green-brown eyes and mass of auburn hair passed slowly behind his eyes. 'Yeah,' he said, a bit guiltily. 'I guess. Sometimes.'

'I still like you,' she repeated, 'such a lot. But I find myself looking at other guys and feeling a bit tied down and – and it's not *fair* to be with you when I feel like that. And I know that feeling – isn't going to go away. It's just going to get bigger. It's been great with you, really great, but . . . but it's time to move on. Don't you feel it?'

'Maybe. Maybe you're right. It's just – God, it's so sudden, this, it's really out of the blue for me . . .'

'I'm sorry Sean. If I'd had the guts, I'd have said something earlier.'

'You sound so *final*.'

'Oh, Sean. I'd sooner finish things between us now than let them drag on until we got so sick of each other we *hated* each other . . .'

'I don't think I'd ever hate you, Aish,' said Sean.

Aisha scrubbed at her eyes again. 'Me neither, I didn't mean that.'

There was a long silence. Sean slowly bent a beermat in two, so that it cracked along the centre. Then he sighed and said, 'You want to have like a – trial split? A break for a month or so? See how it goes?'

'Well – we could – but I think that's just something people do 'cos they can't face making the decision there and then. I mean – I don't really see the point in it.'

'No. Not if you don't fancy me any more.'

'Oh, *Sean*. Come on. Be honest. It's just not been the same, has it? For a couple of months now.'

'No. OK. It's not been the same,' said Sean dully.

'What I would like is to – is to stay friends. 'Cos that's what I think we are underneath. Don't you?'

'Yes,' he said sadly. 'Maybe you're right. I just – I thought maybe if we had a break from each other the feeling would come back.'

'I don't think it works that way,' said Aisha gently. 'If it's gone, it's gone.'

'Aisha – is there someone else?'

'No. No, Sean, there isn't. I'd have told you if there was.'

'It's just – I don't know if I could handle it if I went out tomorrow and saw you with another bloke with his arm round you.'

'Oh, look. I know. I'd feel the same. It's natural. But that's not a good enough reason to stay together, is it?' She took hold of his hand again, urgently. '*Is* it?'

Sean shook his head. 'I s'pose not,' he said.

Guy Makeup

Philly was sitting in her bedroom, hugging the big old bear she'd had since she was a year old. When she heard the doorbell go and her mother's voice, answering it, complaining about how early it was, she looked up, sniffing. Then she heard footsteps pounding up the stairs and the door opened and Ian came into the room.

'Oh, *Ian*,' she said. 'Thank you – for coming over – I really wanted to . . .'

'Hello, Mopey,' he said. 'C'mere.'

He pulled the bear away from her and gathered her up to his chest, giving her a huge hug. 'Hey, what are you looking so upset for? It's Aisha and Sean who've split up, not us.'

'I *know*. But it's just so sad. I mean – they were *made* for each other.'

'No, they weren't, were they?' said Ian, pushing her hair back from her face. 'Not if this has happened.'

'I just can't *believe* it. I mean – she was going on about feeling tied down and stuff the other night, but *dumping* him . . .'

'Yeah, well. Things hadn't been right between them for ages.'

'Oh they *had*. They were great together.'

'No. They were both getting bored.'

'Have you spoken to him?'

'Yeah, last night. He called me. He's OK, honestly. He's a bit cut up and everything, but I think he knows it was the right thing . . .'

'I don't think he wanted to split up at *all*,' Philly burst out. 'I think he's just putting a brave face on it.'

'Yeah? Well, Philly-delphia, you don't know everything.'

'What don't I know?'

'Sean's been getting twitchy too. Really, he has.'

'Twitchy? Who about?'

'Just – generally.'

'When she phoned me last night, Aisha went on

and on about how they were too young to get into something heavy. She said it was stupid.' Philly looked up at Ian. 'Do *you* think it's stupid?'

'Not for us. You know I don't.'

'She went on and on about missing out on life and experience and not wanting to end up all narrow and full of regrets.'

'Blimey. Heavy. Then what did she say?'

'Oh, I don't know. Just stuff about freedom and all. She sounded all relieved and excited and – and . . .'

Ian hugged her to him again. 'Oh, come on, Philly. I mean – it must have been a relief, finally getting up the guts to tell him. And she was just trying to make herself feel she'd done the right thing.'

'So you think it's the right thing?'

'Yeah. For them.'

'And what about us?'

Ian laughed, 'Shut up, Philly. You're talking crap. You know what I feel about you.'

Then he pushed the door shut with his foot, and pulled her onto the bed with him.

* * *

The dress rehearsal was only three days away. Tasha had managed to round up Dave, Andy and Chris and drive them into the green room, so she could try out their stage makeup.

'What d'you have to try it out for?' Dave was complaining. 'Why can't you just slap it on on the night?'

'It's not that easy,' Tasha said. 'I have to play up your features so you don't get lost at the back of the stage under the lights *without* making you look like drag queens.'

'I'll go first, said Andy, settling himself into the chair and tipping his head back. 'I don't care if you make me look like a drag queen.'

'Oh, God,' muttered Dave. 'Spare us.' It was common knowledge now that Andy really fancied Tasha.

Tasha gathered up her tubes of foundation and paint, and started working on Andy's face. He kept kind of smirking as she smoothed on the makeup.

'Andy, keep a straight face,' she snapped. 'It's all going in the creases.'

'Sorry,' he breathed. 'I'll try.'

'*HI* – ya!' Karina appeared at the open door. She

seemed to know instinctively whenever Tasha had any lads in there with her. And even though Chris had been demoted to number two on her Lust List, she still wanted to keep tabs on him. Just in case it didn't work out with Aidan.

'So – how's it going, boys?' she went on. 'Getting all tarted up?'

'Just basic makeup,' said Tasha.

'Lovely! Andy – you look amazing. Hey – Tasha – am I wearing falsies for the show? False *eyelashes*, I mean,' she went on, giggling. 'It's not like I need the other sort!' And she threw her hair back and her chest out.

'Girls like you make me *ashamed* to be female sometimes,' muttered Tasha to herself, cringing. 'Yeah, I thought I'd try eyelashes on all the Pink Ladies,' she said aloud. 'I've got some here.'

'Oooh, goody. Can I see them?' squealed Karina, pushing her way into the room and squeezing past Chris far closer than she needed to. She started rummaging in the makeup box, pulling out tubes and boxes.

'Look, Karina, leave it, can't you? I've just sorted that lot out,' complained Tasha.

'Oh, ratt-*y*. I was only having a look.'

'Well, I can show you later, can't I? This place is getting pretty crowded.'

Karina turned on her heel. 'Sorry, Tasha,' she sniffed. 'Sorry if I crowded out the *room*. Sorry if I cramped your *style*.' And she swaggered out of the door.

'Jesus, that voice,' said Chris, jerking his head towards Karina's departing back. 'It goes right through your head.'

'It's like a car alarm,' added Andy. 'Drives you nuts.'

'OK,' said Tasha, giggling. 'Hold still. Eyeliner.' Carefully, she started outlining Andy's left eye with a thin black line. It was difficult to concentrate, with him breathing up at her. She was very aware of his two hands, lying tense on the arms of the chair. She had this strong instinctive feeling that they'd like to reach up and grab her.

'Wow,' said a deep voice at the door. 'Pretty boy.'

It was Aidan. He lounged in the doorway, arms folded, a sarcastic sort of a grin on his face. Tasha felt such desire when she saw him she could barely stand upright.

She managed to say 'Hi,' and smile. She felt her whole body reaching out towards him, like a plant to the sunlight, just like Andy's was reaching out to her. It's like being in some kind of sex capsule, she thought ruefully, all this lust flying about. She stooped hurriedly over Andy again, pulling his hair back from his forehead so she could work on his other eye. Andy sighed pleasurably.

'He looks too pretty,' repeated Aidan from the doorway.

'I *am* pretty,' murmured Andy. 'I'm a babe.'

'He's like – glowing,' insisted Aidan. 'Like a cornflake ad. He looks like he spends half his time working out.'

Tasha straightened up and glared at Aidan and her eyes melted into his face. 'Well, *I* can't help that,' she retorted. 'He probably *does*.'

Aidan smiled and moved into the room. 'Yeah,' he said, 'but they're supposed to be playing real hard nuts, aren't they?'

'Yeah,' admitted Tasha. 'Guys who smoke fifty a day and eat junk.'

'Well, you should make them look a bit more sick. You want to put some black round their eyes, build up some hollows under their cheek-bones. Here.' And Aidan took the stick of kohl from Tasha's hand, and started to fill in shadows under Andy's eyes and around his face.

Andy was at first seriously annoyed at the switch of makeup artist. But he peered into the mirror as Aidan worked and, despite himself, he was impressed. He looked much rougher, much seedier.

'Hey,' breathed Tasha. 'That's great.'

'You want to have a go on one of the others?' asked Aidan.

Tasha took the kohl stick and started work on Chris, who bent his knees obligingly to get down to her height. Aidan watched her, standing so close that Tasha found it almost impossible to concentrate, indicating with his forefinger where she should shade in the black.

Tasha took a deep breath to give herself courage and said, 'I think you've got yourself a job, Aidan. I could do with your help on the other guys. I'm just – I'm not too good on *guy* makeup.'

Aidan laughed. 'OK. I'll drop by.' Then he turned and made for the door. Tasha let out a long sigh, hoping the three lads hadn't worked out that she'd been on the attempted pull. She thought they probably hadn't. Her pulling techniques were so subtle that usually the guy she was trying it on didn't notice, let alone anyone else.

'Weird bloke,' said Chris, when Aidan was out of earshot. 'Coming in to help with the *makeup*.'

'We should've warned him to go back the way he came,' put in Andy. 'He'll get pounced on. Karina-Hyena went that way.'

Tasha burst out laughing. 'Karina *what*?'

'Hyena. Good, eh? She's ruthless. I reckon if she wants someone, she'll go after them until they drop from exhaustion. And now it's Aidan's turn.'

'How d'you know he doesn't *want* to get pounced on?' said Tasha as casually as she could manage. 'Lots of guys find her really attractive.'

'He can't be interested. No guy could be in any doubt that he had it made with that one, the way she's been acting round him. And as far as I know, he hasn't taken up the offer.'

'Yeah, but you wouldn't know with someone like him,' said Dave, meaningfully. 'I reckon he's a real dark horse.'

A Message From The Heart

Aisha was touring the shopping centre at top speed, looking for new clothes, clothes to suit the new her, telling herself that the adrenaline she was feeling was exhilaration and not sheer panic.

I've done the right thing, I've done the right thing, she repeated to herself, like a mantra. I'm free now, and it's *great*.

She'd felt nothing but exhilaration and relief yesterday evening, right after she'd talked to Sean. She felt like she'd been brave and honest and true to herself; she'd really taken control of her life, just like all the magazines told you to. Now a whole new exciting world was opening out for her, and she'd achieved this without hurting someone she really cared about, because she was sure Sean felt the same way too. They'd finished on such good terms and she was sure they could be friends now, good friends. Who says it's impossible to have it all, she'd thought, almost in triumph.

She'd gone straight home that night and phoned Philly to break the news to her. Philly had been pretty upset, too upset to be all that positive about her decision, but Aisha had expected that. It had been too late to call Tasha by the time she'd got off the phone to Philly, then she'd been all wound up and couldn't sleep properly and her night had been full of troubling, anxious dreams.

The next morning the first thing she saw when she blearily opened her eyes was Sean's picture on the ceiling, one edge peeling down towards her. She'd come to then, in a kind of confused panic, as all the events of yesterday crowded back in on her. And it suddenly felt so strange to be solo again – so weird to think she couldn't just phone Sean and chat to him.

She'd got up and dialled Philly's number instead, meaning to have another talk with her, but Philly's mum told her she'd gone out early to go swimming with Ian. 'They do all this exercise,' Philly's mum had said laughing, 'and then they blow the benefits by having a big fried breakfast afterwards.'

As Aisha put the phone down, this horrible feeling of loneliness came over her. She had a sudden clear vision of Philly and Ian sitting opposite each other in the café, hair all wet, laughing together as they dunked bread in each others' fried egg. I've got no one to do that with now, she thought. No one to just – *be* with.

Then she got dressed at top speed and headed for the shops.

Now she was standing by a rack of party dresses, picking ones at random off the rail to go and try on. They were all short, bright and sensational. It was really hard to choose between them.

In the changing room, she ripped off her jeans and pulled on one of the dresses – a purple one, with a straight, low neckline. Then she stared at her reflection in the mirror, as though she was looking at a stranger, and smiled. She pulled her long, blonde hair over to one side at the front, and tugged the hemline down a bit. 'Wow,' she said to herself. 'This looks brilliant. It'll knock their socks off at the last night party.'

She didn't bother trying any of the other dresses on. The purple one was like a talisman for the new her. She grabbed it, paid for it, then rushed out of the shop. 'I'll get some nail varnish to match,' she said to herself. But she couldn't concentrate on the shiny displays, and her hand shook as she pulled the dress out of its bag and held it up to the little bottles to compare colours.

'Aisha, what is *wrong* with you,' she muttered, walking out of the shop. 'It's OK, it's OK. I'm just jangly 'cos I need to talk to someone. I haven't really spoken to anyone since Sean and I split up. I haven't even *told* Tasha yet. Only Philly, and that was a non-starter. I need to – I need to talk it through, that's all.'

She headed for the shop exit as fast as she could, nearly colliding with a woman with a pushchair as she went out of the door. It was as though she was running away from something, as though if she moved fast enough, the feelings of doubt and panic wouldn't catch up with her again. She sped out of the shopping centre and headed for college, jumping on a bus just as the doors were folding shut.

She went straight to her locker once she got to college, meaning to lock the new dress safely away.

There, tucked into the grille at the front, was a note with 'Aisha' written on it.

Sean's writing. Unmistakable. She seized it, opened it, and read:

Aisha - please meet me at 1pm by the oak tree at the back. I've got something to tell you.
Love Sean.

♥

Karina's Top Tips

Karina was seriously fed up. She was making no headway with Aidan at all. She'd hung around underneath his ladder trying to engage him in conversation about spotlights, and he'd answered in grunts and monosyllables and then given up answering her at all. She'd joined him at his table in the canteen, to be treated to the sight of him wolfing down his food faster than she'd thought humanly possible and then loping off, with a gruff 'See you' tossed back over his shoulder. She'd even waited for what felt like hours in the wings one night for him to finish, to make sure they left college at the same time. But all he'd done was jump on a battered looking motorbike and roar off, with not even the vaguest offer of a lift.

It was awful. It had never happened to her before

– pulling out all the stops to catch a bloke and *still* failing.

Despite not being needed for rehearsals that morning, Karina had cut classes and turned up at the drama studio, just to hang around. But Aidan had kept well out of the way, clambering around in the rafters and then disappearing under the stage, and she'd had no chance at all to get another crack at him. So now she was sitting on the edge of the stage, legs swinging, fed up.

Ness hurried by, head down. She'd just been running through her songs again and it had gone really well.

'Hey, Ness,' called out Karina. 'You sounded good then.'

Ness looked up. 'Oh . . . thanks.'

'You've really got into Rizzo's character, haven't you? Even though she's such a slag.'

Ness looked down, smiling with only one side of her mouth, and didn't reply.

'So – heard the news?' went on Karina. 'The big bust-up.'

'The big . . . ?' Ness stopped walking. She could feel her breathing quicken.

'Sean and Aisha. They've split up. She dumped him last night. Just – out of the blue. She told me this morning.' Karina had actually overheard Ian telling Charley, but she wasn't going to own up to that, eavesdropping not being as cool as sharing confidences. 'He's pretty cut up about it, apparently. What a *bitch*, dropping him right before the show.'

'Did you tell her that?'

'What?'

'That you thought she was a bitch?'

'Well – no I – *anyway*, it won't last. I mean – Aisha was going on about being restless, but it's one thing to feel restless and it's quite another to dump someone who – well, someone like Sean. Those two are *made* for each other. She'll go crawling back, begging him to take her on again.'

'You think? Aisha doesn't seem to me like the type of girl who'd crawl to anyone.'

Karina narrowed her eyes at Ness. She didn't like her attitude. Ness was supposed to be lapping this up, open mouthed, not putting in all these little niggly comments. 'Trust me,' Karina said. 'I know her. She won't last five minutes on her own. And he won't be able to resist, he's so crazy about her. And anyway – it's just *too sad* that they've split. They *have* to get back together again. Don't you think?'

'Only if they both want to,' said Ness.

Karina smiled knowingly. She'd seen Ness and Sean talking together, seen the fireworks between them on stage. Ness probably thinks she can move in now, she thought. Karina didn't like other girls thinking they could be successful with blokes, especially when she wasn't having any success herself.

'No, trust me,' she said again. 'I'll give them three days, and they'll be back in each others' arms. They split up once before, you know, and this other girl tried to move in on Sean and *boy* did she get her fingers burned! I mean – Aisha practically left her for dead! And Sean is just *besotted* with Aisha. I mean – you've only got to look at them together to see that.'

When Aisha arrived at the oak tree at one o'clock, Sean wasn't there. She stood underneath it, with her arms wrapped round herself against the cold, and waited. She could feel her throat tightening. It was their tree, the tree they met under at lunchtime in the summer to share a picnic, the tree they'd sheltered under in the rain on the way home, kissing to pass the time, standing there long after the rain had passed over. She had a sudden vision of Sean standing under it with Ness, arms about each other, and she felt like crying.

Her mind was racing, in confusion. What do I want him to say, she thought frantically, what do I want this to be about? If he comes up and begs me to get back with him, what am I going to say?

'Hey – Aisha!' Sean was walking across the grass towards her, waving. 'How're you doing?' He sounded strained.

'OK,' she said. His face looked so familiar, so warm to her. She had to stop herself throwing her arms round his neck. It was weird, the way that one conversation last night had changed everything between them, just like that.

'Anyway. Thanks for coming, Aish. And look – don't worry – I'm not going to get all heavy. It's just – it was a real bolt out of the blue, last night, and I didn't say all I wanted to, you know?'

She nodded, holding her breath.

'Actually, I've – I've got something for you.' And he drew out of his pocket a slim white box and handed it to her.

She opened it. Inside was a thin silver chain, with a tiny seahorse and two shells hanging from it. 'Oh, Sean,' she began. 'It's lovely – it's . . .'

'I bought that for our six-month anniversary,' he said. 'And last night – well, I was pretty cut up. I was looking for the receipt, thinking I'd take it back to the shop. And then I thought – no, sod it. I bought it for you for the last six months we had together, and just 'cos we've split up now, it doesn't change that. It doesn't change how good that time was, what it meant to me – what *you* meant to me.'

She looked at him, heart pounding, and suddenly with everything in her she wanted him to say 'I want you back, Aisha. Please don't do this to us.'

'Do you like it?' he said. 'Really? I know how much you love the sea. I bought it for you and – I want *you* to have it.'

She nodded, tears starting to come into her eyes. She couldn't speak.

'Look Aisha,' he went on, 'what you did last night was really – it was right. We'd got stale, you were right. It was great, together, and we had a great time, but now it's time to split, and you had the guts to say it. I see that now – now I've, you know, calmed down a bit.'

Then he smiled, and got hold of her by the elbows, like he always did, but this time when he pulled her towards him he only kissed her forehead. 'And I hope we can be friends, like you said,' he said. 'Let's give it a few weeks, eh? Get the play over with and . . . let things settle down. OK, Aish?'

She nodded, forcing herself to smile. Then he was off across the grass, leaving her.

♥

Fast Mover

The next morning Ness was sitting alone in a corner of the canteen, hunched over a cup of cooling coffee. There was less than a week to go now before the first night. I'll be so glad when it's all over, she thought. No, I *won't*. When it's all over I won't see Sean any more. Well – I might *see* him but I won't be able to grab hold of him. I won't have an excuse to kiss him, not like now. Oh, this is such a *mess*. I'm going *mad* with it. And I wish I'd never let myself think about him splitting up with Aisha. Karina's right, he's totally hers. He's probably back together with her already.

She stared gloomily into her coffee cup, wondering whether to bother finishing it. Then, suddenly, shockingly, Sean's face was in front of her, just a few centimetres away across the table. He'd slid into the seat opposite her at the table before she was even aware he'd come into the room.

'Hi, Ness,' he said. 'Mind if I join you?'

'Bit late for that,' she croaked, hoping against hope she sounded normal, while her legs liquefied and her heart hammered. 'I seem to have been joined.'

Sean grinned. 'Can I get you another coffee or something?'

'No thanks. I was just going.'

'Don't. Stay and talk to me. How are your nerves holding up?'

'Nerves? Oh, OK I guess.'

'You're brilliant at it, you know you are. Are you thinking about going in for it – you know – professionally?'

Ness pulled a face. 'Well I'd kind of like to. But I think my mum would disown me if I did. She's always lecturing me on having a steady career.'

'Right. Accounting.'

'Banking.'

'Law.'

They both laughed, then there was a pause. 'Dress rehearsal this Monday,' said Sean.

'Yeah. I know.'

'Well I tell you, I'm freaking out at the thought of it. I mean – it's all getting a bit hyper, isn't it? D'you fancy going for a drink tonight, just to, you know, get out of here and . . .'

Ness stood up, scraping her chair backwards with a head-splitting sound. 'I can't,' she said, hoarsely. 'I – no, I can't.' Then she fled.

Sean leant his elbows on the table and let his face drop into his cupped hands. Then he swore, softly and deliberately, at the empty air.

'Well, you screwed that one up, didn't you?' said a voice behind him.

'What?' Sean looked round angrily. It was Ian standing there.

'I said you screwed that one up.'

'Where the hell did you spring from? What did you do – follow me in here?'

'Ness isn't going to go for you yet, mate. Not right after you've split up from Aisha.'

'Oh, sod off. You superior – git.'

Ian laughed and sat down beside him. 'You know – maybe it would have been better if you'd left – you know – more of a gap. Between girls.'

Sean twisted round and glared at his friend. 'She was the one that dumped me, remember? She wanted out. What does it matter to her what I do now?'

Ian shrugged. 'I wasn't thinking of Aisha, I was thinking of Ness.'

Sean collapsed again into his cupped hands. 'Oh, God, I don't know. What a mess. I mean – part of me knows Aisha's right. It was time to finish. But it's not good being dumped. It's not good at all.'

'You want to just relax, Sean.'

'Oh, shut it.'

'Ness isn't going to go away, you know. She'll keep. And you should let yourself – I dunno . . .'

'If you come out with any more touchy-feely crap, I'll . . .'

Ian laughed. 'OK. Have it your way!'

Aisha was sitting in Tasha's bedroom, hunched into a little ball on the bed. Tasha sat next to her, cradling Sean's silver chain with the seahorse and two shells on it.

'It's absolutely beautiful,' she was saying. 'To

think a *bloke* chose it. He's really something – oh, Aisha – *sorry*!'

Aisha had started weeping again. Tasha put her arm round her shoulders and cuddled her. 'Aisha, ignore me. I've got a hole in the head, seriously.'

'Don't worry,' snivelled Aisha. 'I wanted to have a good cry. That's mostly why I came to see you.'

'Good. Just so long as you didn't come for advice.'

'No. I've been avoiding Philly all day 'cos I knew she'd give me advice. Along the lines of – you have made a serious mistake. Now beg him to take you back.'

'Yeah?' Tasha reached for the tissues. 'And – *if* she said that – would you think she was right?'

'No. No, I wouldn't. Not now I've calmed down, I wouldn't. At least – I don't think I would. Oh, *God*! It's just – it hurt a lot more than I thought it was going to, Tasha. When I saw him yesterday, all I could think of was how nice he was and how good it was going around with him, how safe I felt . . .'

Tasha handed her a tissue. 'Hey, come on. Who wants to feel *safe*, Aisha? You're s'posed to be out there having a *wild time*. Wasn't that what this break-up was all about?'

Aisha smiled wanly. 'Yeah. It was. It's just – I feel so confused, somehow.'

'Course you do. You need to chill for a while and . . . calm down.'

'The thing is . . .'

'What?'

'When I saw him – I just wanted him back again.'

Tasha smiled. 'Well, I think that's natural. Ever bought something at the shops and really loved it, and then decided you hated it and were going to take it back, and then *not* taken it back after all?'

Aisha frowned. 'Yes – but what's that got to do with . . .'

'It's called buyer's remorse, right? It's a – whatsit – a *syndrome*. Well you've got – you've got finishing-with-your-boyfriend remorse. You know it's the right thing to do, you gear yourself up to do it, you do it, and then you get all the flip side coming in, all the doubts. But it was still the right thing to do just like it was a brilliant dress or whatever when you bought it. Oh, God, am I making sense? I told you I was no good at advice.'

Aisha smiled. 'No, I know what you're saying.'

'I mean – all that stuff we were talking about before – how you felt tied down and bored and stuff – that was real, wasn't it?'

'Yeah, that was real.'

'It's just that you're feeling too beat up to feel all that right now. But it'll come back. Really.'

'Yeah. You're right. It's just if I think of him with someone else . . .'

'Someone else?'

'Ness,' Aisha sniffed. 'I found myself just – spilling it all out to her. And she really likes him, I know she does. I think I thought if she got off with him, I'd be off the hook. But now . . .'

'Oh, Aisha. Stop beating yourself up.'

'Yeah. I know you're right. Hey – Tasha?'

'Mmmm?'

'What about you? How's it going with Aidan?'

'Nothing's going anywhere,' said Tasha mournfully. 'And I have never, ever had it this bad. Not ever. Not even that guy from Australia last year.'

'Yeah, well, he wasn't really all that, was he?' said Aisha, distractedly.

'Not compared to Aidan,' mooned Tasha. 'But at least he *spoke* to me. Aidan's so distant, he's so cool and . . .' she tailed off. Both the girls sighed in unison.

'Boys are the pits, aren't they?' grumbled Aisha.

'Yeah. They ruin your life. You're better off without them.'

'Yeah. Much better.'

'Hey,' said Tasha suddenly, 'why don't *we* go out tonight? Eat chocolate – see a film – it's ages since we've done that.'

Aisha smiled. 'Yeah. That's a great idea. No guys – just us. You know Tasha – you give *great* advice.'

Lots Of Love Stuff

Tasha was finding life extremely difficult, because she found herself wanting to behave like Karina. She wanted to hang round Aidan's ladder, lurk in the wings hoping for a glimpse of him, accidentally-on-purpose bump into him. And being anything like Karina so horrified Tasha that it froze her up completely. She kept to her green room like a recluse, only going into the drama studio when she absolutely had to and then keeping her head down and rushing out again.

She thought about Aidan all the time, though. And this was more than was healthy, she told herself. She thought about his voice, and his face, and the way he half-grinned when he looked at her, and she especially thought about the way his shoulders tensed when he lifted his heavy equipment.

There was no doubt about it. She had it bad.

'You carry on at this rate,' she said to her-self severely, 'and you are going to be completely hysterical when he shows up to help with the makeup at the dress rehearsal. IF he shows up.' She'd fixed on that as her big chance – although when she actually thought about trying to move in on him with Dave, Chris and Andy in the room – and Andy still trying to move in on her – she was filled with despair. I can't do it, she thought. Not with that lot there. Not doing their makeup. No one could. Not even Karina.

The technical rehearsal was being held that after-noon. Tasha turned up at the drama studio at two o'clock sharp with a list and a red pen and found herself a seat at the side. Most of the responsibility for the costume changes rested on her and she felt pretty daunted by it.

You could practically reach out and touch the tension in the studio. This was *it* – if this went badly, it didn't auger well for the dress rehearsal. Everyone was talking too loudly and laughing too much, and Bill was stamping around, bossily yelling orders and encouragement.

'OK,' Bill shouted finally. 'I want a clean run through. We'll take it just like the full dress rehearsal – but without the clothes.'

'Get 'em off!' Charley shouted.

'Yes, ha, ha,' said Bill. 'You know what I mean. Now let's GO!'

For the first hour, Tasha concentrated furiously, timing scenes and writing notes in urgent red. Then out of the corner of her eye, she saw Aidan lope across the studio and into the wings. Two minutes later, he crossed back again. She felt her whole self leaning out towards him once more, magnetised by him. 'Concentrate,' she muttered, staring down hard at her list. 'Ignore all distractions.'

But Aidan was a big distraction. He lounged against the wall opposite her, head on one side as he checked the position of the spotlights falling on the stage, then he crossed back again and disappeared into the wings. Tasha sighed and scribbled three large asterisks at random on her list.

On the stage, the boys were into one of their all-singing, all-dancing numbers. Tasha tried to focus on them. The routine had retained an exciting feeling that at any minute all seven would crash into each other.

Suddenly a low voice at her side said, 'It's crap, isn't it?' and Aidan slithered down to a sitting position right next to her.

'What?' Tasha croaked. She felt as if she might hyperventilate with delight – and shock. Why did he go in for such *sudden* appearances?

'It's all crap,' he said. 'The music and the dancing – it's so *dated*.'

'It's meant to be dated,' said Tasha. 'It's set in the fifties.'

There was a pause during which Tasha slid her eyes sideways to look at Aidan and then had to look away again quickly, because if her heart went any faster she thought she'd pass out. He was so close, she only had to lean a little to her left and she'd be touching him.

'I used to dance,' Aidan announced.

'Yeah?'

'Semi-professional.'

'Really? D'you still do it?'

'Nah. It took up too much time – and the ego with dancers, it's all as bad as that lot up there.

Worse.' He grinned. 'I could show them a thing or two, bet they'd've loved me muscling in, wouldn't they. I mean – they'd really appreciate me pointing out to them what crap movers they are.'

Tasha laughed. Aidan turned to look at her. 'That one I put the stage makeup on – Andy is it? He's got the hots for you like – like anything. You noticed?'

Tasha could feel herself going bright, bright red with pleasure. When guys started talking to you about who fancied you it was always, in her experience, a good sign. It meant they might fancy you too. 'Yes. I noticed,' she said. 'How come *you* noticed?'

'How? Have to have your head in a sack not to. He was watching you the whole time I was in your room. You'd better be careful with that one, girl.'

'Yeah? Well – you'd better watch out for Karina.'

'Oh, her – she *scares* me. Lucky for me she always makes so much noise I know she's coming and get time to scarper.'

Tasha laughed, and inside she was crowing. Oh, Karina, too *bad*, she thought.

Up on the stage, the cast had reached the interval. Bill gathered them all around him while he commented on their performances. 'It went OK, I think,' whispered Tasha.

'No major balls-ups then?'

'None that I could see.'

'Yeah. They all look pretty smug, don't they. I guess they'll all be really happy with themselves when they're through. Lots of luvvie kissing, yeah?' And he leant towards her and made a mocking *mwaah mwaah* kiss to each side of her face.

Tasha felt delicious shock waves, even if he hadn't actually made contact with her skin. It was incredible, that breaking of the space boundary between them, just incredible. Aidan didn't draw away from her immediately either – and for one ecstatic moment she thought he was going to end up in the centre and kiss her on the mouth.

But he didn't. He moved back, although not as far as he'd been before. 'You're a real sod,' she said, giggling. 'They're not that bad. I haven't seen a single one of them give a kiss like that *ever*.'

'No – just the other sort, eh?' On the stage, Sean had turned to talk to Ness, who had edged away from him, head lowered, and now Philly had her hand gripped on Sean's arm, holding him back, saying something to him, very intently. Aisha stood to one side, watching them all in silence. Then Bill called for the second half to start.

'Whooo,' muttered Aidan. 'Lots of love stuff there.'

'Yes, there is,' agreed Tasha. 'But what are you, psychic?'

'No. Just a top-grade eavesdropper.' He turned to grin at her, and she managed to meet his eyes. There was so much electricity between them now you could run a generator off it. 'Hey – I'd better go,' he said. 'I'm supposed to be adjusting the spots on Joel, this scene. He wants them brighter. Maybe if I push the volts up I can white him out all together, eh? Bye!'

Tasha laughed and said 'Bye,' as he scrambled to his feet, then she wrapped her hands round her knees and hugged herself as tightly as she could bear. She felt as if she might shoot up to the ceiling in sheer excitement if she didn't. 'That was *fab – u – lous*,' she said to herself.

Aisha Works Out

As soon as the technical rehearsal was over, Ness fled. Sean had tried to talk to her again, then Philly had glared at her and said something very intense to Sean and all the time Aisha was standing at the back all alone and forlorn and silent – it was all absolutely *horrible*.

'No way,' she muttered to herself, '*no* way. I'm not getting caught up in all that. And if Karina's right – I'll be the one that gets hurt. They'll all think I'm a right bitch. I don't care how gorgeous Sean is, I'm not getting involved.'

The next morning, Aisha borrowed her older brother's mountain bike, put on two jumpers and some scratchy woollen gloves, and headed for the woods by the college sports centre. There was a mist in the air and frost on the grass by the roadside, and flurries of tiny birds, stripping the bushes of the last of the berries, flew up as she passed. Aisha laughed with exhilaration as she speeded up a gear. 'It's fine, being on my own,' she said to herself. 'It's more than fine, it's *great*.'

Sitting around moping, she decided, was no way to sort herself out. She was going to get physical. It was harder going in the woods, but Aisha was determined. Crouching low over the handlebars she raced along, her lungs aching from the cold air, and soon she skidded to the end of the lane and rode out onto the huge playing fields.

In the distance by the sports centre building was the running track, with four figures, all spaced out, circling it. As Aisha freewheeled towards it she focused on the tallest of them. It was Dave, she was sure of it, with his broad shoulders and dark hair spiked back in the wind. She felt a pulse of excitement as she stopped by the edge and waited.

Dave circled the track towards her, then slowed for a stride or two and waved. 'Hey – Aisha! What're you doing here?'

'I've come to check out the gym,' she called back. 'See what classes are on offer.'

'I've got two more laps to do – then I'll show you round!' he shouted, then he pounded past her and raced off round the track once more.

Aisha sat back on her bike seat, smiling wryly. God forbid that you cut your training session short for *me*, she thought. She watched as he lengthened his stride, intent on impressing her. Then he was jogging up to meet her, sweaty, gorgeous and grinning. 'So,' he said, 'decided to get fit, have you? Or should I say – fit*ter*?'

He's been working on that for the last five minutes, Aisha thought. 'Well,' she replied, smiling, 'I just thought I should sign up for something. I mean – I do two dance classes a week, but I just don't feel it's enough.'

'Well – three times a week of extended aerobic activity's generally thought to be . . .' and he was off on some technical lecture about balancing fitness levels with upper-body strength. Together they wandered along the edge of the track and up to the sports centre building. Dave showed her where to lock up her bike, and then she followed him inside.

'You look cold,' he said. 'The end of your nose is all red.'

'Well, thanks,' she said sarcastically. 'And actually, I'm freezing.'

'Fancy some hot chocolate?'

'Oh, yeah. Please.'

Dave marched over to a drinks machine standing in the corner, fed in some money, pressed some buttons, them presented Aisha with a little plastic cup of steaming chocolate. Then he punched the buttons for some 'super-isotonic fluid replacement', with pictures of manic athletes all over the can, for himself.

'Come on,' he said. 'I'll show you the gym. I usually do a half-hour workout there after I've been running.'

As they entered the gym, Aisha found herself getting the giggles. 'Aisha, what are you *doing* here,' she muttered to herself, as she stalked self-consciously past a huge guy lifting barbells. 'Dave might be seriously gorgeous, but this isn't exactly your scene is it? Jesus, I'm the only girl here.'

Dave had started to show her the weights, running through his own routine stage by stage as though every detail of it was deeply fascinating. Then he made her sit down at a huge machine, like an upright modern version of the rack, and heave some weights up and down herself. I feel like a complete prat, Aisha thought, as she pulled on the bar. I *am* a complete prat.

'Not bad,' Dave said. 'D'you want me to work you out a routine? You need to do it at least three times a week, and each time you do it, you increase the repetitions by five, and gradually you increase the weights, just by a little each time, say a kilogram or two, and . . .'

In desperation, Aisha looked at her watch and let out a shriek. 'I should've been gone ten minutes ago! Sorry . . . meeting Tasha . . . She'll kill me if I'm late.'

'Well, that's a pity,' said Dave. 'I was going to suggest you hung about while I did my workout and then I could show you the sauna.' And he laid a large hand suggestively on her arm.

Aisha felt something close to panic. 'Sorry,' she said. 'Gotta go! Maybe I'll turn up again, come running with you, eh?'

'Er, OK,' Dave said, confused. 'See you later.

And then maybe we can work you out a pro-gramme.'

'Er – right. OK, then, bye. See you at the dress rehearsal.' Then she fled, jumped on her bike, and raced over the wide spaces of the playing fields.

♥

Avoidance Tactics

The day of the dress rehearsal arrived. Tasha was barricaded into the green room with costumes ranged around her, feeling like she was in a war zone. Aidan was adrift somewhere up in the rafters, trying to sort out a flickering problem, and the whole cast were high as kites and loud as sirens.

But when it finally got started the rehearsal went well, almost without a hitch. Joel stumbled against Chris in one of the dance scenes but Chris managed to bounce him back on his feet with style. Karina muffed up some of her lines but covered it with a high-pitched squeal of laughter quite in character for Marty. Everything else was fine. Bill mopped his brow at the finish, congratulated the whole cast, then told them to get changed, clear off and rest. 'I want tomorrow night's performance to be even more *terrific* than this,' he said. 'The tickets are *sold out*!'

Everyone went off to get changed. Sean cleaned up fast and left the boys' room just in time to see Ness disappearing out of a side door, carrying the old record-player from the sleepover scene. Quickly, he followed her. She skirted the dark corridor behind the stage then disappeared into the props room. Sean walked straight over and went in too.

Ness spun round from the shelves to face him. 'Sean!' she said, shakily, 'what do you want?'

Sean took in a breath. 'I'll tell you what I want,' he said. 'I want you to stop avoiding me.'

'What do you mean?'

'Ness, I just want you to talk to me.'

'I've *been* talking to you.'

'No – you *used* to talk to me, but now you don't. Now you don't say more than two sentences to me. And you head in the opposite direction every time I appear. Why?'

Ness looked down, refusing to answer. He moved towards her. 'What's the matter?' he demanded. 'We used to get on fine.'

'I know . . . I know,' Ness said, flustered. 'But – look – I don't want to get into any complicated stuff, OK? I've seen the way Aisha looks at me. I don't think your girlfriend likes how well we get on together.'

'*Ness*! Don't pretend you don't know. Everyone knows. Aisha isn't my girlfriend now. We split up.'

Ness looked down at the floor and shrugged. 'Yeah, but for how long?'

'What d'you mean, for how long? We're finished. That's why I asked you out for that drink.'

'Well, I don't fancy getting caught up in a collision course when you get back together again.'

'What *are* you on about? We're not getting back together again. I told you – it's over.'

'Like it was last time?'

'*What*? We've never split up before.'

'But Karina said . . .'

'*Karina*? Since when has anyone listened to what old motormouth has to say? What's she been saying, anyway?'

Ness half-smiled. 'I thought you didn't listen to her. She said . . . she said how you and Aisha had split up once before, then got back together again, because you were both so crazy about each other and so right for each other.'

'Well, she made that up. We've never even had a little split over a row or something. And Ness – we're *not* crazy about each other. Not any more. It's over, honestly.'

There was a long stretch of silence. Sean moved across the room and sat down on a pile of folded, old, red curtains. 'Jesus, these are filthy,' he said, batting at the clouds of dust that rose up. 'Ness, now you know the truth – you going to talk to me again? What're you so nervous about?'

Ness turned away, moved in a semicircle round the room, then came to a standstill in front of Sean, staring down at him. She looked as though she'd made up her mind about something.

'Sean – I'm new here,' she said.

'Well, you don't say. I thought you'd been here for years. I thought you'd . . .'

'I'm serious. What I mean is – it's not easy being new. And I really like Aisha and Philly and . . . I don't want to screw things up by – by . . .'

'By going out with me?'

'Look, I know you just asked me out for a *drink*. I'm not saying you and I are *involved* or anything, it's just . . .'

'Just that we could be,' interrupted Sean,' 'and you know it.'

Ness looked down at the ground, heart beating fast. What she'd most wanted to happen was happening, and she wasn't sure she could cope with it. 'Oh, God,' she said. 'I just – I mean – Aisha's been looking *so* upset . . .'

'Aisha and I are over,' Sean said seriously. 'Really over. So you wouldn't be screwing anything up. No one could blame you for anything.'

Ness's heart was pounding. She smiled down at Sean. 'Is that another invitation?' she asked.

He got to his feet. 'Yes,' he said. 'Yes, if you want it to be.'

Ness slowly put out her hand and laid it on Sean's arm, and he covered it with his hand, and then they leant towards each other.

'Yes please,' said Ness. Sean laughed and wound his arms around her. Then – as though they didn't have a choice – they were kissing.

♥

First Night Nerves

Fifteen minutes later, Ness and Sean were still wrapped around each other in the props room. Moving apart was out of the question.

'All right?' asked Sean, as he gently tucked some of her hair behind her ear.

'Yeah,' she breathed, 'definitely.' She still couldn't believe it had happened, that she was kissing him for real, at last. She moved her hands slowly up his arms, then she wound her arms round his neck. He grinned, and bent to kiss her once more.

'Ness,' said Sean after a while, 'this is just – this is so – I've wanted to kiss you properly ever since the first rehearsal. It just about finished me off, you know, when we had to *act* kissing?'

'Yeah, me too,' said Ness. 'I felt like that.'

'Yeah? And all the time we were dancing together

and holding each other – I kept thinking I'd get carried away and you'd whack me one.'

Ness laughed. 'I'm not sure I would've whacked you. I found it pretty hard myself.'

'It was so hot between us on stage, right? And everyone thought we were great actors, but really . . .'

'. . . we just really fancied each other!'

'Yeah. No one's acting's *that* good.'

'No. Well. And I was – I was – oh, you'll think I'm silly.'

'What?' said Sean, grinning.

'I used to think I'd never have the nerve to grab you like Rizzo grabs Kenickie.'

Sean laughed. 'Proved yourself wrong, then?'

'Yep. Definitely.' And she reached up and pulled his head down to hers and proved it all over again.

'Oh, Ness,' Sean sighed, hugging her in really close to him, 'you're fantastic. I thought so the first time I saw you. And then when we got on so well and had such a laugh . . .'

'Yeah. It was too much.'

'Not any more.'

'No. But I don't think we should like – rub Aisha's nose in it, do you?'

♥ 285 ♥

'She dumped me, you know. I was the wounded party.'

'Yeah, yeah. But I mean – I really like her and this is so soon. And there's such a thing as *tact*, you know, and . . .'

Sean laid a finger on her lips. 'I can keep a secret if you can,' he said.

First night. First night. No matter how many first nights you've had, you never really get used to swapping the empty, echoing space of the rehearsal hall for the packed, breathing, heaving lines of the audience. Philly held the curtain up a fraction and peered anxiously out. 'It's like some great *animal* out there,' she whispered, dramatically.

'Well, let's just hope it's friendly,' Ian muttered, then he put his arm round her shoulders and squeezed reassuringly.

Eight o'clock. Right on cue, the music started up. Joel dropped his prima donna first-night-nerves mode and burst on to the stage like a professional. Within ten minutes they had the audience right with them. Lots of laughter, and clapping and catcalls after the musical numbers.

The interval arrived in a heartbeat and Bill gathered all the actors round him like some kind of manic football manager. 'OK, kids, it's going *brilliantly*,' he said. 'Just don't let it go off the boil, OK? Don't get complacent. Keep that *energy* up front. Ness and Sean – what happened to *you*? It was *magic*.'

Charley mimed throwing up and Sean looked down, grinning, not daring to meet Ness's eye. Then they were off on the second half.

The final applause was deafening. 'I know what they mean now when they say it brought the house down,' said Charley triumphantly, as they all finally staggered off the stage. 'I really thought the ceiling was gonna come in.'

'That was just . . . mind blowing,' breathed Philly.

'We did it, we really *did* it,' chanted Ness ecstatically.

'That was brilliant,' gloated Aisha. 'That was

such a *buzz*.' And she threw her arms round Ness and hugged her.

As they clattered off to the changing rooms, Tasha was gathering up all the costumes a bit grumpily. She was very happy that the show had gone so spectacularly well, but she was also just a little fed up at being treated like an invisible housemaid. As she scurried back and forth picking up after everyone, checking for stains and tears, hardly anyone said a word to her. They were still all too full of what had happened on stage.

Well, she could get over that, but she couldn't get over the fact that her plan to get off with Aidan had flopped, just as she'd feared. He'd turned up to help with the makeup like he'd promised, but it had been like trying to get off with someone when you're working side-by-side on a top-speed production line. There was no time for conversation – there was no time to even *look* at each other. The only words he said to her were, 'Got another kohl stick?' To which she replied 'Yeah.' Then, as soon as he'd done the three lads, he was gone, because Bill was shouting about one of the footlights failing.

'Oh, *sod* it,' she muttered, almost in tears, as she

stomped back to the green room. 'I can't *bear* it. It's like trying to make contact with – with *Venus*, he's so out of reach.' She dumped a pile of clothes on the sofa, and miserably began to hook them onto hangers, one by one. 'I've got to make sure he comes to the last-night party,' she muttered. 'It's my last chance before he disappears and I never see him again!'

Sean had his jacket on ready to go. He left the boys' changing room and wandered along the corridor, hands in pockets. Ness was standing there chatting with Aisha and Philly and some of the girls from the chorus, all of them still happily mulling over the evening's success.

'Night, girls,' Sean called out. 'Get some jaw rest before tomorrow.' He laughed at the insults that followed this and walked past them, letting his shoulder knock against Ness's as he did.

Ness looked at his retreating rear view and smiled to herself. Then a few seconds later she announced to the group that she'd better be going or she'd miss the last bus, and followed after him.

The door of the prop room had been left ajar. Ness slid round it into the dark and immediately a pair of arms enfolded her. Then Sean was covering her face in kisses.

'What's the matter?' she laughed. 'Didn't you get enough of me on stage?'

'No,' he said, 'and it's the greasepaint. I can't stand the taste of it.'

She buried her face in his neck, greedily inhaling the scent of his hair, his skin. 'Did you feel weird tonight?' she said. 'Different?'

'It felt great. This feels better.'

'D'you think anyone spotted we weren't acting any more?'

'Nah. They just think we're up for an Oscar.'

'Especially Bill. He's such an idiot, that guy.'

'Don't you knock Bill. I love the man.'

'Yeah?'

'Yeah. He put you in the show didn't he?'

Ness laughed and wrapped her arms tighter round Sean's chest.

♥

Last Night Lust

The second night of the show went off with the
same noisy success as the first and hardly a hitch.
Then the last night arrived. The atmosphere in
the auditorium from the outset was electric, on
stage and off. Joel was going into mega-star mode
because his actor dad had turned up with several
of his cronies.

'This could be my *big* break,' Joel squawked.
'Derek Baskerville's out there, and he's *huge*, he's
like this *huge* director, he makes these *enormous*
films . . .'

'. . . and if you weren't such a *gigantic* prat,'
interrupted Ian, 'he might give you a part in one,
right?'

'My cue,' snapped Joel, and stalked onto the
stage, sticking his chin in the air.

Tucked into a quiet corner behind the scenes, Sean had got hold of Ness again. 'What happened to "I can keep a secret if you can?"' Ness teased.

'OK, OK,' said Sean. 'Just one kiss.'

Minutes later, Charley brushed past them. 'Lay off, we're on next,' he said. 'You'll be done on an obscenity charge.'

Sean laughed. 'He's right. OK, back off Ness, you animal.'

'HAH! Me, an animal?' Ness laughed and she prised herself reluctantly away from him.

When the show finished and the encores were over, Bill strode to the front of the stage. 'I don't want to make a long speech ...' he began. It was hard to hear what he was saying above the cacophony, but his grin told the full story of the show. Philly had remembered to do a quick whip round for him and they'd bought him a bottle of scotch for all his hard work, which Aisha duly presented with a kiss.

'Oh, and one last thing,' bellowed Bill, 'before you all go. As I'm sure you all realise, a lot of work goes on backstage to produce a show like this. And I have two special thanks to give –

to Tasha, our wonderful makeup and costume girl, and to Aidan, who did such a ... er ... such an *innovative* job with the lights. Come on out, you two!' And he flung out both arms, hopefully.

In the wings, Tasha was cringing. 'Oh, God, *no*,' she muttered. She didn't move.

'Get *on* there,' shrieked Aisha, pushing her forwards.

Half pleased, half appalled, Tasha slouched onto the stage. 'OK, here's the lady we owe the look of this thing to – now where's the guy who lit it up?' called Bill.

There was a pause. The stamping in the hall increased. Finally Aidan appeared at the back of the stage.

Over the catcalls, he walked to the front, and grinning, held out his hand to Tasha. She found her hand reaching straight out to take it, then they faced the front and bowed together.

Then the whole cast came back on stage and, in the hubbub, Tasha looked down at her hand, still beautifully enclosed in Aidan's. She wondered if she was supposed to pull it away. She didn't want to. 'All right,' she said urgently to herself. 'You won't get a better chance than this. Now *go for it.*'

'Are you coming to the cast party?' she croaked.

'What cast party?' Aidan asked.

'Oh, *Aidan*. Don't tell me you haven't heard about it!'

'Well – I guess.' He looked at her, and somehow their hands drifted apart.

'Oh – come on. It'll be a laugh. It's in the back room at the *Turks' Head*. You know it? It's only five minutes' walk, it's . . .'

'Yeah, I know it. Look – I'll try,' he said, walking off backstage again.

Aisha had laid her pre-party preparation plans with extreme care. No turning up with black all round the eyes and blobs of cold cream in the hair for *her*. And no schlepping along in stage costume either – Sandy's gear was too naff for words. No, Aisha had it sorted. She had full skincare and makeup kit and the new purple dress she'd bought stashed away in her bag, and now she sought a quiet corner in the girls' toilets to put it all on. And if she was a bit late to the party, so be it. Late entrances were dramatic, right?

Back in the girls' changing room, Ness, Philly and Karina were on a real high. Ness looked in the mirror, wiped off the top layer of her red lipstick and shrugged. 'C'mon, let's go,' she said, turning to the others. 'I can't be bothered to get all this off. I hereby promise myself a face-pack at the weekend to make amends.'

'Yeah,' said Philly. 'Let's just get there.'

'*Yeah*,' squealed Karina. 'And when we get there – stay in character. Let's behave like total tarts all night.'

Resisting the impulse to say so *what would be different for you Karina*? Ness laughed and asked, 'Anyone seen Aisha?'

Philly shrugged. 'Dunno where she is. And I said I'd give Tasha a shout. We were all going to go down there together.'

'Tasha's in the green room still,' said Karina. 'I'll get her. She gets really pissed off if I don't drop in on her, you know. You find Aisha.' And she left.

In the green room, Tasha was in a flap. What-ever interpretation she tried to weld on to them, Aidan's last words had not been encouraging. *I'll try*. Not exactly the passionate avowal of someone keen to get to grips with me, she thought. What happened to that connection they'd made, the day of the technical rehearsal? Had she dreamt it or something?

But just in case he *did* turn up – she needed to look a whole lot better than she did right now. She wanted a shower for a start. She tried tell-ing herself that being hot and sweaty was earthy and animalistic, but didn't quite believe it her-self.

'*Tash*-a!' screeched Karina, jamming her head round the door. 'What are you *doing* in here? Time to go!'

'Oh, God, look at me,' Tasha groaned, peering into the mirror. 'I look like an undercooked chip. Look at my *hair*.'

Karina came and stood behind her and looked into the glass. 'Yeah, I see what you mean,' she said helpfully. 'Never mind. No one's going to notice it's gone all flat.' Then she turned and sashayed out of the room, calling back, 'Anyway, look at *me*! I'm going along in full stage makeup!'

Yeah, thought Tasha sourly, as she followed her, and it doesn't look that different from your normal stuff. If anything, it's more *subtle*.

♥

Party On

'So – anyone asked Aidan along?' asked Philly, glancing at Tasha.

'Yeah,' said Karina. 'I did.'

'And?'

'He didn't sound keen.'

Philly rolled her eyes at Tasha as they pushed open the door to the pub. 'He'll turn up,' she whispered.

'No he won't,' replied Tasha dolefully.

They hadn't found Aisha anywhere, and in the end Tasha, Ness, Karina and Philly had made their way to the party without her. They knew all the lads would be already there, clearing off the food table as fast as possible.

Ness saw Sean as soon as they walked in, but she stopped short of going over and claiming him as hers. There was a great post-show feeling between her and Tasha and Philly now and she didn't want to wreck it. She waited until Ian had jumped on Philly, and Karina was noisily pirouetting round the sporty lads, then she sidled up to Sean and said, 'Alright?'

Sean smiled. 'Yeah,' he said, as he got hold of her hand behind her back and squeezed it, running his fingers over hers.

Tasha stood to the side of the room and watched the door. Even when she turned her back on it, she felt she was watching it, willing it to open and let Aidan come in. It was opening less and less frequently now. Just about everyone had got to the party and the noise level was incredible. She could feel a kind of weight inside her, getting heavier as the minutes ticked by.

'Hey,' said Philly, appearing at her side, 'let's get our plates stacked up. Before the table is cleared completely.'

'I don't feel hungry,' said Tasha.

'Oh, come on, Tasha. Eat something.' Philly grabbed her by the arm and dragged her over to the food table. Now that the first explosion of excitement was over, everyone realised how starved they were and sausages, pizza, bhajis and samosas were disappearing fast. Even the strips of raw vegetables round the dips were looking encroached on.

'Aisha's not here yet, is she,' said Philly, mouth full.

'No,' said Tasha. 'I just hope she doesn't get too upset when she does get here.' And she motioned over to Sean and Ness, on the far side of the table. Their eyes were glued on each other and the magnetism between them was practically visible.

'So are they really an item now?' asked Philly.

'Yeah. I'm sure they are. They're just being . . . . tactful.'

'Aw, bless,' said Philly.

Charley materialised between them. 'They weren't being tactful in the wings tonight,' he said.

'Yeah, well,' said Philly. 'Ian said Sean's fancied her for ages.'

'I'll say he has,' said Charley. He turned to Tasha. 'So, costume queen! You finally got public recognition.'

'Yup.'

'A curtain call with the lighting dude. Is he coming tonight?'

Tasha shrugged. 'Dunno.'

'You don't fool me,' Charley laughed. 'You've been watching that door like a hawk.'

'I have not!'

'Yeah you have. The woman who wouldn't melt ice cubes in her mouth has finally got the hots for someone.'

'Oh, sod off, Charley,' snapped Tasha. 'You don't know what you're talking about.'

'Don't I?' he smirked and wandered off.

'Gobby little git,' she muttered to herself. 'Who's he think he is?'

Then Andy pitched up, making soulful eyes at her. 'Any food left?' he said.

'We haven't had seconds yet,' said Chris.

'Poor *things*,' said Tasha, sarcastically. 'Yeah – a bit.'

'Also – I needed to escape,' said Chris. 'Karina was moving in on me.'

'Like a tank,' added Andy.

'Protect me, Tasha,' said Chris, plaintively.

'Get lost,' laughed Tasha, and the three of them turned to the food table again. Just as they were scooping up the last of the dip, a blast of music filled the room. 'Here we go,' groaned Tasha. 'Bill's turned the sound system up.'

Almost immediately, Bill burst on to the floor, doing a kind of insane, seventies, arm-waving boogie. Karina, screaming with laughter, joined him. 'Oh, sod it,' Tasha said to herself. 'He's not coming!' She took a deep breath. Then she grabbed Andy's and Chris's hands. 'Come on,' she said. 'Let's fill up the floor.'

One of the things that Tasha did really well, and knew she did really well, was dance. When she moved, she responded to every level of the music, fluid and easy. Andy went into turbo-drive beside her, while Chris kept both of them between him and Karina.

Two records later, the door opened once more. Tasha looked up. She felt as though her heart was halfway up her throat, choking her.

But it was Aisha. And Aisha was looking fabulous, with her new dress and her hair long and loose. All the girls in their stage makeup suddenly looked a bit clownish beside her.

'Hey!' yelled Joel, heading over. 'It's my leading lady!'

Dave didn't waste a second either – he was at her side immediately. 'You never made it back to the gym,' he said.

'No – well,' said Aisha. 'I was kind of afraid of straining something.' Like my boredom threshold, she thought.

'You want something to eat?' Joel persevered.

Aisha glanced over at the devastated food table. 'I think I'm a bit late for that. Want to dance?'

'Yeah, great!' said Dave and Joel simultaneously, starting to move.

'Look at Aisha,' said Ness, glancing sideways up at Sean's face, trying to read his expression. '*Two* guys after her. You jealous?'

Sean looked down at Ness, grinning. 'What have *I* got to be jealous about?' he said. 'Come on – let's crowd the floor out some more.'

Within fifteen minutes, the dance floor was packed, everyone heaving and jiving. Bill's wife had moved onto the floor too and was now practically wrestling with him, trying to persuade him it was time to leave. And then the door to the pub backroom swung open yet again and Aidan walked in.

Curtain Down

Aidan stood in the doorway, looking around at everyone. And Tasha knew, ecstatically, looking across the room at him, she knew, without a shadow of a doubt, that he really didn't want to be here at all and the only reason he'd turned up – was because of *her*. She left the crowded floor and headed over to the doorway. She felt full of confidence, bursting with it.

'Hi,' she said.

'Hi,' Aidan replied.

There was a pause, then Tasha grinned. 'You made it then,' she said.

He shrugged. 'Yeah.'

Tasha looked at his face, and she felt as though her legs might fold under her with sheer pleasure. 'You've been ages,' she said.

'Well – I had to lug about fifty light attachments below stage, all by myself.'

'Poor *thing*! No one to help you?'

'No.'

'All the food's gone.'

He smiled. 'I don't care.'

'So you too tired to dance, now?' Tasha said. 'Come on – you said you were a dancer.'

Grinning, Aidan took her hand for the second time that night and they moved onto the floor together. And Aidan proved he could dance. Nothing showy, nothing too energetic – just there with the rhythm, moving with it, at one with it. Tasha was the perfect partner for him. She could feel all eyes on her, feel the amazement and envy from half the girls in the room, and that and the sheer bliss she felt sharpened her performance. She and Aidan prowled round each other, always the same distance apart, as though they were joined by a thread you couldn't see.

Then her pleasure was cut short. Karina sprang across the floor, shrieking 'Ai-*dan*! I thought you weren't com-*ing*!'

Aidan looked at Tasha, his eyes begging – *bail*

me out! Then he turned to Karina. 'Well – I – I kind of made a date,' he said.

'Yeah,' said Tasha, stepping forward and linking her arm through his, 'with me. OK, Karina?'

Karina looked like she'd been slapped round the face. 'O-*K*,' she said, nastily. 'Don't *worry* – I can take a hint.'

'That must be a first – Karina taking a hint,' muttered Aidan, as she flounced off across the floor.

'Oh, don't,' murmured Tasha. 'You could almost feel sorry for her. Almost.'

'So. On our next date . . .'

'Our next date?' she breathed, hardly daring to believe her ears.

'Well, this *is* a date – we just agreed it was.'

Tasha smiled up at him. 'OK. On our next date . . . ?'

'Can we go somewhere where there aren't any actors?'

'Sure,' laughed Tasha, then they started dancing again, even closer than before.

The lights got lower, the music got slower, the

doors to the little terrace outside were flung open despite the cold, and couples started wandering out there for some privacy.

Aisha had managed to dump Joel by the not-so-subtle method of dancing so close to Dave that there wasn't a hair's breadth between them. Then, Joel gone, she'd spun round to include Chris and Andy, who was looking a bit bereft since Tasha's departure, and then other people joined them, and soon they were all dancing about in a big, noisy group. She felt great, dancing and flirting, joking and laughing.

Philly careered across the floor, towing Ian behind her. 'Aisha, you look fantastic,' she said. 'That dress is just *brilliant*! When can I borrow it?'

'Never,' laughed Aisha, turning to dance opposite her. 'Hey – have you seen who Tasha's with?'

'Yes – thank God – isn't it great? And are you – are you . . . ?'

'I'm having a *ball*,' said Aisha, happily spinning away again.

At the first really slow number, Aidan and Tasha faltered, stopped dancing, looked at each other, then Aidan stepped forward and Tasha did too.

Then in one amazing movement their arms were round each other. Tasha sighed with sheer pleasure and rested her face on his chest. She closed her eyes and greedily breathed him in.

'Glad you came?' she whispered, as they started to sway together, and his hands moved slowly up her back, onto her shoulders . . .

'You bet,' he said.

'Even though it's full of egos?'

'I'm not really noticing the egos any more,' he said, then he pulled her in close and bent down to kiss her, slowly, sure of himself, and Tasha kissed him back.

Sean came back from the bar, a drink in each hand. He grinned wickedly at Ness. 'C'mere!' he said.

Ness smiled, took both drinks from Sean and put them down on a side table. Then Sean slid his hands slowly round her waist and pulled her towards him.

For the next hour, Ness and Sean, and Tasha and Aidan were not really conscious of anyone else but the person right in front of them. And all Aisha was conscious of was dancing her feet off and having the most fun she'd had in months.

Then Tasha and Aisha collided together in the Ladies. '*Alright, Tasha*,' crowed Aisha. 'You did it!'

Tasha laughed happily. 'He is – he's amazing, Aisha.'

'Yeah, yeah. I know. I can *see*. Well, you did it Tasha. You held out for the one you really wanted and you got him!'

'I still can't believe it.'

'You'd better. He's out there waiting for you. I saw him when I came in.'

Tasha gave a sort of shudder of pleasure and got her hairbrush out of her bag.

'So,' Aisha went on. 'What's he like, then?'

'Oh – *Aisha!*'

Aisha grinned at her. 'S'OK. I can tell just by looking at you. You jammy cow.'

'Yeah – anyway – what about Dave?'

'What about him? All biceps and no brain.'

Both girls shrieked with laughter. Then they leaned towards the mirror, checking their reflections. 'Oh, Aisha,' said Tasha. 'Are you really OK?'

'Yes,' said Aisha, firmly. 'I feel . . . I feel better

about myself than I have done for ages. I'm just having fun, Tasha.'

'And do you mind about . . .'

'Sean and Ness? No, I don't. I really don't. It's a bit weird, but they were so sweet when I got here – not being really blatant about it. And there was me having a complete ball. I mean – it feels great, being a free agent, Tasha, it really does. Having some space.'

'Yeah?' said Tasha dreamily. 'Lend us your lippy.'

'Here. Yeah, it does. I mean – I know you can't imagine it at the moment. Jesus, you can hardly *focus* at the moment. But it does.'

The girls left the loo and ran straight into Philly and Ian talking to Sean and Ness. Philly was waving her arms about excitedly. 'I *swear* it,' she was saying. 'Come on – I'll show you!'

'What's up?' asked Aisha.

'Follow us,' said Ian, 'and you'll find out.' Aisha and Tasha shrugged at each other. Then Tasha grabbed hold of Aidan and the seven of them made their way out onto the terrace running the length of the pub. They crept to the end of it, then

Philly signalled to them to stop. She peered round the corner, then she stood back and motioned to Sean to look.

Sean stepped forward and craned round the wall. 'Yes – YES!' he breathed ecstatically. 'C'mere – *look*!' He beckoned frantically to the others. Silently everyone crept to the corner and peered round.

The terrace continued round the corner for a couple of metres and at the end of it was a wooden bench under a bower of what would have been roses in the summer. On the bench, heedless of the cold, sat Joel, legs sprawled out in front of him, eyes blissfully closed. And lying half across him, elegantly arranged, lay Karina.

'Oh, blimey,' muttered Tasha, happily. 'Oh, this is great. This is *so – oo* good.'

'Joel's found someone,' said Aisha, linking her arm through Ness's. 'We're safe, Ness. He's found someone dumb enough to take him on.'

'Go, Karina,' whispered Ness 'Go, *girl*!'

Unaware of her audience for once, Karina sat up a little, and smiled at Joel. He opened his eyes and smiled back. 'I mean – I dunno, Joel,' she said, 'I just really think if anyone's going to make it – I mean any of us – it's going to be me or you.'

'Me *and* you,' gurgled Joel. 'Let's both make it.'

Karina giggled shrilly and gave his chest a push. 'I'm being serious, here, Joel!' she squeaked. 'I mean make it in *acting*! The others just aren't committed, are they? Not like we are.'

Joel took hold of one of her hands and pressed it to his lips. Sean ducked back round the corner and started choking. '*Shhhh*!' warned Tasha.

'No one's like you Karina,' slurred Joel. 'Seriously. You're one of the best actresses I've ever seen. If you'd been playing Sandy . . .'

Karina wound her arms gracefully around Joel's neck. 'Yee – es . . . ?' she said.

'. . . we could really have set the stage on fire.'

That did it. The whole group collapsed helpless with laughter, just as Joel was moving in for a major smooch. Sean and Ian started clapping loudly, shouting, 'Encore! Encore!'

Karina shot to her feet, spitting fire. 'You lot are just so *PATHETIC*!' she screeched. 'You're like a lot of *KIDS*. Have you *REALLY* got nothing better to *DO* with your time?'

Still laughing, Tasha laced her fingers through Aidan's, and Ian pulled Philly towards him. Aisha waved happily and headed indoors, summoned by the loud music. 'Yeah,' said Sean, wrapping his arms round Ness with a grin, 'I think maybe we have. A *lot* better!'

Love Money

Sarra Manning

♥

A Recipe For Disaster . . . ?

Atia gave a deep sigh, and trying hard not to breathe in, started to shovel horse manure with an enthusiasm that she didn't really feel.

'That's it, girl,' shouted Mrs Johnson. 'Put some welly into it!' Atia ignored her employer and continued to delicately transfer the horse poop from its pile into thick plastic bin liners. I'm going to cry if any of this gets onto my jeans, she thought with disgust.

Half an hour later, Atia was way beyond tears. Her jeans, which to be honest had seen better days, were liberally specked with the foul-smelling muck.

Atia had been working at the animal sanctuary for the last six months. When her parents had issued the ultimatum to either exist on her below-poverty-level allowance or get herself a job, she'd stuck to her principles and insisted that she'd rather work with animals for no money. Her dad had tried to persuade her to give the pet shop in their local shopping centre a try but Atia stuck to her guns. She couldn't bear to see all those poor little animals cooped up in cages and besides, Atia knew that she'd keep getting into trouble for chatting to her mates when she was supposed to be stocking the shelves with budgie food. But she knew that if she wanted to be a vet (which was her ultimate plan) she'd have to get some creature contact in somehow, so she had decided that she'd spend her Saturday mornings working at Stanhope Animal Sanctuary. OK, there was the occupational hazard of animal dung, but at least it was in the fresh air. And she had even persuaded her 'rents to give her that allowance rise when she'd whinged on at great length about her career goals and how educational working at the animal sanctuary would be.

Huh, if they could only see me now, Atia thought as she trailed horse poo across the yard. After turning the hose on her dung-encrusted wellies, she went in search of Mrs Johnson who ran the sanctuary. Atia couldn't help smirking as she saw Mrs Johnson trying to coax Wilhemina, an elderly Shetland pony, to stand still while she combed out her tangled mane. Mrs Johnson looked more horse-like than most of her equine charges.

'I've finished with the muck pile,' Atia announced, stroking Wilhemina. 'Is it all right if I go now?'

'Of course it is, dear,' boomed Mrs Johnson. 'Do you want to take one of the bags home for your dad? Do his roses the world of good.'

'Er, no thanks,' Atia muttered. There was no way she was getting on the bus with a sackload of horse poo. 'I think there's something wrong with the standpipe in the yard, the water's coming out in a dribble.'

'Bugger!' This was Mrs Johnson's favourite word. 'If it's not one thing, it's another.' The normally stoic Mrs Johnson looked like she was about to burst into tears.

'Is everything all right, Mrs J?' enquired Atia timidly.

'Nothing for you to worry about, Atia love,' said Mrs Johnson heavily. 'It's just that I need to replace the roof on the stable block, we need at least another six kennels and I've just had a whacking great bill from the vet.'

'But I thought that the council gave you money to run the sanctuary,' Atia said, feeling sick. Was this Mrs Johnson's subtle way of telling her that the sanctuary was going to close and that she'd better start looking for new ways to spend her Saturdays?

Mrs Johnson started attacking Wilhemina's mane with renewed vigour. 'Humph,' she snorted. 'They only subsidise us and now they keep going on about cutbacks. They've told me that whatever I can raise, they'll match, but how much do they expect me to make from giving spoilt little brats riding lessons and selling horse muck as garden fertiliser?'

Atia felt a surge of indignation. 'It's ridiculous that they won't give you the money. I mean, they don't mind when we take the overspill from the council's animal shelter.'

Mrs Johnson gave her a gummy smile. 'I know, dear. Well, I'll think of something.'

But Atia hadn't finished. Her big brown eyes were alight with missionary zeal. 'Look, I can help you. I'm brilliant at fund-raising. We can have a sponsored ride and we could charge people to look round the sanctuary and we'll get posters printed up and badges . . .'

Mrs Johnson looked slightly surprised. 'Hmmm, you might be onto something there, Atia love.'

Atia beamed at her. 'Mrs J, I might not be much cop at mucking out but I'm ace when it comes to charity.'

'Well, it's a nice idea,' said Mrs Johnson doubtfully. 'But it isn't really that simple. I suppose I could see if the Rugby Club wives would organise a dinner dance or something.'

Atia sighed to herself. A Rugby Club dinner dance? God, how boring!

'Well, if you think so,' she muttered to Mrs Johnson, without much enthusiasm.

'What did you have in mind then, Atia?' asked Mrs Johnson encouragingly. Maybe she'd been a bit too hasty in dismissing Atia's help.

'There's loads of things we could do!' Atia declared. 'Cake sales and sponsored events. My friend Nick's in a band and they could do a benefit gig.'

Mrs Johnson made an impressed face. 'Hmmm, there might be something in that.'

'Last year, I was leader of the school fund-raising committee and we raised £4,500 for the children's home,' Atia pleaded. 'I have a natural talent for getting people to give me money.'

'So your father tells me,' laughed Mrs Johnson. 'OK, Atia, you're on. I'll organise my dinner dance and you can try out some of your own fund-raising plans. We'll show the council we mean business.'

'Let's face it, chocolate brownies are a licence to print money,' laughed Lorrie. 'I don't know why you're wasting time on that carrot cake, Mai.'

Mai flicked back her long black hair with an annoyed hand. 'Excuse me, Miss Animal Eater, while you shove another packet of butter into your mixing bowl,' she said sarcastically. 'I don't do meat, I don't do fish, I don't do dairy. My carrot cake is 100% organic.'

'You mean you're the caring face of cake-making?' Atia grinned.

Mai shrugged. 'Hey, you know my motto. No food with a face.'

Lorrie plonked a finger into the chocolate brownie mixture and put in her mouth with an ecstatic expression. Her glinting green eyes closed, as she pretended to swoon. 'Mmmm, is there anything in the world better than chocolate?'

Atia consulted her list. 'OK, the chocolate cake, the chocolate cookies and the chocolate truffles are finished. The chocolate muffins and the chocolate roll are in the oven and we've got the chocolate brownies and the carrot cake ready to bake.'

Jo frowned. 'Look, I'm not being picky or anything, but there does seem to be a lot of chocolate and, um, not much else.'

Gillie nodded her head, her brown bob swinging slightly. 'I agree. D'you not think that we've maybe overdone it on the chocolate front, just a tad?' she asked, her Scottish accent becoming very pronounced, as she glanced nervously at Lorrie.

Lorrie shook her head, her riot of red curls gleaming

in the sunlight from the kitchen window. 'But Gillie, people love chocolate,' she protested. 'C'mon, every time we had a cake sale at school, the chocolate cake always went first and people only bought the other stuff once it'd sold out. Our college cake sale will be just the same. But, if it means that much to you, I'm prepared to compromise. We've still got a couple of hours, so I'll go and get some more ingredients and we'll make as many strictly non-chocolate, non-animal cake-type thingies as we can, OK?'

'Cool,' chirped Mai. She'd made a rule in life to never stay mad at anyone for longer than five minutes.

Lorrie was already pulling on her jacket. 'Anyone fancy coming with me to the Stop And Shop?'

'I will,' said Jo. 'I haven't had a can of Diet Coke all day. I'm starting to get withdrawal symptoms.'

The door slammed after them as the other girls continued to work companionably in the kitchen. After a while, Atia peered into the oven. 'Chuck us the oven glove, Gillie, this stuff needs to come out.'

Atia placed the muffins and the roll on a wire tray to cool, while Mai put the brownies and her carrot cake in the oven. Her pale cheeks were flushed and suddenly a dreamy look crossed her face. 'I think Johnny might be a vegetarian,' she announced. Mai had a habit of living in a dippy parallel universe and then expecting the rest of them to follow her unpredictable trains of thought.

'You what?' enquired Atia, exchanging an exasperated smile with Gillie.

'I said, I think Johnny might be a vegetarian,' Mai repeated.

Gillie looked amused. 'Oh and why would you happen to be thinking that?'

'Well, I saw him in the college canteen on Friday and,' – Mai paused for effect – 'he was eating a vegetarian lasagne,' she finished importantly.

Atia was confused. 'And . . . ?'

'Hello, earth to the mother ship. Vegetarian lasagne, meat-free pasta dish, like, d'you see where I'm going with this?' said Mai, as if she was talking to a not-very-bright toddler.

'Mai, honey, seeing as how the other menu choice was a lamb curry that looked as if someone had died in it, I'm not surprised he had the vegetarian lasagne. I mean, I had a cheese salad and I'm not a vegetarian,' Atia insisted.

Gillie snorted. 'I don't know what you see in him anyway. He's always seemed a bit of a jerk to me.'

'Who's a jerk?' announced Lorrie, coming in and dumping a carrier bag down on the worktop.

'No-one's a jerk,' Mai snapped. 'I just happened to remark in passing that I thought Johnny was a vegetarian.'

'Yeah, right.' Lorrie grimaced. 'And I thought he was surgically attached to that flea-bitten leather jacket he always wears. You fancy the pants off him, don't you?'

Mai tried counting to ten. 'I don't fancy him, I merely admire him as one of the college's cultural icons.'

'Oh please,' laughed Atia. 'I don't think so. Anyway, he seems a bit up himself.'

'He's not up himself,' Mai protested. 'He's just shy.'

Lorrie pretended to faint from shock. 'Shy? Just because the boy can barely string a coherent sentence together does not make him shy, Mai.'

'I was sitting on the same table as him and his mates,' Atia went on, 'and he didn't say a word the entire time. He just looked as if he was thinking, "You know what? You *really* bore me."'

Mai was halfway to opening her mouth to dent these accusations (looking as if you were thinking something and actually saying it were two different things) but Lorrie got there first. 'Oh God, talking of which, you'll never guess who we saw lurking outside the Stop And Shop?'

♥ 325 ♥

'No, you're right, we can't guess,' Mai snapped. 'Did you remem—'

'It was that dickweed, Ash,' Lorrie carried on. 'He was showing off as usual.'

Jo looked a bit astonished. 'Lorrie, he was just mucking about on his skateboard . . .'

'Showing off, more like,' Lorrie insisted. 'God, he really thinks he's something. Mind you, he was hanging out with a prime piece of totty.'

The others looked interested. 'What totty? D'you mean Nick?' asked Gillie.

'No, someone called Cameron, he's just moved here,' muttered Jo, going a fetching shade of crimson.

Atia raised her eyebrows. 'Oooh, does that mean there's new totty in the area, Jo?'

Jo tried to look nonchalant. 'He's alright, I s'pose,' she mumbled.

'It's just that you're doing a good impression of a belisha beacon,' Atia persisted.

Jo pressed her Diet Coke can to her cheek. 'Am not. It's hot in here, that's all. Look, are we going to make the rest of this stuff or not?'

Two hours later an impressive array of fairy cakes, flapjacks, scones and oatmeal raisin cookies (Mai's contribution) had been packed into storage containers and old ice-cream cartons. And Atia, after some not-so-gentle persuasion, had convinced her dad to give her a lift into college the next day. The others left and Atia curled up in front of the telly and nibbled on a chocolate brownie. She felt a little guilty as she bit down on a chocolate chunk – she hadn't raised any money yet and she was already eating the profits. She chewed on the brownie and smiled. One brownie wasn't going to make much of a difference, and besides, with the strenuous whirlwind of fund-raising activity that she was planning, she needed to keep her energy levels topped up.

Lorrie planned to stop off for a bag of chips on her way home. As she walked along the High Street, she was so busy visualising the hot greasy chips, liberally doused with salt and vinegar, that she almost cannoned into someone who was skateboarding in the opposite direction.

'Watch it!' she snapped. 'Oh, it's you.' She glared at Ash as he jumped off his skateboard and grinned at her.

'Watch it yourself, ginger-nut.' Ash ran a hand through his floppy blond hair.

Lorrie gave him a withering glance that took in his scuffed trainers, baggy khaki pants and a T-shirt that was about five sizes too big for him. 'Sorry, I thought penny for the guy was in November, they must have started early this year.' One point to me, she thought. 'Oh, and for your information,' she added, 'my hair isn't ginger, it's Titian, after the painter, but I wouldn't expect *you* to know about that.'

'Whatever,' Ash said casually. 'Anyway, you weren't looking where you were going.'

'Well, you shouldn't be riding your skateboard on the pavement,' Lorrie hissed.

'God, you're really uptight,' Ash exclaimed. 'What's your problem?'

Lorrie smirked. 'You are, sad boy. Why don't you get back on your little skateboard and ride off a cliff or something.' With that she tossed back her auburn curls, stuck her nose in the air and flounced off. Ash looked at her departing back with a hurt expression.

Lorrie prided herself on being a pretty fair person, but she'd hated Ash ever since she'd known him, and as they'd both gone to primary school together, that had been a long time. She'd never forgiven him for the hamster incident that had occurred when they were in the blue class. Lorrie had been desperate to take Sammy, the class hamster, home for the

Easter holidays. She'd done an extra good job as milk monitor that term but Ash had pipped her to the post with one extra merit point and taken Sammy home and murdered him. OK, he'd tried to pass it off as a severe case of hamster flu, but Lorrie knew that if Sammy had gone home with her, the worst thing that would have happened to the little furry fella was that he'd probably have overdosed on Easter eggs.

And then there was the time when he'd flipped up her skirt at the end of term disco for a dare. Everyone had seen her pants and it had scarred her for life. Or that stupid gang he'd had that he hadn't let her join. Yup, she loathed Ash with a passion. He was always having a laugh at her expense. Always. Take the first day of college, when he'd sat next to her in English and laughed when she'd dropped her pencil case on the floor. Lorrie had been embarrassed enough as her pens had rolled into the four corners of the room without that, that . . . idiot acting like it was the funniest thing in the world, ever. He seemed to think that he was really laid-back and charming with his goofy grin and lolloping walk, but Lorrie could see right through him. She'd heard Jo tell Gillie that she thought Ash was like a big, friendly puppy, but as far as Lorrie was concerned, he was more like a Rottweiler. The minute that you bent down to pat him, he'd bite your arm off.

Meanwhile Jo had made it back home and was soaking up the last few rays of sun in her back garden. She wriggled about on the sun lounger, trying to get comfortable and hoping that it didn't suddenly collapse, as it had a nasty habit of doing. With a dreamy smile, she thought back to this afternoon when she and Lorrie had bumped into Ash and Cameron at the Stop And Shop. Lorrie had completely mortified her by giving an audible sniff in their direction before stalking into the store. Jo had stopped to say hello. She knew that Lorrie hated Ash but she couldn't help thinking he was kind of cool. He had a Saturday job at the local greengrocer's and she always bumped into him when she was forced to accompany her mother to the shops. He'd always give her a conspiratorial grin because he looked a right divvy in his green overalls and her mum always made a show of her by individually picking each Brussels sprout.

'Hey you,' she greeted Ash. 'How's life in the wonderful world of greengrocery?'

'Oh, you know, it's a thrill a minute,' Ash had said. 'This is Cameron. Cameron, this is Jo.'

The boy he was with stepped forward and smiled at Jo and she'd felt her spiritual self zoom into orbit. He was a complete fox. He had long, dark hair, olive skin and the most beautiful mouth which was smiling . . . at her.

'Hi, you all right?' the vision said to her.

Jo managed to tear her eyes away from his lips and concentrated on a little rip in the collar of his stripy T-shirt instead. 'Er, yeah,' she mumbled. 'Um, you just moved here?'

'My dad's been transferred from Brighton,' said Cameron.

Jo had decided to focus on Cameron's gorgeous brown throat, because she knew that if she looked into his eyes she'd suddenly blurt out something hideously embarrassing like, snog me now. She muttered something that Cameron couldn't catch and turned away as Lorrie came out of the shop.

'Gotta go,' said Jo in a rush and practically sprinted over to Lorrie. 'Wait for me, I'm just going to get my Diet Coke,' she panted, and dived into the shop.

Jo turned over on the lounger and gave a deep sigh. Cameron must think she was a total wuss. She'd stared at him like one o'clock half struck, and she'd barely been able to string a sentence together. Anyway, he was way out of her league. Boys that looked like that didn't go for girls with mousey brown hair, pale skin that went blotchy with nerves on a regular basis and bog standard blue eyes. At least she could worship him from afar at college tomorrow.

Mai was chilling out in her room, watching the omnibus of her favourite soap and carefully stroking a second coat of glittery pink varnish onto her toenails. She'd wear open-toed sandals tomorrow and maybe her long black floaty dress. She might even do something different with her hair, put it up or plait it. Mai looked at herself in the mirror. She knew she was pretty but she wasn't big-headed about it. OK, she had long black hair and clear, fair skin, but as far as Mai was concerned that wasn't enough. Unless you were a good person inside, it didn't matter because, sooner or later, your personality showed on your face. Mai knew that the others thought she was too dippy for words, but she didn't care. She might be dippy but she didn't let people walk all over her.

A picture of Johnny floated into her head and her stomach jolted. It could've been something to do with all the carrot cake mixture that she'd scoffed earlier, but Mai knew better. It was because she and Johnny were meant to be together. She thought of his glossy black hair, blacker even than hers, which he wore slicked back and quiffed, and the little beauty spot underneath his left eye which would have looked girly on another boy but just added to his brooding good looks. She stopped herself. She sounded like one of the wimpy females in her mum's romantic novels. Mai knew that other people thought Johnny was stuck-up, but *she* knew that deep down he was insecure and desperate for the love of a good woman (that would be her) to make him happy. She knew it, he knew it, he just didn't know that he knew it. But he would.

A Bit Of A Bun Fight

Atia bit her lip and looked at the cake stall that they'd set up in the college entrance hall. It wasn't a very inspiring sight. The table that Lorrie had borrowed from the canteen had a folded up newspaper wedged under one leg to stop it from wobbling, and they'd forgotten to bring a tablecloth, so twenty years' worth of cafeteria food was only too visible beneath the paper plates.

The banner was even worse. Jo had volunteered her services and although she was pretty darn hot when it came to art, her efforts to write 'Give hope to the Stanhope Animal Sanctuary. Charity Cake Sale, 1 pm' might be colourful, but she'd misjudged the spacing and the sign actually read, 'Give hope to the Stanhope Ani-mal Sanctuary. Charity cake – sale, 1 pm'.

'That banner looks crap,' she said sulkily to Mai,

who was engrossed in laying out her oatmeal raisin cookies in a geometric pattern on a paper plate.

'Hey, proper sentences are for squares,' Mai replied absently. 'Do you think I should pile up my cookies or lay them flat? I think they look a bit boring flat, don't you?'

Atia didn't have time to worry about the ins and outs of Mai's cookie layout. 'Where's Lorrie and Jo and Gillie?'

'They're putting up posters and stuff.' Mai frowned, still engrossed in her cookies.

All of a sudden, Lorrie emerged with Mr Heckles, the college principal, in tow. 'I just thought I'd see how you were getting on,' he beamed. 'I'm very pleased to see you taking an interest in the community. That's what this college is all about, the community. Education in the community, teaching our students how to be better members of the community, awareness . . .'

Mr Heckles could bore for Britain. Lorrie winked at Atia and gestured at their principal, still droning on about community awareness to Mai, who was more interested in the grated carrot she was arranging on a plate beside her cake, until Jo came up behind her and pointed out that the carrot would go brown in seconds and gross out anyone who'd been tempted by Mai's carrot cake.

'Heckles says he'll officially declare our cake stall open,' Lorrie announced to Atia. Atia visibly blanched at the prospect.

'Oh God, that's all we need,' she moaned. 'He'll scare all our customers away.'

The actual event wasn't as terrible as Atia expected. While a little cluster of trainee hairdressers stood and watched, Mr Heckles droned on, bought a whole chocolate cake (apparently there was a governors' meeting later that afternoon) and then hurried after a foundation art student who'd stubbed out his cigarette in a fire bucket.

For the next half hour the girls were besieged by hungry students with a sugar craving. Atia was too busy counting out change and providing paper napkins to worry about the wobbly table and the drooping banner. Just as she and Lorrie had anticipated, their assorted chocolate creations were the first to go. Mai was starting to fret about the lack of interest in her carrot cake when Ash and Johnny, followed by Nick and Cameron, approached the stall.

Ash was about to make positive noises, until he saw Lorrie sneering at him. He cast a disdainful glance at the crumb-strewn table and a forlorn plate of flapjacks and smirked. 'Well, the animals must be really reassured to know they've got you working for them.'

Lorrie arched an eyebrow. 'You think so?' she spat at him.

Ash shrugged. 'Yeah, I mean you're really going to raise a fortune with this lot.'

Lorrie had to clench her fists to stop herself from smacking the smug expression off his face. 'Well, at least we're trying to do something, instead of spending all our spare time poncing about on a stupid skateboard. You couldn't do any better. You couldn't even run a bath.'

'You wanna bet?' Ash was so angry he could barely get the words out.

Lorrie noticed the angry colour edging along his cheekbones and gave him an insincere smile. 'Yeah, actually I do,' she said.

'I suppose that's a declaration of war,' Ash said icily.

Lorrie tilted her chin. 'I suppose it is.'

'I'll see you later.' Ash turned on his heel and marched down the corridor, the bounce gone out of his step.

Lorrie looked around triumphantly, but the others didn't seem to have noticed. Atia was counting a huge pile of coins, Gillie was putting reduced stickers on the flapjacks, and Mai . . . well, Mai was gazing at Johnny like he was her birthday and Christmas present all rolled into one.

Mai was trying to engage her mouth and her brain at the same time. Speak to him, girl, she thought to herself. She attempted a winning smile, but it kind of came out as a grimace, so she stopped contorting her lips and tried to get a sentence out instead. She needed to make Johnny feel relaxed in her presence, so he could overcome his shyness and maybe even manage the odd, 'Hi, how are you?'

'Would you like to buy a slice of carrot cake?' she said boldly. 'It's all made from natural ingredients.'

Johnny looked at Mai as if her head had started to spin round at 360 degrees. 'Don't like carrots,' he mumbled with a shudder.

Mai looked at him sympathetically. 'That's a pity, they're very good for you. What about my oatmeal raisin cookies?'

Johnny eyed the plate Mai was brandishing at him with some suspicion. 'What about them?'

Mai gritted her teeth. God, this was hard work. 'Would you like to try one? I won't charge you.' She couldn't believe it, she was actually having a conversation with Johnny. This was even better than the time he'd sat opposite her in the college canteen.

Johnny was still looking doubtfully at Mai's culinary wares but, taking his silence as an affirmative answer, Mai wrapped one of the cookies in a paper napkin and handed it to him with a beam.

Johnny cleared his throat as if he was about to say something, thought better of it and walked away. Mai could see him with the wrapped cookie balanced gingerly on his palm as if it was about to leap up and attack him at any moment. That cookie had been a symbol of her love for Johnny and he was acting as if she was trying to poison him. A thought occurred to her. Maybe he was allergic to oatmeal and hadn't wanted to hurt her feelings. That was it. After all, he'd taken the cookie from her, hadn't he? Yay, she thought, he's just as sensitive as I knew he was.

While Mai blissfully imagined the day when she'd coax Johnny out of his shell and help him with his social skills, Jo was turning an attractive shade of red from her forehead to the tips of her toes. The reason? Right in front of her stood Cameron, and he was smiling in such a lopsided kind of way that it made her stomach dip and the blood rush to her head, which would explain the all-over body blush.

'I'll have two flapjacks, a couple of chocolate muffins, a piece of carrot cake and erm, you got any brownies left?' he suddenly blurted out and then looked at Jo expectantly.

Jo tried to be efficient as she wrapped his food in paper napkins. 'God, you *must* be hungry,' she chirped, and then thought, why did I say such a stupid thing? Her words seemed to hang in the air like a bad smell, but Cameron didn't seem to notice.

'I'm always hungry, and this way I get to stuff my face and it's all in the name of charidee,' he finished with a smarmy American accent.

Jo couldn't help but laugh. 'Yup, scoff a muffin and help a lil' animal at the same time.'

They were both giving each other cheesy grins by now. Cameron fumbled for some loose change in his jeans pocket and his T-shirt rode up, giving Jo a glimpse of tanned, taut tummy. She took a couple of deep breaths. God, she was turning into one of those sad old women who went all weak at the knees at the sight of some firm young man flesh. Get a grip on yourself, girl, she told herself, it's just a bit of skin. 'Right, that'll be £3.20 then.'

Cameron pulled out a rather grubby five pound note and handed it to Jo with a flourish. 'Keep the change,' he said, hoping that he sounded caring rather than an arrogant jerk with money to burn, but Jo was beaming at him.

'Aw cheers,' she said. 'You're all heart.'

'I enjoy donating money, it fills me with a sense of enormous well-being,' was Cameron's parting shot as he gathered up cakes and skateboard and departed with a wink. As Jo watched him saunter off down the corridor, she gave a deep sigh. Not only was he cuter than any boy had the right to be, he was also generous and had an ace sense of humour. He had to have a girlfriend back in Brighton, or even here in Stanhope. Someone like Cameron would have been snapped up in an instant, but hey, a girl can dream, can't she? She nudged Mai, who was nibbling the edge of an oatmeal raisin cookie.

'If Atia catches you scoffing the profits, you'll be a goner,' she teased.

Mai gave her a knowing look. 'Hey Jo, why so dreamy? Seen anything you fancy in the boy department?'

Jo grabbed Mai's arm. 'That was him! That was Cameron! Isn't he foxy?'

'Totally foxy and very interested in you, I'd say.'

'And we had a really good conversation,' added Jo.

'I know, I heard,' said Mai. 'Like, give me a muffin and the key to your heart.'

'He did not say that!' Jo squealed.

Mai stuck her tongue out at Jo. 'He might not have said it, but that was what he meant. It's all about body language, hon.'

'He bought a slice of your carrot cake,' said Jo absently. She'd already memorised the whole exchange between herself and Cameron.

'Ooooh, he bought my carrot cake, then he's cute *and* cool,' Mai exclaimed. 'Go for it, girlfriend.'

Jo tried to shrug casually. 'He's probably got a girlfriend. Boys like that have always got a girl.'

'Whatever,' said Mai, raising her eyebrows to indicate that she didn't necessarily think so. 'I think we're just about sold out. How much money have we made?' she called to Atia, who was still counting out coins.

Atia ignored Mai and scribbled a few sums on the back of a napkin. '£90.43p,' she announced triumphantly. 'Yowsa! Where's Lorrie?'

'I'm here,' Lorrie replied. 'I just went to get something out of my locker and found a note from that cretin, Ash.'

'Is he sending you love letters, Lor?' smirked Atia. 'I thought you had a mutual hate thing going on.'

'Very funny,' snapped Lorrie. 'It says that the lads have got a proposition for us and we've got to meet them in the canteen at 3.30 pm.'

There was silence. It didn't take a genius to work

out what Ash was up to. Everyone had heard Lorrie and Ash's high-volume exchange of opinions.

'You know what this is all about,' said Atia. 'Ash is going to start some kind of fund-raising contest. It's obvious.'

'Why is it obvious?' Lorrie asked.

'We all heard you rowing,' Gillie pointed out. 'You know what Ash is like, he's as competitive as you are.'

Lorrie remembered the battle of the merit points over Sammy the hamster and nodded. 'I guess you're right. Sorry.'

'It doesn't bother us,' declared Jo. 'This way we get to raise more money for the animal sanctuary and we get to give the lads a lesson in shame. They couldn't raise enough money to keep a rubber duck.'

'And we get to spend quality time with Johnny and Cameron,' whispered Mai so only Jo could hear, and they both burst out laughing.

At 3.30, the girls sauntered into the canteen. Lorrie had insisted that there was solidarity in numbers. The others followed her as she marched over to where the boys were sitting. She grabbed a chair and sat down, her arms folded across her chest defensively.

The others, with far less aggression, sat down. Lorrie noticed that Johnny, as usual, was sitting slightly away from the others and looking aloof (no change there, then) while Ash was looking at his skateboard as if he'd never seen anything so fascinating in all his life. The others were going to be no use at all, she thought to herself.

'OK, what's with all the intrigue then, skateboy?' she sneered.

Ash looked up. 'It's the animals, you see, we feel really sorry for them.'

Lorrie snorted. 'Yeah, right and . . .'

Ash slouched back in his chair and began to pick at his bitten fingernails. 'No, we do feel sorry for them. 'Cause if your crappy cake sale was anything to go by, they'll be homeless by Christmas.'

The girls gave a collective gasp. What a flaming nerve! 'I don't see you doing anything to help them,' hissed Atia. 'But I suppose slagging us off takes up most of your time.'

Cameron didn't know what to make of all the weird undercurrents that seemed to be wafting round the table. 'Look, we really do want to help,' he said, looking directly at Jo, who immediately glanced away.

'Let's cut the crap,' announced Ash suddenly.

'Here's the deal. We reckon that we can raise more money than you, no contest, so that's what we're gonna do. You hold your girly little bake sales and we'll do our own stuff and the group who raises the least money, ie, you lot, has to fork out an extra fiver . . .'

'Each. Like, per person,' added Nick.

'Wait a minute,' Atia interrupted. 'You're going to help us raise money for the animal sanctuary?'

'Er no,' said Ash sarcastically. 'We're not going to help *you* do anything. We're gonna raise shed-loads of money and show you up for the pathetic wimps you really are,' he finished with relish.

'You're going to be laughing on the other side of your ugly faces when we kick your asses,' Lorrie said furiously. The others looked embarrassed at her outburst.

'OK, I hear what you're saying,' Atia murmured, trying to calm things down. 'I think it's good that you're going to raise some money for the sanctuary although I think your motives are completely dodgy, but if you want a contest then we have to establish some ground rules.'

Ash looked at his mates, who nodded their agreement. 'Fair enough. How about we both have to do the same things?'

Lorrie gave an evil titter. 'God, you really want us to show you up, don't you? Right, you're on. First event will be the council car boot sale, Sunday week. Prepare to be slaughtered.' With that she scraped her chair back and flounced out.

'I s'pose it must be the red hair,' Ash mused, sounding remarkably cheerful for a lad who'd just been at the business end of a hissy fit.

Atia rolled her eyes. 'Goodness me, what an original and unstereotypical thing to say, not.' She narrowed her eyes at the boys. 'OK, let's talk rules. I haven't got all day, you know.'

Johnny gave a deep sigh. All this arguing seemed to be tiring him out. He looked at the girls wearily as if he was in great pain. It was one of the reasons why Mai had such a crush on him. Johnny always seemed as if it hurt his eyes to look at stuff.

Ash ignored Johnny. 'Like we said, we both have to do the same fund-raising activities, and whoever makes the least money has to cough up a fiver each . . .'

'And we have to agree on the activities,' added Jo, blushing. 'We don't want you organising some underhand way of raking in cash without telling us.'

'As if,' muttered Johnny. The others looked amazed. God, he actually speaks, thought Atia.

'We're not suggesting you would,' Mai interjected hastily. 'It's just better to get these things sorted out beforehand. So, what about the proceeds from the cake sale? I mean, if we're going to be doing the same stuff, then it's not really fair if we've got a head start.'

Ash thought for a second. 'We'll treat the cake sale as separate from the contest,' he decided. 'Mind you, I bet you didn't make much money.'

'Actually we made £90.43,' Atia informed him icily.

Gillie and Jo had been nudging each other and talking in whispers. Now they got up. 'We're outta here,' Gillie muttered.

'Yeah, erm, stuff to do,' mumbled Jo indistinctly. She couldn't bear to be near Cameron for a second longer. He just made her feel too weird. Well, she did want to be near him, but she couldn't sit still when he was in close proximity. Instead, she just wanted to climb onto Cameron's lap, pull his arms round her and stay like that forever.

Atia was not going to be left alone with the enemy. 'Wait for me,' she said, gathering up her bag. 'Well, may the best team win,' she added with a significant look at Ash.

'My point exactly,' the lad himself declared. 'I

thought that went rather well,' he said with satisfaction as he watched the girls leave.

'I thought you were well out of order,' blurted out a confused-looking Cameron.

'That Lorrie has it coming,' Ash said with distaste. 'She really reckons herself. She flounces about like she owns the place.'

'Yeah,' agreed Johnny. 'And Atia's bossy, Mai is too dippy for words, Gillie's practically invisible and as for the one, what's her name, Julie . . . ?'

'It's Jo,' pointed out Cameron and Ash.

'Jo then,' sneered Johnny. 'You could heat a block of flats for a week with her face. She should see someone about that blushing.'

Cameron turned a fine shade of red himself. He looked at Johnny challengingly. 'Well, I think she's cute, actually.'

Johnny didn't think that Jo's pigmentation was worth an argument. 'Whatever turns you on, mate,' he said lightly.

Cameron thought about what Johnny had said for a second and smiled to himself.

Pitched Battle

The week leading up to the car boot sale flew by. Collecting stuff to sell could have been tedious if Lorrie and Ash hadn't declared nothing short of total war. Unimportant things like coursework, household chores and kicking back went flying out of the window as they all spent every waking moment hassling rellies, mates and vague acquaintances for 'high quality merchandise' to flog at the car boot sale. If that wasn't enough, Lorrie and Ash were insisting on top-secret United Nations style negotiations to persuade people to donate their junk. The problem was that their social circles were way too small – they all knew the same people and there was only so much bric-a-brac to go round. Ash and Lorrie had even taken to laying elaborate red herrings to fool each other.

Lorrie's name was now officially mud with the boys after she'd tricked them into calling at a false address to collect a box of children's toys. They wandered round the outskirts of town for over an hour before giving up, only to discover that Lorrie had called on their mutual English tutor and swiped a couple of boxes of records that had originally been promised to Ash. This led to a screaming match in the college canteen between Lorrie and Ash, while the others looked on in embarrassed amusement.

'I think those two should try and get some perspective on this,' said Atia wearily as Ash called Lorrie a 'demented pig-woman' and she threw a couple of sachets of brown sauce at him.

'I take it you meant that as an understatement,' laughed Cameron. 'Are we organising two stalls at the local car boot sale or setting our phasers on stun?'

'Sci-fi bore in the area!' teased Jo. So I'm flirting, she thought. So, sue me.

Cameron winked at her. 'Sci-fi's a boy thing, you wouldn't understand.'

'Wouldn't understand or couldn't be bothered?' retorted Jo, sticking her tongue out at him.

Under the table, Mai kicked Gillie. 'God, could those two flirt a little bit more?' she hissed.

'Oh don't be like that,' Gillie murmured. 'Is Johnny still playing hard to get?'

They both glanced across the table to where Johnny was engrossed in a music mag. 'It's not that he's playing hard to get, he isn't playing, full stop.' Mai sighed. 'If only he wasn't so shy.'

Gillie tilted her head and looked sympathetic. 'I don't know. Maybe he's uncomfortable with large groups of people.'

'What are you two whispering about?' asked Nick, who was beginning to feel a bit left out.

'Nothing,' said Mai too quickly.

Atia, who'd been listening to all this, grinned. 'Believe me, Nick, you don't want to know. Anyway, I wanted to ask you, how are you getting your stuff to the car boot sale?'

Nick gave a guilty look in Ash's direction but his mate was still ranting at Lorrie about the devious trick she'd pulled. He lowered his voice. 'Just between you and me, I'm borrowing the band van.' Nick played guitar in a local band and could often be seen careering around the streets in their rickety van which was held together by rust patches and gaffer tape.

Atia made cow eyes at him. 'Any chance of you giving us a lift to the car boot sale?' she pleaded.

'But we've got to be there to set up at six o'clock

in the morning,' he protested. 'And I've got to get our stuff there, too. Ash'll kill me if he finds out that I've been consorting with the enemy.'

'What's he going to do? Withhold your telly privileges and ground you?' Atia asked. 'Look, I know we've got this stupid contest, but we're really doing all this for the same reason aren't we?'

Nick looked blank.

'Duh!' mocked Cameron, who'd finished his not-getting-anywhere flirtation with Jo. 'The animal sanctuary.'

Nick nodded his head. 'Ah yes, it's all coming back to me now. Look, I'll give you a lift, but it'll have to be after I've ferried over all our stuff.'

Atia had wanted to be there dead on six, but beggars who didn't have any transport of their own couldn't be choosers. In fact, Atia was getting fed up with the fund-raising. Sure, she wanted to make some money for the animal sanctuary, but now that this contest with the boys had started, the whole thing had got out of control. Mai and Jo spent all their time mooning over Johnny and Cameron, and as for Ash and Lorrie's stupid one-upmanship! Atia was sick to death of it. She could still hear them behind her.

'Why don't you take your bloody skateboard and

shove it where the sun don't shine,' Lorrie was screaming.

Atia swivelled round in her chair. 'For God's sake, you two, just shut up!' she snapped.

Lorrie and Ash looked a bit shamefaced. 'Sorry, At, just clearing the air with a good, old-fashioned row,' Ash mumbled while Lorrie made apologetic noises.

Atia rolled her eyes. 'Anyone would think you enjoyed baiting each other.'

The two of them looked at each other in horror. 'As if!' they said in unison.

The four decidedly unhappy and bleary-eyed lads kept conversation to a minimum as Nick drove them to the Town Hall car park on the morning of the sale. They managed to grunt at each other a few times as they set the stall up, but it was hardly surprising that no-one noticed when Nick sloped off.

As they laid out their motley wares, they kept throwing glances at the empty pitch beside theirs. They were all kinda hoping that the girls would set up next to them, so they could keep a watchful eye on the competition. Cameron had just finished hauling the last of the boxes into place when he looked up and saw Jo wandering about aimlessly.

'Over here!' he yelled, waving his arms madly to try and catch her attention. Jo gave him a sleepy smile and ambled over to the empty pitch.

She was too tired to even blush at the sight of Cameron. 'I'm absolutely knackered,' she moaned. 'I was so worried that my alarm wouldn't go off, that I spent the entire night tossing and turning. I need matchsticks to keep my eyes open.'

The thought of Jo tossing and turning suddenly made Cameron feel wide awake. 'You look great,' he enthused.

Jo looked surprised. She'd decided to dress for comfort rather than for pulling opportunities, and her thermal anorak and battered jeans could hardly be described as 'great'. A little flicker of hope began to warm her up. 'You silver-tongued devil, you,' she said with a smile.

Cameron smiled back at her and they both stood there for a minute looking into each other's eyes. With a great effort, Cameron managed to tear his gaze away from Jo's. 'So, what's happened to your mob?' he asked.

'They're getting a lift. I said I'd come early and bag a pitch next to you lot, so we could keep an eye on you.'

'We had the same idea,' laughed Cameron. 'So, we're kind of collaborating behind enemy lines, just by talking to each other.'

Jo giggled. 'Not as much as Nick! He's the one who's providing us with transport. But don't tell anyone I told you.'

Cameron was listening with half an ear. He couldn't stop looking at Jo's mouth. He'd never noticed her cute little habit of nibbling on her bottom lip before or how one of her front teeth was slightly chipped. He wondered how it had happened. Jo thought that Cameron seemed a bit distracted and hoped he wasn't about to go back to the lads' stall. He was shifting slightly from foot to foot as if he was agitated. She turned away to see if the others had arrived yet and shivered slightly. Every time she saw Cameron, this funny quivering feeling started. She nearly jumped out of her skin when Cameron put his arm round her.

'You must be freezing. I'll see if the refreshment stall's opened – you obviously need an emergency dose of hot chocolate.'

Jo was just about to mutter something about feeling all right when Cameron whipped off his tartan jacket and placed it round her shoulders.

'I'll be back in a minute,' he promised. Jo watched him run across the car park, the wind blowing his thin T-shirt across his chest. She nuzzled the collar of his jacket. Somehow it seemed to smell warm and friendly. She wondered if Cameron was into random acts of kindness, or whether the loaning of his jacket had some deep and significant meaning – like he fancied her as much as she fancied him.

He certainly wasn't going to declare his undying love for her at half past six on a Sunday morning in the Town Hall car park, but just the weight of his jacket against her back had been worth getting up at the crack of dawn for. She gave a groan and started pulling her fingers through her hair. What did she look like? The boy who haunted her every waking moment was actively being nice to her and she looked like one of the living dead.

Jo was frantically trying to pinch some colour into her cheeks when the others arrived, weighed down by the boxes they were carrying.

'Why didn't you bring the van round instead of lugging all those boxes?' she asked with a frown.

'Because, we're not meant to have come in the van, yes?' said Lorrie as if she was talking to a three-year-old. Lorrie wasn't exactly a morning person. It didn't really matter, 'cause nothing could puncture Jo's good mood. She just beamed at Lorrie's sulky face and went to help Mai who was struggling to lay a piece of red cloth over their table.

'Hey you!' Mai greeted her. 'I love getting up early. The world seems so fresh and clean and new.'

Jo grinned. 'I thought you were cutting down on your sugar intake, Mai.'

Mai gave her a conspiratorial smile. 'Listen, have you seen Johnny anywhere?'

Jo started rummaging in one of the boxes and began laying out china on the table. 'He's around somewhere, why?'

Mai winked and pulled the shoulder of her jacket down to reveal her best vintage dress – a black, beaded number. Mai was a charity shop fiend. 'What d'you reckon?' she asked.

'Don't you think it's a little over the top for a car boot sale?' Jo said in a doubtful voice. 'It's hardly day wear.'

'Huh, I laugh in the face of day wear,' Mai snorted. 'This is Plan A of my Johnny campaign.'

'What's Plan B?' gasped Gillie, who was staggering under the weight of a hideous china dalmatian.

'I haven't got one,' Mai confided. 'I'm putting all my efforts into Plan A.'

'God, can't you think of anything else for, like, one

minute?' Atia said in an exasperated voice. 'Who's got the float?'

'Lorrie has, I think. She was going to ask her dad to change a fiver,' Gillie said.

'So, where is she?' Atia practically screamed. Sometimes talking to her friends was like getting blood out of a stone.

There were raised eyebrows from the other three, who tacitly decided that they didn't want to be in the vicinity of Atia having a temper tantrum and suddenly discovered tasks they just *had* to do.

Thankfully at seven, when the sale started, everyone was in their allotted places and ready to rumble. Atia walked over to the lads' stall to wish them luck, but she hadn't counted on Lorrie accompanying her. The boys' scavenging had paid off. They had a stack of records to sell, a rail of clothes, plus an assorted heap of bits and pieces that included watches, badges and a collection of horse brasses. They also had a life-size china dalmatian that looked kind of familiar.

'We've got one of them,' Atia commented, giving the porcelain monstrosity a pat. 'Mr Heckles gave it to us.'

'He gave us one too,' said Nick. 'Maybe he's got a job lot of them in his office!'

'Anyway, I just wanted to wish you luck and may the best team win and all that,' Atia said.

Nick was just going to make a similar speech when he was interrupted by Lorrie saying in a horribly sneery voice, 'What a bunch of crap! If you give me a fiver, I'll take it to the scrap-yard for you.'

Atia could see that Ash was working up to a crushing retort, so she dragged a wildly protesting Lorrie back to the safety of their own pitch.

'What did you do that for?' said Lorrie, shaking herself free.

'This thing with Ash is getting way out of hand, Lorrie,' Atia told her. 'I never thought you could be such a bitch. Just pack it in.'

Lorrie looked subdued. 'Sorry, At.'

Mai decided that a distraction was called for and suddenly brandished a cake tin. 'This is our secret weapon!' she cried. 'Home-made fudge for every customer.'

Lorrie pulled a can-we-be-friends face, and Atia smiled. 'Cool idea, Mai.' She upped her volume control. 'Free fudge for every customer! C'mon, Ladies and Gentlemen, don't be shy. All proceeds to charity!'

The selling had commenced.

Despite the cold and the uncivilised hour, both teams were rushed off their frozen feet. Some guy who owned a second-hand record shop in Manchester had bought most of the lads' records, and the lady who did the costumes for the local amateur dramatic society was riffling through their clothes rail with evident joy. Meanwhile the girls were cleaning up with Mai and Gillie's home-made jewellery, especially as Mai was making name necklaces while people waited. What that girl couldn't do with a pair of round-nosed pliers, wasn't worth doing!

After Atia's outburst, Lorrie was trying to keep her competitive streak under control, but she couldn't resist the odd haggling contest with Ash.

'I'll let you have the teapot for £2.00,' he was telling an old lady firmly.

'You can have this one for £1.50,' Lorrie yelled across at the old dear. 'And free fudge with every purchase!'

The woman's eyes lit up and she dragged her long-suffering hubby over to the girls' stall.

'How much for the tea set?' she asked Lorrie, indicating the twee, rose-patterned service.

'Ten pounds,' Lorrie decided. 'It's a complete set.'

'I'll give you a fiver,' sniffed the lady. 'I'm sure one of those cups is chipped.'

Lorrie couldn't believe her ears. What a tight old bag! 'Sorry, but at ten pounds I'm practically giving it away,' she insisted. In the end they compromised on nine pounds and Lorrie threw in a tea cosy as well. She looked over at Ash to see if he'd noticed what an ace saleswoman she was, but he was deep in conversation with a well-dressed couple. He kept gesturing in her direction and eventually he called out to her.

'Lorrie, can you come over for a second?'

'Ready for the scrap-yard are you?' she yelled, but Ash was already coming over with the couple in tow.

Lorrie raised her eyebrows enquiringly. 'I'm Mr Geller,' said the man. 'And this is my wife. We're very interested in your dalmatians.'

Lorrie and Ash shared an amazed glance. The dalmatians were revolting – how any sane person could be interested in them was a mystery.

'I'll deal with this, Henry,' the woman announced imperiously. 'These dalmatians are Rockingham. He was a very important craftsman,' she added, seeing their blank expressions. 'Now, I can see that you don't really have a clue when it comes to antiques, but I'm not in the habit of, um, ripping people off, and I understand all your profits are going to charity.'

'They're going to the local animal sanctuary,' said Lorrie in a small voice. If what was about to happen was what she thought was about to happen, then she might burst into flames on the spot.

'I'm going to give you five hundred pounds for the pair, which I think is a very fair price,' said the woman, adjusting her headscarf. 'Do we have a deal?'

'Uh, yeah,' gasped Ash.

Lorrie agreed. 'Yup.'

They both looked on in amazement as the portly gentleman peeled ten fifty pound notes off a massive wad, handed them to Lorrie and then carefully picked up one of the dalmatians.

'We'll be back for the other one,' he muttered.

'I just can't believe that we've found a pair of Rockinghams in a little car boot sale,' declared Mrs Geller as she followed her husband. 'Henry, do be careful!'

Lorrie and Ash looked at each other for a second and then started screaming.

'Can you believe it?'

'Five hundred quid?'

'Who's Rockingham anyway?'

They clasped hands and began to whirl around. Lorrie laughed, her red curls bouncing about. They both stopped and started shouting again.

'We're rich! We are so cool. Wait till we tell the others, they won't believe it!'

Suddenly they both became aware that they were hugging each other and stopped immediately. How embarrassing! Thank God, no-one had seen. They disentangled themselves.

'Hey, watch it, skateboy!' Lorrie snarled.

'Keep your hair on, ginger,' Ash retorted, and they stalked back to their respective pitches.

It was hard to keep the momentum going after the dalmatian incident. It was now 10.30, and the early morning punters had more or less left. Atia assured everyone there'd be a second wave of customers and they decided to go off and get some bacon butties, while no-meat-Mai manned the stall.

Mai fiddled about with her pliers and a length of wire. Her name necklaces had gone down well but she'd been stuck at the side of the pitch and hadn't had more than a glimpse of Johnny all morning. And he was looking particularly spunky today, dressed all in black. She could just bite him, he was so edible. At least the sun had finally come out and she could slip off her jacket and wow him in her beaded fifties cocktail dress. She glanced down at the wire and saw she'd twisted it to spell Johnny's name. An idea suddenly sprang into her head. She stood up and smoothed out the creases in her frock before oh-so-casually sauntering over to the next pitch where Johnny sat looking bored. He looked up as Mai approached and then went back to popping the bubbles in a piece of bubble wrap.

Aw bless, he's so shy, thought Mai. 'I made you a necklace,' she said, making sure she stood in a patch of sunlight so the jet beads on her dress would be shown to their best advantage.

'You what?' muttered Johnny. His attention was caught by Mai's frock. He looked her up and down, then screwed up his eyes as if he was in some kind of deep, existential torment.

'I've made you a necklace with your name on it,' Mai repeated.

'Why?'

'I don't know. You just seemed to look really sad sitting here on your own and I thought it might cheer you up. It's nice getting presents.' Mai wished she could shut up but she couldn't. I'm just going to stand here and talk more and more rubbish until eventually I get so old that I die, she thought.

'Oh, right,' Johnny muttered. There was a long pause. 'Um, thanks.' He seemed to take the afternoon off in between syllables.

'If you don't like it, you don't have to take it,' Mai

said. 'Don't do me any favours.' He might be shy but he could at least make some effort.

Johnny scowled. 'I said thanks. There's no need to make such a big deal about it.'

'I'm not making such a big deal about it,' snapped Mai. 'All I'm saying is that if you didn't like the necklace, you should have said so. And if you do like it, then you've got a funny way of showing it.'

Johnny handed the necklace back to Mai. 'Huh, you're really immature,' he commented.

All of a sudden the sun hid behind a cloud and Mai felt ridiculous in her swank frock, as if she'd gone to a party wearing fancy dress and everyone else had turned up in jeans, which was kind of true in a way. She looked at Johnny in amazement. 'Excuse me, I've had maybe three conversations with you in my whole life, and I don't think that gives you the authority to say whether I'm immature or not.'

'I was just saying . . .'

'Yeah, well, don't!'

Mai squared her shoulders and stalked off with her head held high. Just because Johnny was completely lacking in any social graces, didn't mean that he had to take it out on her. And whose stupid idea had it been to get up at such an ungodly hour anyway? Forgetting her five-minutes-to-be-mad rule, she stomped back to the girls' stall in a huff. Atia was all ready to bawl Mai out for leaving the pitch unattended but she took one look at Mai's mardy face and thought better of it. Whatever had upset Mai was definitely trouser-shaped.

'He ain't worth it, Mai,' Atia said, putting an arm round her friend's shoulders. 'He doesn't deserve you.'

Mai wiped a hand across her eyes. 'I'm fed up. Johnny's so bloody high maintenance. Everybody gets shy, but most of us make some effort to interact with the rest of the human race. And it was a stupid idea to have to get up at the crack of dawn,' she added before snatching up her coat and flouncing off.

The rest of the morning was quiet. The girls were subdued after Mai had run off. They sympathised with Mai over the Johnny business, of course, but they were starting to feel that Johnny wasn't so much shy as just downright rude. Ash tried to start a haggling war with Lorrie again, but her heart wasn't in it. In fact, she even suggested that they pool their leftovers for the last half hour.

'You going soft on me, ginger?' snorted Ash in disbelief.

Lorrie tried to smile. 'Look, I just want this to be over. Mai's really upset over something that Johnny's said or done and I want to go and find her.'

'Johnny's a grade A prat,' chipped in Cameron, who had wandered over, mainly because it gave him a chance to be nearer to Jo.

Jo nodded. 'Yeah, I'm starting to come round to that way of thinking. But I thought he was a friend of yours. Don't you like him then?'

'Not particularly,' replied Cameron, thinking about what Johnny had said about Jo.

'So why do you hang out with him?' she said, bemused.

Cameron tugged his inky black hair agitatedly and took a deep breath. 'Look, Jo, it's hard for me, OK? I've only just moved here and I hardly know anyone. I've only just started sussing out the people who I really want to get close to.'

Jo looked at Cameron and encountered a stare that scorched off the top layer of her skin. 'Significant look', didn't begin to describe it. She was beside herself and really didn't know what to say but could cheerfully have murdered Lorrie, who suddenly came up behind her and dug Jo none too gently in the ribs.

'We wouldn't mind a hand, Jo,' Lorrie said pointedly. 'If it's not too much trouble.'

Jo gave Cameron a rueful smile. 'I suppose I'd better help the others pack up,' she said before turning away.

By twelve o'clock, the entire bunch, girls and boys, were crammed into the van. They'd made an obscene amount of money, but no-one particularly felt like celebrating. Jo and Cameron were locked into their own private little groove, Nick and Ash were furious with Johnny 'cause he'd been worse than useless all morning, and Atia, Gillie and Lorrie were worried about Mai who'd disappeared without a trace. As days go, this one couldn't be classified a roaring success.

Ice-cream And Sympathy

Later that afternoon, once the girls had recovered from the car boot sale, they decided that someone had to go round to Mai's house and sort her out. Originally, the four of them had planned to troop over, but knowing Mai she'd find the attention a bit overwhelming. In the end, they'd all agreed that Jo would be the best candidate. As Lorrie pointed out: 'I'd scream at her, Atia would get annoyed with her and Gillie would just get embarrassed at any highly strung displays of emotion!'

They also had to give the money they'd raised to Mai's dad. Both the lads and lasses had decided that it would be more exciting if they didn't keep a running score on their totals. So, after every event, they'd decided to lodge their takings with an independent party. As Mai's dad was a bank manager, he seemed to be the ideal candidate, even though Ash had been heard to mutter dire warnings about 'parents with vested interests'.

Jo didn't really mind having to assume guardian angel duties. Mai was the easiest person to shake out of a bad mood, and once she was feeling jollier, she wouldn't mind if Jo spent the rest of the afternoon banging on about Cameron. Jo loved Atia, Lorrie and Gillie, but she and Mai had always been best mates. She'd known Mai for ever, quite literally, as their mums had had neighbouring beds on the maternity ward.

Checking for the millionth time that the envelope with all the cash was still in her pocket, Jo was just about to ring Mai's doorbell when Cameron, of all people, suddenly opened the front door!

Jo practically jumped out of her skin. 'God, what are you doing here? You nearly gave me a heart attack.'

'Nice to see you too,' said Cameron, giving Jo a nervous smile. He hadn't been too sure where their last conversation had been heading and he was worried that he might have come on too strong. But no, Jo was smiling and seemed pleased to see him. 'I've just been dropping off the takings,' Cameron explained.

'Oh, right.' Jo nodded. 'Have you seen Mai, is she OK?'

Cameron did his agitated two-step shuffle. 'I guess so.'

Jo nodded again. I feel like one of those stupid toy dogs you see in the back of cars, she thought. Cameron was looking at her in a really intense way and Jo noticed dreamily that although his eyes were green, they had a navy blue ring around the pupil. Oh God, this would be the perfect time for him to kiss me. Cameron was thinking exactly the same thing. He took a step towards her and cleared his throat.

'Jo, I meant what I said earlier about . . .'

'Jo, what a surprise!'

They both jumped as Mr Lee, Mai's dad, suddenly appeared on the doorstep. He seemed to be blithely unaware of the romantic tension happening right there in his front garden and gave the two of them a smile.

'I believe you have something for me?' he enquired jovially.

'Uh?' Jo grunted before remembering about the money. 'Oh, yeah. Um, I've come round to see Mai.'

Mr Lee stood aside to let Jo go through the door. 'Thank God for that. She's taken to her bed and refuses to get up,' he commented. 'I expect it's her hormones.'

How mortifying. Why did parents have to talk about stuff like hormones in front of you? Did they go to special Parentcraft classes that showed them to how embarrass their children, and more importantly, their children's friends? In the circumstances, there wasn't much that Jo could do but give Cameron a helpless shrug and mouth the words, 'See you tomorrow?' at him before she disappeared into the Lees' house. Mai's dad was already peering into the envelope and muttering stuff about balance sheets. It was always a cause of wonder to Jo that someone as logical and straight-edge as Mr Lee could have a daughter as dippy as Mai. And Mai's mother was just as square. Mai had once told her, strictly in confidence of course, that her mother actually ironed her socks. What was all that about? Even her own mother's obsession with cleaning didn't go *that* far.

Jo peered cautiously around Mai's bedroom door. The room was in complete darkness, but as her eyes adjusted she could just make out a miserable looking lump on the bed. Yup, even lying under a twelve-tog duvet, Mai's whole form seemed to encapsulate grief.

'Hey you,' Jo whispered. 'I've got ice-cream, crisps, nail varnish and a big bottle of Diet Coke.'

As she reeled off each item, Mai's huddled body seemed to relax more and more.

Jo continued, 'Fancy some junk-food therapy?' and Mai sat up. Her long black hair was going in all directions. Jo opened the curtains and saw that Mai's face was streaked with tears.

'Oh, come on, Mai, this isn't like you,' Jo said. Mai tried to smile but her bottom lip was wobbling dangerously and Jo hurried over to the bed, just as Mai burst into tears and collapsed in her arms.

After a lot of sobs, interspersed with a lot of spoonfuls of ice-cream, Jo managed to coax the story out of Mai about what Johnny had said to her this morning and how foolish she'd felt.

'I just realised that I'd been chasing after a rainbow, but when I got to the rainbow, I didn't find a crock of gold at all. I found rocks and weeds,' hiccuped Mai dramatically.

Jo curled up on the bed and spooned some of the chocolate and peanut butter ice-cream into her mouth, as she tried to think of the right things to say to Mai.

'Mai, honestly, so he's not exactly communicative – well, you knew that, didn't you?' she enquired tactfully.

Mai sat up and hugged her knees. 'The quiet thing I can handle, but for a second he really turned on me. Maybe I should just forget him.'

'Look, he probably got out of bed on the wrong side. It was a pretty early start this morning,' Jo

♥ 373 ♥

reminded her. 'Don't you think you're kinda blowing this out of all proportion? Honestly Mai, you can be such a drama queen sometimes.'

'To tell you the truth, I'm shattered,' Mai confessed. 'I hate getting up early.'

'Oh, this from the girl who was wittering on about how she loved the fresh feel of a bright new day!'

Mai rolled her eyes. 'So I lied. Seriously, what am I going to do about Johnny? I'm beginning to think that maybe he isn't shy. He might just have nothing to say, full stop. Then again, maybe he just needs the love of a good woman to bring him out of his moody little shell.'

Jo looked knowing. 'And that good woman would just happen to be you, then?' she enquired.

Mai chucked a pillow at her. 'Who else? I'm determined to make him love me.'

'I guess you have to ask yourself if he's as pretty on the inside as he is on the outside. You've got to analyse why you fancy him so much,' Jo advised.

'It's the way he slouches,' sighed Mai. 'And the way he frowns like he's in pain.'

'Hmmm, he does slouch great, but I think the frowning's just a facial tic.'

Mai laughed despite herself. 'I wish I didn't cheer up so easily.'

'I'm bloody glad you do!' said Jo, rolling her eyes for effect.

Mai got out of bed and rummaged through her tapes. She put one on and then clambered back onto the bed, so she and Jo were lying head to head.

'So, come on, spill the beans, Jo.'

'I don't know what you mean,' Jo protested.

Mai gave her a gentle prod. 'Oh, please, you're dying to tell me about Cameron and I'm dying to hear all the sordid details.'

Now it was Jo's turn to sigh. 'There aren't any sordid details, that's the problem. He likes me, but I don't know if there's any more to it.'

'Yeah, right,' sniffed Mai. 'He looks at you like you're on the breakfast menu.'

'Oh, I wish,' Jo moaned. 'It's hard. We seem to get interrupted all the time. We were having this really deep talk this morning and then Lorrie butted in, and I bumped into him a minute ago and just when things were looking promising, your dad put in an appearance.'

Mai sat up. 'Tell me about it,' she laughed. 'He's got this in-built romance radar. When I was going out with Ben he always managed to open the front door at the precise moment we were about to start snogging.'

'Parents just know, don't they?' agreed Jo. 'Oh,

Cameron's so lovely. I've never fancied anyone this much before.'

'Not even that foxy boy who works in Rhythm Records?' asked Mai in a wicked voice.

Jo gave her a gentle kick. 'That was just a crush, this is the real thing. So do you think that Cameron's into me? Because I want to be sure before I do anything about it.'

'No doubt about it!' Mai was practically shouting by now. 'If you want Cameron, go and get him, Jo. I saw the two of you at the car boot sale with his arm round your shoulders.'

'I didn't realise you were there,' said Jo, not bothering to deny it.

Mai smirked. 'I was keeping a tactful distance. Now, any more ice-cream left?'

When Mai breezed into college the next day she was determined to keep her crush on Johnny in perspective. Timing was important, she'd decided. Just when he least expected it, she'd pounce! This was the beginning of a new era in her love for Johnny. As she'd got dressed that morning, she hadn't automatically chosen her outfit with him in mind. Instead she'd plaited her hair, pulled on her favourite jeans and decided that it would be cool to wear her dark green cardie as a jumper. And if Johnny didn't like it, well, who cared?

She was telling Jo about this new philosophy as they were getting stuff out of their lockers when they were interrupted by Gillie, who came running down the corridor, bellowing at them.

'Hey, where's the fire?' exclaimed Mai as Gillie nearly knocked her off her feet.

'Sorry. You'll never guess what the boys have done,' Gillie said breathlessly. 'Lorrie's spitting about it.'

'What have they done?' asked Jo, thinking to herself, boys = Cameron.

'No, I can't explain, you'll have to come and see for yourselves,' huffed Gillie. 'Come on.'

They followed Gillie down the corridor. What the hell was going on? And why did they both have a nasty suspicion that it all had something to do with Lorrie? But when they got to the main noticeboard outside the college canteen, it was obvious that whatever the boys were up to, Lorrie had been left in the dark.

'I don't believe it,' she was saying to Atia. 'Talk about sneaky, two-faced, underhand, conniving . . .'

'Yo! What's up?' enquired Mai brightly.

Atia pointed at a sheet of paper on the noticeboard. 'This is what's up!'

Jo and Mai peered at the notice. It seemed to be advertising a slave auction. There was nothing unusual in that, except the slaves' names were Ash, Cameron, Johnny and Nick, and they were 'willing, available and highly skilled'.

'Johnny – this slave has green fingers and will cater to your every gardening whim for a measly thirty pounds,' Mai read out. 'OK, where do I sign him up?'

'MAI!' shrieked Lorrie. 'That isn't the point – the point is the small print. Look – "all proceeds to the Stanhope Animal Sanctuary". They deliberately flouted the rules of the contest. We're meant to be doing the same things, not going behind each other's backs. There's Ash over there. Right, I'll handle this.'

Atia yanked Lorrie back by her bag strap. 'Actually, Lorrie, I'll handle this,' she said in a scarily firm voice before marching in Ash's direction.

'What's this about a slave auction?' Atia demanded, deciding not to waste time on social niceties like 'hello' and 'how ya doing?'

Ash held up his hands in surrender. 'Sorry, I've been meaning to tell you. Ace idea, you up for it?'

Atia couldn't believe what she was hearing. 'No, we're definitely not up for it,' she spluttered. 'I don't think women died for the right to vote so we could sell ourselves as slaves. And besides, I hate cleaning and gardening.'

Ash scratched his head. 'But I've already been signed up, we can't cancel now.'

'That's your problem,' Atia insisted. 'You should have discussed it with us first. Lorrie was about to land you one.'

'Why doesn't that surprise me?' muttered Ash. 'OK, you organise a girl thing as well.'

'I will,' Atia snapped before turning on her heel and going back to the others.

Lorrie was still threatening to break every bone in Ash's body.

'Calm down, Lor,' Atia begged. 'It was just a communication breakdown, that's all.'

'Huh! If you believe that, you'll believe anything,' snorted Lorrie. 'What's the deal?'

Atia smoothed down her glossy black bob and took a couple of deep breaths. 'We're going to organise our own event, OK? Can we change the subject?'

'Well, you could try talking Mai out of her stupid scheme to buy Johnny for the day,' said Jo.

Mai beamed. 'It's not a stupid idea. It's a genius idea.'

Lorrie looked amused. 'I thought you were into human rights, Mai.'

'Yeah, I'm against slavery,' Mai agreed. 'But I'm not against Johnny spending all day sweating over my mother's flowerbeds. He'll probably take his top off. Yes! Yes! Yes.'

Jo gave Mai a hug. 'She shoots, she scores!'

Mai turned to the others with a big grin on her face. 'Life just suddenly got good again!'

They couldn't help laughing.

'You're mad, Mai.'

'It'll never work.'

'He's gonna be furious when he finds out who's bought him.'

But Mai just smiled – she knew better. She sat in a particularly boring history class and imagined that hot, sunny Saturday afternoon. She'd lie luxuriously on the sun lounger, reading a book and wearing a cute, floaty little dress. As Johnny toiled hard in the heat, his bare chest glistening with little beads of sweat, he wouldn't be able to resist sneaking little looks at her. She'd pretend not to notice but eventually she'd offer him a long, cool drink. She'd saunter off to the kitchen and return with some attractively presented, fruity beverages. She'd put the tray on the grass and call Johnny over. He'd kneel by the lounger and gently brush her hair back from her face.

They'd gaze into each other's eyes for a long second

that seemed to last an eternity, before he'd gather her up in his strong arms and snog her to within an inch of her life. As they came up for air, Johnny would murmur throatily, 'I love you, Mai, I always have.'

Mai came to with a start and decided that she'd better start concentrating on the whys and wherefores of the Russian Revolution before she melted into a pool of gooey slush. She couldn't wait until Saturday.

♥

Mystic Gillie

In the event, Mai had far too much to do to spend the rest of the week daydreaming about what would happen once she'd lured Johnny into her back garden. Lorrie and Atia were determined that their 'girl event' had to happen before Saturday and had to be completely ace. But what could they do that was extremely low maintenance and absolutely stupendous?

They debated the merits of sponsored swims, sponsored runs, sponsored silences (they gave up on that one, pretty sharpish) and even a sponsored chocolate eating session, but as Lorrie pointed out, 'Sponsored stuff is for kids.'

To give them inspiration, they decided that a visit to Maison Blanc, the posh patisserie near the college, might help. If nothing else, the sugar would boost their energy levels. Frothy coffee and cream cakes were consumed while the girls plotted their next move.

'What about a treasure hunt?' offered Jo, after they'd all sat in silence for five minutes.

Lorrie licked a stray blob of cream off her fingers and shook her head. 'It's too time-consuming and we'd have to use some of the money to buy prizes.'

'We could always organise a gig or something,' ventured Atia, before pulling a face. 'Oh, that would take weeks to set up. There must be something.'

Gillie pulled out a magazine. 'I'm just going to check my horoscope and see if it matches the astrological chart I drew up last week.'

Lorrie wound a strand of hair round a finger. 'You drew up your own astrological chart?' she asked incredulously. 'You don't believe all that stuff, do you?'

Gillie wagged a finger in her direction. 'Don't mock what you don't understand. We Campbells are descended from a long line of mystics.'

Mai looked over Gillie's shoulder at the horoscopes. 'Gillie's really good at all this stuff. She did my tarot cards for me and said that I'd come into some money, and the very next day I found a tenner just lying in the street.'

'And remember when I lost my watch and Gillie told me to go home and look under my chest of drawers? There was my watch,' added Jo.

Gillie smiled modestly. 'My Granny Campbell would regularly speak to her own grandfather, even though he'd been dead for twenty years. It's in my blood.'

Lorrie suddenly snapped her fingers. 'That's it! Gillie is going to be our next fund-raising event.'

'Am I?' Gillie looked doubtful.

Atia looked excited. 'You're right,' she said to Lorrie. 'We could set up a fortune-telling booth at college and people could cross Gillie's palm with silver, or a couple of pound coins.'

'I don't think so,' Gillie protested. 'My psychic skills are a gift. It wouldn't be right to make money from them.'

She was shouted down in no uncertain manner.

'It's for charity!'

'If you've got it, exploit it!'

'You know you want to, Gillie!'

Gillie tried to look as if she didn't dig the whole crazy idea, but secretly she was quite pleased. Everyone needs to feel wanted sometimes. And what with Atia spending most of her waking hours immersed in fund-raising schemes, and Jo and Mai mooning over their respective crush objects, and Lorrie being her usual hyperactive self, Gillie had felt a bit surplus to requirements. The others would have been horrified if they'd known about Gillie's insecurities. They loved her faint Scottish accent, which became even more pronounced when she was annoyed or excited. They envied the freckles which marched across the bridge of her nose, and even though she dug all things mystical and shmystical, she was easily the most sensible of the lot of them. As it was, Gillie felt a warm glow of belonging as the others all but begged her to run a fund-raising, fortune-telling booth.

She kept pretending to be iffy about the whole idea but a little smile crept on to her face.

Lorrie peered at Gillie intently. 'Uh-oh, I think she's cracking!' she teased. 'I can definitely see a smile trying to break through.'

Gillie burst out laughing. 'I'll not get a minute's peace till I agree, will I?'

'No!' the others shouted in unison.

Gillie pretended to consider the idea for a minute or two. 'Hmm,' she said contemplatively. 'Oh well, anything for a quiet life.'

'Yay!' squealed Jo. 'And let's face it, you know most people at college, so it won't be too difficult to spin them a line.'

'Spin them a line?' said Gillie indignantly. 'My fortune-telling will be based on the science of the stars, I'll have you know. I don't need to resort to spinning lines. And to show your appreciation of my talents, I think the least you can do is stand me another chocolate eclair!' She smiled winningly.

Lorrie groaned in an exaggerated fashion. 'OK, OK, I'm going.'

When Gillie saw the costume that Atia wanted her to wear, she very nearly called off the whole event. It wasn't the long, flowing purple robes or even the clashing paisley shawl that Gillie objected to. But there was absolutely no way anyone was making her don a tangled black bubble wig and stick-on warts.

'I'm meant to be a psychic,' she protested. 'Not a flaming extra from Macbeth.'

Lorrie twirled the wig invitingly. 'Correction, you're Madame Griselda, soothsayer to the stars. And soothsayers do not have short brown hair.'

'And is there any law that says they have stick-on warts?' Gillie enquired sarcastically. 'Are you sure you don't want me to paint my face green too?'

'Hmmm, that's not a bad idea,' teased Atia.

Gillie didn't see the joke. 'No way,' she stated. 'I refuse. I'm not doing it.'

'Maybe you could wear a scarf on your head,' Mai chipped in, anxious to calm Gillie down. 'You know, gipsy style.'

'I'll wear a scarf,' Gillie agreed. 'But no stick-on warts, no green face paint, no fake hook noses, OK?'

'OK,' said Lorrie. 'Honestly, some people have no sense of humour.'

Eventually Gillie was ensconced in her purpose-built fortune-telling booth. Or rather, a two-person tent that they'd customised with lots of black net and silver spray paint. As she waited for her first customer, Gillie felt a twinge of nervousness. Was she really psychic? So, Mai, had found a tenner – lucky coincidence, and it wasn't that astounding that Jo's watch had been under her chest of drawers. It was so messy under there that Gillie wouldn't be surprised if Jo had found the wreck of the *Titanic* as well. She nibbled on a nail in a worried fashion. God, this was even worse than waiting for the dentist. People had to realise that she was just a bog-standard college student kitted out in some silly clothes. It wasn't like she was a professional mystic or anything.

Suddenly the tent flap was pulled back and Gillie's first victim was ushered in. Gillie grinned to herself. It was Mr Heckles. This actually had the potential to be quite a laugh.

'Who's that under all that make-up?' boomed the college principal.

'You dare to interrogate Madame Griselda?' croaked Gillie in what she hoped was a spooky voice. 'I ask the questions. Now, cross my palm with two pound coins and take a seat.'

Mr Heckles looked suitably chastened and perched on the camping stool opposite Gillie, who indicated that she'd like to see his palm.

She pretended to scrutinise Mr Heckles' hand. 'Hmmm, I see a dog. A large dog.'

Mr Heckles looked confused. 'Are you sure it's a large dog, dear? We've only got a Yorkshire terrier.'

'Silence!' Gillie commanded. 'The dog I see is not alive. It's made of china. I see two dogs made of china, which you recently gave away. These two dogs want you to know that they don't resent being abandoned by you. They've gone to a good home.'

Mr Heckles seemed to be lapping up this information. Gillie racked her brains for some other snippet of information before remembering that Mrs Heckles was pregnant. Bingo, she thought.

'I also see a hospital and many happy faces. Soon you will welcome a new person into your life and this will be a great cause for celebration.'

'My wife's pregnant,' exclaimed Mr Heckles. 'Is it a boy or a girl?'

Help, thought Gillie. She was just about to hazard a guess, thinking that she had a 50/50 chance of being right, when suddenly a little girl's face appeared in her head.

'Er, it's a girl,' she gasped in surprise. 'With dark hair and the bluest eyes.'

The little girl suddenly disappeared.

'Has she got my chin?' asked Mr Heckles.

'Enough!' proclaimed Gillie. 'Madame Griselda must now rest.'

Mr Heckles stumbled out of the tent, seeming a bit shaken. Gillie took a couple of deep breaths until Atia stuck her head through the flap.

'You ready for the next one?' she asked. Gillie nodded and then nearly fell off her stool when Johnny suddenly shot into the tent. Now, this was going to be fun.

'Sit down and cross my palm with a couple of pound coins,' she said icily.

Johnny perched uneasily on the stool. One minute he'd been standing in the canteen wondering why there was an odd looking tent where his favourite table usually was. The next he'd been shoved inside it by Nick and Ash. He made a mental note to give them a wedgie next time he saw them, but for now he'd go along with it. So, here he was, and feeling like a right idiot, too.

Gillie made a show of studying Johnny's palm and then suddenly dropped his hand as if she found it rather disgusting.

'What have we here then?' She sniffed as if there was a bad smell in the tent. 'You are a young man with a communication problem, aren't you? Are you as deep as people think, or are your waters rather shallow?'

As Madame Griselda elaborated on Johnny and the confused messages that he sent out to the rest of the world, the young man in question looked increasingly uncomfortable. OK, this was one of the girls having a huge joke, right? But he wasn't *that* bad, was he?

'Beware of your aloof ways, young man,' Gillie warned. She was beginning to enjoy herself. 'It gets you into trouble. I see a lonely life ahead of you, if you continue this morose way of life. But, look, I see a young girl with a white light around her. She could save you from yourself.'

Johnny perked up. 'A chick? What does she look like?' he enquired eagerly.

'Not a chick!' snapped Gillie. 'She's a young woman with a kind heart. She has long black hair and a lovely smile. Hmmm, I see the letter M . . .'

'Is it Maria from my physics class?'

'No, it's not Maria,' Gillie hissed. Get on the clue train, she thought. 'The girl I see has been hurt by you in the past, but she has a forgiving nature. You were lovers in a former life and it's very rare for people to meet again in another existence. This girl, whose name begins with M, and who has long black hair,' (– Gillie wanted to make sure that Johnny got the message –) 'is your soulmate.'

Johnny was beginning to seem doubtful. 'You what?' he said in a sceptical voice. 'Was I cool in my former life?'

Gillie decided to try another tack. 'Tell me why you shun the company of females?'

Johnny creased his head with the effort of answering the question. Although part of him felt that this fortune-telling business was a load of crap, there was something about Madame Griselda's lilting accent that was completely hypnotic.

'Girls never stop talking,' he told Gillie. 'And I need to be alone with my thoughts.'

'And what are these thoughts?'

'It's funny actually, 'cause once I'm alone with my thoughts, I realise that I don't have as many of them as you'd think.'

Johnny said this with deep sincerity, and it was all

Gillie could do to stop herself from laughing. He had to be having her on.

'Madame Griselda's advice to you is to stop being alone with your thoughts and to explore new experiences and people,' – she informed him. 'Once you find the black-haired girl, your life will change. Madame Griselda now grows weary.'

Johnny got up. His session with Madame Griselda was even more confusing than his sociology coursework. 'Er, bye,' he muttered as he crawled out of the tent.

Gillie rolled her eyes. Well, she'd tried, but what could she do? The boy seemed to be on Planet Wacko.

For the next hour she was kept busy. She got great satisfaction from informing her stroppy sociology teacher to switch to a non-dairy diet to help her oily skin, and put the wind up the college hard nut by telling him that he'd go prematurely bald.

When Lorrie came in, Gillie fiddled about with some old pebbles that she'd found on the beach last summer, before telling her mate that love was found in the most unexpected places. She'd had to suffer a couple of painful heart-to-hearts with Lorrie as her mate lamented her lack of action in the love department, so Gillie reckoned it was sound advice. And when Ash popped in ten minutes later, she told him exactly the same thing. After all, she couldn't be expected to come up with some new prophecy for everyone, could she? Besides, Ash had been experiencing a snog famine ever since Christmas so, again, it seemed like the right thing to say.

Gillie was just about ready to change from Madame Griselda, soothsayer to the stars, back into Gillie Campbell, teenage soap addict, when Cameron ambled into the booth.

Gillie went through the two-pound-coin routine and then sat back and stared at Cameron until he began to shift nervously on the stool. The silence stretched on and Cameron was just about to make a run for it when Gillie spoke.

'You're a stranger in this town and you find it hard to fit in. You have new friends who you will grow close to, but I see someone else. Someone who you would like know better, someone who you want to love, but I see a barrier. A barrier of your own creation, made out of your own doubts.'

'And?' prompted Cameron.

'Your doubts are unfounded,' insisted Gillie. 'The girl – would her name be Jo? – has doubts too. But only because she mistrusts your intentions. In order for you to be happy, it has to be you who breaks down these barriers of doubt. Forget your fears and listen to your heart.'

'What else?' asked Cameron. 'Does Jo really fancy me, or is she just being nice?'

What is wrong with him? thought Gillie. Could I make it any plainer? 'Jo is shy. It has to be you who makes the first move, but I promise that you won't regret it,' she intoned in her best spooky voice.

'What has she said about me? Why does she act like I'm boring her?' Cameron persisted. He knew that it was one of Jo's mates under the pan-stick, but suddenly he was desperate for a bit of advice on how to win Jo round. The lads were all right, but he couldn't really talk to them about anything important.

'As I said, she's shy,' Gillie said wearily. 'But she wants to be with you.'

'Yeah, but has she actually said, "I want to be with Cameron," or has she just hinted at it?'

Gillie couldn't take it any more. She pulled off the scarf and grabbed Cameron by the collar. 'For God's sake, Cameron, get with the programme, she's dying for you to ask her out. What are you – a man or a mouse? Stop dithering about it. If you want her, go and get her. Now stop pestering me.' She suddenly stopped – Cameron was grinning from ear-to-ear.

'Cheers, Gillie,' he beamed.

'If you breathe a word of this to anyone, you're dead,' Gillie said in an angry whisper, but Cameron was already on his way out.

Never, ever again, Gillie decided, as she flopped down on the stool.

Meanwhile, Cameron was a man with a mission. As the bell rang for afternoon classes, he raced around the corridors trying to find Jo, without success. In the end, he decided to write a note and leave it in her locker. But, as he hunted in his bag for a pen, he decided that that was a crap idea. For a start, he couldn't think of what to write, and secondly, Jo might not even get it. The note could languish at the bottom of her locker for the rest of the year, and when she did find it, she might, horror of horrors, be going out with someone else. He could imagine Jo reading his pathetic note and then tossing it into a bin with a derisory laugh. It was a thought too awful to contemplate. It would be a better idea to catch up with her before she went home.

As Jo walked towards the college exit, with nothing more on her mind than her English homework and the sausages that she was going to have for tea, she was surprised to see Cameron running towards her. He's in a hurry, she thought. But, hey, he was stopping and smiling at her.

'Um, hi, er, can I walk you home?' he stammered.

Don't get your hopes up, Jo told herself sternly. 'Yeah, sure,' she mumbled.

They started walking along the High Street, both of them racking their brains for something to say.

I'll speak to him in a minute, thought Jo. Or maybe he'll talk to me first.

What can I say to her that doesn't sound stupid? thought Cameron.

Of course, they both picked exactly the same millisecond to speak.

'I was . . .'

'Did you . . .'

'You go first,' said Cameron.

'Um, I was just wondering if you visited the fortune-telling booth at lunch-time,' Jo said in a squeaky voice.

Cameron tugged at his hair. 'Yeah, I did.'

'Oh yeah, and what does your fortune hold?' asked Jo.

'Well, that kind of depends on you,' said Cameron, suddenly feeling incredibly brave.

'On me? What d'you mean?' enquired Jo, praying

that Cameron was leading up to what she hoped he was leading up to.

'Madame Griselda told me that if I wanted something, I had to go out and get it,' Cameron told her, giving Jo a meaningful look.

Jo's heart was racing. She stopped and turned to face Cameron, unaware of the people bustling around them. To them it was just a normal day. Go to work, go to college, go shopping, but all of a sudden Jo knew that she'd remember this moment forever.

'What do you want?' she asked Cameron in a small voice and then he was smiling at her and taking her hands in his. His face was coming nearer and nearer and then, and then . . . Jo squealed as Nick suddenly dug her in the ribs.

'What are you two up to?' he asked cheerfully, totally unaware this his presence was about as welcome as a plague of killer wasps.

'Nothing,' they said in unison.

The three of them started walking along the High Street. Jo couldn't believe it. There were no two ways about it, Cameron had just been about to snog her when Nick came along. I hope he comes back as an earthworm in his next life, she thought viciously.

'Why were you staring at each other like that?' asked Nick.

Cameron shrugged. 'Jo had something in her eye,' he improvised.

Yup, my love for you, Jo whispered under her breath.

'So are you coming over to my house to jam tonight?' Nick was asking Cameron. 'Cameron might join the band,' he added for Jo's benefit.

'Oh, that's nice,' Jo mumbled. She stopped suddenly. 'Look, I've just remembered, I've got to get some shopping for my mum, so, um, I'll see you both tomorrow.' She stumbled into the nearest shop, leaving Nick and Cameron standing there.

'Ooops! was it something I said?' Nick smirked.

The second that Jo saw Nick and Cameron ambling off, she made a speedy exit from the shop she'd been lurking in. That had to be the most cringeworthy moment of my life, she thought. I am never going to get together with Cameron, ever. We'll still be trying to snog each other ten years from now and every time we get close, we'll be interrupted by someone. She gave a whimper of frustration and started walking home.

Mai Sees The Light

Finally, the day that Mai had been spending all week trying not to think about arrived. When she woke up on Saturday morning, she felt a delicious tremor of excitement run through her. In a few short hours, Johnny would be a slave to her horticultural needs. Suddenly, she sat up in bed with a groan. She'd forgotten to mention her, erm, visitor to her folks.

Now most parents would be only too happy to foist the gardening chores onto a willing helper, but Mai's parents weren't most parents. Her dad lived for his lawn mowing. It was like a religion to him. And her mother's herb patch might just as well have barbed wire around it. Mai's ma was pathologically protective of her lemon-grass and basil and lots of weird Chinese herbs that Mai couldn't even pronounce. Without much enthusiasm, Mai got out of bed, shrugged on her dressing gown and ambled downstairs to get the deed over with.

Her parents were enjoying a leisurely breakfast, as

Mai took her seat at the kitchen table. She looked out of the window at the back garden and gave a deep, dramatic sigh, but her mum was engrossed in her bowl of muesli and her dad was frowning over the crossword.

'The garden's looking a bit wild,' Mai remarked in a casual fashion. Her mother looked up and gave her a vague smile and her dad just grunted.

Mai pulled at the top of the newspaper, so her dad was forced to look at her.

'I just thought I'd let you know,' Mai said with the pathetic smile she used when she was after a favour. 'I've got someone to come round and help with the garden.'

'What are you talking about, Mai?' asked Mr Lee.

'You know we're raising money for the animal sanctuary – there was this, um, slave auction and I hired one of the lads to do stuff in the garden,' she explained in a rush.

'What kind of stuff?' asked her father in an ominous voice.

Mai looked hurt. 'Gardening stuff. Mowing the lawn, weeding, raking, hoeing.'

'No way,' her father declared. 'I'm not having one of your cack-handed friends butchering my lawn and then expecting me to pay for the privilege.'

'And they can steer clear of my herbs,' her mother added.

'Well, that's nice,' huffed Mai. 'I pay, out of my own money, for someone to do the garden for you, so you can have some time to yourselves, and all I get is grief. Cheers.'

'Would this be one of the boys who put holes in my lawn?' was all her father had to say.

'Dad! We were putting up a tent and that was years ago.'

Her father was folding up his paper and giving her one of his looks, and Mai knew that a lecture was coming, so when the phone rang she sprinted to answer it.

'Phew, saved by the bell,' she muttered, as she picked up the phone. 'Hello.'

'What's the matter?' Jo asked. 'You sound really stressed.'

'Oh, don't ask,' Mai groaned. 'I've trying to explain to my folks about Johnny coming round to do a spot of weeding and mowing and all the kinds of hard, strenuous manual activity that work up a bit of sweat on a young man.'

'So, he has no other option but to whip his top off,' added Jo smirking.

'Something like that!' Mai agreed. 'Anyway, what's

been happening in your world? I phoned you last night but your mum said you were in the bath and she had strict instructions not to disturb you. So I immediately knew you were having a traumatic crisis probably caused by something male. Tell me everything in detail and don't skip bits.'

Jo was more than happy to do as she was told and regaled Mai with all the gory details of her near snog. All except what Cameron had told her before Nick ruined everything. There were some things that were too private to share even with your best mate.

'Oh, I'm so happy for you,' cooed Mai once Jo had finished. 'I knew he fancied you something rotten. He's really sweet, Jo. I wouldn't be happy about you going out with someone who didn't deserve you.'

'Aw, shucks,' teased Jo, a bit embarrassed. 'But I wouldn't say we were going out.'

'Rubbish. It's only a matter of time. OK, so you haven't arranged a date, but that's only a formality.'

'Do you reckon?'

'Definitely,' Mai assured her. 'You mark my words, I'll get you alone together.'

'Well, just don't make it obvious,' Jo laughed. 'Now, how are you going to play it this afternoon with Johnny?'

'Very, very cool,' Mai told her. 'The only problem is

the 'rents. They don't seem convinced about the whole thing. Why, I don't know. Anyone would think I had an ulterior motive in wanting the garden to look nice.'

'Yeah, anyone would think that, Mai, especially if they knew you as well as they do,' said Jo. 'Look, I've got to go. I promised I'd take my little brother to the cinema. Give me a ring and let me know what happens.'

'OK, and let's hope that by the end of this afternoon you won't be the only one with a permanent snogging partner!' Mai replied.

'Good luck!' shouted Jo as Mai put the phone down.

Mai replaced the receiver and wandered into the kitchen to continue the conversation with her parents. They were both drinking coffee and reading the papers, but turned and looked at Mai as she walked in. Their expressions weren't exactly encouraging. Mai often wondered if she'd got muddled up with another baby at the hospital. Her parents were so organised. Mai shot a baleful look at her mother's spice rack where the jars weren't just in alphabetical order but also categorised according to national cuisines with curry stuff at the beginning and Italian herbs bringing up the rear. Mai was just thinking about how food could be modern *and* rustic at the same time, when her father gave an impatient cough. That was another thing about her parents – they never seemed to daydream, whereas Mai made sure that most of her day was spent in a parallel universe.

Mr Lee folded his paper and looked at Mai enquiringly. 'Let me get this straight, Mai. You're so worried about the upkeep of our herbaceous borders that you've selflessly employed a young man to spend the entire afternoon toiling in our garden?'

Mai nodded in agreement. When her dad got going like this, there was absolutely no point in interrupting him.

'And not only are you going to pay him for his time, you're willing to supervise both him and his trowel?' her dad continued. 'Who are you and what have you done with our daughter?'

'Well, I think it's very thoughtful of Mai,' said her mother, who had a sneaking suspicion that her daughter was up to something. And knowing her daughter like she did, she had a further suspicion that this something might be to do with the boy coming round. 'So, you don't want to go to that new garden centre with me and have a spot of afternoon tea on the way back, dear?'

Mr Lee disappeared back into his newspaper. 'I'm not saying that. I just smell a rat, that's all,' he said mildly before an article on the New York stock exchange took most of his attention.

Mai shot her mother a grateful look. 'Thanks, Mum,' she said, giving her mother a quick peck on the cheek before racing up to her room. So many things to do, so little time before Johnny arrived on her doorstep.

Two hours later, Mai was peering over the top of her sunglasses as Johnny peeled off his black T-shirt. She quivered slightly as he picked up the rake and his muscles rippled. This was way better than her wildest daydreams. She itched to gently stroke back the hair that flopped into his eyes as he chucked a pile of grass cuttings into the wheelbarrow.

When Mr Lee had opened the door to find Johnny standing on the doorstep and at that exact same moment Mai had wafted down the stairs in her favourite sundress and a cloud of perfume, everything had become apparent. Her dad had just shot her a knowing look and said, 'I'll let you deal with this, Mai.' It could have been a lot worse. Her dad liked to think that he was a real wit. Only last week, as a special treat they'd gone to the new American-style diner that had opened on the High Street and even though Mai liked to think that she was laid-back, her father had made a complete show of her. When the young (and indecently spunky) waiter had brought them the menus, he'd said, 'Hi, I'm Michael and I'm going to be your waiter tonight,' like they do in America. But her father had turned to him and said, 'Hi, I'm Jack and I'm going to be your customer!' Quel embarrassment.

Thank God that Johnny had been spared any examples of her father's humour. The minute he'd walked into the house, her mother had hustled her dad out of the house and into the car for their outing to the garden centre and afternoon tea.

Mai had been left to show Johnny into the garden. And she'd played it so cool that even a cucumber would have been jealous. She hadn't forgotten the immature dig he'd given her at the car boot sale, shyness or no shyness. She'd sauntered ahead of him, so he could admire the nice tan she'd acquired, and showed him round the garden shed before retiring to her lounger to watch him work up a sweat.

She picked up her magazine and pretended to be engrossed in the problem page, but she was way more engrossed in Johnny. She couldn't believe the karmic collision that had led to Johnny, with his top off, in her parents' garden. She must have been very good in a former life. If she looked really carefully, she could see the top of his boxer shorts, poking out the low-slung waist of his jeans, and his chest was just so firm and brown. She took a cooling sip of fruit juice and settled down as if she was asleep. Thank God for dark glasses, she thought.

As Johnny raked up grass cuttings, he couldn't help but sneak little looks at Mai. He'd never realised what a total babe she was. As he bent to tug at a weed he cast a smouldering glance at Mai's legs, which were sprawled over the edge of the lounger, and then up over her body to her long, black hair. She was pretty gorgeous. In fact, she'd be his ideal woman if she didn't talk such a load of dippy drivel.

Johnny knew that Mai fancied him. It was an occupational hazard, he smirked to himself. But girls had to realise that he didn't do commitment. It wasn't fair on the rest of girlkind to tie himself down to one chick in particular. One minute you were getting off with a girl, the next she expected you to hold her hand and remember her birthday and be nice to her mother. Yup, commitment, Johnny decided, was a nothing trip. But that didn't mean that him and Mai couldn't have some fun.

He sauntered over to the sun lounger and plonked himself down on the corner.

'Wotcha doing?' he asked Mai, who pretended he'd woken her from a little snooze. Yeah, right.

Mai gave a little self-conscious stretch. 'Oh, I must have fallen asleep. How's the gardening going?'

Johnny turned to look at the lawn he'd just mowed and raked, so Mai could admire his profile. It was his best side.

'I'm nearly finished,' he said, giving Mai his best smouldering look, the one he'd spent ages perfecting in the mirror.

But Mai was looking at the lawn with a frown. 'Well, you didn't do a very good job,' she said. 'It's terrible. You've missed a great big patch in the middle and all the lines are wonky, and look at the edges – they're all raggedy. I thought gardening was your speciality.'

Johnny scowled at her. What a nerve! 'It's only a stupid lawn,' he muttered. 'It's not that bad.'

'Yeah, right,' said Mai. 'My dad's gonna have a fit when he sees how you've butchered it. You'd better get on with weeding. There's loads of dandelions in the flowerbeds.' She picked up a magazine and started flicking through the pages.

Johnny stood up and shot her a baleful look. Who did Mai think she was, ordering him about like that and dissing his work? She was taking the whole slave thing a bit too literally for his liking. He slunk off in the direction of the garden shed, to find some implement for pulling up weeds. He wasn't too sure what you were supposed to use, but he was pretty confident that he'd find something in there.

Mai watched him saunter shedwards and had to bite her lip to stop herself from laughing out loud. Unaware that he was being watched, Johnny was admiring his reflection in the shed's window and primping his hair. He stepped back and practically preened before disappearing into the shed. Mai shook her head. Maybe she'd been wrong about Johnny. Maybe he wasn't mysterious and shy, maybe he was just shallow and up himself. Could she really fancy a lad who spent so long admiring his own reflection? She spent a good five minutes pondering her crush on Johnny and was just starting to come to a conclusion when she realised that he was still in the shed. What could he be doing in there that took so long? She dreaded to think and realised she'd better investigate.

On opening the shed door, Mai was not best pleased to see Johnny stretched out on the workbench with a cigarette in his hand.

She snatched it from his fingers and stamped on it. 'What are you doing, you idiot?' she shrieked at him.

'What?'

'What do you mean, what?' yelled Mai. 'Firstly, you're meant to be weeding, and secondly you're not supposed to smoke in here. Look, there's paraffin and white spirit and turpentine on that shelf behind you. I don't think my parents would be too happy if they got home and discovered that you'd managed to set the shed and yourself on fire.'

'There's no need to get all mardy,' said Johnny sulkily. 'I was just taking a breather. Keep your hair on.'

Mai gritted her teeth and mentally counted to ten. 'OK, I'm sorry I yelled at you, but please be more careful,' she said in a more normal voice. 'Look, I'll go and get you a cold drink. Now could you please get on with the weeding.'

'Yes, sir!' snapped Johnny.

Rolling her eyes and muttering under her breath, Mai walked back to the house. She'd thought an afternoon with Johnny would be a good chance to break down his barriers and ask him out. She hadn't bargained on finding him so irritating that she wasn't sure if she ever wanted to see him again.

She got a can of Coke out of the fridge, poured it into a glass and was just adding some ice cubes when she glanced out of the window and promptly dropped the ice-cube tray. There was Johnny, spade in hand, digging up the flowerbeds!

Johnny had just finished digging up a nice little pile of weeds when he got the shock of his life. Running towards him was Mai, screaming as if the hounds of hell were snapping at her heels. She was a funny chick. Shrugging, he turned away and began to apply some pressure to the spade. Next thing he knew, Mai had physically thrown him to the ground. Sprawling on the grass, winded, Johnny gaped up at Mai who was literally dancing with temper.

'You cretin!' Mai yelled. 'What the hell do you think you're doing?'

'I'm weeding,' Johnny gasped. 'Duh!'

'Don't you bloody duh me!' screeched Mai. 'You're digging up the flowerbeds!'

She bent down and pulled something out of the little pile of soil that Johnny had amassed.

'What's this?' she asked, waving it in his face.

Johnny failed to see the urgency of the situation and was actually looking a little bored. 'A weed,' he said in an offhand voice, and started to get to his feet. Mai pushed him back.

'It's a marigold, you idiot,' she choked in an angry voice. 'You know sod all about gardening, don't you?'

'That shows how little you know,' bluffed Johnny.

'Oh, excuse me, that's why you were using a spade to dig up the weeds instead of a trowel and your hands.'

'OK, so I don't know about gardening,' Johnny admitted. 'Big deal.'

'It said on the advert for the slave auction that you were skilled at gardening,' Mai pointed out. 'I think the phrase "green-fingered" was mentioned.'

Johnny, who'd decided that it was safe to get up again, looked a bit uneasy. 'Yeah well, I might have exaggerated slightly.'

'So, what are you going to do about it?' Mai growled. She felt like whopping Johnny. If he was any more laid-back, he'd be permanently horizontal.

'Dunno.'

'AAAAARRGH!' screeched Mai, yanking her fingers through her hair. 'Look, just go,' she told Johnny as he slouched in front of her with his hands wedged into his jeans pockets. The slouching wasn't doing that much for her any more – in fact, she felt like shouting at him to stand up straight and put his shoulders back.

She marched Johnny through the house, and even though her hands were on his firmly muscled back as she all but pushed him down the hall, Mai didn't feel one quiver of excitement.

She opened the door. 'Out.'

Johnny didn't budge. 'You owe me thirty quid,' he insisted.

Mai couldn't believe what she was hearing. 'I'm not paying you thirty pounds for mutilating my parents' garden,' she snarled.

'Tight bitch,' muttered Johnny under his breath.

'I heard that!' Mai informed him. 'Not only am I refusing to pay you, I'm going to phone Ash and tell him exactly what I think of you.'

'I know what you think of me. I know you fancy me,' Johnny sneered.

Mai tilted her chin, her dark brown eyes flashing with anger. 'Correction. I did fancy you, until I discovered that you were a brainless, thoughtless, up-himself dickweed,' she spat out. 'And then I went off you – funny, that.'

Johnny wasn't having it. He kicked at the door-frame with one foot. 'Anyway, I could never fancy anyone that lived in a poky little hovel like this,' he jeered, determined to get the last word in.

Mai flared her nostrils and gasped with indignation. 'How dare you?' she hollered at the top of her voice. 'You come here under false pretences, make a complete pig's ear of the gardening and nearly set the shed on fire, and then you slag off me and my home.'

'Yeah, you got a problem with that,' Johnny smirked. 'Let's face it, Mai, you want me!'

'Ha! Like I want a hole in the head,' she told him before slamming the door in his smug face.

Mai wasn't finished with Johnny yet. She might have had a reputation for being easy-going, but push her too far and it was like dancing with the devil. First, she phoned Ash to let him know in no uncertain terms what she thought of him and his untruthful advertising, and then she demanded that he and one of the others get round there so they could restore the back garden to its former pristine state before her parents came home. Ash didn't need telling twice. Mai's icy voice, so different from her usual bubbly tones, had sent shivers down his spine. And the fear of her father's wrath was enough to have him skateboarding furiously in the direction of Mai's house within minutes.

Once Mai was sure that the lads knew what they were doing, she left them toiling in the garden and went to the telephone to tap in Jo's number. Jo picked it up on the second ring.

'That you, Jo?' The minute Mai heard Jo's voice reply she embarked on a rant about the general uselessness of boykind.

'Hey, what's up?' asked Jo when she could get a word in. 'Did something happen with Johnny?'

Mai managed to choke out the entire sorry story while Jo made sympathetic noises.

'So, I refused to pay him and told him exactly what I thought of him,' she finished. 'You don't think I was too hard on him?'

'As if!' Jo spluttered indignantly. 'You know, I didn't like to say anything before, but I did have my doubts about Johnny. I was never completely convinced that all that moodiness was shyness.'

'Tell me about it!' agreed Mai. 'The only reason he keeps so quiet is 'cause he knows that the moment he opens his mouth, his cover's blown. There's nothing between his ears but air.'

'What, you mean he's thick?' asked Jo.

'Well, maybe he's not completely thick,' Mai conceded. 'But all he thinks about is himself and how gorgeous his hair is. I mean, he spent five minutes preening himself in the shed window. I'm surprised he didn't blow himself a kiss! Anyway, I'm going to phone the others and then I'm going to get out a slushy video and eat a vat of chocolate ice-cream. You up for it?'

'I'm on my way now!' said Jo.

Mai started giggling down the line. 'You know what, Jo?'

'What?'

'I don't think I've ever got over anyone so quickly, and I am so over that boy!'

'Atta girl, see you in half an hour,' said Jo before calling off.

Mai went and washed her face with a cold flannel, relieved that she'd finally managed to get her temper under control. She hated blowing up like that, but Johnny had deserved it. She could forgive him for being lazy but he'd been such a creep. How dare he call her a bitch and criticise her home and then think that she'd be so overcome with lust for him that she wouldn't care? The boy had some funny ideas about girls. Thank God I never went out with him, she thought, before going out into the garden to 'supervise' the lads. Or 'boss us to within an inch of our lives' as Nick whispered to Ash.

Five hours after Mai had ordered Johnny off the premises she was ensconced on her velvet beanbag listening to Gillie's confession of Johnny's brush with Madame Griselda.

'If I'd known how arrogant he was, I'd have given him the fortune-telling of a lifetime!' Gille said, laughing. 'I could have told him to join the Foreign Legion or something!'

Mai chucked a handful of popcorn at her. 'Let's declare the subject of Johnny closed. I'm not going to spend any more time mooning over that loser,' she said bravely.

Atia looked up. 'What, are you off lads altogether?'

'Duh!' mocked Mai. 'I'm just off one lad in particular. I'm not going to let one bad apple ruin the rest of the barrel. There's plenty of other lush specimens of boyhood I can have a crush on. What about that bloke who sings in Nick's band, Paul? He's pretty cute.'

Lorrie looked at Mai in amused disbelief. 'God, I thought we were going to spend most of the evening mopping your tears, and you've already picked your next conquest.'

Mai gave a modest shrug. 'Excuse me, but I wouldn't waste my tears on that boy fink. And at least the garden got done for free in the end,' she said with a wink.

'You're my girl hero,' laughed Atia. 'Your powers of recovery are astonishing.'

'So are we going to watch this film or what?' said Mai, settling back onto the beanbag while Lorrie hunted for the zapper. Boys, eh? They were all right in small doses, but she couldn't eat a whole one.

♥

Bath Time

On Monday morning Jo and Mai walked to college together. They had plenty to talk about. After Mai had spent five minutes assuring Jo that she was so over Johnny that she'd spent most of Sunday afternoon compiling a new lust list, Jo squeezed her pal's arm. 'You're not just putting a brave face on the Johnny thing, are you?'

'For maybe one hour on Saturday afternoon I was, but then I thought, hey, life's too short for me to be another notch on Johnny's belt. And that's the honest truth,' Mai told her.

They walked into the college entrance and ambled towards their lockers, moaning about having sociology first thing.

'A sociology lesson is not where I want to be on a Monday morning,' Jo was saying as Mai opened her locker.

'I don't believe it!' Mai exclaimed. 'Ooooh, look, it's a note from Johnny. What a cheek.'

Jo peered over her shoulder to look at the note. 'What's it say?'

Mai smoothed out the note and begun to read: 'Dear Mai, I'm sorry about what happened on Saturday. I guess we got our wires crossed. I've decided to forgive you for the demented way that you acted. I know you're not such a bad person and I'll let you make it up to me. See ya around, Johnny.' She raised her eyebrows at Jo. 'OK, tell me I'm dreaming.'

Jo took the note from her. 'Nah, it's definitely Johnny's handwriting,' she said. 'So, are you pleased that he's forgiven you?'

'Ha!' Mai snorted. 'He's going to have to do some major grovelling if he even wants me to pass the time of day with him. C'mon, let's hit that sociology class.'

By lunch-time there was something new to take everyone's minds off the Mai and Johnny love fiasco. That something was baked beans. Or more specifically bathing in them. 'A sponsored baked bean bath, that is such a sick idea,' declared Gillie. 'Ugh, it makes me feel ill just thinking about it.'

'I think it's an ace idea,' said Atia stoutly. She had decided that all this boy/girl stuff, though highly entertaining, was diverting attention away from the animal sanctuary. She called an emergency meeting of the lads and lasses to launch her, next fund-raising scheme.

'Well, I'll volunteer for us lads, but how long do I have to sit in the baked beans?' said Cameron.

'I've got it all organised,' announced Atia. 'You're going to get money for every quarter of an hour that you can last. And, look at it this way, Mr Heckles has agreed to let the two volunteers off classes that day.'

Mai nudged Jo, who said quickly, 'I don't mind volunteering!'

Lorrie snorted. 'But Jo, you hate . . . ow!' She turned to glare at Mai, who'd just given her a swift kick under the table. Mai looked pointedly at Cameron and then at Jo. Light suddenly dawned and Lorrie gave Jo a wink.

'You lot are obviously too wussy to do it, so I thought I'd save everyone the trouble of having to come up with excuses,' Jo explained. 'But I'm not going naked.'

Atia looked horrified. 'Who said anything about being naked? This is a family event. You can wear shorts and a T-shirt.' She scribbled something down in her notebook. 'Well, I'm glad that's sorted out. I've got to go and talk to the catering manager – the college have promised to donate the baked beans.'

'They're probably going to get them from the slop bucket,' Cameron muttered as Atia hurried off.

'Rather you than me,' said Nick. 'You're going to come out of that bath looking all wrinkly like a prune.'

'An orange prune,' added Mai. Johnny gave a shout of laughter.

'Ha, ha, an orange prune,' he repeated.

'Just cut it out, sickboy,' snapped Mai, getting up to leave. 'The change of character doesn't fool anyone.'

Johnny looked like his whole world had turned to broken biscuit, especially as Gillie and Lorrie flicked him dirty glances as they left the canteen arm in arm.

'I've forgiven her. What more does she want?' he said pitifully to Nick and Ash. 'She really hurt my feelings.'

'Somehow I doubt it,' said Jo scornfully. 'Your ego is the most robust thing about you. You think that you can treat people like dirt and get away with it. Wrong.'

Johnny picked holes in an empty polystyrene cup. 'I didn't treat anyone like dirt. I spent ten minutes mowing her bloody lawn and all she could do was complain,' he mumbled almost to himself. 'But I've changed – no more Mr Nice Guy.'

Jo had just taken a mouthful of coffee, but with Johnny's last remark, she snorted so hard that she showered Cameron with the contents of her mouth. He looked unconcerned as he ineffectually tried to dab the brown stains from his T-shirt.

'Oh God, I'm sorry,' stammered Jo, mortified.

Cameron gave her an easy smile. 'It doesn't matter. If I'd had a swig of coffee when Johnny did his humble routine it'd probably have gone over you.'

They looked at each other and burst out laughing. Johnny glared at them as he got up.

'That's right, laugh,' he hissed. 'You should just grow up.' With that, he marched out of the canteen.

'No more Mr Nice Guy then,' commented Cameron.

'I know, but how can we tell?' asked Jo, still giggling. 'I guess I should be getting off too. I've got to get some Diet Coke before my next lesson.'

'I'll come with you,' Cameron decided. 'We need to get to know each other better, seeing as how we're going to be spending some quality time together.'

Jo's heart started beating at twice the speed of light, or that's how it felt as it thumped away inside her chest.

As they walked out of the canteen, their hands inched towards each other, as if there was a magnetic force field pulling them together. All of a sudden, Cameron grabbed Jo's hand, as if it was the most natural thing in the world. And although neither of them said anything as they walked to the newsagent, their tightly clasped hands said it all.

By the day of the sponsored baked bean bath, Jo was in torment. Every time she'd got near Cameron over the last few days, she was either surrounded by her mates or he was hanging out with his. They'd had no other option but to exchange significant looks and casual chat while the others were about. No girl wants to arrange something important – like a first date with the boy of her dreams – with an audience.

Jo eventually decided that she'd wait until baked bean day before making her move on Cameron. Then it would just be the two of them and nothing could go wrong. Even when Mai rushed over to her to announce that Johnny had been leaving flowers and organic chocolate bars in her locker, Jo merely grunted and tried to concentrate on not thinking about Cameron. This wasn't that difficult because she was more worried about the entire college seeing her, wearing shorts, and submerging herself in a tin bath full of baked beans. With Cameron. Damn, she wasn't going to think about him.

Jo stood shivering in the canteen as the tin bath was prepared. As catering tin after catering tin of beans was emptied into the bath with loud plops, her heart plummeted all the way to the tip of her blue nail-varnished toes. It sank even further when she saw Cameron saunter in to loud cheers and wolf whistles from the assembled crowd. He was wearing a pair of cut-off army trousers and she felt herself go hot and cold as he whipped off his regulation baggy T-shirt. Who'd have thought that underneath his outsize garments, he'd be so . . . fit. Cameron had seen her and was giving her a friendly wave. Miserably she went to join him, blushing the same colour as Lorrie's hair as a crowd of engineering students started wolf-whistling.

'Nice legs, Jo,' one of them yelled.

I wish the ground would open up and swallow me, she thought. 'I can't believe I'm doing this,' she confessed to Cameron, out of the side of her mouth.

Cameron seemed positively chipper at the thought of spending an entire day covered in baked beans.

'Well, at least we get out of lessons,' he said comfortingly.

'Oh yeah, that's right,' Jo muttered. 'I knew there had to be a good reason for making a complete prat of myself.'

'Think of the poor, defenceless animals you'll be helping,' added Atia, coming up behind them.

'I've thought about them,' Jo said. 'I still feel like a complete prat.'

'Stop moaning,' said Atia. 'Come on, they're ready for you.'

To loud claps and cheers, Jo and Cameron climbed into the bath at opposite ends. As their legs brushed, Jo felt a twinge of sexiness. You can stop that right now, she told herself sternly. It's a sick idea; you're trapped in a flaming bath full of baked beans. You do not feel remotely sexy. They sat down, facing each other, their legs touching. Jo tried to move away from Cameron (she didn't want to feel so attracted to him when they had such a huge audience) but it was a small bath and only resulted in a wave of baked beans slopping over the edge. The crowd cheered.

'Stop fidgeting and try and look happy,' whispered Cameron. 'They'll soon get bored.'

Jo gave him a weak smile and stared at a fixed point on the ceiling, pretending that this wasn't happening to her. Maybe if she tried hard enough, she could actually leave her body and perhaps even leave town too, while she was at it. She'd never felt anything quite so disgusting as being submerged in this vat of gloop. It was horrible; the beans felt all slimy and she was sure that some of the little orange blighters had found a way into her shorts. If Cameron isn't my reward for death by baked beans, Jo thought, then there's no justice in the world. After what seemed like an eternity but was actually only five minutes, the bell for morning lessons rang and people mooched off, leaving Jo and Cameron alone, apart from the college cooks who had promised to keep an eye on them.

They sat there for half an hour talking about what had been on telly the night before. Oh, they kept smiling at each other, but both of them had had a sudden attack of shyness. It's all very well fancying someone to bits, but when you find the object of your affections suddenly wedged against you in a bath full of baked beans, it's quite another matter. Jo was intensely aware of Cameron – not difficult when he seemed to be pressed up against her. She gave a deep sigh.

'You still embarrassed?' asked Cameron, wiggling his feet a little bit and causing seismic thrills throughout Jo's body.

Jo attempted nonchalance. 'Nah,' she said, 'I'm fine now.' Bring up the subject of us, she wanted to say to him. You go first.

But Cameron merely nodded and said, 'Fancy a game of I-Spy?'

After an hour of I-Spy they were both feeling a bit less shy. Sharing a bath of cold baked beans was a great leveller (Cameron had pointed out they could have at least warmed the beans up first). And they'd even had a few laughs – there are only so many things you can spy in a college canteen, like drinks machine, tea urn and condiments tray. Something really weird and important was happening between the two of them, Jo decided. They kept exchanging these lingering looks and their legs were now happily entwined in the beany soup.

'OK, I've got a new game,' announced Jo. 'How much would you snog Mrs Heckles for?'

'Urgh!' Cameron pulled a face. 'Two million quid.'

Jo pinched his calf. 'You've got to be realistic, Cam. You would snog Mrs Heckles for far less.'

'Would not.'

'Oh yeah, so if I was only prepared to pay you three thousand quid and no more, you'd turn down the cash?' Jo smirked.

Cameron pursed his lips. 'Well, when you put it like

that, I'd snog her for two thousand quid. OK, how much would you snog that squeaky voiced man who works in the Stop And Shop for?'

'The one with the eyes like hard-boiled eggs,' squealed Jo. 'Five thousand quid.'

'I'd undercut you and snog him for four thousand,' laughed Cameron.

Jo pulled a disappointed face. 'Oh dear. How much would you snog that cook in the green pinny for?'

'Well, a tenner. She's one luverly lay-dee!'

Jo flicked a stray baked bean at him. 'You silver-tongued devil, you. You know, the funny thing is I don't even like baked beans.'

'You don't like baked beans?' asked Cameron incredulously. 'I thought everyone liked baked beans. Mind you, I hate pizza.'

'But pizza's one of the seven wonders of the modern world,' declared Jo.

Cameron shook his head. 'Cooked cheese is the work of the devil. How much would you snog Johnny for?'

'I abstain,' Jo snorted. 'You're allowed one abstention.'

'Oh yeah, says who?' Cameron teased.

'Says me. I invented this game,' said Jo, poking her tongue out at him.

'Anyway, who's going to give us this money for snogging people?' Cameron asked.

'I dunno,' said Jo. 'C'mon, you get to have another go.'

There was a long silence during which they exchanged another deep and meaningful look.

Cameron took a deep breath. 'OK, how much would you snog me for?'

Suddenly Jo realised a fundamental truth about herself. She wanted to snog Cameron more than anything else she wanted in the world, even more than that to-die-for black dress she'd seen in Miss Selfridge. She looked at his mouth. It was made for kisses, her kisses.

She tried to speak, but no words seemed to come out. Suddenly, Cameron was hoisting himself up and kneeling over her. He ran a beany hand delicately down her face, smoothing her hair back. Jo grabbed the back of his neck and pulled him slowly down until their lips were millimetres apart.

Their lips met. Cameron gently brushed her mouth with his and then they were locked together in a kiss that seemed to last for several millennia, much to the shock of the cooks.

Eventually Jo and Cameron came up for air.

Jo exhaled deeply. 'I thought you were never going

♥ 429 ♥

to get around to it!' she exclaimed happily.

Cameron seemed just as pleased. 'It was all a question of timing. I wanted our first kiss to be perfect, but . . .'

'. . . but other people kept getting in the way,' Jo finished for him.

'It was driving me nuts having to sit around and chat about nothing with you because they were all watching.'

Jo grabbed his hand. 'That's exactly how I felt. But I thought about you twenty-seven times between lunch-time and going to bed on Monday.'

The minute Jo said these words, she wished that her gob came with an erase button. Cameron would probably think that she was some kind of mad stalker.

But, no, he was gently tickling her palm and then he raised her hand to his mouth and kissed it.

'I think about you all the time, with no gaps,' he confessed.

'What, all the time, even when you're skateboarding?' Jo asked.

'Yup,' he confirmed. 'Unless I'm negotiating a tricky bit of pavement. Why do you think we got on so well from the start?'

'Because we've both got a warped sense of humour?'

Cameron shook his head and waggled a finger at Jo,

so little drops of tomato sauce splattered her already splattered top. 'Wrong! It was fate. My folks moving down here and then me hooking up with Ash – it was meant to be.' Jo was just about to make puking noises at Cameron's soppy speech when she realised he was laughing at her. 'Well, maybe it was our shared love of Diet Coke, instead!'

'I love a boy who can beat me at my own game,' said Jo with a small smile. 'Why don't you come and sit next to me?'

Cameron tried to manoeuvre himself into place, causing a small tidal wave of baked beans to slop over the edge. By the time the break bell rang and people started to wander in for a mid-morning hot chocolate, Jo and Cameron were wedged side by side and ignoring the whole world as they talked in whispers. They might just as well have had a six foot sign that said 'Bog Off!' suspended over their beany haven.

Despite their uncomfortable and sloppy surroundings, Jo couldn't remember a better day. She and Cameron talked about everything and nothing, from their CD collections to their shared theory that the crunchy bits in the college's chocolate brownies were actually dead ants. And when they got bored with talking, there was always some snogging that could be done.

When Atia came to oversee their ceremonial disembarking from the baked bean bath, they both gave her annoyed looks.

'We don't mind staying here for a bit longer,' Jo protested.

Atia couldn't help but smirk. 'Sorry, love's young dream, but it's time to go home. I take it the sponsored baked bean bath wasn't such an ordeal, then.'

Cameron managed to heave himself from the bath with a loud squelching sound. 'Oh, it had its moments,' he said wolfishly, turning round to give Jo a hand as she clambered out of the bath.

Both of them had gone a strange orange colour and had baked beans clinging to every available inch.

'If this stuff doesn't wash off, we're suing,' Jo told Atia. 'How much did we make?'

Atia looked blank. 'Don't ask me. We'll have a grand ceremony when we reach the final total. I've got one more event planned.'

'Er, what?' Cameron muttered. 'I hope it's something spectacular.'

'It is,' said Atia with a sly smile, and then realised that she was surplus to requirements. 'I'll leave you two to, erm, get it on. I mean, get on with it! See ya.'

After all those intimate hours trapped in a bath of baked beans, it seemed strange to have to go their separate ways, but Jo had already ordered her mother to drive her home and even reminded her to line the back seat of the car with bin bags.

'So, how are we going to leave this?' asked Cameron as he walked her to the car. They made a strange, orange pair.

'I don't know,' Jo replied coyly.

Cameron pulled her into his arms and gave her a quick, hard snog. Her mother honked the horn in horror as she saw her beloved daughter being molested by a gangling, orange youth. Jo disentangled herself, laughing.

'Tell your ma that you've decided to walk home,' Cameron whispered in her ear. And despite her mother's protests, one shower and ten minutes later Jo and Cameron were once again standing stock-still in the middle of the High Street, gazing into each other's eyes. And just when she thought it wasn't going to happen, Jo felt Cameron's lips on hers. At first, it was just a gentle kiss, but then their bags dropped to the floor and Cameron cupped Jo's face between his palms and her fingers were twisting in his hair, just like she'd dreamt of doing since the first time she'd seen him outside the Stop And Shop. It was even better than the kisses that they'd shared amid the baked beans. Their lips fitted perfectly. They stood in the middle of the High Street, kissing, oblivious to the smiles and stares and jokes of the people who had to side-step around them.

Eventually, they came up for air and smiled at each other with dazed expressions.

'You've got lovely hair,' said Cameron, stroking Jo's short brown curls.

'So have you,' whispered Jo dreamily before smiling. 'What happens now, then?'

Cameron picked up their bags and took Jo's hand. They continued with their journey.

'What happens now?' he repeated. 'Well, I tell you that I've fancied you ever since Ash introduced us outside the Stop and Shop. And then you tell me that you felt the same way too.'

'Oh I did,' said Jo hastily.

'And then we kiss a bit more, and then I ask if you fancy going out tonight for fish and chips and you say yes. And I say OK, I'll come round your house to pick you up at about seven.'

Jo decided that if she suddenly dropped down dead right this minute, she'd die with a smile on her face.

'So, what do you think?' asked Cameron, who was a bit alarmed at Jo's silence.

She squeezed his hand. 'It sounds just fine to me,' she told him.

♥

Aaaaargh!!

Two days later, Jo was still floating round in a love-soaked haze. She had to keep pinching herself to make sure that it was really true. The day of the sponsored baked bean bath had been the best day of her life. After their amazing first kiss in the baked beans and then their snogs in the middle of the High Street, she and Cameron had walked back to her place, pausing to kiss every now and again. She'd let him walk her to the top of her road before running home to try and de-orange herself. And even though she'd started angsting about Cameron meeting her family when he called round, it had gone off smoothly. Her mum had taken one look at Cameron and had merely smiled and said, 'I want Jo back at 10.30. It's a college night.' Jo had a sneaking suspicion that her mother had felt like saying, 'So, you're the boy who was mauling my daughter earlier,' but thankfully it never happened.

Even when her parents had given him the third

degree over coffee ('What GCSEs did you do?' 'Are you planning to go to University?'), Cameron had been unfailingly patient and polite. And when her brat of a little brother had shouted, 'Urgh! Have you snogged Jo?' Cameron had still managed to retain his cool.

After their fish and chip supper they'd walked to the park, and in between snogging, made plans to go to the cinema the next evening. Once again, Cameron had proved himself to be one of the finest specimens of boykind by insisting that he didn't really want to see the action movie that was showing and if Jo wanted to see a chick flick then it was all right with him.

Jo had started to laugh. 'Look, Cameron, you don't have to keep up the Mr Perfect act. I'd want to go to the cinema with you, even if you took me to a kung fu triple bill.'

Cameron had pretended to look hurt. 'I don't have a Mr Perfect act,' he'd gasped in mock-indignation. 'I really am perfect!'

'Oh yeah,' Jo had mocked. 'Prove it.'

Cameron had considered the question and then pulled Jo to him, so she was pressed against his taut chest. 'Well, I fancy you,' he'd whispered. 'So that proves that my taste is, well, perfect.' He hadn't said any more because Jo had pressed a kiss onto his lips and then neither of them had talked for quite a while. And the next night, they'd gone to the cinema and it had been even better.

Jo gave a happy sigh as she relived these events and then toddled off to phone Mai. What was the use of going out with the fittest, kindest, funniest lad in the world if nobody knew about it?

'How did your second date with Cameron go? Was it scorchio?' Mai wanted to know.

Jo gave a deep sigh. 'Oh, it was wonderful. I met him outside the cinema and we decided to see that new comedy, the one with the woman from that telly show in . . .'

'Don't skip bits,' Mai ordered. 'What were you wearing?'

'My long check skirt and my dark blue T-shirt and my dark blue hooded top and those trainers I bought last week, OK?' said Jo sarcastically.

'Cool. So did he pay for the tickets?'

'Yeah,' said Jo dreamily. 'But I bought the popcorn and the drinks. And he got the posh tickets so we got to sit in those swank seats at the back. And first he was eating his popcorn but after he'd finished, he put his arm round me, but really casually, and then we held hands. And he just kept squeezing my hand really gently but it was really intense.'

♥   437   ♥

'So, did he snog you?' interrupted Mai.

'No, not in the cinema because that would be tacky,' Jo replied. 'But after the film we went to that new pasta restaurant and Cameron said that he wanted garlic bread but I'd have to have some too, and on the way home when we got to the bottom of my street, he turned to me and looked really deep into my eyes and then we just sort of, um, we just sort of sunk into this kiss. It was wonderful.'

'Wow,' breathed Mai. 'Has he got any friends?'

Everyone was of the same opinion about Jo and Cameron – they were totally made for each other. It was all that Atia, Gillie and Mai could discuss, but Lorrie, although she was pleased for Jo, sat in the canteen on her own, her own personal black cloud firmly in place above her head. It wasn't fair. She hadn't fancied, let alone snogged, anyone for ages. And to make matters worse, she'd had another run-in with Ash over the weekend. She'd been in Rhythm Records and was just about to pick up the latest CD by her favourite band, when Ash had suddenly appeared from nowhere and, ignoring her hand reaching out towards the rack, had snatched it.

'I wanted that!' she'd snapped at him, but he'd just

grinned at her in that infuriating way of his and said, 'Tough, you should have been quicker.'

And of course it had been the last one in stock. She'd seen him careering down the High Street on his poxy skateboard and hoped that he'd veer into the path of a runaway juggernaut. Wherever Lorrie went over the weekend, she'd bumped into Ash. Even when she'd popped to the Stop And Shop at the crack of dawn on Sunday morning to get some milk, he'd been there and smirked at her just-got-out-of-bed hair. At least she had an excuse – his hair was always a mess. She'd spent the rest of the day arguing with Ash in her head and always managing to get the last word in. Next time she saw him, she'd give him a piece of her mind.

But the next time she saw him all the cool put-downs she'd rehearsed in her head suddenly deserted her and she had to pretend to be incredibly engrossed in a poster advertising Nick's band, The In Crowd, who were playing a gig on Saturday. She stared at the poster as if she'd never seen anything quite so fascinating in all her life and mentally willed Ash to go away, but she could feel him standing behind her. She tried sending out hostile vibes, but Ash obviously wasn't in a telepathic mood because he didn't budge. Eventually, Lorrie turned away from the poster, gave Ash a look that suggested that he was something particularly unpleasant she'd found on the sole of her trainer, and stalked off. He followed her. Lorrie whirled around.

'Listen, dogbreath,' she blazed at him. 'Quit following me.'

Ash assumed an air of nonchalance. 'Excuse me, was I following you? No, I was just walking towards my French class, which just happens to be this way. As if I wanted to follow you.'

'Just checking,' Lorrie snarled and carried on walking down the corridor with Ash behind her. This was awful. Lorrie hated Ash more each day. She wondered if she could persuade her parents to emigrate to New Zealand. There was no way she could hold onto her sanity if she had to see Ash every day. She ducked into the girls' toilets, locked herself into a cubicle and sat down on the toilet lid. Maybe she could kill Ash – that would solve everything. All of a sudden there was a bang on the door.

'You in there, Lor?' Atia called. 'It's me.'

'Go away!' yelled Lorrie.

'What's the matter? Let me in.'

'Nothing's the matter, just go away.'

'It's a pretty noisy load of nothing.'

Lorrie realised that nothing was going to budge Atia, who could be like a Rottweiler with a bloodlust when she thought she was missing out on some gossip. She stood up and opened the door. Atia squeezed into the cubicle and pulled the bolt.

'Why are you moping, hon?' she asked in a you-will-tell-me type voice.

'Time of the month,' Lorrie muttered.

Atia stroked back the red curls that were sticking to Lorrie's hot face. 'Your perma sulk wouldn't be over something trouser-shaped, would it? Like Ash, maybe?'

'I don't know what you're talking about,' Lorrie said icily.

'Oh come on,' snorted Atia. 'You spend all your time sniping at each other. I'm not surprised you're depressed. You're obsessed with him, and not in a good way either.'

'I'm not obsessed with him. It's just that everywhere I go, there he is. It's almost like he's lying in wait, so he can torment me. I hate him!' Lorrie blurted out in a rush.

Atia didn't really know what to say. Once Lorrie was depressed, there was no talking her out of it. So she decided to change the subject.

'I've called a meeting at lunch-time, to announce the last completely spectacular fund-raising event,' she said brightly.

'Huh,' grunted Lorrie. 'I'm not going if Ash is going to be there. I just can't face him.'

'Hey, that's not very girl-powered,' Atia retorted. 'OK, you're fed up with him bugging you, but you don't want to show him that. Then he's won. I want you to walk into that canteen like you don't give a damn. And anyway, it's the last event.'

'You're just talking me up so I agree to go to the canteen.' Lorrie sighed. 'But you do have a point. I'm not going to let some dorky skateboy get the better of me.'

'That's more like it,' Atia enthused. 'We are women; hear us ROAR.'

'Grrrr,' said Lorrie, completely deadpan, and gave a little chuckle. 'OK, you've persuaded me. I guess I should go to history and explain why I'm twenty minutes late and why I haven't done my assignment.'

'Sod it,' said Atia, unbolting the door. 'Let's go to the chippy instead.'

Lorrie grinned. 'You know me so well, it's frightening.'

Fortified by a bag of chips, swimming with grease and vinegar, Lorrie felt ready to take on the world as she followed Atia into the canteen – or at least be able to look Ash in the eye without screaming at him.

But as they got nearer to the table where Ash was hanging out with Mai, Nick and Gillie and she saw the sunlight glinting off his haystack hair, Lorrie nearly turned and ran. Atia took a tight hold of her arm and whispered in her ear, 'Remember, I am woman, hear me roar.'

Lorrie made a point of sitting down on the chair furthest away from Ash and engaging Atia in an intense, not to mention completely pointless, conversation.

'OK, look really interested in what I'm saying and smile like I'm really funny,' she instructed Atia.

Atia laughed. 'Well, you got the last bit right. Where are Jo and Cameron? And I suppose Johnny's going to come, too.'

Mai looked up. 'He left another bar of organic chocolate in my locker this morning,' she informed Lorrie and Atia. 'And a note which says, "Mai, I'm wearing black because I'm in mourning for my life."'

'Are you convinced?'

'As if!' snorted Mai. 'He *always* wears black. Oooh, look, here he comes.'

As Johnny pulled a chair out, all the girls automatically looked in the other direction. Only Ash nodded at him and Nick threw him a casual, 'All right, mate?' Johnny sat down and eyed Mai sorrowfully, looking for all the world like a little puppy that had been abandoned in a motorway lay-by.

Atia began to fidget. 'Where's Cameron and Jo?'

'They've probably gone to Casualty to get their lips surgically separated,' said Lorrie sourly, but Cameron and Jo were walking in, hand in hand, and then sitting down with a flurry of apologies.

'Never mind that,' said Atia impatiently. 'I know you're all dying to find out what I've arranged for our last fund-raising event.'

'We're on the edge of our seats, At, just tell us,' interrupted Jo.

Atia had a smug look on her face. 'You're going to love this. Sometimes I amaze even myself, 'cause this is fantastic.'

'What the bloody hell is it?' shouted Nick.

Atia grinned beatifically. 'Keep your hair on. All right, all right' (as the others shot her filthy looks) 'it's a sponsored bungee jump!' she finished triumphantly. 'Well, what do you think about that?'

The others didn't seem to be reacting as ecstatically as she'd expected.

'I'd like a few more details before I commit myself to a comment,' said Cameron slowly.

Atia rolled her eyes. What a bunch of ingrates! 'It's all organised. On Saturday one of us girls, and one of you lot, gets strapped together, tied to a rope and then jumps from a great height. How cool is that?'

'No way!'

'Uh, uh!'

'I get vertigo!'

'I'm allergic to ropes!'

Atia waited until the protests had died down and then produced two paper bags. 'I knew you were a bunch of wusses, so we're going to draw names out of a hat. This bag is for us girls and this bag has got the boys' names in it.'

Nick had his head between his knees and was taking deep breaths but managed to gasp, 'So, we pick names, like, democratically?'

'Give the man a prize,' said Atia sarcastically, before beckoning over a girl who was in her media studies group. 'Julie has very kindly agreed to pick out the names, haven't you?'

Julie seemed very happy to be picking out the names, so much so that she gave Atia a huge wink before she shoved a hand into each bag.

'OK, Lorrie will be jumping for the girls,' she proclaimed, 'and Ash will be the boys' bungee jump-er!'

'That's not fair!' Lorrie and Ash both shouted in unison.

Julie pulled a face at them. 'Hey, don't shoot the messenger, I'm outta here.'

They both turned to Atia. 'I'm not bungee jumping with her,' Ash insisted. 'I meant what I said, I get really bad vertigo.'

'And I am not being strapped to him,' yelled Lorrie. 'I'll do it with one of the others.'

Cameron, Nick and Johnny weren't having it. 'Sorry, Lor, but you know, drawing the names out of a bag was the fairest way,' said Cameron.

'And we're playing a gig on Saturday night,' Nick reminded her. 'I can't play guitar with a broken arm.'

'And you hate me even more than you hate Ash,' Johnny pointed out. 'So you wouldn't want to be strapped to me either.'

'The judge's decision is final and I will not have mutiny in the ranks,' snapped Atia. 'If you don't do this bloody bungee jump and raise some serious cash for the animal sanctuary then I will never, ever speak to either of you again.'

'Well, if you put it like that,' said Ash.

'Yeah, all right,' sniffed Lorrie.

Atia gave them a pleasant smile. 'I knew you'd see things from my point of view.'

'Like, you gave us any choice,' Lorrie started to say but Atia was already leaving with the others in tow. Only Ash was left.

'She's evil and she must be stopped,' he said to Lorrie.

Lorrie wrinkled her nose. 'Do you get the feeling that there's something weird going on? Like, there's this joke and no-one's told us the punch line?'

Ash stared at Lorrie for a long moment. 'What are you asking me for? I mean, why should you care about what I think? You're always said that I'm total scum,' he said slowly.

'I've never *said* that about you,' objected Lorrie.

'Well, you might not have said those exact words, but your meaning's always been pretty clear.'

'You go out of your way to wind me up,' she accused.

'Ah, but that's because it's so easy to get a reaction out of you,' said Ash with a smile.

'I wonder if I dropped a brick on your head from a great height whether you might actually feel something,' Lorrie bit out.

'Oh, I feel plenty of things,' Ash told her.

'Yeah, and all of them are for your skateboard. You care more about a lump of wood with four wheels than you do about . . .' Lorrie had been about to say, 'me' – why, she didn't know, but that was the little word that had been forming in her head. And Ash knew it, if the ginormous grin on his face was anything to go by.

'Well, that is interesting!' he said. 'You're jealous of my skateboard!'

'I am not jealous!' Lorrie protested. 'I was just trying to point out that your cognitive thought processes were somewhat underdeveloped.'

Her words fell on deaf ears.

'Yeah, right,' said Ash mockingly. 'You're jealous of my skateboard. Now why could that be?'

Lorrie got up so hurriedly she knocked over her chair with a loud bang. 'I think you're pond life, and after the bungee jump, if I never see you again, it'll be too soon for me,' she screeched, patches of red dancing along her cheekbones.

She stormed out of the canteen, leaving Ash sitting there with a dopey expression on his face. Lorrie was ace. He loved winding her up because it never failed to get a reaction from her. He decided to get the bungee jump out of the way and then, ignoring all of Lorrie's protests, let her know in no uncertain terms that it was time to draw up a peace treaty.

It was weird, thought Lorrie, but when you hated someone as much as she hated Ash, you ended up thinking about them all the time.

She lay in bed that night, unable to sleep. Just get out of my head, Ash, she thought with a groan. In a funny kind of way, she loved bickering with him. When she argued with Ash, she always felt so intensely alive. She saw him careering around the college grounds on his stupid skateboard wearing one of his shapeless baggy tops and his combats and generally acting like he didn't have a care in the world. Lorrie wondered if Ash thought about her to the same degree and decided he didn't. He probably had more important things to think about, like where to find T-shirts that were five sizes too big and how to get his hair long enough to look cool but short enough not to look like a hippy. It wasn't fair! How come Ash got to think about other stuff, when all she could think about was Ash?

Lorrie managed to get through the rest of the week by avoiding places where Ash might be. This meant a lot of ducking into doorways and diving down corridors. She also spent a large amount of time talking to Ash in her head. Or rather, she called him a dickweed and demolished his entire belief system while he sat there and meekly took it. But, hey, it was her imagination. With so much to do, Lorrie didn't really have time to worry about the imminent bungee jump, so she had a bit of a shock when she woke up on Saturday morning and realised that today was the day that she got to be suspended from a very long and (she hoped) industrial-strength rubber band.

Deciding to skip breakfast because she'd probably chuck it up later, Lorrie rummaged through her wardrobe. She wanted to look drop-dead gorgeous because she'd heard on the grapevine that Atia was trying to get the local paper to send a photographer down. This was the kind of thing you never read about in magazines, Lorrie decided. They never explained how to put together an outfit that could withstand a bungee jump yet would be alluring enough to make it onto the front page of the *Stanhope Echo*. In the end, she decided to wear her new check trousers and her skinny fit black jumper with her trainers.

By the time she heard Nick honking his horn, she'd just finished putting her hair into a messy ponytail that had taken half an hour to achieve. Promising her mother that she'd ring the moment her feet touched firm ground again, she ran out to the van and jumped in the back where the others were sitting. Ash, she was pleased to notice, was looking a particularly fetching shade of green.

'Are you nervous, then?' asked Mai, and Lorrie replied quite honestly that she wasn't. She hadn't had time to feel nervous.

'I'm quite looking forward to it actually,' she confessed with a sly glance in Ash's direction. 'I can't wait to see the ground plunging towards me.'

Ash gave a groan and stuck his head out the window, and the rest of them decided to remain diplomatically silent. After a short drive they reached the leisure complex where the bungee jump was. And suddenly Lorrie did feel nervous, but excited at the same time.

After big hugs from the girls and good-luck pats on the back from Cam, Nick and even Johnny, Ash and Lorrie began the long trek up to the platform.

Before the man in charge could even greet them, Ash was ready to call the whole thing off.

'I didn't realise it would be so high up,' he whimpered, looking over the edge of the platform. The rest of the gang were nothing but tiny specks. Despite everything, Lorrie felt sorry for him. She grabbed his ice-cold hand and gave it a comforting squeeze.

'You can't chicken out now,' she said. 'Just don't look down.'

'That's right, love,' said the organiser. 'My name's

Dave and it's my job to make sure you're safe as houses. We've never had an accident here.'

'Hmm, there's always a first time,' muttered Ash.

'He doesn't like heights,' Lorrie explained, the wind tugging at her hair. 'But I think you've got to look the devil in the face.'

Dave gave her a wry smile and then proceeded to strap them into their safety harnesses and explain in detail the back-up procedure in case anything went wrong. Lorrie was literally dancing on the spot she was so psyched up. This was gonna be ace. It was just a pity that Ash didn't think so.

'Come on, hon,' she said comfortingly as Ash suddenly grabbed onto her. She didn't flatter herself that it was because Ash suddenly found her completely desirable. The poor guy was bricking it. She gave him a hug as they inched towards the edge of the platform.

'Don't be so bloody nice to me,' he moaned. 'At least if you were hollering at me, it would take my mind off being so scared.'

Lorrie could see Dave nodding at her and knew that the moment was upon them, but Ash was rooted to the spot. Every inch of his body seemed to be clinging to her.

'You're so chicken,' she crowed.

'Yeah, I am.'

'You're not such a big talking man, are you?'

'Go to hell, Lorrie, you . . . AAAAAAAARGH!'

Lorrie had decided to distract Ash with an argument, and just as he was easing into a bit of verbal cut and thrust, she'd seen Dave give her the signal and had jumped off the platform. And as Ash was strapped to her, he'd had to go too!

As the world below rushed to meet them, they both screamed loud and long. Just as it seemed inevitable that they'd hit the ground with a sickening crunch, the rope jerked them back up and then they were plunging down again and shrieking fit to burst.

'Lorrie?' Ash yelled in her ear as the wind made a wooshing noise around them.

'What?'

'I fancy you so much!'

Still jerking around in mid-air, Lorrie and Ash snogged. They were still clinging together, lips locked, as the rope slowly descended to the ground. Once they'd been released from the harness, still clutching at each other for dear life, they made the mutual decision that their legs had turned to jelly and collapsed on the ground in hysterics.

The others could only look on in amazement as Lorrie and Ash rolled about on the grass and on top of each other, screaming with laughter. Every time they appeared to have calmed down, Ash would suddenly jump on Lorrie and tickle her until they both began rolling around and burbling again.

'I think the jump must have addled their brains,' said Cameron eventually. But no, Ash was pulling Lorrie to her feet and then they were running over to the others and jumping around, trying to hug everyone at once.

'It was ace! It was, like, the best thing ever!'

'And we've called a truce!' shouted Ash.

'Tell us something that we can't work out for ourselves,' whispered Atia to Gillie.

After ten more minutes of Ash and Lorrie acting like hyperactive toddlers, they all piled into the van and drove to the nearest phone box so Lorrie could assure her worried mother that she hadn't broken every bone in her body. As Lorrie jumped back into the van, Atia clapped her hands to get everyone's attention.

'OK, everyone back to mine!' she announced. 'It's time for the big count.'

There was silence for a moment as both gangs eyed each other up. How much moolah had they raised? And, more importantly, who had made the most dosh?

Flash That Cash

Once they arrived at Atia's house, everybody charged up the stairs like a horde of marauding wildebeests, except for Lorrie and Ash, who jumped out of the van and promptly started smooching in the middle of the pavement.

Mai and Jo watched them from Atia's bedroom window.

'You owe me a fiver!' Jo informed Mai.

'Is anyone going to actually tell them that all the pieces of paper in those bags had their names on them?' asked Mai with a giggle.

'You don't stick your head in a lion's mouth, do you?' retorted Cameron, coming up behind them and putting his arms round Jo's waist. 'We knew that they'd only get together if they were given an almighty push, but they might not see it like that.'

'Hmmm, you've got a point,' Mai decided. 'I hope somebody gets an almighty push in my direction tonight.'

'Well, there's always Paul. He's just split up with his girlfriend, so you might catch him on the rebound,' said Jo. 'I guess you're not going to give Johnny another chance?'

'In a word, no,' sniffed Mai. 'OK, the organic chocolate was a nice idea, but once a creep, always a creep.'

'Put the poor bloke out of his misery then,' said Cameron. ''Cause all I get twenty-four hours a day, seven days a week is a detailed and anguished account of how he screwed up and why he can't live without you.'

'My heart bleeds for him, but the answer's still no,' Mai said decisively.

She was prevented from enlightening them further on her non-feelings for Johnny by Atia and Gillie staggering into the room, laden down with drinks and munchies. Atia left Gillie in charge of hostess duties and joined them by the window.

'Those two look like they're trying to swallow each other whole,' she observed, looking out at Lorrie and Ash who were still locked together in a clinch. 'Do you think we should turn the hose on them?'

Cameron gave an evil smile. 'I've got a better idea,' he said, sliding the window open. 'Oi, you two!' he bellowed. 'Stop snogging and get your butts up here!'

Lorrie and Ash managed to prise themselves apart, and even though Ash made a two-fingered gesture at Cameron, he was grinning as he and Lorrie wandered up Atia's garden path hand in hand.

Eventually they all settled down, and as Nick tapped out a ceremonious drum roll on the edge of Atia's dressing table, Atia unfolded a piece of paper.

'OK, I'm going to put you out of your misery immediately. We raised the grand sum of £3,484!'

'Yowsa!'

'Ace!'

'How brilliant is that?'

After everyone had calmed down, Lorrie raised a hand. 'All right, I have a question – who made the most moolah?'

'I was coming to that,' said Atia. 'The boys made £1,720.28. which is good but not good enough, and us girls, being completely fab with added bits of fabness, raised £1,763.72.'

Lorrie turned round to face Ash, who was sitting next to her with his arm around her shoulders. 'OK, cough up, skateboy, you owe me a fiver!'

'I hope you're using that term as an affectionate nickname,' Ash said with a smile.

Lorrie nuzzled her head against his shoulder. 'I think you realise that I'm just a teensy bit smitten, Ash, but you'll always be skateboy to me.'

For the next few moments the girls clamoured for their fivers, until Cameron got to his feet.

'Look, we're all going to see Nick's band tonight, so how about we all go out for a meal first, on us lads?'

There were murmurs of agreement from the girls.

'You're on,' announced Gillie. 'And I, for one, am going to order the most expensive things on the menu!'

'We're only going for a pizza,' Nick said hastily. 'I'm off, I've got to soundcheck.'

Within five minutes of Nick's departure, Atia had the house to herself. She hurried to phone Mrs Johnson to give her the good news.

'Well done!,' exclaimed Mrs Johnson. 'And the Rugby Club dinner dance and raffle made over five thousand pounds.'

'So the animal sanctuary will be all right?' Atia asked anxiously.

'It's going to be more than all right, dear,' boomed Mrs Johnson. 'There'll even be some money left in the kitty for next year. I'm very proud of you. I had my doubts about all this fund-raising, but you've proved me wrong.'

Atia grinned to herself. 'Thanks, Mrs J.'

'Anyway, give yourself a pat on the back and I expect to see you bright and early next Saturday morning.'

After gorging themselves on pizza (or spaghetti bolognese in Cameron's case), they hit the gig. Nick sloped off to be reunited with his guitar, before he could be whinged at for refusing to put them on the non-existent guest list.

'It wouldn't have killed him to let us in for free,' muttered Atia to Mai as they pushed their way to the front.

'Oh, I got in for nothing,' announced Mai smugly. 'Paul gave me a free ticket when I bumped into him in town earlier.'

Atia shrieked as someone trod on her toe and then gave Mai a knowing look.

'Oh, like that, is it?'

'I don't know what you mean!'

'Yeah, right.'

They were interrupted by the band bounding on-stage and blasting into their first number. Mai smiled as she caught Paul's eye and he winked at her. He was so foxy, and she had it on good authority from Nick that he thought she was 'really cute'. And he'd nearly got himself run over when he'd darted across the High Street to talk to her this afternoon. Paul was definitely an ace face around town, and he was way cooler than anyone else she knew.

'Look at Mai giving Paul the eye,' Lorrie bellowed in Ash's ear. 'That girl has no shame!'

'Like you,' teased Ash. 'You chased me so mercilessly, I didn't have any say in the matter.'

'Yeah, right,' protested Lorrie, digging him in the ribs. 'You fancied me first.'

'I love arguing with you, Lor!'

'I noticed!'

Meanwhile Jo and Cameron were dancing together and pausing every now and again to lock lips, and Johnny was gazing at Mai, entranced. After the band went off-stage, he decided to tell Mai that she didn't have to apologise and then, well, then they'd be snogging the rest of the night away.

Gillie and Atia, keen to get in on some boy action themselves, had slammed, accidentally on purpose, into a group of lads from the art foundation course at college.

'Buy us a drink,' shouted Gillie, smiling at a blond guy with a stud through his lip who'd been staring at her for the last fifteen minutes.

Atia rolled her eyes. Gillie could be so unpredictable sometimes. Most of the time she was quiet and sensible and then, all of a sudden, she'd get really lairy. She could just make out Gillie saying to the guy as they went to the bar, 'So, you got anything else pierced then?' She looked around at the rest of the art students and then at Nick, back on-stage again. She'd always thought Nick was cute in a scruffy sort of way. They'd even snogged once during a game of sardines at Mai's birthday party. Hmmm, it'd been a pretty good snog too, Atia remembered with a grin.

With a triumphant drum roll, the band came to the end of their set and Atia and Lorrie whooped vigorously to show their appreciation. Nick looked up, saw Atia and grinned at her. She made a do-you-want-a-drink motion and he nodded.

'Sorted!' she said cheekily to Lorrie.

'What, you and Nick?'

'Why not?' asked Atia. 'I'm not madly in love with him, but he might be all right for a snog.'

Lorrie laughed. 'Life's great, isn't it?'

'You said it, Lor,' said Ash, coming up behind Lorrie and then picking her up and whirling her around until they both collapsed in a heap on the floor.

'Honestly, Ash, you're going to have to start treating

me a bit better,' teased Lorrie. 'Your skateboard might put up with all this rough treatment, but I won't.'

'Let's get one thing straight,' said Ash in a mock serious voice. 'No girl comes between me and my skateboard.'

'Yeah, that's 'cause no girl would want to!'

They happily started to bicker again. OK, so they might not be as lovey-dovey as Jo and Cameron, but the way Lorrie saw it, arguing had brought them together. Just because she and Ash had actually admitted that they fancied each other, didn't mean that they had to stop disagreeing. When Atia had told them to cut it out as they argued furiously over the last piece of garlic bread, they'd both smirked at her. 'Hey, we enjoy it!' Ash had said. 'Just because we're going out with each other, doesn't mean we can't disagree now and again.'

'Yup, it just clears the air,' Lorrie had remarked, adding to herself, 'And making up is a lot of fun too!'

Only Johnny was left on his own. He skulked about the club for a while and then he saw Mai sitting on the edge of the stage, looking pensive. He sauntered over.

'Wotcha, Mai,' he said.

Mai turned and looked at him. 'Hi,' she said without much enthusiasm.

Johnny didn't seem to notice and sat down next to her.

'I've been thinking,' he announced. 'All that stuff you said, it doesn't matter. I'm willing to give you another chance.'

'Excuse me,' spluttered Mai, not quite able to believe her ears.

'Look, I don't fancy you as much as you fancy me, but we could maybe see each other on a casual basis.'

'And why would I want to do that?' queried Mai.

'You fancy me,' said Johnny, suddenly a bit unsure of himself.

Mai tossed back her hair. 'If you say so.'

'Is this guy bothering you, Mai?' said a voice behind Johnny.

Johnny turned around to see the lead singer from Nick's band walking across the stage towards him. He was dressed all in black and looked at Johnny menacingly.

'What's it to you?' Johnny asked belligerently.

Paul jumped off the stage and faced Johnny. 'I just told Mai to wait for me so I could buy her a drink, and I come back to find her being pestered.'

Mai put a hand on Paul's arm. 'I can handle this,' she said firmly, before turning to the hapless Johnny.

'Look, Johnny, get this into your thick skull. I used to fancy you, then I found out what a prat you were and I stopped fancying you. End of story. Oh, and stop leaving those stupid bars of organic chocolate in my locker.' She smiled at Paul, who smiled back. His eyes were a gorgeous green colour and his hair was all tousled like he'd just got out of bed. 'Shall we go and get that drink?' Mai said.

Johnny watched them, with a disgruntled expression on his face, as they walked across the dance floor, arm in arm. He pulled the collar of his jacket up and scrunched up his eyes, then he noticed a cute girl looking at him. He ran a hand through his hair and looked pained. Out of the corner of his eye, he could see the girl coming towards him and he slumped his shoulders as if he had to bear the weight of the world's problems on them. Yup, she was definitely coming towards him, he smirked to himself. Girls loved the mean and moody approach. It never failed – well, almost never . . .